FRANZ KAFKA

THE MAN WHO DISAPPEARED
(AMERIKA)

A new translation from the German with an introduction by
MICHAEL HOFMANN

PENGUIN BOOKS

PENGUIN BOOKS

Published by the Penguin Group
Penguin Books Ltd, 27 Wrights Lane, London w8 5tz, England
Penguin Books USA Inc., 375 Hudson Street, New York, New York 10014, USA
Penguin Books Australia Ltd, Ringwood, Victoria, Australia
Penguin Books Canada Ltd, 10 Alcorn Avenue, Toronto, Ontario, Canada m4v 3b2
Penguin Books (NZ) Ltd, 182–190 Wairau Road, Auckland 10, New Zealand

Penguin Books Ltd, Registered Offices: Harmondsworth, Middlesex, England

This translation first published by Penguin Books 1996
1 3 5 7 9 10 8 6 4 2

Grateful acknowledgement is made to A. P. Watt Ltd
on behalf of Michael Yeats for permission to reprint an extract from
'Towards Break of Day', from *The Collected Poems of W. B. Yeats*

The moral right of the translator has been asserted

Set in 10/12.5pt Monotype Janson
Typeset by Rowland Phototypesetting Ltd, Bury St Edmunds, Suffolk
Printed in England by Clays Ltd, St Ives plc

CONTENTS

INTRODUCTION

Der Verschollene (*The Man Who Disappeared*), is the Cinderella among Kafka's three novels: the earliest begun and earliest abandoned; the last to achieve posthumous publication (as *Amerika*), edited by Max Brod, in 1927; the least read, the least written about and the least 'Kafka'. That said, I agree with Edwin Muir, whose English translation first came out in 1928, that it is 'the most purely delightful of Kafka's books', and there is a weightier case to be made for it as well – not that delight should be lost sight of in the search for meaning.

It seems that Kafka worked on a version (which is now lost) of *Der Verschollene* from 1911 into the summer of 1912. It went slowly, and he was never happy with it. Then, following the writing of *Das Urteil* (*The Judgement*) in a single night (22–3 September 1912), he embarked on a second version, which went swimmingly. Brod reports on his friend's progress:

I quote from my diary notes of the time. 29 September: 'Kafka in ecstasy, writing all night. A novel set in America.' 1 October: 'Kafka in incredible ecstasy.' 2 October: 'Kafka, continuing very inspired. A chapter finished. I am happy for him.' 3 October: 'Kafka doing well.' On the 6 October he read me *The Judgement* and *The Stoker.*

By 17 November he had completed six chapters and thought he could finish the novel by Christmas, when he had a week off. In the event, things happened differently. For three weeks, he was distracted by *Metamorphosis*, experienced increasing difficulties with the novel, and finally put it aside on 24 January 1913. In June, the first chapter, *The Stoker*, was published as 'a fragment' by Kurt Wolff, and there was some talk of putting it out in another volume, along with *The Judgement* and *Metamorphosis*, to be called perhaps *Die Söhne* (*The Sons*) – a suggestion of how

Kafka expected to be read. When his copy of *The Stoker* arrived, Kafka read it aloud to his parents and noted:

Exuberance, because I liked *The Stoker* so much. In the evening I read it to my parents, there is no better critic than myself, reading aloud to my most reluctantly listening father. Many shallows, in amongst obviously inaccessible depths.

Kafka didn't take up the manuscript again until October 1914, when he completed the '"Up, up!" cried Robinson' section (from 'This was most unfair'), and worked on the two final fragments before finally giving up, this time for good. Some of his subsequent judgements were spectacularly harsh – as with all his work – but he never actually destroyed *The Man Who Disappeared*, and the time came when he thought his revulsion came from incapacity, and it turned on himself: 'strength apparently (already) beyond me today.' In 1920, reading Milena Jesenská's translation of *The Stoker* into Czech, he approved of her rendition of 'in his exuberance, and because he was a strong lad', while suggesting she should leave it out altogether, so little sympathy did he have left for his strikingly young, forthright, cheerful and brave hero. Not only did Kafka expect his writing to reflect himself (and to be better than himself), but to go on doing so.

The version that Brod published in 1927 differs from the present one in at least one matter of substance, and many of detail – if there is such a thing as a detail with Kafka. The substance is the section '"Up! Up," cried Robinson' and the first of the fragments, 'Brunelda's Departure', never previously presented in English. The details range from the title of the book – which, though he may have spoken to Brod about his 'American novel', is only twice referred to in writing, both times as *Der Verschollene* (it is a book about a person, not a place) – to the through-numbering and titles of the later chapters, including 'The Nature Theatre of Oklahoma', which were supplied by Brod. In the text, there are some thousands of differences – most of them merely corrections of such things as spelling and punctuation – from the age of the hero given in the first sentence ('seventeen' instead of 'sixteen') to the very last – Brod originally ended the book 'Such a carefree journey in America they had never known,' a falsely and quite preposterously un-Kafkaesquely ringing summary, instead of where Kafka actually broke off, 'so close that the chill breath of them made their faces shudder', characteristically menacing, peculiar, physical, ambivalent, something visual becoming palpable, words growing teeth, and an odd resemblance too to Yeats's poem of disenchantment, 'Towards Break of Day':

> Nothing that we love over-much
> Is ponderable to our touch.
>
> I dreamed towards break of day,
> The cold blown spray in my nostril.

It may seem an odd thing to do, to go back to a rough, unedited and error-strewn manuscript version of a book: to reintroduce inconsistencies of spelling in the names of Mack and Renell (not to mention Lobter), to situate San Francisco in the East instead of the West, to have a bridge linking New York with Boston instead of Brooklyn, to talk of 'quarter pounds' instead of 'quarter dollars', to provide floor numbers that don't add up and so forth, but for the translator, himself putting out a rough new text, it is pleasing to have a rough old one. Theatre people in particular will understand the importance of freshness of language. Muir's version of Brod has had years to weather and settle; I like to think there is compatibility, if not parity, between the speed and unevenness of Kafka and what I've done. Anyway, this is only a partial exercise. I haven't written 'Newyork' or 'Occidental' in minuscule letters, there is no way of usefully suggesting 'Austriacisms' in English, and so forth. (Nor, incidentally, have I fallen for the obvious temptation – not available to Muir or Kafka – of trying to make my translation sound 'American': that would have been to strive for a misleading verisimilitude. I may have meant 'elevator', but I enjoyed writing 'lift'.) Brod's work is often unarguable and always well-intentioned – and but for him we wouldn't have had most of Kafka at all – but I am still glad to have been able to slip past it.

The prevailing sense of *Amerika* – Muir's certainly – is that of a much sunnier book altogether than the other two, full of open space and forward movement and real people and things as against confinement, inertia and allegory. 'The Nature Theatre of Oklahoma', with its women on pedestals (where else!) blowing trumpets (what else!) promises to be

Kafka's vision of Heaven, and the happy ending he discussed with Brod has been widely reported:

In enigmatic language Kafka used to hint smilingly, that within this 'almost limitless' theatre his young hero was going to find again a profession, a stand-by, his freedom, even his old home and his parents, as if by some celestial witchery.

As if it were Kansas, not Oklahoma. Muir goes so far as to claim: 'His story is the story of innocence, as that of the heroes of the other two books is the story of experience,' but I think the opening sentence establishes Karl's guilt beyond all doubt. He may feel and sound and act innocent, and think of himself as innocent, but when was that ever any defence in Kafka, in whom, here as elsewhere, guilt is assumed at the outset?

There is an opposing reading of *The Man Who Disappeared*, very effectively advanced in Hartmut Binder's *Kafka Kommentar*, that, far from being a jolly picaresque or Chaplinade, its events actually describe a pitiless descent through American society, towards a probable catastrophe every bit as grim and ineluctable as those in *The Trial* or *The Castle*. The chapters are in triads: wandering, adoption and expulsion. The first six chapters that Kafka completed thus comprise two whole such cycles; and there is evidence – in Karl's arrival at 'Enterprise No. 25', in the names 'Fanny' and 'Negro', in Karl's reticence about his last place of employment and so forth – that in his novel Kafka was looking at a spiral of descent comprising four complete cycles: a young man with expectations, a lift-boy (what a symbol of forlorn aspirations!), a skivvy, and then, it has been conjectured, a fence and brothel-attendant. While – especially in Kafka – the book's plunging onward movement breeds hope, its cyclical organization guarantees doom. Binder points out that this book which – compared to his others – seems everywhere improvised ('free improvisation without any or without much serious afterthought', writes Muir), fanciful and airy, is actually extremely tightly and purposefully composed, full of careful echoes; that objects and relationships are not haphazard, but more like deformed replicas of one another. One thinks of the meals at Mr Pollunder's house, outside the hotel, Robinson's picnic on the balcony, and the welcome feast at Clayton (each one a last supper); the way the action takes place in what might be one room (one basic stage-set would certainly be enough), high up, balconied, over-furnished, with views (and no doubt Kafka would have brought the floor-numbers into conformity with one another!); the washings, Karl's high-tech shower at his uncle's, his wash in the Head Cook's room, Brunelda's medieval bath; such details as tickets, passports and visiting cards, music, drink and beards.

It seems likely – remember *The Sons* – that far from being free ('the most worthless condition' (p. 88), albeit) and in the land of the free (though quite how it deserves the label in the book is unclear), Karl is continually being made to replay his drama of expulsion, now with the Senator and the stoker as his 'parents', now with Mr Green and Mr Pollunder, now with the Head Cook and the Head Waiter, the implacable father and the mother who is, finally, no defence. There is a possibility that Kafka meant Karl to die at the end of the book – or perhaps already to be dead, with the Oklahoma Theatre a sort of afterlife – and if that sounds far-fetched, one should think about the fact that the lavish and pointless-seeming description of the box in the theatre that so fascinates Karl in Clayton is of the place where Lincoln – also described – was assassinated; that the Oklahoma Theatre was part-based on a large sanatorium called 'Just's Jungborn' where Kafka spent the summer of 1912, that according to him gave its occupants some taste of America, and might not be heaven at all but a penal colony by other means, as Kafka loved to subvert expectation; that one of Kafka's sourcebooks had a photograph labelled 'Idyll in Oklahoma' of a lynched black man surrounded by happy white faces (and Karl had just given his name as 'Negro'). Binder suggests that Kafka was either telling the perennial optimist Brod what he wanted to hear, or maybe he was even winding him up. Perhaps the reconvening of the cast would be to witness a horrible judicial murder – as elsewhere in Kafka: why else would Liberty in the opening paragraph carry a sword? Where we leave the book – where the book leaves us – is with a *mélange* of *Schlaraffenland* (Cockaigne), bureaucracy *in excelsis* and – incredibly – *Judentransporte*.

This meaning, typically, seems about as far removed as possible from the experience of reading *The Man Who Disappeared*. 'They are pictures, just pictures,' Kafka remarked to Janouch. The French critic Claude David, quoted in Binder, writes:

Le roman de Kafka est comme construit sur deux plans. D'une part les aventures, une agitation incohérente ... Mais, en dessous, règne un strict système de relations, un monde de signes, où rien n'est gratuit, où tout porte un sens, où tout invite à l'exégèse. ('Kafka's novel [*The Man Who Disappeared*] has two levels. On the surface, there is the action, the story, an incoherent agitation ... But buried underneath it, an ineluctable network of relationships exists, a world of signs where nothing is casual, where everything carries meaning and demands to be interpreted.')

(Perhaps Kafka was referring to something like this when he wrote about shallows and inaccessible depths.) Nowhere in Kafka is this gulf greater than in *The Man Who Disappeared*, with its pantomime vividness and gusto. Although there is quite a bit of the fluid, bewildering and hilariously destabilizing description that one thinks of as Kafkaesque, playing Zeno-like games with space and time and event, more striking is the number of sentences that do nothing but advance the action: '"What's your name?" he asked, tucking his truncheon under his arm, and slowly pulling out a notepad.' It's an almost parodically meticulous transcription of an action, very nearly as modest as Kingsley Amis's ideal novel sentence, 'He put out his cigarette and left the room,' except for its quotient of joy and its deliberate slowness. A lot of *The Man Who Disappeared* consists of direct speech – and Kafka's characters like to talk, in Seamus Heaney's line, 'like a book of manners in the wilderness' – interspersed with descriptions of gesture. Here, it doesn't resemble epic (the novel) so much as drama, with speech and action (Kafka was going to the Yiddish theatre a lot in 1912). Almost more than action and gesture is the emphasis on blocking, grouping, distance, movement, positioning. It's thus less like a playscript (one in which the dialogue, admittedly, is half-concealed in endless paragraphs – another thing Brod did was break up these prose blocks, exactly as a British editor would have done) than a director's notes. Often the effect is absurd: the movements – and one's awareness of them – are as artificial and elaborate as the speech itself, and quite often at variance with it: Karl 'repeatedly pushing down a little pair of scales, for sheer delight', Robinson and Delamarche 'clinking glasses and keeping them touching in mid-air awhile'. In addition to its dramatic aspect, there is lyricism in the way the prose will sometimes strike an almost random note that reverberates powerfully in the reader's mind.

Cruelty, sex and homesickness are most often sounded, but there are also moments of dense, almost inexplicable peace:

In the empty lanes one occasionally saw a policeman on a horse, motionless, or the carriers of flags and banners spanning the whole street, or a workers' leader surrounded by colleagues and shop stewards or an electric tramcar, which hadn't managed to flee in time, and was now standing there dark and empty, with the driver and conductor sitting on the platform.

America, when Kafka wrote about it, was a mythical place, a promised land to Europeans. Joseph Roth has a character called Zwonimir in his early novel, *Hotel Savoy* (1924): 'He loved America. When a billet was good he said "America". When a position had been well fortified he said "America". Of a "fine" lieutenant he would say "America", and because I was a good shot he would say "America" when I scored bullseyes.' Karl May's tremendously popular cowboy stories of the 1880s were written without his having been there (his Wild West peopled by Indians and Saxons is oddly like Kafka's America, an exploded Bohemia). The youthful Brecht's frontier ballads likewise. *The Man Who Disappeared* was written at the height of the immigration from Eastern Europe. Some of Kafka's relatives had gone to the new world – one had helped build the Panama Canal – and had gone into family lore (see Anthony Northey's book, *Kafka's Relatives: Their Lives and His Writing*). The cult of American speed, scale, novelty, machinery and brutality had entered European consciousness. But even beyond that, Kafka tried to make his book up to the minute, with its telephones and gramophones, electric bells and electric torches, lifts, the Brooklyn Bridge (now misnamed again, but only completed in 1910), an early reference to Coca-Cola perhaps (available in Europe since 1892). But then Kafka already had to his credit the first description of aeroplanes in German literature in 'Aeroplane in Brescia' in 1907.

One of the harmless incidental sidelines of translating the book was doing much of it in America. To be thinking of Kafka in a jumbo jet banking over Ellis Island, or while watching ten tiny aeroplanes flying round and round a 100,000 seater sports stadium in the middle of nowhere, all towing banners for pizzas, for judges or for true love; to be spiralled round the immigration hall at La Guardia with an Italian delegation already in cowboy boots, string ties and ten-gallon hats, or visiting Dean and Deluca on Broadway with its pressed tin ceilings, wires, strings and pipes; or be listening to an NPR report on the case of a 340 lb. Louisiana woman who used to bring her own chair into the local cinema because she couldn't fit into a cinema chair, bursting into tears when the manager told her it was a fire hazard. I mention these things not because there is any distinction in them, but precisely the opposite, because there is none.

MICHAEL HOFMANN
London, July 1995

BIBLIOGRAPHY

Hartmut Binder: *Kafka Kommentar*, Munich, 1976.

Max Brod: *Über Franz Kafka*, Frankfurt, 1974.

Jiri Grusa: *Franz Kafka of Prague*, London, 1983.

Franz Kafka: *Tagebücher*, Frankfurt, 1948.

Franz Kafka: *Amerika*, translated with an introduction by Edwin Muir and a postscript by Max Brod, London, 1928.

Gustav Janouch: *Conversations with Kafka*, London, 1953.

Anthony Northey: *Kafka's Relatives: Their Lives and His Writing*, London, 1991.

THE MAN WHO DISAPPEARED
(AMERIKA)

I

THE STOKER

As the seventeen-year-old Karl Rossmann, who had been sent to America by his unfortunate parents because a maid had seduced him and had a child by him, sailed slowly into New York harbour, he suddenly saw the Statue of Liberty, which had already been in view for some time, as though in an intenser sunlight. The sword in her hand seemed only just to have been raised aloft, and the unchained winds blew about her form.

'So high,' he said to himself, and quite forgetting to disembark, he found himself gradually pushed up against the railing by the massing throng of porters.

A young man with whom he had struck up a slight acquaintance during the crossing said to him in passing: 'Well, don't you want to get off yet?' 'I'm all ready,' said Karl laughing to him, and in his exuberance and because he was a strong lad, he raised his suitcase on to his shoulder. But as he watched his acquaintance disappearing along with the others, swinging a cane, he realized that he had left his umbrella down in the ship. So he hurriedly asked his acquaintance, who seemed less than overjoyed about it, to be so good as to wait by his suitcase for a moment, took a quick look around for his subsequent orientation, and hurried off. Below deck, he found to his annoyance that a passage that would have considerably shortened the way for him was for the first time barred, probably something to do with the fact that all the passengers were disembarking, and so he was forced instead to make his way through numerous little rooms, along continually curving passages and down tiny flights of stairs, one after the other, and then through an empty room with an abandoned desk in it until, eventually, only ever having gone this way once or twice previously, and then in the company of others, he found that he was totally and utterly lost. Not knowing what to do, not seeing anyone, and hearing only the scraping of thousands of human feet overhead and the last, faraway wheezings of the engine, which had already been turned off, he began without thinking to knock at the little door to which he had come on his wanderings. 'It's open!' came a voice from within, and Karl felt real relief as he opened the door. 'Why are you banging about on the door like a madman?' asked an enormous man, barely looking at Karl. Through some kind of overhead light-shaft, a dim light, long since used up in the higher reaches of the ship, fell into the wretched cabin, in which a bed, a wardrobe, a chair and the man were all standing close together, as though in storage. 'I've lost my way,' said Karl. 'I never quite realized on the crossing what a terribly big ship this is.' 'Well, you're right about that,' said the man with some pride, and carried on tinkering with the lock of a small suitcase, repeatedly shutting it with both hands to listen to the sound of the lock as it snapped shut. 'Why don't you come in,' the man went on, 'don't stand around outside.' 'Aren't I bothering you?' asked Karl. 'Pah, how could you bother me?' 'Are you German?' Karl asked to reassure himself, as he'd heard a lot about the dangers for new arrivals in America, especially coming from Irishmen. 'Yes, yes,' said the man. Still Karl hesitated. Then the man abruptly grabbed the door handle, and pulling it to, swept Karl into the room with him. 'I hate it when people stand in the corridor and watch me,' said the man, going back to work on his suitcase, 'the world and his wife go by outside peering in, it's quite intolerable.' 'But the passage outside is completely deserted,' said Karl, who was standing squeezed uncomfortably against the bedpost. 'Yes, now,' said the man. 'But now is what matters,' thought Karl. 'He is an unreasonable man.' 'Lie down on the bed, you'll have more room that way,' said the man. Karl awkwardly clambered on to the bed, and had to laugh out loud about his first vain attempt to mount it. No sooner was he on it, though, than he cried: 'Oh God, I've quite forgotten all about my suitcase!' 'Where is it?' 'Up on deck, an acquaintance is keeping an eye on it for me. What was his name now?' And from a secret pocket that his mother had sewn into the lining of his jacket for the crossing, he pulled a calling-card: 'Butterbaum, Franz Butterbaum.' 'Is the suitcase important to you?' 'Of course.' 'Well then, so why did you give it to a stranger?' 'I forgot my umbrella down below and went to get it, but I didn't want to lug my suitcase down with me. And now I've gone and gotten completely lost.' 'Are you on your own? There's no one with

4

you?' 'Yes, I'm on my own.' I should stay by this man, thought Karl, I may not find a better friend in a hurry. 'And now you've lost your suitcase. Not to mention the umbrella,' and the man sat down on the chair, as though Karl's predicament was beginning to interest him. 'I don't think the suitcase is lost yet.' 'Think all you like,' said the man, and scratched vigorously at his short, thick, black hair. 'But you should know the different ports have different morals. In Hamburg your man Butterbaum might have minded your suitcase for you, but over here, there's probably no trace of either of them any more.' 'Then I'd better go back up right away,' said Karl and tried to see how he might leave. 'You're staying put,' said the man, and gave him a push in the chest, that sent him sprawling back on the bed. 'But why?' asked Karl angrily. 'There's no point,' said the man, 'in a little while I'll be going up myself, and we can go together. Either your suitcase will have been stolen and that's too bad and you can mourn its loss till the end of your days, or else the fellow's still minding it, in which case he's a fool and he might as well go on minding it, or he's an honest man and just left it there, and we'll find it more easily when the ship's emptied. Same thing with your umbrella.' 'Do you know your way around the ship?' asked Karl suspiciously, and it seemed to him that the otherwise attractive idea that his belongings would be more easily found on the empty ship had some kind of hidden catch. 'I'm the ship's stoker,' said the man. 'You're the ship's stoker,' cried Karl joyfully, as though that surpassed all expectations, and propped himself up on his elbow to take a closer look at the man. 'Just outside the room where I slept with the Slovak there was a little porthole, and through it we could see into the engine-room.' 'Yes, that's where I was working,' said the stoker. 'I've always been terribly interested in machinery,' said Karl, still following a particular line of thought, 'and I'm sure I would have become an engineer if I hadn't had to go to America.' 'Why did you have to go to America?' 'Ah, never mind!' said Karl, dismissing the whole story with a wave of his hand. And he smiled at the stoker, as though asking him to take a lenient view of whatever it was he hadn't told him. 'I expect there's a good reason,' said the stoker, and it was hard to tell whether he still wanted to hear it or not. 'And now I might as well become a stoker,' said Karl. 'My parents don't care what becomes of me.' 'My job will be going,' said the stoker, and coolly thrust his hands into his pockets and kicked out his legs, which were clad in rumpled, leather-like iron-grey trousers, on to the bed to stretch them. Karl was forced to move nearer to the wall. 'You're leaving the ship?' 'Yup, we're off this very day.' 'But what for? Don't you like it?' 'Well, it's circumstances really, it's not always whether you like something or not that matters. Anyway you're right, I don't like it. You're probably not serious about saying you could become a stoker, but that's precisely how you get to be one. I'd strongly advise you against it myself. If you were intending to study in Europe, why not study here. Universities in America are incomparably better.' 'That may be,' said Karl, 'but I can hardly afford to study. I did once read about someone who spent his days working in a business and his nights studying, and in the end he became a doctor and I think a burgomaster, but you need a lot of stamina for that, don't you? I'm afraid I don't have that. Besides, I was never especially good at school, and wasn't at all sorry when I had to leave. Schools here are supposed to be even stricter. I hardly know any English. And there's a lot of bias against foreigners here too, I believe.' 'Have you had experience of that too? That's good. Then you're the man for me. You see, this is a German ship, it belongs to the Hamburg America Line, everyone who works on it should be German. So then why is the senior engineer Rumanian? Schubal, his name is. It's incredible. And that bastard bossing Germans around on a German ship. Don't get the idea' – he was out of breath, and his hands flapped – 'don't you believe that I'm complaining for the hell of it. I know you don't have any influence, and you're just a poor fellow yourself. But it's intolerable.' And he beat the table with his fist several times, not taking his eyes off it as he did so. 'I've served on so many ships in my time' – and here he reeled off a list of twenty names as if it was a single word, Karl felt quite giddy – 'and with distinction, I was praised, I was a worker of the kind my captains liked, I even served on the same clipper for several years' – he rose, as if that had been the high point of his life – 'and here on this bathtub, where everything is done by rote, where they've no use for imagination – here I'm suddenly no good, here I'm always getting in Schubal's way, I'm lazy, I deserve to get kicked out, they only pay me my wages out of the kindness of their hearts. Does that make any sense to you? Not me.' 'You mustn't stand for that,' said Karl in agitation. He had almost forgotten he was in the uncertain hold of a ship moored to the coast of an

6

unknown continent, that's how much he felt at home on the stoker's bed. 'Have you been to see the captain? Have you taken your case to him?' 'Ah leave off, forget it. I don't want you here. You don't listen to what I say, and then you start giving me advice. How can I go to the captain.' And the stoker sat down again, exhausted, and buried his face in his hands. 'But it's the best advice I know,' Karl said to himself. And it seemed to him that he would have done better to fetch his suitcase, instead of offering advice which was only ignored anyway. When his father had given the suitcase into his possession, he had mused in jest: I wonder how long you'll manage to hang on to it for? And now that expensive suitcase might already be lost in earnest. His only consolation was the fact that his father couldn't possibly learn about his present fix, even if he tried to make inquiries. The shipping company would only be able to confirm that he had reached New York safely. But Karl felt sad that there were things in the suitcase that he had hardly used, although he should have done, he should have changed his shirt for example, some time ago. He had tried to make false economies; now, at the beginning of his career, when he most needed to be in clean clothes, he would have to appear in a dirty shirt. Those were fine prospects. Apart from that, the loss of his suitcase wasn't so serious, because the suit he was wearing was better than the one in the suitcase, which was really nothing better than a sort of emergency suit, which his mother had even had to mend just before his departure. Then he remembered there was a piece of Verona salami in the suitcase as well, which his mother had given him as a last-minute gift, but of which he had only been able to eat a tiny portion, since for the whole crossing he had had very little appetite and the soup that was doled out in the steerage had been plenty for him. Now, though, he would have liked to have had the salami handy, to make a present of it to the stoker, because his sort are easily won over by some small present or other. Karl knew that from the example of his father who won over all the junior employees he had to deal with by handing out cigars to them. Now the only thing Karl had left to give was his money, and if he had indeed already lost his suitcase, he wanted to leave that untouched for the moment. His thoughts returned to the suitcase, and now he really couldn't understand why, having watched it so carefully for the whole crossing that his watchfulness had almost cost him his sleep, he had now permitted that same suitcase to be taken from him so simply. He recalled the five nights during which he had incessantly suspected the little Slovak, who was sleeping a couple of places to his left, of having intentions on his suitcase. That Slovak had just been waiting for Karl, finally, sapped by exhaustion, to drop off for one instant, so that he could pull the suitcase over to himself by means of a long rod which he spent his days endlessly playing or practising with. That Slovak looked innocent enough by day, but no sooner did night fall than he would get up time and again from his bed and cast sad looks across at Karl's suitcase. Karl saw this quite clearly, someone, with the natural apprehensiveness of the emigrant, was forever lighting a little lamp somewhere, even though that was against the ship's regulations, and trying by its light to decipher the incomprehensible pamphlets of the emigration agencies. If there happened to be one such light close by, then Karl would be able to snooze a little, but if it was some way off, or even more if it was dark, then he had to keep his eyes open. His efforts had exhausted him, and now it seemed they might have been in vain. That Butterbaum had better look out, if he should ever run into him somewhere.

At that moment, the complete silence that had so far prevailed was broken by the distant sound of the pattering of children's feet, that grew louder as it approached, and then became the firm strides of men. They were obviously walking in single file, in the narrow passage, and a jangling as of weapons became audible. Karl, who was almost on the point of stretching out on the bed and falling into a sleep freed of all worries about suitcase and Slovaks, was startled up and nudged the stoker to get his attention at last, because the head of the column seemed to have reached the door. 'That's the ship's band,' said the stoker, 'they've been playing up on deck, and now they're packing up. That means everything's done, and we can go. Come on.' He took Karl by the hand, at the last moment removed a picture of the Virgin from the wall over the bed, crammed it into his top pocket, picked up his suitcase and hurriedly left the cabin with Karl.

'Now I'm going to the purser's office to give those gents a piece of my mind. There's no one left, no point in hanging back any more.' This the stoker repeated with variations in various ways and he also attempted to crush a rat that crossed their path with a sideways swipe of his boot, but he only succeeded in propelling it into its hole which it had reached

8

just in time. He was generally slow in his movements, for if his legs were long they were also heavy.

They came to a part of the kitchen where a few girls in dirty aprons – which they were spattering on purpose – were cleaning crockery in large vats. The stoker called out to one Lina, put his arm around her hip, and walked with her for a few steps, as she pressed herself flirtatiously against him. 'We're just off to get paid, do you want to come?' he asked. 'Why should I bother, just bring me the money yourself,' she replied, slipped round his arm and ran off. 'Where did you get the good-looking boy from?' she added, not really expecting an answer. The other girls, who had stopped their work to listen, all laughed.

They for their part carried on and reached a door that had a little pediment above it, supported on little gilded caryatids. For something on a ship, it looked distinctly lavish. Karl realized he had never been to this part of the ship, which had probably been reserved for the use of first and second class passengers during the crossing, but now the separating doors had been thrown open prior to the great ship's cleaning. They had in fact encountered a few men carrying brooms over their shoulders who greeted the stoker. Karl was amazed at all the bustle, between decks where he had been he had had no sense of it at all. Along the passages ran electrical wires, and one continually heard the ringing of a little bell.

The stoker knocked respectfully on the door, and when there was a shout of 'Come in' he motioned Karl to step in and not be afraid. Karl did so too, but remained standing in the doorway. Through the three windows of the room he could see the waves outside and his heart pounded as he watched their joyful movement, as though he hadn't just spent the last five days doing nothing else. Great ships kept crossing paths, and yielded to the motion of the waves only insofar as their bulk allowed. If you narrowed your eyes, the ships seemed to be staggering under their own weight. On their masts were long, but very narrow flags, which were pulled tight by their speed through the air, but still managed to be quite fidgety. Greeting shots rang out, probably from warships, the guns of one such ship not too far away and quite dazzling with the sun on its armour, seemed soothed by the safe and smooth, if not entirely horizontal movement. The smaller ships and boats could only be seen if they were some distance away, at least from the doorway, multitudes of them running into the gaps between the big ships. And behind it all stood New York, looking at Karl with the hundred thousand windows of its skyscrapers. Yes, you knew where you were in this room.

Seated at a round table were three men, one a ship's officer in a blue marine uniform, the two others were port officials dressed in black American uniforms. On the table lay a pile of various documents, which were perused first by the officer with his pen in hand and then passed on to the other two, who would read, copy and file them away in their briefcases whenever one of them, making an almost incessant clicking noise with his teeth, wasn't dictating something in protocol to his colleague.

At a desk by the window, his back to the door, sat a smaller man who was doing something with great ledgers that were lined up in front of him, at eye level, on a stout bookshelf. Beside him was an open cash till, which at first glance anyway appeared to be empty.

The second window was untenanted and afforded the best views. But in the proximity of the third stood two gentlemen, conducting a muffled conversation. One of them was leaning beside the window, he too in ship's uniform, toying with the handle of a sabre. His collocutor was facing the window and by occasional movements revealed some part of a row of medals on the other's chest. He was in a civilian suit and had a thin bamboo cane, which, as he had both hands on his hips, stood out like a sabre as well.

Karl had little time to take in all of this, because a servant soon approached the stoker and, frowning, as though he didn't belong there, asked him what he was doing. The stoker replied, as quietly as he could, that he wanted a word with the chief cashier. The servant declined this wish with a movement of his hand but, nevertheless, on the tips of his toes, and giving the round table a wide berth, went up to the man with the ledgers. The man – it was quite evident – froze at the servant's words, then finally turned to face the man who wanted to speak to him, but only in order to make a vehement gesture of refusal to the stoker, and then, to be on the safe side, to the servant as well. Whereupon the servant went back to the stoker and in a confiding sort of tone said: 'Now get the hell out of here!'

On hearing this reply the stoker looked down at Karl, as if he were his own heart, to whom he was making silent plaint. Without any more ado, Karl broke away, ran right across the room, actually brushing the officer's chair on his way, the servant swooped after him with arms outspread, like a rat-catcher, but Karl was first to the chief cashier's table, and gripped it with both hands in case the servant should attempt to haul him away.

Naturally, with that the whole room suddenly sprang to life. The ship's officer leapt up from the table, the men from the port authority looked on calmly and watchfully, the two men by the window drew together, while the servant, who believed it was not his place to carry on when his superiors were themselves taking an interest, withdrew. Standing by the door, the stoker waited nervously for the moment at which his assistance might become necessary. Finally the chief cashier swung round to the right in his swivel chair.

Karl reached into his secret pocket, which he had no fear of revealing to the eyes of these gentlemen, and pulled out his passport which he opened and laid out on the table, by way of an introduction. The chief cashier seemed unimpressed by the document, flicking it aside with two fingers, whereupon Karl, as though this formality had been satisfactorily concluded, pocketed his passport once more. 'I should like to say', he began, 'that in my opinion the stoker here has been the victim of an injustice. There is a certain Schubal who oppresses him. He himself has served, to complete satisfaction, on many ships, which he is able to name to you. He is industrious, good at his work and it's really hard to understand why, on this of all ships, where the work isn't excessively onerous, the way it is for instance on clipper ships, he should let anyone down. There can only be some slander that is in the way of his advancement, and is robbing him of the recognition he should otherwise certainly not lack for. I have kept my remarks general, let him voice his particular complaints himself.' Karl had addressed all the men in the office, because they were all listening, and the odds that one of their number should prove just were much better, than that the chief cashier should be the man. Cunningly, Karl had failed to say that he had only known the stoker for such a short time. He would have spoken far better if he hadn't been confused by the red face of the man with the cane, whom he could see properly, really for the first time, from his new position.

'Every word he says is true,' said the stoker before anyone could ask, even before anyone looked at him. Such precipitateness on the stoker's part might have cost him dear, had not the man with the medals, who, as it dawned on Karl, must be the captain, already decided for himself that he would listen to the stoker's case. He put out a hand and called out: 'Come here!' in a voice so firm you could have beaten it with a hammer. Now everything depended on the conduct of the stoker, for Karl had no doubt as to the rightness of his cause.

Happily, it became clear that the stoker was well versed in the ways of the world. With exemplary calmness he plucked from his little case a bundle of papers and a notebook, and, completely ignoring the chief cashier as though there was no question of doing anything else, went straight to the captain, and laid out his evidence on the window-sill. The chief cashier had no option but to join them there himself. 'That man is a well-known querulant,' he explained. 'He spends more time in the office than in the engine-room. He has driven that easy going man Schubal to a state of despair. Listen, you!' he turned to the stoker, 'You're really taking your importunity a stage too far. The number of times you've been thrown out of the accounts offices, quite rightly, with your completely and utterly, and with no exception, unjustified claims! The number of times you've come from there straight to the head office here! The number of times we've taken you aside and quietly reminded you that Schubal is your immediate superior, that you work to him and must deal directly with him! And now you barge in here in the presence of the captain himself, and you start pestering him, you've even had the neck to bring with you this well-rehearsed spokesman for your stale grudges, in the form of this little chap here, whom I've never even seen before.'

Karl had to restrain himself forcibly. But there was the captain, saying: 'Let's just listen to the man, shall we. Schubal's been getting a little too independent for my liking lately, which isn't to say that I accept your case.' This last remark was meant for the stoker, it was only natural that he couldn't take his part at once, but things seemed to be going well. The stoker embarked on his explanations, and right at the outset he even managed to refer to Schubal as 'Mr Schubal'. What joy Karl felt, standing by the chief cashier's now deserted desk, repeatedly pushing down a little pair of scales, for sheer delight. Mr Schubal is unjust. Mr Schubal favours the foreigners. Mr Schubal dismissed the stoker from the engine-room and made him clean lavatories, which was surely not part of his job as a stoker. On one occasion, the diligence of Mr Schubal was alleged to be more apparent than real. At that point Karl fixed the captain as hard as he could, frankly, as if he were his colleague, lest he be influenced by the stoker's somewhat clumsy way of expressing himself. Because, though he said much, nothing of substance was revealed, and while the captain went on looking straight ahead, showing in his expression his determination to hear the stoker out for once, the other men were becoming restless and the stoker's voice was now no longer in sole command of the room, which did not bode well. First of all, the man in the civilian suit activated his cane, and began softly tapping it on the floor. Of course the other men couldn't help looking in his direction now and again. The men from the port authority, obviously in a hurry, reached for their files and went back to looking through them, though in a slightly distrait manner; the ship's officer moved back to his table; and the chief cashier, scenting victory, heaved a deep and ironic sigh. The only one unaffected by the general air of distraction that was setting in was the servant, who had some sympathy with the sufferings of the underdog at the hands of the powerful, and nodded earnestly at Karl as though to assure him of something.

In the meantime the life of the harbour was going on outside the windows. A flat barge carrying a mountain of barrels, which must have been miraculously laden so as not to start rolling, passed by and plunged the room into near-darkness. Little motorboats, which Karl would have been in a good position to examine if he'd had the leisure, pursued their dead straight courses, responsive to every twitch of the hands of the men standing up at their wheels. Strange floats surfaced occasionally from the turbulent water, only to become swamped again and sink astonishingly from sight. Boats from the great liners were rowed ashore by toiling sailors, full of passengers who obediently kept their places and sat quietly and expectantly, even though a few couldn't refrain from turning their heads this way and that to look at the changing scene. All was endless movement, a restlessness communicated by the restless element to the helpless men and their works.

Everything enjoined haste, precision, clarity of representation – and what was the stoker doing? He was talking himself into a lather, his trembling hands could no longer hold the papers by the window-sill. He was deluged with complaints about Schubal that came to him from every direction, any one of which in his opinion would have sufficed to completely bury Schubal, but all he could put across to the captain was just a mishmash of all of them. The man with the bamboo cane had begun whistling quietly up at the ceiling, the men from the port authority had the officer at their table again, and showed no sign of relinquishing him, the chief cashier was obviously only constrained by the calm of the captain from the intervention he was all too eager to make. The sergeant was waiting at attention for an imminent order from the captain regarding the stoker.

At that Karl could no longer stand idly by. He walked slowly up to the group, rapidly considering how best to approach the affair. It was really high time to stop. Much more of it and the two of them might easily find themselves slung out of the office. The captain was a good man and he might at that very moment have some particular grounds, so Karl thought, to show himself to be a fair master, but for all that he wasn't a musical instrument to be played into the ground – which was precisely how the stoker was treating him, albeit from a soul that was illimitably indignant.

So Karl said to the stoker: 'You'll have to explain it all much more clearly and simply, the captain can't respond to what you're telling him now. In order to be able to follow your account, he would have to know the first and last names of every single machinist and errand boy. Put your complaints in order, say the most important thing first, and then go through the others in order of decreasing importance, perhaps you won't even be called upon to mention most of them that way. You always explained it so clearly to me.' If America was the sort of place where they stole suitcases then the occasional lie was permissible, he thought in extenuation.

If only it had helped! But was it not already too late? The stoker broke off the moment he heard the familiar voice, but with eyes dimmed with the tears of offended male honour, of frightful memories and the dire need of the moment, he barely even recognized Karl. How could he, Karl suddenly thought as the two of them silently confronted one another, how could he suddenly change his whole manner of speaking, it must seem to him that he had already said all there was to say, without anything to show for it, and, conversely, that he had said nothing at all, and he couldn't presume that the gentlemen would willingly listen to

14

everything. And at such a moment, his solitary supporter, Karl comes along wanting to give him a piece of advice, but instead only shows that all is lost.

If only I'd come earlier, instead of looking out of the window, Karl said to himself, he lowered his gaze before the stoker, and smacked his hands against his trouser seams in acknowledgement that all hope was gone.

But the stoker misunderstood him, he probably sensed some veiled reproach from Karl and hoping to reason him out of it, he now, to cap everything, began quarrelling with Karl. Now: with the gentlemen at the round table incensed at the pointless noise which was interrupting them in their important work, with the chief cashier increasingly baffled by the captain's patience and on the point of erupting, with the servant once more back in the camp of his masters, wildly eyeing the stoker, and finally, even the man with the little bamboo cane, to whom the captain sent friendly looks from time to time, seeming completely indifferent to the stoker, yes, even disgusted by him, and pulling out a little notebook, and clearly engaged with something entirely different, continually looking between the notebook and Karl.

'I know, I know,' said Karl, who had difficulty in warding off the tirade which the stoker now directed at him, but still keeping a friendly smile on his face. 'You're right, you're right, I never doubted that.' He felt like grasping the gesticulating hands of the other, for fear of being hit, even better he would have liked to go into a corner with him and whisper one or two quiet soothing words into his ear, that none of the others needed to hear. But the stoker was out of control. Karl even started to draw comfort from the thought that in an emergency the stoker, with strength born of desperation, could vanquish all the other seven men in the room. Admittedly, on the desk there was, as he saw at a glance, a centrepiece with far too many electrical buttons on it. Simply pressing a hand down on that could turn the whole ship against them, and fill its corridors with their enemies.

Then the so entirely uninvolved man with the bamboo cane stepped up to Karl and asked, not loudly, but quite audibly over the stoker's shouting: 'What is your name please?' At that moment, as though it had been a cue for someone behind the door, there was a knock. The servant glanced at the captain, who nodded. So the servant went over to the door and opened it. Outside, in an old frogged coat, stood a man of medium build, not really suited, to go by his appearance, to working with machines, and yet – this was Schubal. If Karl hadn't known it from looking at everyone's eyes, which showed a certain satisfaction – from which even the captain himself was not exempt – he must have learned it from the stoker who, to his alarm, tensed his arms and clenched his fists, as though that clenching was the most important thing to him, something for which he would willingly give all the life in his body. All his strength, even what kept him on his feet, was invested there.

So there was the enemy, sprightly and snug in his Sunday suit, with an account book under his arm, probably the wages and work record of the stoker, looking round into the eyes of all those present, one after the other, quite shamelessly gauging the mood of each one of them. All seven were his friends, for even if the captain had entertained, or had seemed to entertain, certain reservations about him before, after what the stoker had put him through, Schubal probably seemed free from any stain. One couldn't be too hard on a man like the stoker, and if Schubal was guilty of anything, then it was the fact that he hadn't been able to break the rebellious spirits of the stoker in time to prevent him from daring to appear before the captain today.

It was perhaps still reasonable to expect that the confrontation between the stoker and Schubal would have much the same effect before this company as before a higher assembly, because even if Schubal was a skilful dissembler, he surely couldn't keep it up right to the end. Just a quick flash of his wickedness would be enough to make it apparent to the gentlemen, and Karl wanted to provoke it. He was already acquainted with the respective acuity, the weaknesses and the moods of the company, so, at least from that point of view, his time here hadn't been wasted. If only the stoker had been in better shape, but he seemed completely out of commission. If Schubal had been dangled in front of him, he would probably have been able to split his hated skull open with his bare fists like a nut in a thin shell. But even to walk the few paces to reach him seemed to be beyond him. Why had Karl failed to predict the wholly predictable eventuality, that Schubal would at some stage present himself in person, either under his own steam, or else summoned by the captain. Why hadn't Karl formulated a precise plan of attack with the stoker on their way here instead of turning up hopelessly unprepared, thinking it was enough to step through the door? Was the stoker even still capable of speech, could he say yes and no under a cross-examination, which itself would only become necessary in the most favourable circumstances. He stood there, feet apart, knees slightly bent, head a little raised, and the air coming and going through his open mouth, as though he had no lungs in him with which to breathe.

Karl for his part felt stronger and more alert than he had ever done at home. If only his parents could see him, fighting for a good cause in a strange land before distinguished people, and while he hadn't won yet, he was absolutely ready for the final push. Would they change their minds about him? Sit him down between them and praise him? For once look into his eyes that shone with devotion to them? Doubtful questions, and hardly the time to start asking them now!

'I have come because I believe the stoker is accusing me of some dishonesty or other. One of the kitchen maids told me she had seen him on his way here. Captain, gentlemen, I'm prepared to refute any accusation against me with the help of these written records, and, if need be, by the evidence of some impartial and unprejudiced witnesses, who are waiting outside the door.' Thus Schubal. It was the clear speech of a man, and to judge by the change in the expressions of the listeners, it was as though they had heard human sounds for the first time in a long while. What they failed to realize was that even that fine speech was full of holes. Why was 'dishonesty' the first important word to occur to him? Perhaps the charges against him should have begun with that, rather than with national bias? A kitchen maid had seen the stoker on his way to the office, and straightaway drawn the right conclusion? Was it not guilt sharpening his understanding? And he had come with witnesses, and impartial and unprejudiced witnesses at that? It was a swindle, one big swindle, and the gentlemen stood for it and thought it was a proper way to behave? Why had he almost certainly allowed so much time to elapse between the maid's report and his arrival here, if not for the purpose of letting the stoker so tire everybody out that they lost their power of judgement, which was what Schubal would have good reason to fear? Had he not been loitering behind the door for a long time, and only knocked when that one gentleman's irrelevant question suggested to him that the stoker was finished?

It was all so clear, and in spite of himself Schubal only confirmed it, but the gentlemen still needed to have it put to them even more unambiguously. They needed shaking up. So, Karl, hurry up and use the time before the witnesses appear and muddy everything.

Just at that moment, though, the captain motioned to Schubal 'enough', and he – his affair for the moment put back a little – promptly walked off and began a quiet conversation with the servant, who had straightaway allied himself with him, a conversation not without its share of sidelong glances at the stoker and Karl, and gestures of great conviction. It seemed that Schubal was rehearsing his next big speech.

'Didn't you want to ask the young man here a question, Mr Jakob?' said the captain to the man with the bamboo cane, breaking the silence.

'Indeed I did,' he replied, thanking him for the courtesy with a little bow. And he asked Karl again: 'What is your name please?'

Karl, believing it was in the interest of the principal cause to get the stubborn questioner over with quickly, replied curtly and without, as was his habit, producing his passport, which he would have had to look for first, 'Karl Rossmann'.

'But,' said the man addressed as Jakob, taking a step backwards with a smile of near-disbelief. The captain too, the chief cashier, the ship's officer, even the servant clearly displayed an excessive degree of surprise on hearing Karl's name. Only the gentlemen from the port authority remained indifferent.

'But,' repeated Mr Jakob and rather stiffly walked up to Karl, 'then I'm your Uncle Jakob, and you're my dear nephew. Didn't I know it all along,' he said to the captain, before hugging and kissing Karl, who submitted quietly.

'What's your name?' asked Karl, once he felt he had been released, very politely but quite unmoved, and trying to see what consequences this new turn of events might have for the stoker. For the moment there was at least no suggestion that Schubal could draw any advantage from it.

'Don't you see you're a very lucky young man,' said the captain, who thought the question might have hurt the dignity of Mr Jakob who had gone over to the window, obviously in order to keep the others from seeing the emotion on his face, which he kept dabbing at with a handkerchief. 'The man who has presented himself to you as your uncle is the state councillor Edward Jakob. You now have a glittering career ahead of you, which you surely cannot have expected. Try to understand that, though it isn't easy, and pull yourself together.'

'I do indeed have an Uncle Jakob in America,' said Karl to the captain, 'but if I understood you correctly, it was the state councillor's surname that was Jakob.'

'That's correct,' said the captain expectantly.

'Well, my Uncle Jakob, who is my mother's brother, is Jakob by his first name, while his surname is of course the same as my mother's maiden name which is Bendelmayer.'

'Gentlemen, I ask you,' cried the state councillor, returning from his restorative visit to the window, with reference to Karl's explanation. Everyone, with the exception of the port officials, burst out laughing, some as though moved, others more inscrutably.

But what I said wasn't so foolish, thought Karl.

'Gentlemen,' reiterated the state councillor, 'without your meaning to, or my meaning you to, you are here witnessing a little family scene, and I feel I owe you some explanation, seeing as only the captain here' – an exchange of bows took place at this point – 'is completely in the picture.'

Now I really must pay attention to every word, Karl said to himself, and he was glad when he saw out of the corner of his eye that animation was beginning to return to the figure of the stoker.

'In the long years of my stay in America – although the word stay hardly does justice to the American citizen I have so wholeheartedly become – in all those years I have lived completely cut off from my relatives in Europe, for reasons that are firstly not relevant here, and secondly would distress me too much in the telling. I even dread the moment when I shall be compelled to relate them to my nephew, when a few home truths about his parents and their ilk will become unavoidable.'

'He really is my uncle, no question,' Karl said to himself, as he listened. 'I expect he's just had his name changed.'

'My dear nephew has simply been got rid of by his parents – yes, let's just use the phrase, as it describes what happened – simply got rid of, the way you put the cat out if it's making a nuisance of itself. It's not my intention to gloss over what my nephew did to deserve such treatment – glossing over isn't the American way – but his transgression is such that the mere naming of it provides an excuse.'

'That sounds all right,' thought Karl, 'but I don't want him to tell them all. How does he know about it anyway? Who would have told him? But let's see, maybe he does know everything.'

'What happened,' the uncle went on, resting his weight on the little bamboo cane and rocking back and forth a little, which robbed the matter of some of the unnecessary solemnity it would certainly have otherwise had – 'what happened is that he was seduced by a maidservant, one Johanna Brummer, a woman of some thirty-five years of age. In using the word seduced, I have no wish to insult my nephew, but it's difficult to think of another word that would be applicable.'

Karl, who had already moved quite close to his uncle, turned round at this point to see what impact the story was having on the faces of the listeners. There was no laughter from any of them, they were all listening quietly and gravely: it's not done to laugh at the nephew of a state councillor at the first opportunity that comes along. If anything, one might have said that the stoker was smiling very faintly at Karl, but, in the first place, that was encouraging as a further sign of life on his part, and, in the second place, it was excusable since back in the cabin Karl had tried to keep secret a matter that was now being so openly aired.

'Well, this Brummer woman,' the uncle continued, 'went on to have a child by my nephew, a healthy boy who was christened Jakob, I suppose with my humble self in mind, because even my nephew's no doubt passing references to me seem to have made a great impression on the girl. Just as well too, let me say. For the parents, to avoid paying for the child's upkeep or to avoid being touched by the scandal themselves – I must state that I am not acquainted either with the laws of the place, or with the circumstances of the parents, of whom all I have are two begging letters that they sent me a long time ago, to which I never replied, but which I was careful to keep and which now constitute the only, one-sided, written communications between us in all these years – to resume then, the parents, to avoid scandal and paying maintenance, had their son, my dear nephew, transported to America with, as you may see, lamentably inadequate provision – thus leaving the boy, saving those miracles that still happen from time to time and particularly here in America, entirely to his own devices, so that he might easily have met his death in some dockside alleyway on his arrival, had not the maid written to me, which letter, after lengthy detours, came into my possession only the day before yesterday, and acquainted me with the whole story, together with a personal description of my nephew, and, very sensibly, also with the name of the ship on which he was travelling. Now, if it were my purpose at this point to entertain you, gentlemen, I might well read out some choice passages from this letter' – he pulled from his pocket two enormous, closely written pages, and waved them around – 'It would certainly make a hit, written as it is with a certain low, but always well-intentioned, cunning and with a good deal of affection for the father of her child. But neither do I want to amuse you more than is necessary, nor do I want to injure any tender feelings possibly still entertained by my nephew, who may, if he cares to, read the letter for himself in the privacy of his own room, which already awaits him.'

Actually, Karl had no feelings for the girl. In the crush of an ever-receding past, she was sitting in the kitchen, with one elbow propped on the kitchen dresser. She would look at him when he went into the kitchen for a glass of water for his father, or to do an errand for his mother. Sometimes she would be sitting in her strange position by the dresser, writing a letter, and drawing inspiration from Karl's face. Sometimes she would be covering her eyes with her hand, then it was impossible to speak to her. Sometimes she would be kneeling in her little room off the kitchen, praying to a wooden cross, and Karl would shyly watch her through the open door as he passed. Sometimes she would be rushing about the kitchen, and spin round, laughing like a witch whenever Karl got in her way. Sometimes she would shut the kitchen door when Karl came in, and hold the doorknob in her hand until he asked her to let him out. Sometimes she would bring him things he hadn't asked for, and silently press them into his hands. Once, though, she said 'Karl!' and led him – still astonished at the unexpected address – sighing and grimacing into her little room, and bolted it. Then she almost throttled him in an embrace, and, while asking him to undress her she actually undressed him, and laid him in her bed, as though she wanted to keep him all to herself from now on, and stroke him and look after him until the end of the world. 'Karl, O my Karl!' she said as if she could see him and wanted to confirm her possession of him, whereas he couldn't see anything at all, and felt uncomfortable in all the warm bedding which she seemed to have piled up expressly for his sake. Then she lay down beside him, and asked to hear some secret or other, but he was unable to tell her any, then she was angry with him or pretended to be angry, he wasn't sure which, and shook him, then she listened to the beating of his heart and offered him her breast for him to listen to, but Karl couldn't bring himself to do that, she pressed her naked belly against his, reached her hand down, it felt so disgusting that Karl's head and neck leapt out of the pillows, down between his legs, pushed her belly against his a few times, he felt as though she were a part of him, and perhaps for that reason he felt seized by a shocking helplessness. He finally got to his own bed in tears, and after many fond goodnights from her. That had been all, and yet the uncle had managed to turn it into a big deal. So the cook had thought of him, and informed his uncle that he was arriving. That was nice of her, and one day he would like to pay her back.

'And now,' said the Senator, 'I want to hear from you loud and clear, whether I am your uncle or not.'

'You are my uncle,' said Karl and kissed his hand, and was kissed on the forehead in return. 'I'm very glad I've met you, but you're mistaken if you think my parents only say bad things about you. But there were a few other mistakes in what you said, I mean, not everything happened the way you described it. But it's difficult for you to tell from such a distance and anyway I don't think it matters if the gentlemen here have been given an account that's inaccurate in a few points of detail, about something that doesn't really concern them.'

'Well spoken,' said the Senator, and took Karl over to the visibly emotional captain, and said, 'Haven't I got a splendid fellow for a nephew?'

The captain said, with a bow of the kind that only comes with military training, 'I am delighted to have met your nephew, Senator. I am particularly honoured that my ship afforded the setting for such a reunion. But the crossing in the steerage must have been very uncomfortable, you never know who you've got down there. Once, for instance, the first-born son of the highest Hungarian magnate, I forget his name and the purpose of his voyage, travelled in our steerage. I only got to hear about it much later. Now, we do everything in our power to make the voyage as pleasant as possible for steerage passengers, far more than our American counterparts, for example, do, but we still haven't been able to make a voyage in those conditions a pleasure.'

'It did me no harm,' said Karl.

'It did him no harm!' repeated the Senator, with a loud laugh.

'Only I'm afraid I may have lost my suitcase –' and with that he suddenly remembered all that had taken place, and all that still remained to be done, and looked around at all those present, standing in silent respect and astonishment. None of them had moved and all were looking at him. Only in the port officials, inasmuch as their stern and self-satisfied faces told one anything, could one see regret that they had come at such an unsuitable time; the wristwatch they had laid out in front of them was probably more important to them than anything that had happened, and that might yet happen, in the room.

The first man, after the captain, to express his pleasure was, extraordinarily, the stoker. 'Hearty congratulations,' he said and shook Karl by the hand, also wanting to show something like admiration. But when he approached the Senator with the same words, the latter took a step back, as though the stoker had taken things too far, and he stopped right away.

But the others saw what had to be done, and they crowded round Karl and the Senator. Even Schubal offered Karl his congratulations in the confusion, which he accepted with thanks. When things had settled down again, the last to appear were the port officials who said two words in English, and made a ridiculous impression.

To make the most of such a pleasant occasion, the Senator went on to describe, for the benefit of himself and everyone else present, various other, lesser moments, which weren't only tolerated but listened to with interest. He pointed out, for instance, that he had copied down in his notebook some of Karl's distinguishing features as they were described in the cook's letter, in case they should prove useful to him. During the stoker's intolerable tirade he had taken out the notebook for no other purpose than to amuse himself, and for fun tried to match the cook's less than forensically accurate descriptions with Karl's actual appearance. 'And so a man finds his nephew,' he concluded, as though expecting a further round of congratulations.

'What's going to happen to the stoker now?' asked Karl, ignoring his uncle's latest story. It seemed to him that in his new position he was entitled to say whatever was on his mind.

'The stoker will get whatever he deserves,' said the Senator, 'and whatever the captain determines. But I'm sure the company will agree we've had enough and more than enough of the stoker.'

'But that's not the point, it's a question of justice,' said Karl. He was standing between the captain and his uncle, and perhaps influenced by that position, he thought the decision lay in his hands.

But the stoker seemed to have given up hope. He kept his hands half tucked into his belt, which his excited movements had brought into full view along with a striped shirt. That didn't trouble him in the least, he had made his complaint, let them see what rags he wore on his back, and then let them carry him off. He thought the servant and Schubal, the two lowliest persons present, should do him that final service. Then Schubal would have peace and quiet, no one to drive him to the brink of despair, as the chief cashier had said. The captain would be able to engage a crew of Rumanians, everyone would speak Rumanian, and maybe everything would go better. There would be no more stoker to speechify in the office, only his last tirade might live on fondly in their memories because, as the Senator had stated, it had led indirectly to the recognition of his nephew. That very nephew had tried to help him several times before that, and so he didn't owe him anything for his help in having made him recognized; it never occurred to the stoker to ask anything more of him now. Anyway, Senator's nephew he might be, but he wasn't a captain, and it was the captain who would be having the final say in the affair – So the stoker wasn't really trying to catch Karl's eye, only, in a room filled with his enemies, there was nowhere else for him to look.

'Don't misunderstand the situation,' said the Senator to Karl, 'it may be a question of justice, but at the same it's a matter of discipline. In either case, and especially the latter, it's for the captain to decide.'

'That's right,' muttered the stoker. Anyone who heard him and understood smiled tightly.

'Moreover, we have kept the captain from his business for long enough, which must be particularly onerous at the moment of arrival in New York. It's high time we left the ship, lest our completely unnecessary intervention may turn this trifling squabble between a couple of engineers into a major incident. I fully understand your behaviour, dear nephew, but that's precisely what gives me the right to lead you swiftly from this place.'

'I'll have them get a boat ready for you right away,' said the captain, astonishing Karl by not offering the slightest objection to the uncle's self-deprecating words. The chief cashier hurried over to the desk and telephoned the captain's order to the boatswain.

'Time is pressing,' Karl said to himself, 'but without offending them all there is nothing I can do. I can't leave my uncle who's only just found me. The captain is being polite, but really nothing more. When it's a matter of discipline, his kindness will come to an end, I'm sure uncle was right about that. I don't want to talk to Schubal, I'm even sorry I shook hands with him. And everyone else here is just chaff.'

So thinking, he walked slowly over to the stoker, pulled his right hand out of his belt, and held it playfully in his own. 'Why don't you say anything?' he asked. 'Why do you let them get away with it?'

The stoker furrowed his brow, as though looking for words for what he wanted to say. He looked down at his hand and Karl's.

'You've suffered an injustice, more than anyone else on the ship, I'm convinced of that.' And Karl slipped his fingers back and forth between those of the stoker, whose eyes were shining and looking around as though feeling inexpressible bliss and at the same time daring anyone to take it away from him.

'You must stand up for yourself, say yes and no, otherwise people will never learn the truth. I want you to promise me to do that, because I'm very much afraid that soon I won't be able to help you any more.' Karl was crying as he kissed the stoker's cracked and almost lifeless hand, holding it and pressing it to his cheek, like some dear thing from which he had to be parted. His uncle the Senator appeared at his side, and, ever so gently, pulled him away. 'The stoker seems to have put you under his spell,' he said, and looked knowingly across to the captain over Karl's head. 'You felt abandoned, then you found the stoker, and you're showing your gratitude to him, it's all very laudable. But please for my sake don't overdo it, and learn to come to terms with your position.'

Outside the door, there was a commotion, shouting, and it even seemed as though someone was being viciously pushed against it. A rather wild-looking sailor came in, wearing a girl's apron. 'There's people outside,' he said, pumping his elbows as though still in the crowd. Finally he came to his senses, and was about to salute the captain, when he noticed his girl's apron, tore it off, threw it on the ground, and said: 'That's disgusting, they've tied a girl's apron on me.' Then he clicked his heels together and saluted. Someone stifled a laugh, but the captain said sternly: 'Enough of these high jinks. Who is it who's outside?' 'They are my witnesses,' said Schubal stepping forward, 'I'd like to apologize for their behaviour. At the end of a long sea voyage, they sometimes get a little unruly.' 'Call them in right away,' ordered the captain, and turning quickly to the Senator, he said kindly but briskly: 'Would you be so kind now, my dear Senator, as to take your nephew and follow the sailor who will escort you to your boat? I can't say what happiness and honour your personal acquaintance has brought me. I only wish I may have another opportunity soon of resuming our discussion of the American Navy, and then perhaps to be interrupted as pleasantly as we were today.' 'One nephew's enough for me for the moment,' said the uncle laughing. 'And now please accept my thanks for your kindness, and farewell. It's by no means out of the question that we' – he pressed Karl affectionately to himself – 'might spend a little longer in your company on the occasion of our next visit to Europe.' 'I should be delighted,' said the captain. The two gentlemen shook hands, Karl took the captain's hand quickly and silently because he was then distracted by about fifteen people who had come into the office, a little chastened but very noisily still, under Schubal's leadership. The sailor asked the Senator to let him go first, and cleared a way for him and Karl, who passed quite easily through the crowd of bowing people. It seemed these cheerful souls thought the quarrel between Schubal and the stoker was a joke that even the captain was being permitted to share. Among them Karl spotted Line the kitchen maid, who winked merrily at him as she tied on the apron which the sailor had thrown down, because it was hers.

With the sailor leading the way, they left the office and went out into a little passage, which after a few steps took them to a small door, after which a short flight of steps led them down to the boat which had been prepared for them. The sailors in the boat – into which their escort leapt with a single bound – rose to salute them. The Senator was just telling Karl to be careful as he climbed down, when Karl started sobbing violently on the top step. The Senator took Karl's chin in his right hand, hugged him tight, and stroked him with his left hand. They went down together, one step at a time, and in a tight embrace got into the boat where the Senator found Karl a good seat directly facing him. At a signal from the Senator, the sailors pushed off from the ship, and straightaway were rowing hard. Barely a few metres from the ship, Karl discovered to his surprise that they were facing the side of the ship where the head office looked out. All three windows were occupied by Schubal's witnesses, shouting goodbye and waving cheerfully, the uncle even waved back and one sailor managed to blow a kiss without interrupting the rhythm of his rowing. It really was as though there was no stoker. Karl examined his uncle a little more closely – their knees were almost touching – and he wondered whether this man would ever be able to replace the stoker for him. The uncle avoided his eye, and looked out at the waves, which were bobbing around the boat.

2

THE UNCLE

Karl soon got used to his new circumstances in his uncle's house, and his uncle was also very kind to him in every little matter, so Karl never had to learn from bitter experience, which is the lot of so many when they begin a new life in a new country.

Karl's room was on the sixth floor of a building, whose five lower floors, and three more which were subterranean, were taken up by his uncle's business concern. The light that came into his room through two windows and a balcony door never ceased to astound Karl when he emerged from his little bedroom in the morning. Think of where he might have had to live, if he'd climbed ashore as a poor little immigrant! His uncle, from his knowledge of the immigration laws, even thought it highly probable that he might not have been admitted into the United States at all, but would have been sent straight back again, never mind the fact that he no longer had a home. Because one couldn't look for pity here, and what Karl had read about America was perfectly correct in this regard; here the fortunate few seemed quite content to enjoy their good fortune with only the pampered faces of their friends for company.

A narrow balcony ran along the entire length of the room. But what would probably have been the highest vantage point in Karl's hometown here did not afford much more than a view of a single street, which ran in a dead straight line between two rows of lopped-off houses until it vanished in the distance where the massive forms of a cathedral loomed out of the haze. In the morning and evening, and in his dreams at night, that street was always full of swarming traffic. Seen from above, it appeared to be a swirling kaleidoscope of distorted human figures and the roofs of vehicles of all kinds, from which a new and amplified and wilder mixture of noise, dust and smells arose, and all this was held and penetrated by a mighty light, that was forever being scattered, carried off and eagerly returned by the multitudes of objects, and that seemed so palpable to the confused eye that it was like a sheet of glass spread out over the street that was being continually and violently smashed.

Cautious as the uncle was in all things, he urged Karl for the moment, in all seriousness, to avoid all manner of commitments. He was to absorb and examine everything, but not allow himself to be captured by it. The first days of a European in America were like a new birth, and while Karl shouldn't be afraid, one did get used to things here faster than when entering the human world from beyond, he should bear in mind that his own initial impression did stand on rather shaky feet, and he shouldn't allow them any undue influence over subsequent judgements, with the help of which, after all, he meant to live his life. He himself had known new arrivals, who, instead of sticking by these useful guide-lines, would for instance stand on the balcony for days on end, staring down into the street like lost sheep. That was certain disorientation! Such solitary inactivity, gazing down on an industrious New York day, might be permitted to a visitor, and perhaps even, with reservations, recommended to him, but for someone who would be staying here it was catastrophic, one could safely say, even if it was a slight exaggeration. And the uncle actually pulled a face each time when, in the course of one of his visits, which he made at unpredictable times but always once a day, he happened to find Karl on the balcony. Karl soon realized this, and so he denied himself, as far as possible, the pleasure of standing out on the balcony.

After all, it was far from being the only pleasure in his life. In his room there was an American writing desk of the very finest sort, one of the kind his father had been longing for for years, and had tried to find at an affordably cheap price at various auctions, without ever having been able to afford one with his small means. Of course his desk was nothing like those so-called American desks that turn up at European auctions. For instance the top part of it had a hundred different compart-ments of all sizes, so that even the President of the Union would have found room for each of his files in it, but even better than that, it had an adjuster at the side, so that by turning a handle one could rearrange and adjust the compartments in whatever way one wanted or needed. Thin lateral partitions slowly descended to form the floors of newly created compartments or the ceilings of enlarged ones; with just one turn of the handle, the appearance of the top would be completely transformed, and one could do it either slowly or at incredible speed, depending on how one turned the handle. It was a very modern invention, but it reminded Karl vividly of the nativity scenes that were demonstrated to astonished children at the Christmas Fairs at home. Karl himself, warmly dressed, had often stood in front of these nativities, and had incessantly compared the turning of the handle, which an old man performed, with the effect it had on the scene, the halting progress of the three Kings, the shining star of Bethlehem and the shy life in the holy stable. And always it had seemed to him as though his mother standing behind him wasn't following the events closely enough and he had pulled her to him, until he felt her against his back, and he had drawn her attention to various more subtle manifestations by loud shouts, say a rabbit that was alternately sitting up and making to run in the long grass at the front, until his mother put her hand over his mouth and presumably reverted to her previous dullness. Of course the desk hadn't been designed to recall such things, but the history of inventions was probably full of such vague connections as Karl's memory. Unlike Karl, the uncle was not at all pleased with the desk, but he had wanted to buy Karl a proper desk, and all desks were now fitted with this contraption, which had the added advantage of being inexpensive to mount on older desks. Still, the uncle kept urging Karl preferably to avoid using the adjuster at all; to back up his advice the uncle claimed that the machinery was very delicate, easily broken and very expensive to repair. It wasn't hard to see that such claims were mere excuses if one reminded oneself that it was very easy to immobilize the adjuster, which the uncle never did.

In the first few days, there were of course frequent conversations between Karl and his uncle, and Karl had mentioned that he had played the piano at home, not much but with enjoyment, although he only knew the basics, which his mother had taught him. Karl was well aware that to mention this was tantamount to asking for a piano, but he had already seen enough to know that his uncle didn't need to economize. Even so, his wish was not immediately fulfilled, and it wasn't till a week later that the uncle said, and it sounded like a reluctant admission, that the piano had arrived and if Karl wanted to he could supervise its move up to his room. It was an undemanding job, but really no more demanding than the moving itself, because the building had its very own service lift, in which a whole removal van might have fitted with ease, and this lift carried the piano up to Karl's room. Karl could have gone on the same lift as the piano and the removal men, but since there was an ordinary lift just next to the other, standing empty, he took that, using a lever to remain constantly at the same level as the other lift, and looking through the glass walls at the beautiful instrument that was now his own. When it was installed in his room, and he played a few notes on it, he was seized with such a crazy joy that instead of continuing to play he leaped up and gazed at it from a distance, standing with his hands on his hips. The acoustics of the room were excellent, and that helped to take away his initial unease at living in an iron house. In fact, though the building might look very iron from outside, inside it one had not the slightest sense of its iron construction, and no one could have pointed to any features of the decor that were anything other than completely cosy. In the early days, Karl had high hopes of his piano playing, and while lying in bed, at any rate, he thought it might have a direct effect upon his American environment. But it did sound very peculiar when, with the windows letting in the noisy air from outside, he played an old ballad from his homeland, which the soldiers sing to each other in the evenings as they lean out through the barrack windows gazing at the dark square outside – but then, when he looked out on to the street, it was just the same, a tiny piece, no more, of a gigantic circulatory system that couldn't be arrested without understanding all the forces operating on its totality. The uncle put up with his piano playing and made no objection to it, especially as, quite unprompted, Karl only rarely allowed himself the pleasure of it. Yes, he even brought Karl the scores of American marches and of course of the national anthem, too, but it couldn't just have been love of music that made him one day ask Karl perfectly seriously if he wouldn't care to learn the violin or the French horn as well.

But naturally Karl's first and most important task was learning English. A young teacher from a trade school would appear in Karl's room at seven in the morning, to find him already seated at his desk, among his notebooks, or else walking up and down the room, committing something to memory. Karl understood that he couldn't learn English quickly enough, and that his rapid progress at it was also his best way of pleasing his uncle. At first the English content of his early conversations with his uncle had been confined to hello and goodbye, but he was soon able to increase the English portion of their conversations, and also to move on to more personal subjects. The first time Karl recited an American poem to his uncle one evening – the subject of it was a conflagration – it made him quite sombre with satisfaction. They both stood by a window in Karl's room, the uncle looked out into the darkened sky, and in sympathy with the verse, he slowly and rhythmically clapped his hands, while Karl stood beside him with expressionless eyes and struggled with the difficult poem.

The more Karl's English improved, the more inclined the uncle was to introduce him to his circle of acquaintances, decreeing that his English teacher should always accompany Karl. The very first acquaintance to whom Karl was introduced was a slim young man of astounding suppleness, whom the uncle ushered into Karl's room with a whole shower of compliments. He was obviously one of those millionaire's sons who from their parents' point of view have gone wrong, and whose life was such that no normal person could have followed so much as a single day of it without pain. As though in recognition of this, there was about his lips and eyes a continual smile for the good fortune that seemed to have been granted to him, to those he met and indeed to the whole world.

The young man, one Mr Mak, suggested, with the uncle's express approval, that they go out riding together at half past five in the morning, either in a riding school, or in the open air. Karl was a little loath to agree to this as he had never in his life sat on a horse, and wanted to learn to ride a little first, but in the face of the urgings of his uncle and Mack, both of whom said it was just for pleasure and a healthy form of exercise, nothing artistic, he finally agreed. It meant, unfortunately, that he had to get out of bed by half past four, and he often regretted that, because he seemed to be afflicted by a veritable sleeping sickness here, probably a consequence of having to be on his toes all day – but once in his bathroom, he quickly got over his regret. The sieve of a shower extended over the whole length and breadth of the bathtub – which of his former schoolmates, however rich, had anything like that, still less all to himself – and Karl would lie stretched out, he could even spread his arms in the tub, and let streams of warm, hot, warm and finally ice-cold water descend on him, all or part, just as he liked. As he lay there in a kind of half-sleep, what he liked best was to feel the last few drops falling on his closed eyelids, and then open them, and let the water run down his face.

Waiting for him at the riding school, where the lofty automobile of his uncle dropped him, would be his English teacher, while Mak invariably only turned up later. He could afford to, because the truly animated riding would only begin once he was there. Didn't the horses leap out of their doze on his entry, didn't the whip crack more percuss-ively through the arena, while the surrounding gallery was suddenly populated by various spectators, grooms, riding pupils, or whoever they were? Karl used the time before Mack's arrival for some very basic riding exercises. There was a long tall man who could reach the highest horseback almost without raising his arm, and he always gave Karl that fifteen-minute preparation. Karl was not overly successful with him, a pretext for learning English lamentations, which he kept uttering in a breathless way during this tuition to his English teacher, who was always leaning on the same doorpost, generally dog-tired. But almost all his frustration with riding would disappear when Mak arrived. The tall man was dismissed, and soon nothing would be heard in the still half-dark hall except the sound of galloping horses, and little was seen except Mak's raised arm as he gave Karl some order. After a delightful half an hour of this had passed almost like sleep they called a halt, Mak was in a tearing rush, he said goodbye to Karl patting him on the cheek if he were particularly pleased with his performance, and disappeared, in too much of a hurry even to go out through the door with Karl. Karl then took the teacher in his car, and they drove to their English lesson, usually by some roundabout way, because the big street, which actually led straight from the uncle's house to the riding school, was so choked with traffic that they would have lost too much time. He didn't have the company of the English teacher for very much longer, because Karl reproached himself for dragging the tired man along to riding school to no purpose, as the English communication with Mak was on a very simple level, and so he asked his uncle to relieve the teacher of this duty. After some thought, the uncle agreed.

It took rather a long time before his uncle decided to give Karl any insight at all into the nature of his business, though Karl often asked him about it. It was a sort of commissioning and forwarding business, of a kind that Karl thought probably didn't even exist in Europe. The actual business consisted of intermediate trade, but not delivering goods from producers to consumers or even to retailers, but the supplying of goods and raw materials to the great factory cartels, and from one cartel to another. It involved buying, storing, transporting and selling on a vast scale, demanding constant telephone and telegraph communications with its customers. The telegraph room was not smaller but actually larger than the telegraph office of his home town, through which Karl had once walked guided by a fellow pupil who knew his way around it. And wherever one looked in the telephone room, the doors of telephone booths were continually opening and closing, and the sound of so many telephones ringing was quite bewildering. The uncle opened the door of the nearest booth, and in the fizzing electric light sat an employee, quite indifferent to the sound of the door, his head gripped by a steel band that clamped the headphones to his ears. His right arm lay on a little table, as though it was particularly heavy, and only the fingers holding a pencil moved with inhuman speed and fluency. He spoke very sparingly into the tube and one often saw that he wanted to make some objection to the speaker, or to ask him some question, but certain words he heard forced him instead, before he could say anything, to lower his eyes and write. It wasn't his job to talk, as the uncle quietly explained to Karl, because the information that he was gathering was also simultaneously being taken down by two other employees and then collated, so that errors were as far as possible eliminated. Just as Karl and his uncle were stepping out of the door, an apprentice slipped in and emerged with the completed message on a piece of paper. People were criss-crossing the middle of the floor, in all directions, at great speed. No one offered a greeting, greetings had been abolished, each one fell into the tracks of the man ahead of him and kept his eyes on the floor, across which he wanted to make as rapid progress as possible, or else he picked up, at a glance, single words or figures from the fluttering piece of paper he held in his hand.

'You really have achieved a lot,' said Karl, on one of his visits to the business, the full inspection of which must take many days, merely to take in each individual department.

'And, you know, I set it all up myself thirty years ago. I owned a little store in the harbour district, and if five chests were unloaded there in the course of a day, that was a lot, and I would go home feeling very full of myself. Today I own the third largest warehouse in the port, and that shop now serves as the canteen and toolroom for the sixty-fifth group of my dockworkers.'

'It's like a miracle,' said Karl.

'Things develop very fast over here,' said the uncle, terminating the conversation.

One day his uncle turned up just as it was time for dinner, which Karl was about to eat by himself as usual, and told him to get into a dark suit and eat with him and a couple of business friends of his. While Karl was changing in the room next door, the uncle sat down at his desk and looked through an English exercise Karl had just completed, slammed his hand down on the desk and called out, 'Really excellent!' His dressing seemed to go better when he heard that praise, but in fact he was now pretty confident of his English.

In his uncle's dining-room, which he remembered from the evening of his first arrival, two large fat gentlemen rose to greet them, the one was a certain Green, the other a certain Pollunder as became clear during the conversation. It was his uncle's habit never to say very much by way of introduction, and to leave it to Karl to find out essential or interesting things about people. Over dinner, only private business matters were discussed – it was a good opportunity for Karl to master some business expressions – and Karl was left in peace to get on with his dinner, like a child for whom the most important thing is that it should eat its fill, but afterwards Mr Green leaned across to Karl, and evidently at pains to speak slowly and clearly, asked Karl about his first impressions of America. In the deathly silence that followed Karl replied, giving the occasional look at his uncle, pretty fully and tried to please his listeners by using some New Yorkish expressions. At one such expression all three gentlemen burst out laughing and Karl was afraid he had made some blunder, but no, he had, as Mr Pollunder explained, said something very felicitous. In fact, he seemed to conceive a special fondness for Karl and while the uncle and Mr Green returned to their business discussion Mr Pollunder had Karl move his chair closer to him, first asking him questions about his name, where he was from and the journey here, and then, to let him relax, he talked hurriedly, coughing and laughing, about himself and his daughter, with whom he lived on a little estate outside New York where he was only ever able to spend the evenings because he was a banker and his work kept him in the city all day. Karl was cordially invited to come out to this country estate, such a recent American as Karl must surely need to recover from New York from time to time. Karl asked his uncle for permission to accept this invitation, and his uncle, apparently happily, gave it, though without stipulating or raising the question of a date, as Karl and Mr Pollunder had expected him to do.

But the very next day Karl was summoned to one of his uncle's offices – there were ten of them, just in this one building – where he found his uncle and Mr Pollunder lounging rather silently in two armchairs. 'Mr Pollunder,' said his uncle, whom it was difficult to recognize in the evening gloom, 'Mr Pollunder has come to take you up to his estate, as we discussed yesterday.' 'I didn't know it was going to be for today,' replied Karl, 'otherwise I should have been prepared.' 'If you're not ready, then perhaps we'd better put off your visit for another time,' said the uncle. 'What kind of preparations!' exclaimed Mr Pollunder. 'A young man is always prepared.' 'It isn't on his account,' said the uncle to his guest, 'but he would have to go up to his room, and that would delay you.' 'There's plenty of time for that too,' said Mr Pollunder, 'I allowed for a delay, and left work early.' 'You see', said the uncle, 'the kind of inconvenience your visit has caused already.' 'I'm sorry,' said Karl, 'but I'll be back in a trice' and was just on his way. 'Don't be in too much of a hurry,' said Mr Pollunder. 'You haven't caused me the slightest inconvenience, on the contrary your visit will make me very happy.' 'You'll miss your riding-lesson tomorrow, have you cancelled that yet?' 'No,' said Karl. The visit he had been looking forward to was becoming a burden, 'I didn't know –' 'But you still intend to go?' the uncle asked. The amiable Mr Pollunder came to his assistance. 'We can stop by at the riding school on our way and sort it out.' 'That's an idea,' said the uncle. 'But Mak will still be expecting you.' 'Not exactly expecting me,' said Karl, 'but he will be there.' 'Well?' said the uncle, as though Karl's reply hadn't made the slightest justification. Once again Mr Pollunder intervened: 'Klara' – this was Mr Pollunder's daughter – 'is expecting him too, tonight, and surely she takes precedence over Mak?' 'Absolutely,' said the uncle. 'So run off to your room,' and he banged the armrest of his chair, almost involuntarily, a few times. Karl was already at the door when the uncle fired one more question at him: 'But you will be back in time for your English lesson tomorrow morning?' 'Oh!' Mr Pollunder exclaimed, and spun round in his chair in astonishment, inasmuch as his bulk made it possible. 'Can't he even stay for tomorrow? I'd bring him back on the morning of the day after.' 'That's out of the question,' replied the uncle. 'I can't permit his studies to be affected. Later on, once he's established in an orderly, professional way of life, I'll be very glad to allow him to accept such kind and flattering invitations as yours even for longer periods.' 'What contradictions!' thought Karl. Mr Pollunder was sad now. 'It's almost not worth it, just for one evening.' 'That was what I thought too,' said the uncle. 'But you have to take what you can get,' said Mr Pollunder, laughing again. 'I'm waiting for you,' he called to Karl, who, as his uncle didn't say anything this time, rushed off. By the time he got back, ready to go, he found his uncle had gone, and only Mr Pollunder was left in the office. Mr Pollunder happily shook him by both hands, as though to be sure that Karl really would be going with him. Hot himself from rushing about, Karl shook both Mr Pollunder's hands, he was looking forward to going on the excursion. 'Was uncle really not angry at me for going?' 'Oh no! He didn't really mean it. It's just that he cares about your education.' 'Did he tell you himself that he didn't mean what he said earlier?' 'Oh yes,' said Mr Pollunder in a drawn-out way, to prove that he was incapable of lying. 'It's strange how reluctant he was to give me permission to visit you, even though you're his friend.' But even Mr Pollunder, though he didn't admit it, couldn't find an explanation either and both pondered the matter for a long time afterwards as they drove through the warm evening in Mr Pollunder's car, though their conversation was on other things.

They sat close together, and Mr Pollunder held Karl's hand in his while he talked. Karl wanted to hear all about Miss Klara, it was as though he felt impatient on account of the long drive, and believed that by listening to Mr Pollunder's stories he would be able to arrive earlier than he really could. Although he had never before driven through the streets of New York at night and the noise pulsing over pavements and roads and changing direction like a whirlwind was more like a distinct element than something caused by men, as Karl tried to follow Mr

Pollunder's every word, he concentrated all his attention on Mr Pollunder's dark waistcoat, which had a gold chain calmly draped across it. From the streets where people, showing an open fear of arriving late, hurried their steps and drew up outside theatres in speeding vehicles, they passed some transitional areas and then reached the suburbs, where their car kept being diverted off on to side-streets by mounted policemen, as the main thoroughfares were all occupied by striking metalworkers, and only the most essential traffic could be allowed to pass at the crossroads. When their car emerged from one of the dark echoey side-streets on to one of these main avenues that was as broad as a whole square they saw in endless perspective on either side of them a great column of people walking in tiny steps, their massed voices more in unison than a single human voice. In the empty lanes one occasionally saw a policeman on a horse, motionless, or the carriers of flags and banners spanning the whole street, or a workers' leader surrounded by colleagues and shop stewards or an electric tram car, which hadn't managed to flee in time, and was now standing there dark and empty with the driver and conductor sitting on the platform. A long way away from the actual demonstration stood little groups of onlookers, all of them reluctant to leave the spot, even though they had no idea of what was going on. But Karl rested happily against the arm Mr Pollunder had thrown around him, the conviction that he would shortly be a welcome guest in a well-lit, high-walled, dog-guarded country house making him very happy, and even if he could no longer, on account of his growing sleepiness, follow every word of what Mr Pollunder was saying to him, he did still pull himself together from time to time and rubbed his eyes to check whether Mr Pollunder had noticed his sleepiness because that was what he wanted to avoid at all costs.

3

A COUNTRY HOUSE NEAR NEW YORK

'We've arrived,' said Mr Pollunder, in the middle of one of Karl's absences. The car had stopped in front of a country house, which, in the manner of rich people's country houses around New York, was bigger and higher than country houses for single families needed to be. As only the lower part of the house was lit up, it was impossible to gauge how high it was. There were rustling chestnut trees in front of it, and between them – the gates were already open – a short drive leading to a flight of stairs at the entrance. Judging by the tiredness he felt on getting out, Karl thought the drive there had probably been quite long. In the dark of the chestnut avenue, he heard a girl's voice beside him saying: 'At last, Mr Jakob.' 'My name is Rossmann,' said Karl, and took the hand held out to him by the girl, whom he could just see in outline. 'He is only Jakob's nephew,' Pollunder explained, 'and his name is Karl Rossmann.' 'We're still very pleased to welcome him here,' said the girl, who didn't much care what people were called. But Karl still inquired, as he walked up to the house flanked by Mr Pollunder and the girl: 'Are you Miss Klara then?' 'Yes,' she said, and a little differentiating light from the house just reached her face which she held up to him, 'but I didn't want to introduce myself in the darkness.' Then why did she meet us at the gate? wondered Karl, gradually waking up because of the walk. 'By the way, we have another guest tonight,' said Klara. 'Not possible!' exclaimed Mr Pollunder angrily. 'Mr Green,' said Klara. 'When did he got here?' asked Karl, almost with foreboding. 'Just a moment ago. Didn't you hear his car ahead of you?' Karl looked up at Pollunder to see how he was taking the news, but he had his hands in his pockets and seemed to be stamping rather. 'It's really no good living just outside New York, you're not spared any interruptions. We'll definitely have to move further out. Even if I have to drive half the night to get home.' They stopped at the foot of the stairs. 'But Mr Green hasn't been to see us for ages,' said Klara, who was obviously in complete agreement with her father, but still wanted to calm him down. 'Why did he have to come tonight,' said Pollunder, and the words tripped out over his fat lower lip, which being loose and fleshy easily became agitated. 'Quite!' said Klara. 'Perhaps he'll go away again soon,' observed Karl, and was astonished at the sympathy he felt with these people, who even yesterday had been complete strangers to him. 'Oh no,' said Klara, 'he has some kind of big business with Papa, and the discussion will probably go on for a long time, because he told me in jest that I'll have to stay and listen till tomorrow morning if I'm to be a good hostess.' 'Then he's spending the night with us. That too,' cried Pollunder, as if the depths had really been plumbed. 'Really,' he said, and the thought cheered him up, 'really, I feel like taking you straight back to the car, Mr Rossmann, and taking you back to your uncle. The evening is completely ruined, and who knows when your uncle will next let us take you away from him. But if I bring you back now, tonight, then he won't be able to refuse next time.' And he reached for Karl's hand to put the plan into effect. But Karl made no move, and Klara asked her father to let him stay because she and Karl at least wouldn't be put out by Mr Green in the slightest, and finally Pollunder realized that his resolve wasn't unshakeable. Besides – and this was perhaps the decisive factor – Mr Green came out on to the top step and called out into the garden: 'What's keeping you?' 'Come on,' said Pollunder, and began climbing the steps. Karl and Klara followed him, scrutinizing one another in the light. 'Such red lips she has,' Karl said to himself, and he thought of Mr Pollunder's lips and how beautiful they had become in his daughter. 'After supper,' she said, 'if it's all right with you, we can go up to my room, then we'll be rid of Mr Green and can leave Papa to talk to him. And I hope you'll be kind enough to play the piano for me, because Papa has already told me how good you are, unfortunately I can never bring myself to practise and I never go near my piano, even though I really love music.' Karl was in full agreement with Klara's suggestion, even though he would have preferred it if Mr Pollunder had been able to join them too. But faced by the enormous figure of Green – Karl had become used to Pollunder's size – which gradually grew towards them as they climbed the stairs, all Karl's hopes of somehow enticing Mr Pollunder for the evening from such a man quickly faded.

Mr Green received them in a great hurry, as though there was much catching up to do, he took Mr Pollunder's arm and pushed Karl and Klara ahead of him into the dining-room, which, with the flowers on the table half-peeping out of strips of fresh foliage, looked very festive, and made Mr Green's presence doubly regrettable. As he stood by the table waiting for the others to sit down, Karl was glad that the big glass door into the garden would be left open, because a powerful scent blew up to them as in an arbour, when Mr Green, puffing and panting, busied himself with shutting it, bending down to the lowest bolts, reaching up on tiptoe for the top ones, and all with such youthful speed that by the time the servant rushed up to help it was all done. Mr Green's first words at table were expressions of surprise that Karl had been permitted by his uncle to make this visit. Rapidly, he spooned soup into his mouth and explained to Klara on his right and Mr Pollunder on his left why he was so surprised, how closely the uncle watched over Karl, and how the uncle's love for Karl really surpassed the usual love of uncles. Not content with making mischief by being here, he's making mischief between me and my uncle, thought Karl, and he couldn't swallow a mouthful of the golden soup. But as he didn't want to draw attention to his irritation he began dumbly pouring soup into himself. The dinner dragged on like a plague. Only Mr Green, and to some extent Klara, showed any degree of animation and managed the odd short laugh. Mr Pollunder only became snarled up in the conversation on the few occasions when Mr Green turned to business matters. But he quickly withdrew again, and Mr Green had to surprise him into it a little later. He was at pains to emphasize – and here Karl, who was listening as if to a threat, had to be reminded by Klara that there was roast meat in front of him and that this was dinner – that it hadn't been his intention at any stage to make this surprise visit. For even if the business they still had to discuss was of particular urgency, then at least the principal part of it could have been negotiated in town today, and the details kept for tomorrow or some other day. Accordingly he had gone to see Mr Pollunder long before the close of business, but had found him gone, so that he had been compelled to ring home to say that he wouldn't be back that night and had then driven out here. 'Then I owe you an apology,' said Karl aloud, and, before anyone could reply, he went on, 'because it's my fault that Mr Pollunder left his business early and I'm very sorry.' Mr Pollunder covered most of his face with his napkin, while Klara smiled at Karl, but it wasn't a sympathetic smile, but rather one that sought to influence him in some way. 'No need to apologize,' said Mr Green, who was just carving up a pigeon with a few brisk strokes of his knife, 'on the contrary, I'm glad to be spending the evening in such pleasant company, rather than having my evening meal by myself at home, waited on by my old housekeeper who is so ancient that even the few steps from the door to my table seems to take her forever, and I can if I am minded to, sit back in my chair and follow her progress. Just recently I arranged for the butler to carry my food as far as the dining-room door, but the way from the door to my table she seems to think is hers by rights.' 'My God!' exclaimed Klara, 'such loyalty!' 'Yes, there is still some loyalty in the world,' said Mr Green lifting some food to his mouth, where, Karl happened to see, his tongue curled round and gripped it. He felt rather sick and stood up. Almost instantly Mr Pollunder and Klara each seized one of his hands. 'You must remain seated,' said Klara. And once he had sat down again, she whispered to him: 'We'll soon be able to get away. Be patient.' Mr Green was quietly getting on with his dinner meanwhile, as though it were the responsibility of Mr Pollunder and Klara to calm Karl down each time he made him feel sick.

What made the dinner go on was the thoroughness with which Mr Green treated each course, although he always seemed ready for another one afterwards, never slackened, and really gave the appearance of wanting to recover from his old housekeeper. Now and again he would praise Miss Klara's management of the house, which visibly flattered her, while Karl attempted to ward off these compliments as though they were attacks on her. Nor did Mr Green confine his attention to her, he repeatedly, without looking up from his plate, deplored Karl's striking lack of appetite. Mr Pollunder defended Karl's appetite, though, as Karl's host, it should have been his role to encourage him to eat more. Karl felt under considerable strain throughout the meal, and that made him so sensitive that, against his better judgement, he saw Mr Pollunder's words as hostile to himself. And it was purely on account of this that he suddenly consumed a great quantity of food with prodigious speed, then dropped his knife and fork exhausted and was the most lethargic member of the company, which made things very difficult for the waiter.

'Tomorrow I will tell the Senator how you offended Miss Klara by not eating,' said Mr Green and the only clue to his humorous intention was the way he handled his cutlery. 'Look at the girl, see how sad she looks,' he went on, and chucked Klara under the chin. She let him do it, and closed her eyes. 'Little thing you,' he cried, leaned back in his chair, and laughed red-faced and with the vigour of one who has eaten. Karl couldn't understand Mr Pollunder's behaviour at all. There he sat staring at the plate in front of him, as though the important events were all taking place there. He didn't pull up Karl's chair, and when he spoke he spoke to the generality, but he had nothing particular to say to Karl. And yet he allowed Green, that old New York bachelor roué, blatantly to fondle Klara, to insult Karl, his guest, or at least to treat him like a child, and Lord knows to what acts he was gearing himself up.

With dinner over – when Green sensed the general mood, he was the first to get up, and as it were pulled all the others up with him – Karl went off by himself to one of the great windows, divided up by little white strips, that looked out on to the terrace, and that turned out, on closer inspection, to be doors. What was left of the revulsion Mr Pollunder and his daughter had initially felt for Green, and which had seemed so incomprehensible to Karl at first? Now there they were standing with Green nodding at him. The smoke from Mr Green's cigar, a present from Pollunder, of a thickness that his father would occasionally affirm existed, but had probably never witnessed with his own eyes, spread throughout the room, and carried Green's influence into nooks and corners in which he would personally never set foot. In spite of the distance, Karl felt the smoke tickle his nose, and the behaviour of Mr Green, at whom he cast another quick glance across the room, seemed to him quite dastardly. Now he no longer excluded the possibility that his uncle had only refused to let him make this visit because he knew Mr Pollunder for a weak character, and so foresaw, if not in detail, then at least in general, the possibility of Karl's being insulted. Nor did he care for the American girl, although her appearance had hardly been a disappointment to him. Since Mr Green had taken up with her he had been surprised by the beauty which her face was capable of, especially by the lustre of her constantly darting eyes. He had never seen a skirt as clinging as the one that clasped her body, little creases in the yellow, delicate, resistant fabric showed the strain. But Karl felt nothing for her, and would happily have declined to go up to her room with her, if instead he could open the door, the knob of which he held in both hands just in case, and climb into the car, or if the chauffeur was asleep already he could have gone to New York on foot by himself. The clear night with the favourable full moon was free for anyone, and to be afraid out in the open seemed idiotic to Karl. He pictured to himself – and for the first time he felt happy in that room – how he would arrive in the morning – he could hardly get there any sooner on foot – and surprise his uncle. He had never seen inside his uncle's bedroom, in fact he didn't even know where it was, but he would find out from someone. Then he would knock on the door, and on hearing the formal 'Enter', he would run into the room and surprise his dear uncle, whom he had previously only seen buttoned up and fully dressed, sitting up in bed, startled eyes on the door, in his nightshirt. Just by itself that might not be much, but imagine the possible consequences! Perhaps he would have breakfast with his uncle for the first time, his uncle in bed, himself on a chair, the breakfast on a low table between them, then perhaps they would breakfast together regularly, perhaps as a consequence of these breakfasts, it was almost inevitable in fact, they would meet more than the once a day it had been up until now, and then of course they would also be able to talk more openly with one another. It was really only because of the lack of frankness between them that he had shown a little dis-obedience to his uncle, or rather just stubbornness. And if he had to spend the night here – which unfortunately seemed probable, even though they left him to stand alone by a window and amuse himself – perhaps this unfortunate visit would become the turning point in his relations with his uncle, and perhaps his uncle in his bedroom tonight entertained similar thoughts himself.

He felt slightly comforted and turned round. Klara was standing in front of him, saying: 'Do you really not like it here with us at all? Couldn't you feel a little more at home? Come with me, I'll make one final effort.' She led him across the room to the door. The two men were sitting at a side table with tall glasses full of gently effervescent drinks, which were unfamiliar to Karl and which he would have liked to try. Mr Green had his elbow on the table, and the whole of his face as close as possible to Mr Pollunder; if one didn't know Mr Pollunder, one might easily have supposed that what these two were talking about was not business at all, but something of a criminal nature. Whereas Mr Pollunder's eyes followed Karl tenderly as he went to the door, Green didn't make the slightest move to look at Karl – even though one quite involuntarily tends to follow where one's partner is looking. Karl saw in this behaviour the expression of a creed of Green's that everyone should try to get by on his own abilities, Karl for himself and Green for himself, the necessary social connection between them would be established in time by the victory or destruction of one or other of them. 'If he thinks that,' Karl said to himself, 'then he's a fool. I want nothing to do with him, and I wish he would leave me in peace.' No sooner had he emerged into the corridor than he thought he had probably behaved badly, because he had had his eyes glued to Green and had made Klara practically drag him out of the room. To make amends, he walked eagerly beside her now. Walking down the corridor, he at first didn't believe his eyes when he saw at every twenty paces a richly liveried servant standing with a candelabra, holding its thick stem in both hands. 'Electric power has so far only been connected to the dining-room,' explained Klara. 'We only recently bought the house, and had it completely converted, inasmuch as you can convert such an old and idiosyncratically constructed house like this.' 'So there are some old houses in America,' said Karl. 'Of course,' said Klara laughing, and pulling him on. 'You've got some strange ideas about America.' 'You're not to laugh at me,' he said crossly. After all, he knew both Europe and America, whereas she only knew America.

Klara put out her hand to push open a door in passing, and said: 'This is where you'll be sleeping.' Of course Karl wanted to take a look at the room right away, but Klara explained, almost shouting with impatience, that that could wait, and he was to come along now. They had a little tug of war in the corridor, finally Karl thought he mustn't just do whatever Klara said, and he broke loose and ran into the room. It was surprisingly dark outside, because just beyond the window was a treetop which was swaying to and fro. There was birdsong. In the room itself, which the moonlight hadn't penetrated, one could make out very little. Karl was sorry he hadn't brought along the electric torch his uncle had given him. Torches were essential in a house like this, if they had a few torches all the servants could be packed off to bed. He sat down on the window-seat and looked and listened. A frightened bird seemed to drill its way through the foliage of the old tree. The whistle of a New York suburban train sounded somewhere out in the distance. Apart from that all was quiet.

But not for long, because Klara ran in. Clearly angry, she cried: 'What do you think you're playing at?' and smacked at her skirt. Karl wasn't going to answer until she changed her tone. But she strode up to him and cried: 'Well, are you coming or not?' and either intentionally or in her excitement, she shoved him in the chest, so that he would have fallen out of the window, if his feet hadn't gripped the floor at the last moment as he slipped backwards off the window-seat. 'I almost fell out of the window just now,' he said, reprovingly. 'Well, I wish you had. Why are you so naughty. I'm going to push you down again.' And she put her arms round him, he was so surprised he forgot to make himself heavy, and with her sport-toughened body she carried him almost as far as the window. Then he came to his senses, freed himself with a twist of his hips, and then grabbed her. 'Oh stop it, you're hurting me!' she said right away. But this time Karl thought he'd better not let her go. He allowed her to move her feet and take steps, but he went with her and didn't let go. It was so easy to hold on to her in her tight dress. 'Let me go,' she whispered, her flushed face just by his, he had to strain to see her, she was so close, 'Let me go, and I'll give you a present.' 'Why is she sighing like that,' thought Karl, 'it can't be hurting her, I'm not pressing at all,' and he didn't let go. But suddenly after a moment of careless silent standing, his body felt her strength returning and she slipped free, and held his upper body in a practised grip, warding off his legs with foot movements of some exotic fighting style, and panting for air with wonderful regularity, she drove him back towards the wall. There was a sofa there, on which she laid Karl, and said to him, 'Now try and escape.' 'You cat, you wildcat,' Karl cried in a bewilderment of shame and rage. 'You wildcat, you're mad.' 'Watch your words,' she said, and one of her hands slipped round his throat and began choking him so hard that Karl was reduced to gulping for air, while with the other hand she touched his cheek as though to try it out, and then withdrew it far enough for her to slap him at any moment. 'How would you like it,' she said, 'if for your behaviour towards a lady I were to send you home with a good slap for punishment. Perhaps it would be a useful lesson for future reference, though it wouldn't be a pleasant memory.

I'm sorry for you, you're quite a good-looking boy really, and if you'd learned ju-jitsu, you would probably have given me a thrashing. Even so, even so – seeing you lying there, I feel an enormous urge to smack your face. I'll probably regret it, but if I do it, I want you to know that it will almost have been in spite of myself. And of course I wouldn't content myself with just one slap then, but hit you left and right till your cheeks are swollen. Maybe you're a man of honour – I almost think you are – and you won't be able to go on living after you've been slapped, and you'll have to do away with yourself. But why did you have to treat me like that? Don't you like me? Didn't you want to come up to my room with me? Woops! I almost slapped you by accident. But if I let you off for now, you'd better behave in future. I'm not your uncle whom you can defy with impunity. Lastly I want to point out to you that if I let you go without slapping you, you're not to think that in point of honour you might as well have been slapped, because if you were to think that, I'd prefer actually to slap you. I wonder what Mack will say when I tell him all this.' At the name of Mack she let go of Karl, to whose confused mind Mack seemed like a saviour. He could still feel Klara's hand round his throat, so he went on writhing for a while and then lay still.

She told him to get up, but he didn't move or reply. Somewhere she lit a candle, and the room grew light, a blue zigzag pattern appeared on the ceiling, but Karl lay there, his head on the sofa cushion, just as Klara had left it, and didn't move it an inch. Klara walked about the room, her skirt swishing against her legs, then she stopped for a long time, probably by the window, he guessed. 'Snapped out of it?' she could be heard to ask. It was a heavy blow to Karl that in this room, where Mr Pollunder had put him for the night, he could get no rest. This girl was walking about in it, then she would stop and talk, it was all so inexpressibly tedious. He wanted to get to sleep quickly, and then get out of here, nothing more. He didn't even want to go to bed, just stay where he was on the sofa. He was just lying there, waiting for her to leave, then he would leap across to the door, bolt it, and fling himself back on the sofa. He had such a need to stretch and yawn, but he didn't want to do that in front of Klara. And so he lay there, staring up, feeling his face becoming ever more rigid, sensing a fly buzzing in front of his eyes, without really knowing what it was.

Klara went over to him again, leaned across to see where he was looking, and if he hadn't disciplined himself, he would have had to look at her. 'I'm going now,' she said. 'Maybe you'll feel like seeing me later. The door to my rooms is the fourth one along on this side of the corridor. So you pass three doors, and the next one is mine. I won't be going down to the salon again, I'm staying up in my room. You've really taken it out of me. I won't exactly be waiting for you, but if you want to, then come. Remember, you promised to play the piano for me. But maybe you're fed up with me, and you can't move any more, then stay here and sleep. For the moment I'm not going to tell my father about our fight; I'm just saying that in case you're worried.' Then, in spite of her alleged tiredness, she was out of the room in two bounds.

Straightaway Karl sat up, lying had become impossible for him. For a little exercise he went to the door and looked out into the passage. It was pitch-black out there! He felt relieved when he had shut the door and bolted it, and was back by his table in the candlelight. He had decided not to stay in the house any longer, but to go downstairs to Mr Pollunder, to tell him quite openly how Klara had treated him – he didn't mind admitting his defeat – and with probably sufficient justification, ask for permission to drive or walk home. If Mr Pollunder should have any objection to his immediate return, then Karl would ask to be shown to the nearest hotel by a servant. This wasn't how one normally behaved to a friendly host, but it was still more unusual for a guest to be treated as he had been by Klara. She had even thought her promise not to mention the fight to Mr Pollunder was doing him a favour, and that was shocking enough. Was it some kind of wrestling bout to which Karl had been invited, so that it would have been embarrassing for him to have been thrown by a girl who probably spent most of her waking hours learning wrestling holds? She had probably received tuition from Mack. Let her tell him everything, he would understand, Karl was sure of that, even though he'd not yet had an opportunity to try him. But Karl also knew that if Mack had given him coaching, he would have been a far better pupil than Klara; and one day he would come back here, most probably uninvited, he would first reconnoitre the area, local knowledge was a prime advantage of Klara's, and then he would grab that selfsame Klara, and dust that same sofa with her which she had laid him on today.

Now it was just a matter of finding his way down to the salon, where, in his initial distraction, he had probably also left his hat in some unsuitable place. He would take the candle with him of course, but even with its light, it wouldn't be easy to find the way. For example he didn't even know whether this room was on the same floor as the salon or not. Klara had kept pulling him on the way here, so that he had been unable to look around. He had also been distracted by the servants with their candelabras, in short, he really didn't know if they had climbed one flight of stairs or two, or none at all. Judging from the view, the room was quite high up, and he tended therefore to imagine that they had climbed some steps, but then there were steps leading up to the front door, so perhaps that accounted for the height on this side of the house. If only there was a glimmer of light from a doorway or a faint voice in the corridor.

His wristwatch, a present from his uncle, showed eleven o'clock as he took up the candle and went out into the corridor. In case his search should be unsuccessful, he left his door open, so that he would at least be able to find his room again, and thereby, in an extreme emergency, Klara's as well. Lest the door should fall shut, he pushed a chair in the way. In the passageway Karl found that he had to contend with a draught – naturally he had turned left, away from Klara's door – that was quite weak, but still well capable of extinguishing the candle, so that Karl had to shield the flame with his hand, and also to stop at intervals to allow the guttering light to recover. He made slow progress, and the way back seemed to be twice as long. Karl passed great stretches of wall that had no doors at all, so that one couldn't imagine what lay behind them. Then it was one door after another, he tried several of them, but they were all locked, and the rooms evidently unoccupied. It was an extraordinary waste of space, and Karl thought of the eastern districts of New York, which his uncle had promised to show him, where one small room apparently housed several families and a corner was home to a whole family, with the children huddling round their parents. And here there were so many empty rooms, whose sole purpose was to make a hollow sound when you knocked on their doors. Karl thought Mr Pollunder had been led astray by false friends, besotted with his daughter, and thus corrupted. His uncle had surely judged him correctly, and only that principle of his of not influencing Karl's own judgements was responsible for this visit and his wanderings along these passages. Karl decided to tell his uncle all this straight out tomorrow, because his uncle's own principle meant that he would listen to his nephew's opinion, even of himself, calmly and gladly. That principle was perhaps the only thing that Karl didn't like about his uncle, and even that feeling was not unqualified.

Suddenly the wall on one side of the corridor came to an end, and was replaced by an ice-cold marble balustrade. Karl put the candle down on it and carefully leaned forward. Empty darkness blew towards him. If this was the entrance hall of the house – by the light of the candle he saw what seemed to be a bit of vaulted ceiling – why hadn't they come in through it? What was this large and lofty room for? It was like standing in the gallery of a church up here. Karl almost regretted that he couldn't stay in the house till morning, he would like to have had a guided tour of it by daylight from Mr Pollunder.

The balustrade did not go on for very long, and soon Karl was swallowed up by the enclosed corridor again. Suddenly it made a sharp turn, and Karl walked smack into a wall, only the vigilance with which he held the candle upright kept it from falling from his grasp and being extinguished. As the corridor seemed never ending, without a window anywhere and no sign of movement either high or low, it occurred to Karl that he was going round in a circle, he hoped to come upon the open door of his room soon, but neither that nor the balustrade returned. So far Karl had refrained from calling out, as he was reluctant to make a noise in a strange house at this late hour, but he now realized that it would be a forgivable thing to do in this unlit house, and he was just about to halloo loudly down the corridor in both directions, when he saw, from where he had come, a small light coming ever nearer. Karl's joy at this salvation was so great that he forgot all his caution and started running towards it, which caused his candle to go out after a few steps. He didn't care, he didn't need it any more, here came an old retainer with a lantern who would show him the way.

'Who are you?' asked the retainer and held the lantern in Karl's face, thereby simultaneously lighting up his own. His face seemed rather stiff on account of a long white beard which only broke up into silky ringlets when it hit his chest. He must be a trusty servant to be allowed to wear such a beard, thought Karl, and he stared at its length and breadth, without being inhibited by the fact that he was being stared at himself.

He replied right away that he was a guest of Mr Pollunder's, that he had left his own room to go back to the dining-room, but had been unable to find it. 'Oh yes,' said the servant, 'we haven't introduced electric light yet.' 'I know,' said Karl. 'Wouldn't you care to light your candle at my lantern?' asked the servant. 'Yes please,' said Karl, and did so. 'There is such a draught in the corridors,' said the servant, 'a candle is easily extinguished, and so I have a lantern.' 'Yes, a lantern is far more practical,' said Karl. 'You're all spattered with wax too,' said the servant, passing the lantern over Karl's suit. 'I never noticed that,' said Karl, and he was very sorry as it was his black suit, which his uncle had said fitted him best of all his suits. The fight with Klara couldn't have done much for the suit either, he now thought. The servant was kind enough to give the suit a quick clean; Karl kept turning round in front of him, drawing more stains to his attention, which the servant duly removed. 'Why is there such a draught here?' asked Karl, once they were on their way again. 'There's a lot of building work still to be done,' said the servant, 'they've begun on the conversion, but it's going very slowly. And now the building workers have gone on strike, maybe you've heard. A building job like that is nothing but trouble. They've made a couple of major openings, but there's no one to wall them up, and so there's a draught all over the house. If I didn't have cotton wool in my ears, I wouldn't be able to survive.' 'Would you like me to speak up?' said Karl. 'No, your voice is very clear,' said the servant. 'But to get back to the building, the draught is quite intolerable, especially here in the vicinity of the chapel, which will certainly have to be separated from the rest of the house later.' 'So the balustrade you pass in this corridor opens out into the chapel?' 'Yes.' 'I thought so right away,' said Karl. 'It's well worth seeing,' said the servant. 'If it hadn't been there, I doubt whether Mr Mack would have bought the house.' 'Mr Mack?' asked Karl, 'I thought the house belonged to Mr Pollunder.' 'Yes, it does,' said the servant, 'but Mr Mack was the moving force behind the purchase. Do you not know Mr Mack?' 'Yes I do,' said Karl. 'But what is his relationship with Mr Pollunder?' 'He is the young lady's intended,' said the servant. 'I had no idea of that,' said Karl, and stopped. 'Does it come as such a surprise to you?' asked the servant. 'I just want to take account of it. If you're not aware of such relationships, you can make very serious blunders,' replied Karl. 'I'm surprised you weren't informed about it,' said the servant. 'No I wasn't,' said Karl, embarrassed. 'They probably thought you knew about it,' said the servant, 'it's not a recent development. By the way, we've arrived,' and he opened a door, behind which a flight of steps led steeply down to the back door of the dining-room, which was brightly lit, as it had been on their arrival. Before Karl had entered the dining-room, from which the voices of Mr Green and Mr Pollunder could be heard, as they could two hours previously, the servant said: 'If you like, I'll wait here for you, and take you back to your room. It is difficult to find your way around on your first evening with us.' 'I won't be going back to my room,' said Karl, and he didn't know why the statement made him feel sad. 'Surely it's not that bad,' said the servant, smiling in a gently superior way and patting him on the arm. He probably took Karl to mean that he intended to spend the whole night in the dining-room, talking and drinking with the gentlemen. Karl didn't want to make any admissions, and besides, he thought this servant, whom he liked better than any of the others, might be able to show him the way to New York later, and so he said: 'If you wouldn't mind waiting here, that would be very kind of you, and I'm happy to accept. I'll be out in a little while, and tell you what's to be done then. I think I'll be needing your help.' 'Very good,' said the servant, and set the lantern down on the floor and seated himself on a low plinth, whose unoccupied condition was probably something to do with the conversion of the house, 'I'll be waiting for you here.' 'You can leave the candle with me too,' he added, as Karl was about to enter the salon with his burning candle in his hand. 'I am being absent-minded,' said Karl, and passed the candle to the servant, who merely nodded to him, although it wasn't clear whether it was deliberate, or merely the result of stroking his beard.

Karl opened the door which rattled loudly, not through his own fault, but because it consisted of a single pane of glass which almost broke when the door was quickly pulled open held only by the handle. Karl let go of the door in fright, because he had meant to make a particularly quiet entrance. Without turning round, he noticed how behind him the servant must have got off his plinth to close the door carefully, without making the slightest noise. 'Excuse the interruption,' he said to the two gentlemen, who stared at him with large astonished faces. At the same time he scoured the room to see whether he might not quickly find his hat lying somewhere. But it was nowhere to be seen, the table had been cleared, there was the disagreeable possibility that it had been carried off into the kitchens. 'What have you done with Klara?' asked Mr Pollunder, who seemed to welcome the interruption, as he straightaway shifted in his chair to face Karl. Mr Green feigned indifference, pulled out his wallet, by size and thickness a monster of its kind, and seemed to be looking for some particular item in its various compartments, but as he looked he also perused whatever else came to light. 'I've got a favour to ask you, you mustn't take it amiss,' said Karl, and he went hurriedly across to Mr Pollunder, and to be as close as possible to him he laid his hand on the armrest of his chair. 'What favour is that?' asked Mr Pollunder, looking candidly at Karl. 'Of course it's already granted,' and he put his arm round Karl, and made him stand between his legs. Karl didn't mind, although he thought he was generally a little too old for such treatment. But it made it harder to ask the favour. 'How do you like it here with us?' asked Mr Pollunder. 'Wouldn't you agree that the country has a liberating effect, when you come here from the city. In general' – and he sent an unambiguous look at Mr Green, half-obscured by Karl's body – 'in general I feel like that every time I come here in the evening.' 'The way he talks,' thought Karl, 'it's as though he didn't know about the big house, the endless corridors, the chapel, the empty rooms, the darkness everywhere.' 'Now then!' said Mr Pollunder. 'That favour!' and he gave Karl a friendly shake as he stood there silently. 'The favour,' said Karl, and however much he tried to lower his voice, he was unable to prevent everything he said from being overheard by Green, who might construe his request as an insult to Pollunder so that Karl would have dearly liked to keep it from him – 'the favour I want to ask is to let me go home right now, tonight.' And since the worst had been spoken, everything else tumbled out too, he spoke, without any recourse to lying, things he hadn't even thought previously. 'More than anything I want to go home. I will be happy to come on another occasion, because anywhere you are, Mr Pollunder, I am glad to be myself. Only today I can't stay. You know that my uncle didn't willingly give me permission for this visit. He must have had his reasons too, as he does for everything, but I ventured, against his superior understanding, to force his permission. I simply abused his love for me. It doesn't matter any more why he was against the visit, I just know that there was nothing in his reasons to cause you any offence, Mr Pollunder, because you are the best, the very best of my uncle's friends. None of my uncle's other friends can remotely compare with you. That's the only excuse for my disobeying him, but it's not a sufficient excuse. Your understanding of the relationship between my uncle and me may not be very thorough, so let me just mention some salient points. Until my English studies are complete, and I have seen something of the workings of business, I am utterly dependent on the kindness of my uncle, which as a blood-relation I have a certain right to enjoy. You must bear in mind that I am as yet unable to make my own way in life respectably – and may God save me from all else. Unfortunately my education has been too unpractical for that. I have had four years as a middling pupil at a European second-ary school, and in terms of a qualification for earning money, that means less than nothing, because our schools follow a very antiquated syllabus. If I told you what I'd studied it would only make you laugh. If you continue, and finish the secondary school and go on to university, then everything probably balances out somehow and you end up with a decent education that is of some use, and also gives you the resolve to go out and earn money. Unfortunately I was plucked out of such a coherent education prematurely, at times I believe I know nothing at all, and everything I might possibly know would still be too little for America. In my home country a few progressive secondary schools have recently been introduced, where modern languages and perhaps some business studies are taught, but at the time I left elementary school they didn't yet exist. My father was keen for me to learn English, but firstly I had no way of knowing what catastrophe would befall me, and with what urgency I would need English, and secondly I had to study hard at secondary school, so that it didn't leave me with much time for other pursuits – I tell you all this to show you how dependent on my uncle I am, and correspondingly how indebted to him. You will surely agree that under such circumstances I could not permit myself to do the slightest thing against his wishes, or even his presumed wishes. And that is why to try and partly atone for my transgression against him, I must go home right away.' Mr Pollunder had listened carefully to Karl's long speech, he had pressed Karl to himself imperceptibly, especially when the uncle was mentioned, and occasionally and as though expectantly and seriously looked over to Green, who continued to be engaged with his wallet. Karl though, the more his position towards his uncle had become clear to him as he spoke, had become more and more restless, and tried involuntarily to break away from Mr Pollunder's hold, everything here was constricting him, the way to his uncle through the glass door, down the stairs, through the avenue, along the country roads, through the suburbs to the big thoroughfare, ending up in his uncle's house, seemed to him to constitute an indivisible entity, lying empty, smooth and ready for him, and it called out to him in a loud voice. Mr Pollunder's goodness and Mr Green's vileness blurred together, and he wanted nothing more from this smoky room than permission to leave it. He felt impervious to Mr Pollunder and ready to fight Mr Green, and yet he was filled with the sensation all around him of a vague fear, whose throbbings dimmed his eyes.

He took a step back and was now equidistant from Mr Pollunder and Mr Green. 'Didn't you have something to say to him?' Mr Pollunder asked Mr Green, as though imploringly taking Mr Green's hand. 'I wouldn't know what I had to say to him?' said Mr Green, finally pulling a letter from his wallet, and laying it on the table. 'It's all very laudable of him to want to go back to his uncle, and one might go so far as to predict that he will give his uncle great pleasure by so doing. Unless, that is, he has previously so angered his uncle by his disobedience, which is also possible. In that case, he would be better advised to stay here. It's difficult to say anything definite, both of us are friends of his uncle's, and it would be a tricky thing to establish some pecking order between my friendship with his uncle and Mr Pollunder's, but finally we can't see inside the uncle, least of all so many miles away from New York.' 'Mr Green, please,' said Karl, and overcoming his reluctance, he approached Mr Green, 'I understand you to be suggesting that the best course for me would be to return right away as well.' 'That's not what I meant at all,' said Mr Green, and focused his attention on the letter, sliding two fingers up and down the edge of it. He seemed to be suggesting with that that he had been asked a question by Mr Pollunder and given him his reply, and that he had nothing to do really with Karl.

In the meantime Mr Pollunder had gone up to Karl and had gently pulled him away from Mr Green to one of the big windows. 'Dear Mr Rossmann,' he said, bending down to Karl's ear, giving his face a preparatory wipe with his handkerchief, stopping at his nose, which he blew.

'Surely you can't believe that I want to detain you against your will. There's no question of that. I am afraid I can't put the car at your disposal, because it is kept at a public garage some way from here, as I have yet to build my own garage here, where everything is still at an early stage. Moreover, the chauffeur doesn't sleep here either, but somewhere near the garage, I'm not exactly sure where myself. Besides it's no part of his duties to be here, all he has to do is to pick me up at the right time each morning. But all of that needn't impede your immediate return home in any way because, if you insist, I will accompany you straightaway to the nearest suburban line railway station, although that is actually so far away from here that you wouldn't arrive home much earlier than if you came along with me in the morning – we leave by seven o'clock – in the car.' 'That being so, Mr Pollunder, I'd still like to take the train,' said Karl. 'I never thought of the train. You just said yourself that I'd get there quicker by train than if I came in the car in the morning.' 'It's only a very tiny difference.' 'Never mind, Mr Pollunder, never mind that,' said Karl, 'remembering your kindness to me, I will always be very glad to come here, assuming of course that after my behaviour of today you will still want to invite me, and perhaps in the future I will better be able to explain why every minute by which I might see my uncle the sooner is so vital to me.' And, as though he had already been granted permission to leave, he added: 'But you mustn't accompany me. It's quite unnecessary. There is a servant outside who will be happy to walk me to the station. Now I just have to find my hat.' And with these last words, he started across the room, just for one last look to see where his hat might be. 'Perhaps I could help you out with a cap,' said Mr Green, pulling a cap out of his pocket, 'maybe this one fits you.' Karl stopped in astonishment and said: 'I'm not about to deprive you of your cap. I can perfectly well go bareheaded. I don't need anything.' 'It's not my cap. Go on take it!' 'In that case, thank you,' said Karl so as not to delay matters, and he took the cap. He pulled it on, and then he had to laugh because it fitted so well, then he took it in his hand and looked at it, but he couldn't find whatever feature he was looking for; it was a completely new cap. 'It fits so perfectly!' he said. 'Good, it fits!' said Mr Green and pounded the table.

Karl was on his way to the door to fetch the servant when Mr Green got to his feet, stretched himself after the lavish meal and the long rest, noisily thumped his chest, and said in a tone couched between advice and command: 'Before you leave, you must say goodbye to Miss Klara.' 'Yes, you must,' concurred Mr Pollunder, who had also stood up. You could tell with him that the words didn't come from his heart, he let his hands drop listlessly against his trouser seams, and he kept buttoning and unbuttoning his jacket, which, in the latest fashion was barely hip length, which on such a fat person as Mr Pollunder was unbecoming. One got the distinct impression, on seeing him standing alongside Mr Green, that Mr Pollunder's fatness was no healthy fatness, his massive back was bowed, his belly looked soft and unsustainable, a real weight, while his face looked pale and anxious. Mr Green was perhaps even fatter than Mr Pollunder, but it was a convincing, mutually supportive fatness, his feet were together in soldierly fashion, he carried his head erect and swaying, he looked like a great gymnast, a real team leader.

'So first you go and look in on Miss Klara,' continued Mr Green. 'That ought to be a pleasure for you, and it also fits in nicely with my own timetable. Because it so happens I have something interesting to tell you before you leave here, which may well affect your decision to return home. Only unfortunately I'm bound by a higher command not to reveal anything to you before midnight. You can imagine how I regret that, because it eats into my night's sleep, but I must stick to my instructions. The time now is a quarter past eleven, therefore I can finish discussing my business with Mr Pollunder, where you would only be in the way, while you can spend an agreeable few minutes with Miss Klara. On the dot of twelve you present yourself back here, where you will be told all that is needful for you.'

Could Karl refuse this demand, which really asked of him only the minimum of politeness and gratitude towards Mr Pollunder, which, furthermore, was put to him by a coarse man who was unconcerned in the matter, whereas Mr Pollunder, whom it did concern, stayed out of it, in both word and look? What was the interesting news he would only be allowed to hear at midnight? Unless it speeded his return home by the three quarters of an hour by which it delayed him now, it was of little interest to him. But his greatest doubt was whether he could go to Miss Klara at all, seeing as she was his enemy. If only he'd had the life-preserver with him which his uncle had given him as a paperweight. Klara's room might be a dangerous den indeed. But now it was impossible to say the least thing against Klara, seeing as she was Pollunder's daughter, and, it seemed, Mack's betrothed as well. She would only have had to behave slightly differently towards him, and he would have openly admired her on account of such connections. He was still pondering all this when he realized that no further pondering was required of him because Green opened the door and said to the servant who sprang up from his plinth: 'Take this young man to Miss Klara.'

'That's the way an order should be carried out,' thought Karl, as the servant led him at a brisk trot, though groaning with old age, by some particularly short route to Klara's room. As Karl passed his own room, whose door was still open, he wanted to step inside for a moment, perhaps to calm himself a little. But the servant wouldn't allow that. 'No,' he said, 'you must go to Miss Klara. You heard it yourself.' 'I only wanted to stay there a minute,' said Karl, and he thought he would throw himself on the sofa for a change, to while away some of the time to midnight. 'Don't make it any harder for me to carry out my instructions,' said the servant. 'He seems to think a visit to Miss Klara is a punishment for me,' thought Karl. He took a few more steps, and then stubbornly stopped again. 'Now come along, young sir,' said the servant, 'seeing as you've got this far already. I know you wanted to leave tonight but you can't always have everything the way you want it. I told you right away that that would be very difficult.' 'Yes, I want to go away, and I will go away,' said Karl, 'and now I just want to say goodbye to Miss Klara.' 'There,' said the servant, and Karl could tell he didn't believe a word of what he'd just said, 'so why are you so reluctant to say goodbye, come along.'

'Who's that in the corridor?' Klara's voice inquired, and she appeared leaning out of a nearby doorway, with a large table-lamp with a red shade in her hand. The servant rushed over to report to her, Karl dawdled along in his wake. 'You're late,' said Klara. Without answering her for the moment, Karl said to the servant quietly, but, now knowing something of his character, in tones of strict command: 'You're to wait for me outside!' 'I was just going to bed,' said Klara, putting the lamp down on the table. As he had downstairs with the dining-room door, the servant carefully closed the door from outside. 'It's gone half past eleven.' 'Gone half past eleven,' Karl repeated doubtfully, as though alarmed by the numbers.

'Then I have to say goodbye right away,' said Karl, 'because on the dot of twelve I have to be down in the dining-room.' 'What urgent business you have,' said Klara, and absent-mindedly arranged the folds of her loose nightgown, her face glowed and she kept smiling. Karl sensed that there was no danger of a resumption of hostilities with Klara. 'Couldn't you play something for me on the piano, as Papa promised me yesterday and you yourself did earlier today?' 'Isn't it too late for that?' asked Karl. He would have liked to oblige her, because she was quite different from the way she had been before, as though she'd risen into the circle of Pollunder's, and of Mack's too. 'Well, it is late,' she said, and her desire for music seemed to have abated. 'And then every note echoes through the whole house, if you did play I'm sure it would wake all the servants in the attic.' 'Then I'll leave the piano-playing, I hope to come back sometime, and if it's not out of your way, why don't you visit my uncle some time, and then you could pop in and see me too. I've got a magnificent piano in my room. Uncle gave it to me. If you like, I could play you all my little pieces on it, unfortunately there aren't very many of them, and they're not really suitable for such a great instrument, on which only virtuosos should be heard. But you would be able to have that pleasure too, if you arrange your visit ahead of time, because uncle wants to hire a famous piano teacher for me – just imagine how much I'm looking forward to that – and his playing would be an inducement to you to visit me during a lesson. To be honest, I'm glad it's too late to play now, because I can hardly play anything, you'd be amazed at how little I know. And now you must allow me to say goodbye, after all it is your bedtime.' And because Klara looked at him kindly, and seemed to bear him no ill will as a result of their fighting, he added with a smile as he gave her his hand: 'As they say in my country: sleep well and sweet dreams.'

'Wait,' she said, without taking his hand, 'maybe you should play after all,' and she disappeared through a little side-door directly beside the piano. 'What's the matter?' thought Karl, 'I can't wait much longer, however sweet she is.' There was a knock on the outer door, and the servant, not quite daring to open the door, whispered through a crack in the door: 'Excuse me, I've just been called away, so I can't stay here any longer.' 'Off you go then,' said Karl, who by now trusted himself to find the way to the dining-room unescorted, 'just leave the lantern by the door for me. What time is it, by the way?' 'Almost a quarter to twelve,' said the servant. 'How slowly the time passes,' said Karl. The servant was on the point of closing the door, when Karl remembered he hadn't tipped him yet, took a schilling from his trouser pockets – he had acquired the American habit of carrying his loose change jingling in his trouser pocket, and banknotes in the pocket of his waistcoat – and handed it to the servant with the words: 'This is for your services.'

Klara had come back in the meantime, her hands in her rigid coiffure, when it occurred to Karl that he shouldn't have sent the servant away, because who would walk him to the suburban railway station now? Well, Mr Pollunder would probably be able to drum up a servant from somewhere, perhaps this very servant had been called down to the dining-room to be put at his disposal later. 'I would like you to play something for me. We have so little music here, I don't want to miss an opportunity of hearing some now.' 'Then it's high time,' said Karl, and without further ado he sat down at the piano. 'Would you like some sheet music?' asked Klara. 'No thank you, I can't even read music properly,' replied Karl, and began playing. It was a little tune, which as Karl probably knew, was meant to be played quite slowly, particularly so that foreigners could understand it, but he hammered it out as mechanically as a march. When he'd finished, the shattered silence of the house slunk back. They sat there stunned and motionless. 'Pretty good,' said Klara, but there was no platitude that might have comforted Karl after playing like that. 'How late is it?' he asked. 'A quarter to midnight.' 'Then I've still got a bit of time,' he said, and privately he thought: It's either or. I don't have to play all ten of my tunes, but there is one I can try and play nicely. And he embarked on his beloved soldier's song. So slowly that the hearer's alerted expectations lengthened towards the next note, which Karl would hold back as long as he could before squeezing it out. As with all his tunes, he first had to locate the notes by eye, but he also felt sorrow being born within him that sought its definition beyond the end of the song and couldn't find it. 'I'm no good,' Karl said when he'd finished this time, and looked at Klara with tear-filled eyes.

Then there came the sound of loud clapping from the next door room. 'Someone else is listening!' cried Karl in consternation. 'Mack,' said Klara quietly. And Mack's voice rang out, calling: 'Karl Rossmann, Karl Rossmann!'

Karl swung himself off the piano stool and opened the door. He saw Mack sprawling on a large four-poster bed, with the coverlet draped loosely over his legs. The blue silk canopy was the only thing remotely feminine about the angular, simple, heavy bed. There was a single candle burning on the bedside table, but the bedlinen and Mack's shirt were so white that its light reflected off them in a dazzle; even the edges of the canopy gleamed with its slightly ruched, not quite stretched silk. Behind Mack the bed and everything else was lost in complete darkness. Klara leaned against the bedpost, and only had eyes for Mack.

'Hello there,' said Mack, and gave Karl his hand. 'You play pretty well, so far I've only known your horsemanship.' 'I do equally badly at both,' said Karl. 'If I'd known you were listening, I would certainly not have played. But your' – he broke off, as he was reluctant to say 'betrothed', since Mack and Klara were obviously already sleeping together. 'I thought so,' said Mack, 'that's why Klara had to lure you away from New York, otherwise I'd never have got to hear you play. You're only a beginner, and even in those pieces which you must have practised a lot, and which are in very rudimentary arrangements you made a few mistakes, but I was still very glad to hear you, quite apart from the fact that I despise no one's playing. Won't you sit down and keep us company for a while. Klara, give him a chair.' 'Thank you,' said Karl hesitantly. 'But I can't stay, however much I'd like to. I never knew this house had such cosy rooms.' 'I'm having everything converted to this style,' said Mack.

At that moment, a bell chimed twelve times in quick succession, each ring falling into the noise of its predecessor. Karl felt the wind from those great bells brushing his cheeks. What village was it that could boast of such bells!

'High time,' said Karl, held his hands out to Mack and Klara without touching them, and ran out on to the corridor. There was no lantern there, and he was sorry he had tipped the servant too soon. He was feeling his way along the wall towards his own room, but was still only halfway there, when he saw Mr Green hurriedly swaying towards him with a candle held high in his hand. In the same hand he carried the letter.

'Rossmann, why aren't you coming? Why are you keeping me waiting? What have you been up to with Miss Klara?' 'Questions, questions!' thought Karl, and now he'll push me against the wall, because he was standing right in front of Karl, whose back was indeed against the wall. In this corridor Green took on a quite ridiculous size, and Karl was even wondering flippantly to himself whether he might not have eaten up nice Mr Pollunder.

'It appears you are not a man of your word. You promise to come down at twelve o'clock, instead of which you're prowling around Miss Klara's door. I on the other hand promised you something interesting at midnight, and lo, here I am.'

And with that he handed Karl the letter. On the envelope it said: 'To Karl Rossmann. To be delivered to him at midnight, wherever he may be met'. 'Finally,' said Mr Green, while Karl was opening the letter, 'I think it's noteworthy that I've driven all the way here from New York on your account, so you really shouldn't make me chase you up and down corridors on top of that.'

'It's from my uncle!' said Karl, no sooner than he'd opened the letter. 'I was expecting it,' he said, turning to Mr Green.

'I really couldn't care less whether you were expecting it or not. Just read it,' he said, and held the candle up to Karl.

By its light Karl read: 'Beloved Nephew! As you will have realized during our unfortunately far too brief life together, I am a man of principle. That is a very disagreeable and a very sad thing, not only for those around me, but for myself as well, however, I owe everything I am to my principles, and no one has the right to ask of me that I deny myself out of existence, no one, not even you, my dear nephew, though you should be the very first if it ever occurred to me to allow such a general assault on myself. Then I would love to take you with these same two hands that are holding and writing on this piece of paper, and lift you high up in the air. However, as there is no suggestion that this might ever occur, I am bound to send you away from me after what has happened today, and I must ask you neither to seek me out in person nor to attempt to communicate with me by letter or through an intermediary. Against my wishes, you decided to leave me this evening, so be true to your decision all your life, only then will it have been a manly decision. For the conveyor of this news, I chose my best friend, Mr Green, who will surely find sufficiently sparing words for yourself, I have none left in me at the moment. He is a man of influence, and will, for love of me, support your first independent steps by word and deed. In order to understand our separation, which as I end this letter seems to me once more unfathomable, I have to keep saying to myself: No good can come from your family, Karl. Should Mr Green forget to give you your suitcase and umbrella, then remind him to do so. With best wishes for your future well-being, I remain

Your faithful uncle Jakob.'

'Have you finished?' asked Green. 'Yes' said Karl, 'have you got the suitcase and umbrella for me?' asked Karl. 'There you are,' said Green, and set Karl's old suitcase, which he had kept hidden behind his back in his left hand, on the floor beside Karl. 'And the umbrella?' asked Karl. 'It's all here,' said Green, and pulled out the umbrella, which was dangling from a trouser pocket. 'The things were brought in by one Schubal, a chief engineer with the Hamburg–America Line, he claims he found them on the ship. Thank him if you ever get the chance.' 'Well, at least I have my old things back,' said Karl, and laid the umbrella on the suitcase. 'The Senator suggests you might look after them better in future,' remarked Mr Green, and then asked, obviously out of personal curiosity: 'What kind of strange suitcase is that?' 'It's a suitcase that soldiers in my home country enlist with,' replied Karl, 'it's my father's old army suitcase. It's very practical.' Smiling, he added: 'If you remember not to leave it somewhere.' 'Well, you've had enough instructions now,' said Mr Green, 'and I don't suppose you have another uncle in America. Lastly, here is a third-class ticket to San Francisco. I chose that as your destination, firstly because the chances of employment are far better for you in the east, and secondly because your uncle is involved in everything here that you might be considered for, and a meeting is to be avoided at all costs. In Frisco, you'll be able to work undisturbed, just start at the bottom and gradually work your way up.'

Karl could hear no malice in these words, the bad news that had been inside Green all evening had been delivered, and now Green seemed a harmless man, one with whom it was perhaps possible to talk more openly than anyone else. The best of men, who through no fault of his own is made the bearer of such a secret and painful decision, is bound to be suspicious for as long as he contains it within himself. 'I will leave the house at once,' said Karl, expecting the confirmation of an experienced man, 'because I was only invited into it as the nephew of my uncle, whereas as a stranger I have no business here. Would you be so good as to show me the way out, and point me in the direction of the nearest inn.' 'Will you get on with it,' said Green, 'you're putting me to a great deal of trouble.' On seeing the enormous stride that Green had taken right away Karl stopped, such haste was suspicious, and he grabbed Green by the coat-tails and said, suddenly grasping the true state of things: 'There is one more thing you must explain to me. On the envelope of the letter you were told to give me, it just says that I am to be given it at midnight wherever I am met. Why, then, pleading those instructions, did you detain me here when I wanted to leave at a quarter past eleven? You went beyond your instructions.' Green introduced his reply with a gesture indicating in an exaggerated way the fatuity of Karl's observation, and then said: 'Does it say anywhere on the envelope that I am to be rushed into an early grave on your account, and do the contents of the letter allow one to conclude that the instructions are to be taken in such a way? If I hadn't detained you, then I would just have had to give you the letter at midnight on the highway somewhere.' 'No,' Karl insisted, 'not quite. If you were too tired, you might not even have been able to set off after me, or, though Mr Pollunder denies it, I might have been back with my uncle by midnight, or it might have been your duty even to drive me back to my uncle in your automobile – which seems to have been unaccountably ignored – seeing as I was insistent on returning. Don't the words on the envelope declare quite unambiguously that midnight was the deadline for me? And you must take the blame for making me miss it.'

Karl looked hard at Green, and he saw that shame at his unmasking was struggling in him with joy at the success of his project. Finally he pulled himself together and said in a tone as if he were cutting off Karl in mid-flow, though he had been silent for some time: 'Not another word,' and propelled Karl, who had taken up his suitcase and umbrella, through a little door which he had pushed open for him.

Karl stood in the open, astonished. A flight of stairs without a railing led downwards. He needed only to go down it, and then turn right on to the avenue which led to the road. In the bright moonlight it was impossible to go wrong. Down in the garden he heard the barking of dogs running around in the shadow of the trees. There was silence otherwise, so that one could hear the sound of their impacts on the grass as they leapt about.

Without being molested by these dogs, Karl emerged from the garden. He couldn't say with any certainty in which direction New York lay, on the way here he had paid little attention to details which might have been useful to him now. Finally he told himself he didn't necessarily have to go to New York where no one was expecting him, and one person definitely was not. So he chose a direction at random, and set off.

4

THE MARCH TO RAMSES

In the little inn that Karl reached after a short walk, which was actually the last little way-station for vehicular traffic to New York, and was thus rarely used for overnighting, Karl asked for the cheapest billet available, because he thought he had to start economizing right away. The landlord accordingly ushered him, like an employee, up the stairs, where a dishevelled old baggage, annoyed at having her sleep disturbed, received him and almost without listening to him, with incessant instructions to him to tread softly, led him to a room, and breathing one last 'Ssh!' at him, shut the door after him.

At first Karl wasn't sure whether it was because the curtains were drawn, or the room had no windows, it was so dark; at last he noticed a small dormer window, he drew away the cloth veiling it, and a little light entered the room. It had two beds in it, but both were already occupied. Karl saw a couple of young fellows lying fast asleep in them. They struck him as untrustworthy, not least because for no obvious reason they were both sleeping in their clothes, one of them even in his boots.

Just when Karl pulled aside the curtain, one of the sleepers raised his arms and legs in the air a little, which looked so ridiculous that Karl, for all his worries, had to laugh silently to himself.

He soon saw that, apart from the lack of anywhere else to sleep, no sofa, no couch, he wouldn't be able to sleep anyway, because he couldn't expose his newly returned suitcase and the money he carried on him to any danger. Nor did he want to leave, because he didn't think he could slip past the woman and the landlord and leave the building unnoticed. But surely he wouldn't be at greater risk here than on the open road. There was, though, as far as he could tell in the half-light, a striking absence of any other luggage in the room. Perhaps the likeliest solution was that these two were house-servants, who would have to get up soon to look after the guests, and therefore slept in their clothes. In which case he wasn't in particularly prestigious company, but at least he was safe. But so long as there was any doubt about it, he mustn't go to sleep.

At the foot of one of the beds was a candle and matches, which Karl crept over and got. He felt no compunction about striking a light, because the landlord had given the room to him as much as to the two others, and they had already enjoyed half a night's sleep, and had the inestimable advantage of being in beds anyway. He did, though, by moving and behaving cautiously, make every effort not to wake them.

First he wanted to examine his suitcase to take a look at his belongings, of which he only had a vague memory, and of which the most valuable were surely already gone. Because once Schubal lays his hand on something, there's little chance of getting it back in its original condition. Admittedly, he probably stood to get a large tip from the uncle, and the blame for any individual missing items he could always pin on the original minder of the suitcase, Mr Butterbaum.

When he opened the suitcase Karl was appalled by what met his eyes. All those hours he had spent during the crossing, packing and repacking it, and now everything was crammed in in such a higgledy-piggledy fashion that the lid flew up when he opened the catch. But Karl soon saw to his joy that the sole cause of all this disorder was the fact that the suit he had worn during the crossing, and for which of course the suitcase had not allowed had been crammed in afterwards. Nothing at all was missing. In the secret pocket of his jacket there was not only his passport but also the money he had brought from home, so that, when Karl added it to what he already had on him, he was for the moment plentifully provided with money. The linen he'd been in on his arrival was also there, washed and ironed. He immediately put his wristwatch and money into the tried and tested secret pocket. The only lamentable circumstance was that the Verona salami, which was not missing either, had imparted its smell to everything in the suitcase. If that couldn't be removed by some means, Karl faced the prospect of going around for the next several months shrouded in that smell.

As he looked out a few items in the very bottom of the suitcase, a pocket Bible, letter paper and photographs of his parents, his cap slipped off his head and into the suitcase. In its old setting he recognized it at once, it was his cap, the cap his mother had given him as a travelling cap. He had been careful not to wear it on board ship, as he knew that in America caps are generally worn in place of hats, and he hadn't wanted to wear his out before he even got there. Now Mr Green had used it to amuse himself at Karl's expense. Had his uncle put him up to that too? And in an unintentionally furious movement he banged the lid of the suitcase, which clicked loudly shut.

There was nothing for it now, both sleepers had been woken by this. At first one of them stretched and yawned, and then the other. And almost the entire contents of his suitcase were spread out on the table, if they were thieves they needed only to make their way to it and help themselves. Not just to pre-empt this possibility, but also to establish a few facts, Karl went over to their beds, candle in hand, and explained his right to be there. They seemed not to have expected any such explanation, and, far too tired to speak, they just stared at him without being taken aback in the slightest. They were both very young fellows, but hard work or hunger had made the bones stand out prematurely in their faces, they had scruffy beards on their chins, their long-uncut hair was rumpled on their heads, and in their sleepiness they rubbed and pressed their knuckles against their deep-set eyes.

In order to exploit their momentary weakness, Karl said: 'My name is Karl Rossmann, and I am German. Since we are sharing this room together, please tell me your names and nationalities. I would like to assure you that I have no interest in claiming a bed, since I arrived late, and I do not in fact intend to sleep. Please do not be misled by my good suit, I am very poor and have no prospects.'

The shorter of the two – he was the one with his boots on – intimated with his arms, legs and general demeanour that none of this had any interest for him, and that this was no time for such a palaver, lay down and was asleep at once: the other, a dark-skinned fellow also lay down again, but before going to sleep he casually waved his hand: 'That's Robinson and he's Irish, my name's Delamarche, I'm French, and now goodnight.' No sooner had he said this than with a huge breath he blew out Karl's candle, and fell back on his pillow.

'So that danger has been averted for the time being,' Karl told himself, and went back to the table. Unless their sleepiness was feigned, all was well. Too bad that one of them had to be Irish. Karl couldn't quite remember what book at home had warned him to beware of Irishmen in America. His stay with his uncle would have given him an excellent opportunity of going into the question of the dangers of Irishmen, but because he'd thought himself in security for good, he had neglected to do that. Now he at least wanted to take a closer look at the Irishman, with the candle that he had re-lit, and found that he looked if anything more palatable than the Frenchman. There was still a trace of roundness in his cheeks, and he had a friendly smile as he slept, as far as Karl could make out standing on tiptoe some way away.

For all that, still determined not to sleep, Karl sat down on the one chair in the room, put off the repacking of his suitcase, for which he had the rest of the night, and leafed around in his Bible without reading it. Then he picked up the photograph of his parents, in which his little father stood very tall, while his mother sat shrunken in the armchair in front of him. One of his father's hands was on the back of the armchair, the other, making a fist, rested on an illustrated book which was open on a fragile ornamental table beside him. There was another photograph that depicted Karl and his parents together, one in which his father and mother were both glaring at him, while he had been instructed by the photographer to look into the camera. But then he hadn't been allowed to take that photograph with him on the journey.

The more minutely he now examined the one in front of him and tried to catch his father's gaze from various angles. But try as he might, even moving the candle to different points, his father refused to become any more alive, his heavy horizontal moustache didn't look anything like the real thing, it wasn't a good photograph. His mother had been better caught, her mouth downdrawn as though she'd suffered some injury, and forcing a smile. Karl thought that that must be so obvious to anyone looking at the picture, that a moment later, it seemed to him that it was too blatant and actually illogical. How could a picture give one an irresistible sense of the concealed feelings of its subject. And he looked away from the photograph for a while. When he looked at it again he was struck by his mother's hand, dangling from an armrest in the very foreground of the picture, close enough to kiss. He wondered whether he shouldn't after all write to his parents, as both of them had demanded, his father with particular sternness in Hamburg, at the end. Admittedly he had vowed to himself that terrible evening when his mother had told him that he would be going to America, irrevocably, that he would never write, but what did the vow of an inexperienced boy count in these new circumstances. He might just as well have vowed that after two months in America he would be a general in the American army, whereas in fact he was sharing an attic room with a couple of tramps, in an inn outside New York, and moreover, he had to concede that this was just the right place for him. Smilingly he interrogated his parents' faces, as though one might tell from them if they still craved news of their son.

So looking, he soon noticed that he was in fact very tired, and would scarcely be able to stay awake all night. The photograph slipped from his hands, he laid his face against it so that its coolness soothed his cheek, and with that pleasant sensation he fell asleep.

In the morning a tickling in his armpit woke him up. It was the Frenchman who permitted himself this intimacy. But the Irishman too was standing by Karl's table, and they were both looking at him with as keen an interest as Karl had shown in them the night before. Karl wasn't surprised that their getting up hadn't woken him; their quietness didn't necessarily imply any evil intent on their part, because he had been in a deep sleep, and they clearly hadn't taken too much trouble dressing or, for that matter, washing.

They now greeted each other properly and with a certain formality, and Karl learned that the two of them were fitters who had been out of work for a long time in New York, and so were pretty much on their uppers. By way of demonstration, Robinson opened his jacket and one could see he had no shirt on underneath, which one might also have concluded from the loose fit of his collar, which was attached to his jacket at the back. They were on their way to the little town of Butterford, two days' walk from New York, where apparently there were jobs to be had. They had no objection to Karl joining them, and promised him firstly that they would carry his suitcase some of the time, and secondly, if they should get jobs themselves, to get him a place as a trainee, which, if there was any work going at all, would be a simple matter. No sooner had Karl agreed to this, than they were counselling him to take off his good suit, which would only be a disadvantage to him in looking for a job. In fact, there was a good opportunity to get rid of it here and now, because the cleaning woman ran a clothes stall. They helped Karl, who wasn't altogether convinced in the matter of the suit, to get out of it, and they took it away. As Karl, alone now and still a little groggy with sleep, slowly got into his old suit, he reproached himself for selling the other which might disadvantage him in applying for a traineeship, but could only be of assistance in the search for a better sort of job, and he opened the door to call the two of them back, but there they were already, laying half a dollar as the proceeds of the sale on the table, but looking so pleased with themselves that it was impossible not to believe that they hadn't also earned their share from the sale, and an irritatingly large one at that.

There was no time to argue because the cleaner came in, every bit as sleepy as she'd been in the night, and ushered them all out into the corridor, on the grounds that the room had to be got ready for new guests, a specious reason of course, it was pure malice on her part. Karl, who had just wanted to put his suitcase in order, was compelled to look on as the woman gathered up his things in both hands and slung them into the suitcase with such force, as if they were wild animals being brought to heel. The two fitters danced around her, plucked at her skirts, patted her on the back, but if their purpose was to help Karl, it had the opposite effect. When the woman had shut the suitcase she pushed the handle into Karl's hand, shook off the fitters and drove them all out of the room, threatening them with no coffee if they didn't leave. The woman seemed to have completely forgotten that Karl hadn't been with the fitters all along, because she treated them all as one band, although the fitters had sold Karl's suit, which did at least imply a certain common purpose.

They had to walk up and down the corridor for a long time, and the Frenchman in particular, who had linked arms with Karl, was swearing incessantly, threatening to punch the landlord to the ground if he should show his face, a moment he seemed to be preparing for by furiously grating his fists together. At last an innocent little boy came along, who had to get up on tiptoe to hand the Frenchman the coffee can. Unfortunately there was only that one can available, and the boy couldn't be made to understand that glasses were wanted as well. So only one person could drink at a time, and the other two had to stand and watch. Karl didn't want any, but not wanting to offend the others, he raised the can to his lips when it was his turn, but didn't drink from it.

When it was finished, the Irishman tossed the can on to the flagstones and they left the inn unseen by anyone, and walked out into a thick yellowish morning fog. For the most part they walked abreast and in silence along the side of the road, Karl had to carry his suitcase, the others probably wouldn't relieve him without being asked, the occasional automobile shot out of the fog, and all three turned their heads towards these cars, which were usually enormous, and so striking in appearance and so fleetingly present there was no time to notice whether they had any occupants or not. A little later, the columns of vehicles bringing food to New York started up, and in five lanes that took up the whole breadth of the road, they rolled by so solidly that no one could get across. From time to time the road widened out into a square, in the middle of which on a tower-like elevation a policeman strode up and down, directing everything and ordering the traffic on the main road and the side roads too, which then remained unsupervised until the next square and the next policeman, but was voluntarily kept in sufficient order by the silent and watchful coachmen and drivers. It was the prevailing calm of it all that most surprised Karl. Had it not been for the cries of the carefree animals going to the abattoirs, perhaps nothing would have been heard save the clatter of hooves and the hissing of the tyres. Although of course, the speed was anything but constant. At some of the junctions, because of the excessive pressure of traffic from the side roads, extensive rearrangements had to be undertaken, whole columns would grind to a halt, and only inch forward, but it also happened that for a while everything would hurtle past at lightning speeds, until, as though stopped by a single brake, it was all becalmed once more. The road didn't throw up a single speck of dust, the air remained crystal clear. There were no pedestrians, no market women making their way into town, as existed in Karl's home, but there were some large flat-backed automobiles, carrying up to twenty women at a time, all with baskets on their backs, perhaps they were market-women after all, craning their necks to see the traffic, and hoping to make faster progress. There were also automobiles of a similar type on which a few men rode, strolling about with their hands in their pockets. On one of these automobiles, which bore various inscriptions, Karl gave a little cry when he read: 'Dock workers hired for Jakob's shipping company'. The car was just travelling very slowly and a short, bowed, lively man beckoned to the three travellers to come on board. Karl took refuge behind the fitters, as though his uncle might be on the car and see him, and he was relieved when the others refused the invitation, although their arrogant expressions when they did so somewhat offended him. They shouldn't think themselves too good to work for his uncle. He immediately gave them to understand as much, although in veiled terms. Thereupon Delamarche told him not to concern himself in matters he didn't understand, that way of hiring people was a shameful swindle and Jakob's company was notorious throughout the whole of the United States. Karl made no reply, but from now on he inclined to the Irishman and asked him to carry his suitcase for a while, which, after Karl had repeated his request a few times, he did. Only he complained incessantly about the weight of the suitcase until it became clear that all he had in mind was to lighten it of the Verona salami, which had already drawn his favourable attention in the hotel. Karl was made to unpack it, the Frenchman took possession of it, set about it with a sabre-like knife, and ate almost the whole thing. Robinson was given the occasional slice, while Karl, who was left to carry the suitcase again if it wasn't to be abandoned on the highway, got nothing at all, as though he had already had his portion in advance. It seemed too petty to him to beg for a bit of it now, but it did gall him.

The fog had quite disappeared now and a high mountain range glittered in the distance, its wave-like crest lying under a still more distant heat haze. Lining the road were poorly cultivated fields around large factories, smoke-blackened, and all alone in open country. In tenement houses dotted about, the many windows trembled with all sorts of movement and light, and on all the small frail balconies women and children busied themselves, while around them, covering and uncovering them, pieces of washing, hanging and lying, fluttered in the morning wind and ballooned hugely. Leaving the houses, one could see larks high in the sky and swallows diving not far above the heads of the travellers.

Many things reminded Karl of his home, and he wasn't sure whether it was a good idea for him to leave New York and make for the interior. New York had the sea and the possibility of going home at any time. And so he stopped and told his companions he wanted to stay in New York after all. When Delamarche tried to push him forward he refused to be pushed, and said he must have the right to determine what he did for himself. The Irishman had to intervene between them, and explain that Butterford was far more beautiful than New York, and they both had to plead with him before he agreed to go on. And even then he wouldn't have gone if he hadn't told himself that it was probably better for him to go to a place from which it would be less easy to return home. It would be better for his work and his general progress, if he had no useless thoughts to distract him.

And now it was his turn to pull the others along, and they were so pleased with his eagerness that, quite unasked, they took it in turns to carry his suitcase, and Karl didn't understand what he had done to make them so happy. The road started to climb and when they stopped from time to time they could see, looking back, the panorama of New York and its harbour continually unfolding. The bridge that connected New York with Boston lay slender across the Hudson, and trembled if you narrowed your eyes. It seemed to be carrying no traffic at all, and below it was the smooth unanimated ribbon of water. Everything in both metropolises seemed empty, useless construction. There was almost no distinction to be drawn between the big buildings and the little ones. In the invisible canyons of the streets, life probably continued on its way, but above them there was nothing to be seen except a thin haze which didn't move, but seemed easy enough to dispel. Even in the harbour, the world's largest, peace had returned, and only sporadically did one have the impression, probably influenced by earlier, closer views, that one could see a ship sliding forward a little. But it was impossible to trace, because it eluded one's eyes and couldn't be found again.

But Robinson and Delamarche evidently saw much more, they pointed this way and that, and with their hands they arced towards squares and gardens, which they referred to by name. It was incomprehensible to them that Karl had been in New York for over two months, and had seen nothing of the city but one single street. And they promised him that once they had made enough money in Butterford, they would take him to New York and show him the sights, and in particular certain places of paradisal entertainment. Thereupon Robinson started singing at the top of his voice, Delamarche gave a clapping accompaniment, and Karl recognized it as an operetta tune from his home, but he liked the English version better than he ever had the original. So they gave a little open air performance in which they all participated, only the city below them, for whose benefit it was supposed to be, seemed unaware of it.

Once Karl asked where Jakob's shipping company was, and straightaway the index fingers of Delamarche and Robinson shot out, pointing perhaps at the same place, perhaps at places that were miles apart. When they resumed their march, Karl asked when would be the earliest they might expect to return to New York with sufficient funds. Delamarche said it might easily be no more than a month, because there was a shortage of labour in Butterford and wages were high. Of course they would pool their money, so that chance differences in earnings between the three of them would be ironed out. Karl didn't like the idea of pooling their money, in spite of the fact that as a trainee he would of course be earning less than they would as qualified workers. Robinson then observed that if there was no work to be had in Butterford, they would of course have to go on looking further afield, either to find work as agricultural labourers, or maybe on to the goldfields of California, which, going by Robinson's detailed explanations, seemed to be his favourite plan. 'Why did you become a fitter, if you want to go to the goldfields?' asked Karl, who didn't like to hear of the need for such long and hazardous journeys. 'Why I became a fitter?' said Robinson. 'Certainly not so that my mother's son would starve. There's a fortune to be made in the goldfields.' 'There was,' said Delamarche. 'Still is,' said Robinson, and talked of many acquaintances who had made their fortunes, were still there, and of course didn't need to lift a finger, but for old friendship's sake would help him, and his friends as well, to a fortune. 'We'll wangle our way into jobs in Butterford,' said Delamarche, and that was what Karl wanted to hear, although the way he expressed it didn't inspire much confidence.

In the course of the day they stopped at an inn just once, with an outdoor table that seemed to Karl to be made of iron, and ate practically raw meat that one couldn't cut but only tear with knife and fork. The bread was in the shape of a cylinder and every loaf had a sharp knife stuck in it. The meal was washed down with a black liquid that burned in one's throat. Delamarche and Robinson liked it, though, and drank to the fulfilment of various wishes, clinking glasses and keeping them touching in the air awhile. On neighbouring tables sat workers, in chalk-spattered shirts, all drinking the same black liquid. The many automobiles driving past spread clouds of dust over the tables. Large newspapers were passed around, and there was excited talk about the construction workers' strike, the name Mack was used several times, Karl asked about him and learned that he was the father of the Mack he had known, and was the greatest property developer in New York. The strike was costing him millions, and even threatened him with bankruptcy. This was the talk of ill-informed and malevolent people, and Karl didn't believe a word of it.

The meal was further spoiled for Karl by the fact that it was rather open to question how it would be paid for. The fair and natural thing would be for each of them to pay his share, but Delamarche, and Robinson too, had occasionally let drop that the last of their money had gone on the previous night's lodgings. No watch or ring or anything else that might be turned into money was to be seen on either of them. And Karl couldn't complain that they had kept some money from the sale of his suit. That would have been an insult to them and would have meant goodbye for good. The astounding thing was that neither Delamarche nor Robinson showed any sign of anxiety about the bill, rather they were sufficiently high-spirited to make frequent advances to the waitress, who with a proud and heavy gait kept walking between the tables. Her hair would fall forward over her brow and cheeks, and she kept pushing it up and back again. Finally, just when one might have expected a friendly word from her, she walked up to the table, rested both hands on it, and said: 'All right, who's paying?' Never did hands move faster than those of Delamarche and Robinson as they pointed to Karl. Karl wasn't alarmed, he had seen it coming, and seen nothing wrong with it; his comrades, from whom he was expecting certain advantages, had every right to expect a few trifles to be paid for by him, even though it would have been better to discuss it fully, in advance. The awkward thing was that the money had to be got out of his secret pocket. His original intention had been to keep it for an emergency, and for the time being place himself on the same footing as his comrades. The advantage that the money, and especially his having kept quiet about it, had given him over his comrades they more than made up for by the fact that they'd been in America since childhood, had sufficient expertise and knowledge to enable them to earn money themselves, and finally that they were not used to any better living standard than they were presently enjoying. Karl's prior plan with regard to the money shouldn't automatically be affected by this bill, because he could spare a quarter pound, and could lay a quarter pound on the table and declare it was all he had, and that he was prepared to make a sacrifice for their joint journey to Butterford. For a trek on foot, such a sum was perfectly adequate. But now he wasn't sure if he had enough change, and besides, his coins were with his folded banknotes somewhere in the depths of his secret pocket, and the easiest way of finding anything in it was to empty the entire contents of it out on to the table. It was quite unnecessary for his comrades to learn of the existence of this secret pocket. Happily, it appeared that his comrades were still more interested in the waitress than in how Karl would find the money with which to pay for their meal. By calling for the bill, Delamarche had brought her to stand between himself and Robinson, and she could only repel their intrusiveness by putting her spread hand on the face of one or other of them, and pushing him away. In the meantime, hot with the effort, Karl was collecting in one hand the money he was fishing for and pulling out of the secret pocket with the other. Finally he thought he had enough, though he wasn't that familiar with American currency, and laid it on the table. The sound of money straightaway put an end to the horseplay. To Karl's annoyance and the general surprise there was almost a whole pound on the table. No one actually asked why Karl hadn't mentioned the money, which was enough to pay for the three of them to travel to Butterford in comfort on the railway, but it was still very embarrassing for Karl. He paid for the meal and slowly pocketed his money, although Delamarche managed to take a coin out of his hand, which he needed as a tip for the waitress, whom he embraced and squeezed and gave the money to from the other side.

Karl was grateful to them for not saying anything about the money when they walked on, and for a time he even toyed with the idea of confessing to them his entire fortune, but, finding no opportunity to do so, he didn't. By evening they were in more rural, fertile countryside. All around were unbroken fields, covering gentle slopes with their first green, rich country seats abutted the road, and for hours they walked between the gilded fences of the gardens; they crossed the same sluggish river several times, and often heard the trains thundering overhead on high arched viaducts.

The sun was just setting over the level top of distant forests when they flung themselves down on a patch of grass surrounded by a copse of trees on a plateau, to rest from their labours. Delamarche and Robinson lay there and stretched for all they were worth while Karl sat up and watched the highway a few feet below, on which, as they had all day long, cars kept rushing past one another, as though a certain number had been despatched from some faraway place, and the selfsame number were expected someplace equally faraway. During the whole day, from early in the morning, Karl hadn't seen a single car stopping or a single passenger getting out.

Robinson suggested spending the night there, as they were all tired enough, and they would be able to set off bright and early the next morning, and finally as they wouldn't be able to find any cheaper or better-located campsite before nightfall. Delamarche agreed with him, and only Karl felt obliged to reveal that he had enough money to pay for them all to stay in a hotel. Delamarche said they would be needing the money later, and he should hold on to it for the time being. Delamarche quite openly gave it to be understood that they were counting on Karl's money. As his initial suggestion had been accepted, Robinson went on to declare that, to gain strength for the morrow, they should have themselves a good bite to eat, and one of them should procure something for their supper from the hotel that was very close by them on the highway, with the luminous sign 'Hotel Occidental'. As the youngest, and in the absence of any other volunteers, Karl didn't hesitate to offer himself for this errand, and went across to the hotel, having been told to get bread, beer and bacon.

There must be a large town nearby, because the very first lounge that Karl set foot in at the hotel was full of a crowd of noisy people, and at the buffet, which ran down the length of the room as well as its two shorter sides, numerous waiters in white aprons were running about ceaselessly, and still they couldn't satisfy the impatient guests, as one could hear from the swearing on all sides and the noise of fists being banged on tables. No one paid the slightest attention to Karl; nor was there any service in the room itself, rather the guests, who were seated at tiny tables, swamped by other tables on all sides, foraged for themselves at the buffet. All the tables had a large bottle of oil, vinegar or somesuch on them, and all the dishes that were obtained from the buffet were doused with the liquid before being eaten. In order for Karl to reach the buffet, where the difficulties which faced him, with such a large order, would really only begin, he first had to squeeze his way through many tables, which, for all his caution, couldn't be done without grossly disturbing the guests, who took it all as if they were completely insentient, even on the occasion when Karl, albeit pushed from behind, stumbled against one of the little tables and almost upset it. He apologized of course, but no one seemed to understand, nor did he understand anything that they called out to him either.

With much difficulty, he managed to find a little space at the buffet, although his view was restricted for a long time by the propped elbows of the people either side of him. It seemed to be the custom here to rest one's elbows on the table, and to press one's fists against one's temples; Karl remembered how much Dr Krumpal, his Latin teacher, had hated that posture, and how he would quietly and surreptitiously sneak up, and with a suddenly brandished ruler brush an offending elbow abruptly and painfully from the table.

Karl stood pressed against the buffet, because no sooner had he reached it, than another table was set up immediately behind him, and one of the customers sitting down at it brushed Karl's back with the broad brim of his hat each time he threw his head back while speaking. But there was so little hope of getting anything from the waiters, even once his two rude neighbours had gone away satisfied. A few times Karl had reached across the table and grabbed at a waiter's apron, but it was simply torn free with an angry frown. You couldn't get a grip on any of them, all they did was keep running and running. If there had been anything suitable to eat and drink anywhere near Karl he would simply have taken it, asked how much it cost, paid and gone away happily. But the dishes in front of him were full of some herring-like fish, with black scales that had a golden gleam at the edges. They might be very expensive and probably wouldn't satisfy anyone's hunger. And to drink there were only little barrels of rum, and he wasn't taking any rum back to his companions, they seemed avid enough as it was for the most highly concentrated alcoholic drinks, and he wasn't about to help them in their quest.

So Karl had no option but to look for another place, and begin afresh. But a lot of time had passed. The clock at the other end of the room, whose hands could just be made out through the smoke if you looked hard, showed that it was already past nine o'clock. Elsewhere at the buffet the crush was even greater than at his previous, somewhat marginal position. Besides, the room seemed to be filling up more and more as it got later. New guests kept coming through the main doors with a great commotion. At some points, the guests simply cleared the buffet, sat down on the tables, and toasted one another; they were the best places, from there they could see across the whole room.

Karl was still pressing forward, but he no longer hoped to achieve anything by doing so. He cursed himself for volunteering for this assignment in spite of his ignorance of local conditions. His companions would quite rightly tell him off, and maybe even think that he hadn't bought them anything in order to save money. And now he was standing in a region where warm meat dishes with fine yellow potatoes were being eaten, and he had no notion of how people had come by them.

Then he saw, a couple of steps ahead of him, an elderly woman, obviously part of the hotel staff, talking and laughing with one of the guests. All the time she kept working away at her coiffure with a hairpin. Karl immediately resolved to present his order to this woman, partly because as the only woman, she seemed to him to be an exception to the general noise and bustle, and partly for the simpler reason that she was the only hotel employee within reach, always assuming that she didn't suddenly run off somewhere the second he addressed her. In fact, just the opposite happened. Karl hadn't even addressed her, only listened in a little bit, when she, just in the way one sometimes looks to one side while talking, looked at Karl, and breaking off her conversation, asked him in friendly tones and in English of textbook purity whether he wanted something. 'I do indeed,' said Karl, 'I can't seem to get anything here.' 'Then come with me,' she said, took her leave of her acquaintance, who doffed his hat to her — it seemed an act of incredible gallantry in the prevailing circumstances — took Karl by the hand, went to the buffet, pushed a customer aside, opened a hatch in the buffet, crossed the passage behind the tables with Karl, where you had to look out for the indefatigably rushing waiters, opened a double curtain, and there they were, in a large, cool storeroom. 'It's just a matter of knowing how it's done,' said Karl to himself.

'So what is it you want then?' she asked, and leaned down encouragingly towards him. She was terribly fat, her body rippled, but her face, of course only by comparison, was almost delicate in its modelling. Karl was tempted, in view of the many foodstuffs that were carefully piled on shelves and tables here, to improvise some more delectable supper, especially as he suspected he might be offered a good deal by this influential woman here, but then he couldn't think of anything, and he stuck to the original bacon, bread and beer. 'Nothing else?' asked the woman. 'No thank you,' said Karl, 'but enough for three.' When the woman asked who the other two were, Karl told her in a few words about his companions, he was happy enough to be asked some questions.

'But that's a meal fit for convicts,' said the woman, now obviously awaiting further requests on Karl's part. However, he was afraid that she might give them to him and refuse payment, and so he said nothing. 'Well, I'll soon have that ready for you,' said the woman, and with mobility remarkable for someone of her bulk she went to one of the tables, cut off a large piece of streaky bacon with plenty of lean on it, with a long, thin, sawblade-like knife, took a loaf of bread from a shelf, picked up three bottles of beer from the floor, and put everything in a light straw basket, which she handed to Karl. Meanwhile, she explained to Karl that she had led him in here because the food out on the buffet always spoiled, because of the smoke and the many smells there, in spite of its being consumed so quickly. For the people outside it was still good enough. Karl lapsed into silence now, because he didn't know what he had done to be given such special treatment. He thought of his companions, who, however well they might know America, might never have reached this storeroom, and would have had to content themselves with the spoiled food out on the buffet. In here, you couldn't hear a thing from the hall, the walls must be very thick to keep these cellars cool enough. The straw basket had now been in Karl's hands for some little time, but he didn't think of paying and made no other move. Only when the woman went to add another bottle, similar to those that were on the tables outside, to the basket, did Karl shudderingly refuse.

'Have you got far to go?' asked the woman. 'To Butterford,' replied Karl. 'That's a very long way,' said the woman. 'Another day's walk,' said Karl. 'No more?' asked the woman. 'Oh no,' said Karl.

The woman rearranged a few things on the tables, a waiter came in, looked around for something, was directed by the woman to a large bowl where a great heap of sardines lay sprinkled with a little parsley, and then carried the bowl out in his raised hands.

'Why are you so keen on spending the night outdoors?' asked the woman. 'We have plenty of space here. Come and sleep here in the hotel with us.' Karl was very tempted, especially as he'd had so little sleep the previous night. 'I have my luggage outside,' he said reluctantly, if also with a little pride. 'Just bring it here,' said the woman, 'that's no obstacle.' 'What about my companions!' said Karl, and he sensed right away that they indeed presented an obstacle. 'They can stay here as well of course,' said the woman. 'Come on! Don't make me keep asking.' 'My companions are decent enough people in most respects,' said Karl, 'but they're not terribly clean.' 'Didn't you see all the dirt in the hall?' asked the woman, pulling a face. 'Honestly, we take in all sorts here. I'll have them make up three beds right away. It'll be up in the attic, I'm afraid, because the hotel is full, I've had to move up to the attic myself, but it's still preferable to being out in the open.' 'I can't bring my companions,' said Karl. He imagined the noise those two would make on the corridors of this classy hotel, how Robinson would besmirch everything and Delamarche inevitably molest even this woman here. 'I don't know why that should be so out of the question,' said the woman, 'but if you like, why not leave your companions outside, and come to us on your own.' 'I can't, I can't,' said Karl, 'they are my companions, and I have to stay with them.' 'How obstinate you are,' said the woman, averting her head, 'someone tries to be kind to you, to help you out, and you resist as hard as you can.' Karl saw this was true, but he could think of no solution, and so he just said: 'Thank you very much indeed for your kindness,' then he remembered that he hadn't paid yet, and he asked how much he owed. 'You can pay when you return the basket,' said the woman. 'I need it back by tomorrow morning at the latest.' 'Very well,' said Karl. She opened a door that led straight outside, and said to him as he left with a bow: 'Good night. But you're making a mistake.' He was already a few steps away when she shouted after him: 'See you tomorrow!'

No sooner was he outside than he could hear the full noise from the buffet room again, which by now had had a brass band added to it. He was glad he hadn't had to leave through the hall. The hotel's five storeys were all lit up, brightening the road in front of it. Cars were still going by, though no longer in an unbroken stream, growing out of the distance even faster than by day, feeling their way with the white beams of their lights, which dimmed as they entered the illuminated area in front of the hotel, and brightened again as they returned to darkness.

Karl found his companions already fast asleep, he really had been gone far too long. He was just about to lay the food out appetizingly on some paper napkins he found in the basket, and wake his companions when everything was ready, when he saw that his suitcase, which he had left behind locked, and the key to which he had in his pocket, was wide open, with half its contents scattered about on the grass. 'Get up!' he shouted. 'Thieves have been here while you were asleep.' 'Is anything missing?' asked Delamarche. Robinson, not fully awake, put out a hand for the beer. 'I don't know,' said Karl, 'but the suitcase is open. It was very reckless of you to go to sleep and leave the suitcase standing unprotected.' Delamarche and Robinson both laughed, and the former said: 'Well, you shouldn't stay out so long. The hotel is no more than ten paces away, and it takes you three hours to get there and back. We were hungry and we thought there might be something to eat in your suitcase, so we tickled the lock till it opened. But there was nothing there, and you can pack it all up again.' 'I see,' said Karl, staring at the rapidly emptying basket, and listening to the peculiar noise Robinson made while drinking as the liquid first rolled down his throat, then sped back upwards with a whistling sound, before finally gathering itself and plunging back into the deep. 'Have you finished eating?' he asked, as the others paused for breath. 'Didn't you eat in the hotel?' asked Delamarche, thinking Karl was claiming his share. 'If you still want to eat, then hurry up,' said Karl, and walked to his suitcase. 'He's in rather a bad mood,' Delamarche said to Robinson. 'I'm not in a bad mood at all,' said Karl, 'but I don't think it's right to break open my suitcase in my absence, and scatter my belongings on the ground. I know there's always some give and take between companions, and I was prepared for it too, but this is going too far. I'm spending the night in the hotel and I'm not going on to Butterford with you. Now eat up, I have to return the basket.' 'Will you listen to that, Robinson, that's the way to talk,' said Delamarche, 'that's a fine way to talk. You can tell he's German. You warned me off him early on, but like a fool I took him along. We put our trust in him, dragged him along with us for a whole day and lost

83

at least half a day as a result, and now – just because someone's lured him to the hotel – he says goodbye, he just simply says goodbye. But because he's a perfidious German, he doesn't do it openly, but he uses the suitcase as a pretext, and because he's a vicious German, he can't leave without offending our honour and calling us thieves, just because we had a little laugh with his suitcase.' Karl, packing his things, said without turning round: 'Just go on talking like that, you make it easier for me to leave. I know very well what companionship is. I had friends in Europe, and no one can say I behaved perfidiously or rudely to them. We've lost touch now of course, but if I ever return to Europe, they'll be glad to see me, and we'll be friends again right away. According to you, Delamarche and Robinson, I betrayed you when, as I will never cease to proclaim, you had the kindness to take me up and offer me the prospect of an apprenticeship at Butterford. But what really happened was something different. You have nothing, and while that doesn't lower you in my estimation, it makes you envious of my few possessions, and so you try to humiliate me, and that's what I can't stand. Having broken open my suitcase, you offer not a word of apology, but rather go on insulting me and insulting my people – and that finally makes it quite impossible for me to remain in your company. All this doesn't really apply to you, Robinson, my only objection to your character is that you are too much influenced by Delamarche.' 'So now we know,' said Delamarche, walking right up to Karl and giving him a little push, as though to get his attention, 'so now we know who you really are. All day long you've been walking behind me, you've held on to my coat-tails, you've followed my every move, and apart from that there wasn't a squeak out of you. But once you think you've found some sort of support in the hotel, you start making big speeches to us. A slyboots is what you are, and I'm not sure we're going to take it lying down. Perhaps we should demand a tuition fee for everything you've picked up from watching us. Say, Robinson, he says we're jealous of his possessions. A single day in Butterford – not to mention California – and we'll have ten times more than what you've shown us, and whatever else you've got sewn into the lining of your jacket. So watch your words with us!' Karl had got up from his suitcase, and watched as Robinson, still sleepy but becoming animated by the beer, also approached him. 'If I stay around here much longer,' he said, 'I might get some further surprises.

You seem half inclined to beat me up.' 'Our patience has limits,' said Robinson. 'You'd better stay out of it, Robinson,' said Karl, keeping his eyes on Delamarche, 'I know you're really on my side, but you have to pretend to support Delamarche.' 'Are you trying to bribe him?' asked Delamarche. 'I wouldn't dream of it,' said Karl. 'I'm glad I'm going, and I want nothing more to do with either of you. I only want to say one more thing, you accused me of having money and hiding it from you. Assuming that was the case, wasn't it the right way to behave with people I'd only known for a few hours, and hasn't your present behaviour fully vindicated me?' 'Keep your cool,' said Delamarche to Robinson, although the latter hadn't budged. Then he asked Karl: 'You're being so shamelessly frank, why not, as we're standing so companionably close together, take your frankness a stage further and admit to us what you're going to the hotel for.' Karl had to step back over his suitcase, so close had Delamarche come to him. But Delamarche wasn't to be thrown off, he pushed the suitcase aside, took another stride forward, putting his foot on a white shirt-front that was lying on the grass, and repeated his question.

As though in answer a man with a bright torch approached the group from down on the road. He was a waiter from the hotel. No sooner had he spotted Karl than he said: 'I've spent half an hour looking for you. I've combed the embankments on both sides of the highway. The head cook sends me to say that she needs the basket she lent you back urgently.' 'I've got it here,' said Karl, in a voice shaking with nerves. Delamarche and Robinson had stepped modestly to one side, as they always did when in the presence of powerful strangers (to whom they hadn't been introduced). The waiter took the basket and said: 'And then the head cook would like to know whether you've had second thoughts, and did want to stay the night in the hotel after all. The other two gentlemen would also be welcome, if you wanted to bring them too. Beds have been made up. Admittedly, it is a mild night but there are some dangers attendant on sleeping out, there are often snakes on these embankments.' 'In view of the cook's kindness, I would like to accept her invitation after all,' said Karl, and waited for his companions to chime in. But Robinson just stood there, and Delamarche had his hands in his trouser pockets and was gazing up at the stars. Both of them were obviously relying on Karl simply to take them with him. 'In that case,' said the waiter, 'I have been instructed to show you to the hotel, and to carry your baggage for you.' 'Then just a minute please,' said Karl, and stooped to pick up one or two things that were lying around, and put them in the suitcase.

Suddenly he stood up. The photograph was missing, it had been lying uppermost in the suitcase, and now it was nowhere to be seen. 'I can't find the photograph,' he said beseechingly to Delamarche. 'What photograph do you mean?' he asked. 'The photograph of my parents,' said Karl. 'We saw no photograph,' said Delamarche. 'There was no photograph there, Mr Rossmann,' Robinson confirmed beside him. 'But that's not possible,' said Karl, and his beseeching glances drew the waiter nearer. 'It was right at the top, and now it isn't there any more. If only you hadn't played your joke with the suitcase.' 'An error is out of the question,' said Delamarche, 'there was no picture in the suitcase.' 'It mattered more to me than everything else I have in that suitcase,' said Karl to the waiter, who was walking around, looking in the grass. 'It's irreplaceable, you see, I'll never get another one.' And as the waiter gave up the pointless search, he added: 'It's the only picture of my parents that I had.' Thereupon the waiter said perfectly undiplomatically, 'Perhaps we should check the two gentlemen's pockets'. 'Yes,' said Karl right away, 'I must find the photograph. But before I start looking through your pockets, I'd like to say that whoever gives me the photograph of his own volition will get the entire suitcase plus contents.' After a moment of general silence, Karl said to the waiter: 'My companions obviously want to be searched. But even now, I promise the person who has the photograph in his pocket the whole suitcase. I can do no more.' The waiter straightaway set about searching Delamarche, who seemed to him a trickier customer than Robinson, whom he left to Karl. He pointed out to Karl the necessity of searching them both at the same time, because otherwise one of them could discreetly get rid of the photograph somewhere. The instant Karl put his hand into Robinson's pocket he pulled out a necktie that belonged to him, but he didn't take it back, and added to the waiter, 'Whatever you may find on Delamarche, please leave it with him. I want only the photograph, nothing but the photograph.' As he searched through the breast-pockets, Karl felt Robinson's hot and fatty breast with his hand, and he thought he might be perpetrating a great injustice on his companions. He tried to hurry. It was all in vain anyway, the photograph was not found on Robinson or Delamarche.

'It's no use,' said the waiter. 'They've probably torn up the photograph and thrown away the pieces,' said Karl, 'I thought they were my friends, but secretly they were only out to do me harm. Not so much Robinson, it probably wouldn't even have occurred to him that the photograph would be so precious to me, but Delamarche all the more.' Karl saw only the waiter in front of him, whose torch lit up a small circle, whereas everything else, including Delamarche and Robinson, was in pitch blackness.

Of course that put an end to any idea that the two might be taken along to the hotel. The waiter swung the suitcase on to his shoulder, Karl took the straw basket and they set off. Karl was already on the road when, reflecting, he stopped and called into the darkness: 'Listen to me! If one of you should still have the photograph on him, and would like to bring it to me in the hotel, he'll still get the suitcase and – I give you my word – immunity from prosecution.' There was no reply as such, just a blurted word, the beginning of a reply from Robinson before Delamarche obviously stopped his mouth. Karl still waited for a long time for them to reconsider. Twice more he called out: 'I'm still here.' But there was no answering sound, just once a stone rolled down the slope, perhaps by chance, perhaps it was a misaimed throw.

5

IN THE HOTEL OCCIDENTAL

On reaching the hotel, Karl was taken straightaway to a kind of office, where the Head Cook, holding a notebook in her hand, was dictating a letter to a young typist. Her very precise dictation, the subdued and elastic tapping of the keys overtook the intermittently audible ticking of a clock on the wall, which now indicated almost half past eleven. 'There!' said the Head Cook, and she snapped the notebook shut. The typist leapt to her feet, and draped the wooden lid over the typewriter, without taking her eyes off Karl as she performed this mechanical action. She looked like a schoolgirl still, her apron for example had been very carefully ironed, with little ruches on the shoulders, her hair was piled up on her head, and after such particulars it was quite a surprise to come upon the serious expression on her face. First bowing to the Head Cook, and then to Karl, she left the room, and Karl involuntarily looked inquiringly at the Head Cook.

'I am glad you decided to come after all,' said the Head Cook. 'What about your companions?' 'I didn't bring them,' said Karl. 'They probably have to make a very early start,' said the Head Cook, as though to explain it to herself. 'Won't she suppose that I'll be setting off with them?' Karl wondered, and therefore, to settle any doubts, he added: 'We had a falling out.' The Head Cook seemed to treat this as good news. 'So you're at liberty?' she asked. 'Yes, I'm at liberty,' said Karl, and it seemed the most worthless condition. 'Listen, wouldn't you like to get a job here in the hotel?' asked the Head Cook. 'Very much,' said Karl, 'but I am shockingly unqualified. I don't even know how to type, for example.' 'That's not the point,' said the Head Cook. 'For the time being you would start off in a very small job, and then it will be up to you to try and work your way up by industry and application. To say the least, though, I think it would be better for you to settle somewhere than to go tramping through the world. You don't seem to me to be cut out for that.' 'My uncle would agree with that,' Karl said to himself, and he nodded his consent. At the same time, he remembered that he – the object of such concern – had yet to introduce himself. 'I'm so sorry,' he said, 'I haven't introduced myself, my name is Karl Rossmann.' 'You're German, aren't you?' 'Yes,' said Karl, 'I've only been in America for a little while.' 'Where do you come from?' 'From Prague in Bohemia,' said Karl. 'Well I never,' exclaimed the Head Cook in German with a very strong English accent, and almost threw up her arms, 'then we're compatriots, my name is Grete Mitzelbach, and I come from Vienna. I know Prague extremely well, for half a year I worked at the Golden Goose on Wenceslas Square. Just imagine!' 'When was that?' asked Karl. 'It's many, many years ago now.' 'Because the old Golden Goose,' said Karl, 'was torn down two years ago.' 'Oh really,' said the Head Cook, lost in memories of bygone times.

Then suddenly becoming animated again, she seized Karl's hands and cried: 'Now that it has emerged that you are my fellow countryman, you mustn't leave here at any price. I won't let you do that to me. How would you like to be lift-boy, for example? You only have to say the word. If you've been around a bit, you will know that it's not particularly easy to get jobs like that, because they are really the best openings imaginable. You get to meet all the guests, you're always on view, you keep getting little jobs to do, in short, every day you get a chance to better your status. Leave all the rest to me!' 'I wouldn't mind being a lift-boy,' said Karl, after a short pause. It would have been very foolish of him to hold out against the job of lift-boy on the strength of his five years in secondary school. Here in America it would be more appropriate to be ashamed of those five years of school. And in point of fact, Karl had always liked lift-boys, he thought of them as an ornament of hotels. 'Don't you need languages?' he asked. 'You speak German and good English, that's perfectly adequate.' 'But all my English I've learned in just two and a half months in America,' said Karl, thinking he shouldn't hide his one light under a bushel. 'That says everything about you,' said the Head Cook. 'When I think of the trouble I had learning English. Admittedly that was thirty years ago now. I was talking about it only yesterday. Yesterday was my fiftieth birthday.' And with a smile she turned to see what impression such a great age made on Karl. 'I wish you many happy returns,' said Karl. 'That would always come in useful,' she said, shook Karl's hand, and was once again half melancholy at the old phrase from home, which had come to her as she spoke German.

'But you mustn't let me detain you,' she cried. 'I expect you're very tired, and we can talk about everything much better in the daytime. My delight at meeting a fellow countryman has made me quite inconsiderate. Come on, I'll take you to your room.' 'I have another favour I'd like to ask you, cook,' said Karl, looking at the telephone apparatus on the table. 'It is possible that tomorrow, perhaps very early, my former companions may bring in a photograph that I need urgently. Would you be so kind and telephone the porter to send them up to me, or have me brought down to them.' 'Of course,' said the Head Cook, 'but wouldn't it do if he just took receipt of the photograph? What is the photograph of, if I may ask?' 'It's a photograph of my parents,' said Karl, 'but no, I need to talk to them myself.' The cook made no reply, and telephoned the porter's lodge with the instructions, giving Karl's room number as 536.

They went out through a door opposite the one he had come in at, on to a little passage where a little lift-boy was asleep on his feet, leaning against the railing of a lift. 'We can help ourselves,' said the cook quietly, and ushered Karl into the lift. 'A ten or twelve hour day is just a bit much for a boy like that,' she said, as they rode up. 'But America's odd like that. Take that little boy, for instance, he only arrived here with his parents six months ago, he's Italian. At the moment, it looks as though he couldn't possibly stand up to his work, his face is gaunt, he falls asleep on his shift, even though he's a very willing lad by nature – but give him another six months of working here or somewhere else in America, and he'll take it with ease, and in five years' time he'll be a strong man. I could regale you for hours with cases like that. I'm not even considering you, because you're a strong lad. You're seventeen, aren't you?' 'Sixteen next month,' replied Karl. 'Only sixteen!' said the cook. 'Well, courage!'

Upstairs, she took Karl to an attic room with a sloping ceiling that looked very cosy in the light of two electric lamps. 'Don't be put off by the furnishings,' said the cook, 'it's not a regular hotel room, but one of the rooms in my apartment, which consists of three rooms, so you won't be bothering me in the least. I'll lock the connecting door, so you'll have absolute privacy. When you join the hotel staff tomorrow you will of course be given a little room of your own. If you had brought your companions, I would have had beds made up for all of you in the staff dormitory, but as you've come on your own, I think you will be better off here, even though you'll be sleeping on the sofa. And now I hope you sleep well, so you'll be refreshed for work tomorrow. It won't be too tough to begin with.' 'Thank you for all your kindness.' 'Wait,' she said, stopping on her way out, 'you would almost have been woken up.' And she went over to one of the side doors of the room, knocked and called: 'Therese!' 'Yes, Head Cook,' the voice of the little typist replied. 'When you come to wake me tomorrow morning, will you go via the corridor, I have a guest sleeping in this room. He's terribly tired.' She smiled at Karl as she said this. 'Do you understand?' 'Yes, Head Cook.' 'Good night, then!' 'Good night.'

'You see,' said the Head Cook, by way of explanation, 'for the past few years I've been sleeping extremely badly. I am happy in my job, and don't really have anything to worry about. So my sleeplessness must be caused by the worries I had earlier. I count myself lucky if I fall asleep by three in the morning. But seeing as I need to be back on the job by five or half past at the latest, I have to be woken up, and very carefully at that, so that I don't become even more nervous than I am already. And so I have Therese wake me. But now you're fully informed, and I'm holding you up. Goodnight!' And in spite of her bulk, she positively skipped out of the room.

Karl was looking forward to his sleep, because it had been a long day. And he couldn't wish for any cosier place in which to have a long and untroubled sleep. His room wasn't intended as a bedroom, it was more of a living-room, or really a salon for the Head Cook, and a washstand had kindly been provided especially for that one evening but in spite of that, Karl didn't feel like an intruder, but all the better cared for. His suitcase was in order, and it probably hadn't been so secure for some time. There was a low chest of drawers with a loosely woven woollen rug thrown over it, with various framed photographs standing on it, Karl stopped to study them as he was inspecting the room. For the most part they were old photographs, and they were mainly of girls in uncomfortable old-fashioned clothes, with little hats perched on their heads, their right hands resting on parasols, facing the viewer but still somehow avoiding his glance. Among the male portraits, Karl was particularly struck by the picture of a young soldier who had set his cap down on a little table, standing there stiffly with his wild black hair, and a proud and repressed humour. The buttons on his uniform had been retouched in gold on the photograph. All these pictures probably came from Europe, you could probably read on the back just where, but Karl didn't want to pick them up. He would have liked to display the picture of his parents in his own room in just the same way as these photographs were displayed here.

He was just stretching out on the sofa, looking forward to his sleep after thoroughly washing himself all over, as quietly as possible on account of his neighbour, when he thought he heard a quiet knocking on the door. He wasn't quite sure which door it was, and it might also have been just a noise. There was no immediate repetition of it, and Karl was on the point of sleep when it happened again. This time there could be no question but that it was a knock, coming from the door of the typist's room. Karl went over to the door on tiptoe and asked, in a voice so quiet that it wouldn't have woken his neighbour if she had happened to be asleep: 'What can I do for you?' Straightaway, and just as quietly, came the reply: 'Won't you open the door? The key is on your side.' 'Of course,' said Karl. 'Just let me get dressed first.' There was a slight pause, and then: 'You don't have to. Open the door and go and lie down in your bed again, I'll wait a moment.' 'Very well,' said Karl, and did as she suggested, only he turned the electric light on as well. 'I'm ready,' he said, a little louder. And at that the little typist emerged from her dark room, wearing exactly the same clothes she had had on downstairs in the office, she probably hadn't thought about going to bed in all that time.

'Do please excuse me,' she said, standing at Karl's bedside, leaning over him a little, 'and please don't give me away. I won't keep you long, I know you're dead tired.' 'It's not that bad,' said Karl, 'but perhaps it would have been better if I had got dressed after all.' He was forced to lie flat, in order to remain covered up to the neck, as he didn't have a nightshirt. 'I'll just stay for a moment,' she said, and reached for a chair, 'or can I sit down on your sofa?' Karl nodded. And then she sat down on the sofa, so close to him that Karl had to move right back against the wall in order to be able to look up at her. She had a round face, and regular features, only her forehead was unusually high, but that might just be on account of her hairstyle, which didn't quite suit her.

Her dress was very clean and tidy. In her left hand she was squeezing a handkerchief.

'Are you going to be staying here for long?' she asked. 'I'm not sure yet,' replied Karl, 'but I think I'd like to stay.' 'That would be a very good thing,' she said, and passed her handkerchief over her face, 'because I'm so lonely here.' 'You surprise me,' said Karl, 'the Head Cook is very nice to you. She doesn't treat you like an employee at all. I thought you might be a relation.' 'Oh no,' she said, 'my name is Therese Berchtold, I come from Pomerania.' Karl introduced himself too. Thereupon for the first time, she looked him full in the face, as though by telling her his name he'd become a little stranger to her. For a while neither spoke. Then she said, 'You're not to think of me as ungrateful. But for the Head Cook, I'd be in a far worse position than I am. I used to be a kitchen maid here in the hotel, and I was in grave danger of being sacked, because I couldn't do the heavy work. They ask an awful lot of you here. Last month a kitchen maid fainted through sheer over exertion, and spent two weeks in hospital. And I'm not very strong, I had a difficult childhood and I'm a bit underdeveloped as a result, you'd never guess I'm eighteen now would you. But I'm getting stronger now.' 'The work here must be very demanding,' said Karl. 'Just now I saw the lift-boy downstairs asleep on his feet.' 'But it's the lift-boys who have the best of it,' she said, 'they get a pretty penny from tips, and don't need to slave away nearly as much as the people down in the kitchen. But I was really lucky, the Head Cook needed a girl once to fold the napkins for a banquet, and she sent down to the kitchen where there are about fifty of us girls, and I just happened to be available and she was very pleased with me because I've always been good at folding napkins. And from that time on she kept me at her side and gradually trained me to be her secretary. I've learned a great deal.' 'Is there such a lot of writing to do?' asked Karl. 'Oh, a great deal,' she replied, 'you probably can't imagine it. You saw how I was working up until half past eleven, and today's just an ordinary day. Admittedly I don't spend all my time writing, I also have a lot of errands to run in the town.' 'What town is that?' asked Karl. 'Don't you know?' she said, 'Ramses.' 'Is it a big town?' asked Karl. 'Very big,' she replied, 'I don't like going there. But are you sure you don't want to sleep now?' 'No, no,' said Karl. 'You haven't told me why you came in yet.' 'It's because I don't have anyone to talk to.

I don't feel sorry for myself, but if you don't have anyone, it makes you happy to find someone who will listen to you. I saw you when you were in the dining-room downstairs, I was just on my way to collect the Head Cook, when she led you off to the storerooms.' 'That dining-room is an awful place,' said Karl. 'I hardly notice it any more,' she replied. 'But I wanted to say that the Head Cook is as good to me as my dear departed mother. Only the difference between our ranks is too great for me to be able to talk to her freely. I used to have some good friends among the kitchen maids, but they've all moved on, and I don't really know the new girls. Sometimes I think my new job is even more demanding than my old one, and I'm even less up to it, and that the Head Cook only keeps me in it because she feels sorry for me. You really need a better education than mine to be a secretary. It's a sin to say so, but very often I'm afraid I may go mad. For God's sake,' she suddenly said much faster, and clutched Karl's shoulder, as his hands were under the bedclothes, 'you mustn't breathe a word of this to the Head Cook, because otherwise I really would be done for. It would be unpardonable if, on top of the dissatisfaction she must feel with my work, I were to hurt her feelings as well.' 'You may rest assured that I won't say anything to her,' replied Karl. 'Thank you,' she said, 'and I hope you do stay. I'd be pleased if you stayed, and if you like, we could be friends. The first time I saw you, I felt I could trust you. But at the same time – honestly, this is how bad I am – I was afraid that the Head Cook might make you her secretary in my stead, and get rid of me. Only when I was alone for a long time when you were downstairs in the office, I thought it over, and it seemed to me it would be just as well if you did take my job, because you'd be much better at it than I am. If you didn't want to run errands in the city, I could go on doing those. Apart from that I'm sure I'd be far more useful in the kitchen, especially as I'm a bit stronger now.' 'The matter's taken care of,' said Karl, 'I'm going to be a lift-boy, and you'll go on being a secretary. But if you so much as hint of your plans to the cook, then I will go and tell her all that you've told me today, even though it would make me very upset.' Therese was so shaken by his tone that she threw herself down on his bed, pressed her face against the sheets and sobbed. 'I won't give anything away,' said Karl, 'but you're not to say anything either.' Now he couldn't remain completely hidden under the bedclothes any more, he stroked her arm a little, and could think of nothing comforting he could say to her, and only thought how bitter life here must be. Eventually she calmed down enough to be ashamed of her tears, and she looked gratefully at Karl, told him to sleep in tomorrow morning, and promised him, if she got a chance, to come up at around eight and wake him. 'You're famous for waking people up, I've heard,' said Karl. 'Yes, there are one or two things I'm good at,' she said, ran her hand gently over the blanket in farewell, and scurried back to her room.

The next day Karl insisted on beginning work right away, even though the Head Cook wanted to give him the day off for sightseeing in Ramses. But Karl replied frankly that there would be opportunities for that later, and the most important thing for him now was to start work, because he had already once had to break off a career in Europe without anything to show for it, and he was starting as a lift-boy at an age in which the more advanced boys at any rate were almost ready to move on to better jobs. It was perfectly right and proper that he should be starting off as lift-boy, but by the same token he was in a hurry. Under the circumstances, sightseeing in the city would be no pleasure to him at all. He wasn't even prepared to go for a short walk with Therese. Always at the back of his mind was the thought that, if he didn't apply himself, he might finish up like Delamarche and Robinson.

At the hotel tailor's, he tried on the lift-boy's livery, which looked very splendid, with gold braid and gilt buttons, but Karl shuddered a little as he put it on, because the little jacket was cold and stiff and at the same time chronically damp under the arms from the sweat of the lift-boy who had worn it before him. The uniform had to be altered for Karl, particularly across the chest, because not one of the ten available jackets was anything like wide enough. In spite of the sewing that was necessary – and the tailor seemed very pernickety, twice sending the finished article back to the workshop – it all took barely five minutes, and Karl left the workshop already looking like a lift-boy, dressed in tight trousers, and, the tailor's firm assurances to the contrary, a constricting little jacket, which kept making Karl do breathing exercises as he wanted to ascertain whether it was possible to breathe in it at all.

Then he reported to the Head Waiter under whom he was to serve, a slim, handsome man with a big nose, who was probably already in his forties. He had no time for any conversation whatsoever, and merely rang for a lift-boy, it happened to be the very one Karl had seen the day before. The Head Waiter called him by his christian name, Giacomo, as Karl only learned later, because the name in its English pronunciation was unrecognizable. That boy was given the task of showing Karl the essentials of lift work but he was so bashful and so hasty, that, though there was little to learn, Karl didn't even learn that. Giacomo was probably annoyed besides at having to leave the lift service to make way for Karl, and to be assigned to helping the chambermaids, which seemed to him, on the basis of some experiences he didn't care to divulge, dishonourable. It came as a particular disappointment to Karl that the lift-boy's only contact with the machinery was the simple pressing of a button, whereas for any repairs to the mechanism, the hotel's team of engineers were exclusively responsible, so that Giacomo for instance, after six months on the lifts, had not seen the motor in the basement or the machinery inside the lift with his own eyes, even though he would have liked to very much, as he stressed. All in all the work was monotonous, and because of the twelve-hour shifts that alternated between day and night, it was so exhausting that according to Giacomo's reports it was completely unendurable without the odd catnap on one's feet. Karl said nothing to this, but it was clear to him that it was this skill of Giacomo's that had cost him his job.

Karl was very glad that the lift to which he had been assigned was one that travelled to the upper floors only, so that he would be spared any dealings with the wealthier and more demanding hotel guests. Granted, he would learn less as well, and so it was only good for a start.

By the end of the first week, Karl could see that he was well up to the job. The brass trim on his lift was the most highly polished of all, none of the other thirty lifts could compare with it, and it might have gleamed still more if the boy who worked on the same lift as him had been anything like as conscientious, instead of taking Karl's diligence as an excuse for his own sloppiness. He was an American by birth, Rennel was his name, a vain boy with dark eyes and smooth, somewhat concave cheeks. He had an elegant suit of his own, in which on his evenings off he would hurry, lightly perfumed, into the city; occasionally too he would ask Karl to fill in for him in the evening, as he had to go off for family reasons, and it didn't bother him that his appearance seemed to be rather at variance with such claims. In spite of that, Karl liked him, and he liked it when, on such evenings, Rennel would stand around by the lift with him in his going-out clothes, say a few more words of apology as he pulled his gloves over his fingers and then stroll off down the corridor. Besides, in covering for him, Karl was only doing a favour, as seemed prefectly natural to start off with, for a colleague older than himself, it wasn't meant to become a permanent state of affairs. For this continual riding up and down in the lift was tiring enough anyway, and in the evening there were almost no interruptions.

Soon Karl also mastered the quick, deep bows that the lift-boys were expected to perform, and he could catch tips in mid-air. The money vanished into his waistcoat pocket, without anyone being able to tell from his expression whether it was a large sum or small. For ladies he opened the door with a little show of gallantry, and swung himself into the lift slowly behind them, as they tended to get into it more hesitantly than men, afraid for their dresses, their hats and wraps. During the ride, he would stand, as this was least obtrusive, hard by the door, with his back turned to the guests and hold the handle so as to be able to push it aside the instant the lift stopped, without causing any undue alarm. It was rare for anyone to tap him on the shoulder during a ride to ask for some piece of information, in which case he would promptly turn round, as though expecting it, and reply in a clear voice. Often, in spite of the great number of lifts, especially after the theatres let out, or after the arrival of certain express trains, there would be such a crush, that barely had the guests got out at the top than he had to race back down to pick up more waiting downstairs. By pulling at a wire that ran through the lift, he had the option of increasing the usual speed, although this was forbidden by the lift regulations, and was supposed to be dangerous as well. Accordingly Karl never did it when he had any passengers on board, but when he had dropped some off upstairs, and there were others waiting below, he would be ruthless, and pull strongly on the wire, hand over hand, like a sailor. He knew that the other lift-boys did this as well, and he didn't want to lose his passengers to the other boys. Certain guests, who had been staying in the hotel for some time, which seemed to be quite common practice here, would occasionally smile at Karl, to show that they recognized him as their lift-boy. Karl was grateful for their attention, but took it with a stern face. Sometimes, when there was less traffic, he was able to take on little special errands, for instance, in the case of a hotel guest who didn't want to go all the way back up to his room to fetch some small item that he'd left behind, he would rush up alone in the lift, which seemed particularly close to him at such moments, step into the strange room, which usually contained extraordinary things he had never seen before, strewn around or hanging from coat-hangers, breathe the characteristic smell of a particular soap, perfume or mouthwash, and without loitering at all, hurry back down again, having found the object in spite of the generally unclear instructions. He was often sorry not to be able to take on larger commissions, because there were waiters and errand-boys specially set aside for these, who did their work on bicycles or even motorbikes, it was only for errands involving the rooms and dining-rooms or gaming-rooms that Karl was able, unless otherwise engaged, to be used.

When he came off the twelve hour shifts, at six in the evening on the first three days, and at six in the morning for the three following, he was so tired that he went straight to bed without paying any attention to anybody else. He was in the dormitory for lift-boys. The Head Cook, whose influence wasn't perhaps as great as he had thought that first evening, had endeavoured to find him a room of his own, and might even have succeeded, but when Karl saw the trouble it put her to, and the number of times she spoke on the telephone to his superior, that terribly busy Head Waiter, on his account, he abandoned the idea and convinced the Head Cook that he was serious by arguing that he didn't want to incur the envy of the other boys by obtaining a privilege he wouldn't have been able to secure for himself.

Now this dormitory was anything but a quiet place to sleep. For, since each of them divided up his twelve hours off, between eating, sleeping, pleasure and work on the side, there was a loud and continual commotion in the dormitory. There were some who were asleep, with the blankets pulled up over their ears in order to eliminate the noise; but if one of these was awakened, then he would scream so angrily at the shouting of the others, that none of his fellow sleepers could remain so. Almost every one of the boys owned a pipe, pipes were their luxury, Karl had acquired a pipe for himself too, and soon got a taste for it. Now smoking on duty was not allowed, and as a result everyone in the dormitory who wasn't asleep would be smoking. Each bed was swathed in its own individual cloud of smoke and a general pall hung over the whole room. In spite of a theoretical agreement to that effect, it proved impossible to maintain the principle of having light at only one end of the room. If that suggestion had prevailed, then the ones who wanted to sleep could have done so quietly in the darkness of one half of the room – which was a large one, containing forty beds – whereas the others could have played dice or cards in the lighted half, and whatever else they needed a light for. If one whose bed was in the light part of the room wanted to sleep, he could have lain down on a vacant bed in the dark half, because there were always sufficient beds, and no one ever objected to the temporary borrowing of a bed by someone else under such circumstances. But there was never a night on which such a division was practised. There would always be a couple of boys, say, who having used the darkness to get some sleep, then felt like a game of cards in their beds, laying a board between them and of course switching on a handy electric light, whose piercing beams would startle the sleepers on whom they fell and wake them up. A sleeper would toss and turn for a while, but in the end there was nothing for it but to start a game with his neighbour, who had been similarly awakened, and with additional illumination. And of course all puffed away on their pipes. There were some – Karl usually among them – who wanted to sleep at any price, and who instead of laying their heads on their pillows covered their heads or rolled them inside their pillows. But how could you remain asleep when your next door neighbour would get up in the dead of night in order to seek some pleasure in town before the beginning of his shift, when he washed at the ewer at the end of your own bed, splashing loudly, when he not only pulled on his boots with much clattering, but stamped his feet to get them properly in – almost all of them had boots that were too small for them despite being of American design – and then finally, missing some item of apparel, raised the pillow of the sleeper, who by now would be long awake and only waiting to have a go at him. And then they were all athletic, young, strong lads, reluctant to let slip any opportunity for physical exercise. So you could be sure that when a great noise startled you out of your night's sleep you would find two boys wrestling on the floor beside your bed, bright lights, and all around standing up on their beds in shirt and underpants, giving expert commentary. In the course of one such nocturnal bout, one of the combatants fell across Karl's bed as he lay sleeping, and the first thing Karl saw on opening his eyes was the blood pouring from the boy's nose, and soaking the bedclothes before anything could be done to prevent it. Often Karl would spend his entire twelve hours attempting to get a couple of hours of sleep, though he was also very tempted to join in the amusements of the others; but he kept thinking that in their lives they had an advantage over him, which he needed to make up for by greater industry and a certain self-denial. Even though his sleep was very important to him, principally for the sake of his work, he didn't complain about conditions in the dormitory either to the Head Cook or to Therese, because in the first place all the boys more or less endured them without serious complaint, and secondly the torments of the dormitory were an integral part of his job as lift-boy, which he had gratefully accepted from the hands of the Head Cook.

Once a week, when the shift pattern changed, he got twenty-four hours off, which he used to pay one or two visits to the Head Cook and to have a few little chats with Therese whose precious free time he would share, in some corner somewhere, in the corridor, or more rarely in her room. Sometimes too he would accompany her on her errands in the city, though these had to be done in a great hurry. They would almost run, Karl carrying her bag, to the nearest underground station, the ride was over in a flash, as though the train was being pulled by an irresistible force, and already they were out, clattering up the stairs instead of waiting for the lift which was too slow for them, the great squares appeared, out of which the roads flew apart in stellar patterns, and with them a bewildering confusion of traffic all of it flowing in straight lines, but Karl and Therese hurried, close together, into various offices, laundries, storerooms and shops, to place orders or make complaints where it wasn't possible by telephone, things that were usually less than momentous. Therese soon realized that Karl's assistance on these missions was not to be despised, rather it brought a great acceleration to many things. In his company, she was never made to wait, as happened often when she was alone, for over-occupied business people to listen to her. He stepped up to the counter and drummed on it with his knuckles until someone came, he shouted in his utterly distinctive, over-precise English across walls of humanity, he went unhesitatingly up to people, even if they had arrogantly withdrawn into the furthest recesses of seemingly endless premises. He didn't do it out of hubris, and he respected resistance, but he felt he was in a strong position, the Hotel Occidental was a client that couldn't be mocked, and finally Therese, for all her business experience, needed his help. 'I wish you could always come along with me,' she said sometimes, smiling happily when they returned from a particularly well executed campaign.

Only on three occasions during the month and a half that Karl spent in Ramses did he stay longer than a couple of hours in Therese's little room. It was of course far smaller than any of the Head Cook's rooms, the few belongings of Therese's were grouped around the window, but after his experiences in the dormitory, Karl keenly appreciated the value of a comparatively quiet room of one's own, and though he didn't say anything to Therese directly, she still understood how much he liked her room. She had no secrets from him, and indeed it would have been difficult for her to have any after her visit to him that first evening. She was an illegitimate child, her father was a builder's foreman, and had sent for the child and her mother from Pomerania, but then as though that represented the limit of his obligation, or he had expected other people than the exhausted woman and sickly child he greeted at the harbour, he had emigrated to Canada shortly after their arrival, without much explanation, and they had received no letter nor any news of him, which wasn't all that surprising as they were hopelessly lost in the cramped ghetto in the Eastern part of New York.

Once – Karl was standing next to her at the window, gazing down on the street – Therese had talked about the death of her mother. The way that one winter evening her mother and herself – she must have been five at the time – each carrying a bundle, chased down the street, looking for a place to sleep. The way her mother at first led her by the hand (there was a blizzard and it was hard to make any headway) till her hand relaxed and she let go of Therese without looking to see what became of her, and she had to strive to grab hold of her mother's skirts. Often Therese stumbled and even fell but her mother seemed possessed and wouldn't stop. And the snowstorms in the long straight streets of New York! Karl hadn't experienced a winter in New York. If you walk into a swirling headwind, you can't open your eyes even for a second, the wind is incessantly rubbing snow in your face, you walk and walk and get nowhere, it's quite desperate. Of course a child has a certain advantage over a grown-up, it can walk underneath the wind, and is still able to enjoy everything. And so Therese hadn't quite been able to understand her mother at the time; and she was firmly convinced that if she had behaved more sensibly that evening with her mother – but she was just a little girl – she wouldn't have had to suffer such a miserable death. Her mother had already been without work for two days, they didn't have a penny piece, they had spent the day in the open without a bite to eat, and all they had in their bundles were useless rags which they were only afraid to throw away because of superstition. Now her mother had been offered work on a building site the following morning, but as she told Therese all day long, she was afraid she wouldn't be able to take up this good opportunity because she was dead tired, that morning to the alarm of passers-by on the pavement she had coughed up a lot of blood, and all she wanted was to get in the warm somewhere and rest. But on this one evening it was proving impossible to find a place. Anywhere that the janitor hadn't evicted them from the doorway of a building, and in which there was at least a little protection from the weather, they would hurry through narrow icy passages, climb long flights of stairs, circle the narrow courtyards, knocking randomly on doors, sometimes not daring to speak, at others asking anyone they met, and once or twice her mother would squat down breathless on the steps in a quiet staircase, pull Therese, in spite of her resistance, to herself, and press her lips against her so hard that it hurt. When she knew later that those were the last kisses, she couldn't understand how even if she were a little shrimp, she could have been so blind as not to see that. In some of the rooms they passed, the doors were open to let out some suffocating fumes, and from the haze that filled the room like smoke from a fire, a human figure would loom in the doorway, and either with a curt word or by its mute presence communicate the impossibility of finding shelter in that particular room. Looking back it seemed to Therese that her mother had only been serious in her search for the first few hours, because after midnight or thereabouts, she no longer asked anyone, although she didn't stop rushing around till dawn, with short interruptions, and even though there is always life in those buildings where neither the gates nor the doors to individual rooms are ever locked, and you keep running into people. Of course it wasn't as though they made much headway with their scurrying about, it was simply the utmost exertion of which they were capable, and perhaps in reality it was no more than a crawl. Nor could Therese be sure whether they had tried their luck in twenty houses between midnight and five o'clock, or two or even just one. The corridors of those tenements are cleverly designed to make the most of the space, but without regard to easy orientation, so how many times they might have gone down the selfsame passages! Therese had a dim memory of leaving the entrance of a building having spent an eternity looking up and down inside it, but she could also remember how they had turned on the pavement, and plunged straight back inside the building again. For the child it was incomprehensible suffering, now held by her mother, now holding on to her, without so much as a comforting word, being dragged along, and in her incomprehension the only explanation she could find for the whole thing was that her mother was trying to run away from her. Therefore Therese held on as hard as she could, even when her mother had her by the hand, she still gripped on to her skirts with her other hand, just to be sure, and cried at intervals. She didn't want to be abandoned here among the people who stamped up the stairs ahead of them, or came up behind them, still hidden behind a turn in the stairs, who would meet and quarrel in the corridors outside a door, and push one another into rooms. Drunks wandered round the building singing faintly, and Therese and her mother were just able to slip through a group of them as it was closing around them. They could surely, late at night when people weren't so absolutely insistent on their rights, have found their way into one of the general dormitories, that were rented out by speculators, of which they passed several, but Therese didn't understand, and her mother didn't want to rest any more. At daybreak on a fine winter morning, they both leaned against the wall of a house, and perhaps slept a little, perhaps just stared in front of them. It turned out that Therese had lost her bundle, and her mother was going to punish her for her carelessness with a beating, but Therese heard no blows, and could feel none. They went on through streets that were just beginning to wake up, her mother walking by the wall, they crossed a bridge, where her mother's hand brushed the frost from the railing, and finally, Therese at the time accepted it, today she couldn't understand it, they arrived at the building site where her mother was supposed to start that morning. She didn't tell Therese whether she wanted her to wait for her or to go away, and Therese took that as an order to wait, which was what she wanted to do anyway. So she sat down on a pile of bricks and watched as her mother untied her bundle, took out a coloured rag and tied it over the kerchief she had worn all night. Therese was too tired even to think of helping her mother. Without reporting in the site office, as was customary, and without asking anyone, her mother had climbed straight up a ladder, as though she already knew what task had been allotted to her. Therese was puzzled, because women helpers were usually kept on ground level and told to slake lime, pass bricks and do other simple things. So she thought her mother wanted to do some other, better paid form of work today, and she smiled sleepily up at her. The construction was no great height yet, the ground floor was barely completed, though the scaffolding for the upper floors soared up into the blue sky, although as yet without any cross planking. Up there, her mother skilfully went round the masons laying brick on brick, who surprisingly didn't ask what she was doing, she held delicately on to a wooden crate that served as a railing, and Therese in her doze below, marvelled at the sure-footedness of her mother, and thought she caught a friendly glance from her. Then her mother came to a little pile of bricks marking the end of the railing and probably the path as well, but she didn't stop, she walked up to the bricks, her sure-footedness seemed to have deserted her, she kicked over the bricks and fell with them over the edge. Many bricks fell after her, and some time later a heavy board became detached and crashed down on top of her as well. Therese's last memory of her mother was of her lying there with legs apart in the checked skirt she had brought with her from Pomerania, the rough plank on top of her, almost covering her, people running together from all directions, and from up on the site some man angrily shouted something.

It was late when Therese came to the end of her story. It had been unusually detailed for her, and, especially in unimportant places, for instance the description of the scaffolding poles each soaring into the sky, she had had to stop with tears in her eyes. After ten years, she still remembered every detail of what had happened, and because the sight of her mother up on the partly finished ground floor was her last memory of her mother's life, and she couldn't relate it clearly enough to her friend, she wanted to go back to it again after the end of her story, but she faltered, buried her face in her hands and didn't say another word.

But there were happier times in Therese's room as well. On his very

PARAGON - daňový doklad č.: ....
ODBĚRATEL:
DIČ:

Zboží	Počet	Cena za MJ	Celkem Kč
The man			
Who Disappeared			
(America)			
217			

Cena bez DPH:		K úhradě Kč	

Datum uskut. zdanit. plnění:	DPH %	Kč

DODAVATEL: **KNIHKUPECTVÍ ACADEMIA**
Václavské nám. 34, 110 00 Praha 1
DIČ: **Tel.: 2422 3511-2, Fax: 2422 3520**
DIČ: 002-62933752
④

Tisk Baloušek, s.r.o.. tel.. fax: 069/ 97 42 651   razítko a podpis dodavatele

first visit there, Karl had seen a manual of business correspondence lying there, and had asked to borrow it. It was then arranged that Karl would do the exercises in the book and take them for approval to Therese, who had already studied the book for what was relevant to her own little tasks. Now Karl would spend whole nights with cotton wool in his ears, downstairs on his bed in the dormitory, in all possible positions for variety, reading the book, and scribbling out exercises in a little notebook with a fountain pen the Head Cook had given him as a reward for organizing one of her large inventories in a tidy and practical way. He was able to turn the interruptions from the other boys to good account, by asking them for little English tips, until they got bored and left him alone. It often surprised him how reconciled they were to their present position, seemingly oblivious to its provisional nature – there were no lift-boys older than twenty at the hotel – and didn't see the need for a decision about any future employment, and, in spite of Karl's example, read nothing but detective stories at best, tattered copies of which were passed from bed to bed.

When they met now, Therese would go over his work with excessive pedantry, they had differences of opinion, Karl called in evidence his great New York professor, but his views on grammar counted for no more with Therese than those of the lift-boys. She took the fountain pen out of his hand and crossed out the passage she was convinced was wrong, while in such doubtful instances, though there was usually no higher authority than Therese who would see the exercises, Karl usually put a line through her crossings-out to record his disagreement. Sometimes though the Head Cook would turn up and she invariably decided in Therese's favour, which didn't prove anything at all, as Therese was her secretary. But at the same time she did effect a general reconciliation, because they had tea and biscuits, and Karl was made to tell her about Europe, albeit with many interruptions from the Head Cook, who kept asking questions and exclaiming in surprise, which made Karl aware of how much had changed there, quite fundamentally, in a relatively short space of time, and how much must have changed already in his own absence, and was changing all the time.

Karl had been in Ramses for perhaps a month, when one evening Renell told him in passing that he had been spoken to outside the hotel by a man called Delamarche, who had asked after Karl. Renell had no reason to keep quiet about anything, and he had truthfully reported that Karl was working as a lift-boy, but, as he enjoyed the protection of the Head Cook, he had excellent prospects of promotion. Karl noticed how carefully Delamarche had treated Renell, even asking him to dinner this very night. 'I'm not having anything more to do with Delamarche,' said Karl. 'And you should be on your guard with him!' 'Me?' said Renell, and he stretched and hurried off. He was the most delicate boy in the hotel, and there was a rumour circulating among the other boys, whose source was unknown, that he had, to put it no higher than that, been kissed in the lift by a posh lady who had been living in the hotel for some time. For anyone who knew the rumour, a great part of its charm was in watching that self-possessed lady, whose exterior gave no clue to the possibility of such behaviour, going past with her light quiet tread, delicate veils, and sternly corseted waist. She lived on the first floor, and so Renell's lift was not hers, but of course if their own lifts happened to be engaged, one couldn't forbid the guests from stepping into another. And so it happened that the lady did occasionally ride in Karl and Renell's lift, and in fact only ever when Renell was on duty. It might be pure chance, but no one thought so, and when the lift went up carrying the two of them in it, a barely suppressed commotion went along the whole line of lift-boys, which had necessitated the intervention from one of the head waiters. Now, whether it was the lady or the rumour that was the cause, Renell had changed, he was even more self-confident, he left all the cleaning and polishing to Karl, who wanted to have a word with him about it, and he never set foot in the dormitory any more. No one else had so completely quit the normal orbit of the lift-boys, because in general, in questions of duty they all stuck together, and had a union that was recognized by the hotel management.

All this passed through Karl's mind, and he thought of Delamarche as well, as he went on doing his work. At midnight he had a little relief, because Therese, who would often come with little surprises, gave him a large apple and a bar of chocolate. They chatted awhile, barely put out by the interruptions of his taking the lift up and down. Conversation turned to Delamarche, and Karl realized that, in thinking of him as a dangerous person for some while now, he had allowed himself to be influenced by Therese, because that was how he appeared to her from what Karl had told her about him. Basically, though, Karl thought he was nothing worse than a scamp who had been turned to the bad by his misfortune, but with whom one could perfectly well get along. Therese though, took issue with that, and in long speeches pleaded with Karl to promise her that he would never exchange another word with Delamarche. Instead of making such a promise, Karl pressed her to go to sleep, it was already long past midnight, and when she refused he threatened to leave his post and take her up to her room himself. When she finally agreed to go, he said: 'Why do you worry yourself unnecessarily, Therese? If it makes you sleep any better, I'll gladly promise you that I won't speak to Delamarche unless I absolutely have to.' Then many rides were required of him, because the boy in the next door lift was called away on some errand, and Karl had to look after both lifts. Some hotel guests spoke of disorganization and one gentleman who was escorting a lady went so far as to tap Karl with his walking stick to make him hurry, something that was not called for at all. If only the guests would see that there was no boy standing by the other lift and would all come over to Karl's, but no, they went to the other lift and remained there, with their hands on the door handle, or they even walked straight into it, which was something the lift-boy had to prevent at all costs, it was the strictest item in the rule book. The result for Karl was a lot of very fatiguing coming and going, and even then he didn't feel he was discharging his duty properly. At about three in the morning, a porter, an old man with whom he was vaguely friendly, asked him for some help with something, but he was unable to give it, because there were groups of guests standing in front of both his lifts, and it needed great presence of mind to decide in favour of one of them, and promptly stride towards it. He was relieved, then, when the other boy returned and he called out a few words of reproach to him for his long absence, although it probably wasn't his fault. After four o'clock there was a small lull, and not before time. Karl leaned against the railing beside his lift, slowly eating his apple, from which a strong sweet aroma rose from the very first bite, and looked down the lift-shaft, which was surrounded by the large windows of the storerooms, behind which great bunches of bananas glimmered faintly in the dark.

6

THE ROBINSON EPISODE

Just then, someone tapped him on the shoulder. Karl, thinking of course it was a guest at the hotel, quickly stuffed the apple into his pocket and hurried off back to his lift, not bothering to give the man behind him a glance. 'Good evening, Mr Rossmann,' said the man, 'it's me, Robinson.' 'You have changed,' said Karl, shaking his head. 'Yes, I'm doing fine,' said Robinson, and looked down at his clothes, which although individually they might have been choice items, made a positively shabby impression together. The most striking part of the ensemble was a white waistcoat he was obviously wearing for the first time, which had four small black-rimmed pockets, to which Robinson tried to draw attention by puffing out his chest. 'You are expensively dressed,' said Karl, and thought briefly of his beautiful dark suit in which he could have stood comparison with Renell, and which his two bad companions had sold. 'Yes,' said Robinson, 'almost every day I buy myself something new. How do you like the waistcoat?' 'It's very nice,' said Karl. 'The pockets aren't real, mind, they just look like pockets,' said Robinson, and took Karl's hand so that he might convince himself of this. Karl, though, shrank back, because an intolerable brandy smell wafted out of Robinson's mouth. 'You're drinking again,' said Karl, standing by the railing now. 'No,' said Robinson, 'not much,' and contradicted his previous self-satisfaction by saying: 'What else can a man do in this world.' A ride on the lift interrupted their conversation, and no sooner had Karl come down again than he was summoned by telephone to fetch the hotel doctor, as a lady had fainted on the seventh floor. On his way, he secretly hoped that Robinson might have left before he got back, because he didn't want to be seen with him, and, mindful of Therese's warning, he wanted to hear nothing from Delamarche either. But Robinson was still there, standing in the stiff attitude of one completely drunk, just as a senior hotel employee in black tails and top hat passed by, fortunately without apparently taking any notice of Robinson. 'Wouldn't you like to visit us some day, Rossmann, we're doing very well now,' said Robinson, and looked invitingly at Karl. 'Are you asking, or is it Delamarche?' Karl asked. 'Delamarche and I. We are of one mind in this,' said Robinson. 'Then let me tell you, and please pass it on to Delamarche: our parting, while it may not have seemed so at the time, was final. I have suffered more at the hands of the two of you than from anyone else. Will you not finally leave me in peace?' 'But we are your companions,' said Robinson, and repulsive drunken tears welled up in his eyes. 'Delamarche says to say that he wants to make up for everything that's happened in the past. We're living with Brunelda now, she's a wonderful singer.' And he was on the point of delivering a tune in a high falsetto when Karl hissed at him: 'Shut up, don't you realize where you are.' 'Rossmann,' said Robinson, deterred from singing but nothing else, 'I'm your companion, whatever you say. And here you are with such a fine job, couldn't you spare me a bit of money.' 'You'll only spend it on drink,' said Karl, 'in your pocket I can see you've got a bottle of some brandy, from which I'm sure you had a drink while I was gone, because to begin with you were still relatively sober.' 'It's just to give me strength on my mission,' said Robinson apologetically. 'I've given up trying to better you,' said Karl. 'Then what about some money!' said Robinson with staring eyes. 'I suppose you've been instructed by Delamarche to get some money. Very well, I'll give you money, but only on condition that you leave the premises right away and never try to see me here again. If you have anything to say to me, you may write. Karl Rossmann, lift-boy, Hotel Occidental, that should get there. But you mustn't, I repeat, mustn't, try and find me here again. I work here, and have no time for visits. Will you accept the money, under those conditions?' asked Karl, and reached into his waistcoat pocket, having decided to sacrifice whatever tips he had received that night. Robinson merely nodded in answer, and breathed noisily. Karl was unable to interpret this, and he said again: 'Yes or No?'

Then Robinson beckoned him nearer and whispered with unmistakable heaving movements: 'Rossmann, I feel sick.' 'Goddamnit!' Karl exclaimed, and with both hands he dragged him to the railing.

And already vomit spewed forth from Robinson's mouth into the deep.

Helplessly, in the intervals allowed him by his nausea he blindly felt for Karl. 'You're really a good chap,' he would say or 'it's almost over,' which then turned out not to be the case at all, or 'those bastards have poisoned me!' Karl couldn't stand to be near him, he felt such apprehension and disgust, and he began pacing up and down. Robinson was slightly concealed in the corner by the lift, but what if someone were to notice him, one of those rich highly strung hotel guests, who were only waiting to voice a complaint to a passing hotel employee, who would then take it out on the whole staff, or if one of the continually changing hotel detectives happened to pass, incognito to all but the management, but whom one suspected in every man who screws up his eyes, even when it's out of short-sightedness. While, down below, some member of the round-the-clock catering staff needed only to go into the foodstores, remark on the foulness in the light-shaft and telephone Karl to ask what the Hell was going on up there. Could Karl deny all knowledge of Robinson? And if he did, wouldn't Robinson in his stupidity and desperation, instead of apologizing, appeal to Karl for help? And wouldn't Karl then be faced with instant dismissal, in view of the shocking fact that a lift-boy, from the lowest and most expendable rank in the enormous hotel hierarchy, had, through the agency of a friend, sullied the hotel and alarmed or even driven away its guests? Was a lift-boy to be tolerated who had such friends, and from whom he received visits even while on duty? Wouldn't it seem likely that such a lift-boy was himself a drinker or worse, for what could be more logical than to suspect that he supplied his friends from the hotel's stores to the point where they did such things in random places in the scrupulously clean hotel, as Robinson had just done? And why should such a lad content himself with stealing victuals, since the possibility for thieving was almost limitless, what with the notorious negligence of the guests, the wardrobes standing open, valuables left lying on tables, gaping coffers and keys thoughtlessly thrown around?

Just then Karl saw some guests emerging from a basement bar, where a variety performance had just ended. He took up his position by his lift and didn't dare even look at Robinson, afraid of what might meet his eyes. It was of little comfort to him that there was not a sound, not so much as a sigh that could be heard from that direction. He attended to his guests, ferried them up and down, but he was unable to disguise his absent-mindedness, and every time he rode down, he expected to find an embarrassing surprise awaiting him.

Finally he got a chance to see to Robinson, who was crouching in his corner, with his face pressed against his knees, making himself as small as possible. His round hard hat had been pushed right back on his head. 'You must leave now,' said Karl quietly and decisively, 'here's some money. If you're quick about it, I'll show you the short cut myself.' 'I can't move,' said Robinson, mopping his brow with a tiny handkerchief, 'I just want to die. You have no idea of how awful I feel. Delamarche always takes me along to smart bars, but I can't stomach the fancy stuff they serve, I tell Delamarche so every day.' 'Well, you certainly can't stay here,' said Karl, 'consider where you are. If you're found, you'll be punished, and I'll lose my job. Where will that get us?' 'I can't go,' said Robinson, 'I'd sooner jump down there,' and he pointed between the bars of the railing, down the light-shaft. 'So long as I sit here like this I can just about take it, but I can't get up, I tried it once while you were gone.' 'Then I'll get a car, and you can go to hospital,' said Karl, pulling a little at the legs of Robinson, who threatened to lapse into complete stupor at any moment. No sooner did Robinson hear the word hospital though, which seemed to awaken terrible associations for him, than he started crying out loud, and thrust out his hands to Karl for pity.

'Quiet,' said Karl, and smacked his hands aside, ran to the lift-boy he had stood in for earlier in the night, asked him to return the favour for a little while, hurried back to Robinson, pulled him, still sobbing, to a standing position (which took all of his strength) and whispered to him: 'Robinson, if you want me to look after you, make an effort to walk upright for a little way. I'll take you to my bed, you'll be able to stay there until you feel better. You'll be surprised how quickly you'll recover. But now act sensibly, because there are a lot of people in the corridors, and my bed is in a common dormitory. If you attract any attention to yourself at all, I will be unable to do anything more for you. And you must keep your eyes open, I can't carry you around as though you were at death's door.' 'I'll do all you say,' said Robinson, 'but you won't be able to move me by yourself. Couldn't you get Renell to help you?' 'Renell isn't here,' said Karl. 'Oh, yes,' said Robinson, 'Renell is with Delamarche. It was them that sent me to you. I'm getting everything mixed up.' Karl took advantage of this and other incomprehensible burblings of Robinson's to push him along, and succeeded in getting to a corner from where a rather dimly lit corridor led to the lift-boys' dormitory. Just then a lift-boy came running towards them full pelt, and continued past. Otherwise they had only harmless encounters; things were at their quietest between four and five o'clock, and Karl knew that if he couldn't manage to remove Robinson now, there was no hope of being able to do so later on when it grew light and the morning rush began.

At the far end of the dormitory there was a big fight in progress or something similar, you could hear rhythmic clapping, excited drumming of feet and partisan cries. Near the door there were only a few resolute sleepers in their beds, most were lying on their backs staring into space, while now and then, dressed or undressed as he might be, someone would leap out of bed to check how things were progressing at the far end of the room. So Karl was able to take Robinson, who was by now a little used to walking, relatively unobserved to Renell's bed, which was very near the door and fortunately unoccupied, whereas in his own bed, which he saw from a distance, there was some boy he didn't know at all quietly asleep. No sooner did Robinson feel the bed under him than – one leg still dangling out of it – he fell into a deep sleep. Karl pulled the blanket right up over his face, and thought he wouldn't have to worry about him for the immediate future, as Robinson would certainly not wake up before six o'clock in the morning, and by then he would be back here and would find some means, perhaps in concert with Renell, of removing Robinson from the hotel. Inspections of the dormitory by the authorities only took place in extraordinary circumstances, they had been routine once in the past, but the lift-boys had secured their abolition, and so there was nothing to fear in that way.

When Karl was back downstairs by his lift, he noticed that both it and that of his neighbour were at that moment on their way up. Anxiously he waited for the reason for this to become clear. His lift came down first, and out of it came the boy who had run down the corridor a minute ago. 'Hey, Rossmann, where have you been?' he asked. 'Why did you go away? Why didn't you report it?' 'But I asked him to stand in for me for a while,' replied Karl and pointed to the boy from the next lift who was now approaching. 'I've just stood in for him for two hours at peak time.' 'That's all very well,' said the boy thus referred to, 'but it's not enough. Don't you know that the least absence from your post must be reported to the Head Waiter's office. That's what you've got a telephone for. I would have been happy to deputize for you, but it's not that easy, you know. Just now there were guests off the 4.30 express standing in front of both lifts. I couldn't go to your lift, and leave my passengers waiting, so I took my own lift up first.' 'Well?' asked Karl tensely, as both boys were silent. 'Well,' said the boy from the other lift, 'the Head Waiter is going past, he sees the people queuing in front of your lift, which is unattended, he is furious, he asks me as I come running up where you are, I haven't a clue, you never told me where you were going, and so he telephones up to the dormitory for another boy right away.' 'I passed you in the corridor,' said Karl's replacement. Karl nodded. 'Of course,' insisted the other boy, 'I said right away that you'd asked me to stand in for you, but you can be certain he doesn't listen to excuses like that. You probably don't know him yet. And we're to tell you to go and see him in his office right away. So get a move on and don't hang around. Maybe he'll forgive you, you really were only gone for two minutes. It's best not to say that you stood in for me earlier, nothing will happen to me, I had permission to go, but it isn't good to bring up something like that, still less to mix it up with this affair which has got nothing to do with it.' 'But I've never left my post before,' said Karl. 'That's always the way, only no one ever believes it,' said the boy, and ran to his lift, as people were approaching. Karl's stand-in, a boy of about fourteen, obviously feeling sorry for Karl, said: 'There have been many instances of similar incidents being forgiven. Usually you are just assigned to other duties. So far as I know, only one person has actually been dismissed for such a thing. You just have to think up a good excuse. On no account say you suddenly felt sick, he'll just laugh at you. You'd be better off saying a guest sent you on an urgent errand to another guest, and you can't remember who the first guest was, and you were unable to find the second.' 'Oh well,' said Karl, 'it won't be that bad,' after what he had heard, he no longer believed things might take a good turn. And even if he should be forgiven for his breach of duty, there was still Robinson lying in the dormitory, as living proof of his guilt, and considering the splenetic character of the Head Waiter it was all too likely that he wouldn't be content with any superficial investigation, and Robinson would be discovered. There was probably no actual rule that said strangers were not to be taken up to the dormitory, but that was only because the unimaginable was not expressly forbidden.

As Karl stepped into the Head Waiter's office, he was drinking his morning coffee, from which he had just taken a sip, and was looking at an inventory that the Head Porter, who was also present, had given him to examine. This was a big man, made even broader in the shoulders than he was already by his lavish and richly decorated uniform which had gold chains and ribbons twining all over his shoulders and down his arms. His shiny black moustache, teased into long points in the Hungarian style, didn't move, however quickly he turned his head. In actual fact, because of the weight of his apparel, the man could only move with difficulty, and accordingly stood with his feet apart, to keep the weight evenly distributed.

Karl had made a swift and easy entrance, as he had become accustomed to doing in the hotel, because the slowness and circumspection that in other walks of life signify politeness are taken for laziness in lift-boys. Besides, he didn't want his guilty conscience to be immediately apparent. The Head Waiter had glanced at the door, but immediately went back to his coffee and his reading, without taking any more notice of Karl. The porter, though, seemed to feel bothered by Karl's presence, perhaps he had some confidential piece of news or favour to ask, at any rate he kept turning stiffly to send angry looks in Karl's direction, and when these looks duly met Karl's, he would look back at the Head Waiter again. But Karl thought it would make a bad impression if, having got here, he left the office again without being ordered to do so by the Head Waiter. He, though, carried on studying the inventory and eating a piece of cake from which he occasionally shook the sugar without stopping reading. Once a page of the inventory fell to the ground, the porter didn't even make a move to pick it up, he knew that was entirely beyond him, nor was it necessary either as Karl had already done it, and passed the page back to the Head Waiter who took it from him with a motion of his hand that suggested it had flown back to him from the floor all by itself. The little service achieved nothing whatsoever, because the porter still carried on with his angry glances.

Even so, Karl felt calmer than before. Even the fact that his affair seemed to have so little importance for the Head Waiter might be a good sign. One could see why it should be so. Of course a lift-boy is utterly insignificant and therefore may not step out of line, but by virtue of his insignificance what could he do anyway. And then the Head Waiter was a former lift-boy himself – which made him the pride of the present generation of lift-boys – he was the one who had organized the lift-boys for the first time, and he must certainly have left his post without permission on the odd occasion, even if no one could compel him to remember it now, and one shouldn't forget either that, as an erstwhile lift-boy, he saw that his duty lay specifically in keeping that rank in order, even by occasionally draconian means. Karl also pinned some hope on the advancing time. By the office clock it was already a quarter past five, Renell might be back at any time, perhaps he was back already, because it must have struck him that Robinson had failed to return, and, it further occurred to Karl, Delamarche and Renell must have been in the proximity of the Hotel Occidental, because otherwise Robinson in his wretched state would not have got there. Now, if Renell found Robinson in his bed, as must surely happen, then all would be well. For Renell was a practical character, particularly when his own interests were at stake, and he would find a way of speedily getting Robinson out of the hotel, which would be easier as Robinson would have got his strength back by now, and besides Delamarche would probably be waiting for him outside the hotel as well. Once Robinson was gone, Karl would be much more comfortable with the Head Waiter, and might get away with a severe reprimand this time. Then he and Therese might discuss whether he could tell the Head Cook the truth – he for his part couldn't see why not – and if that was possible, the whole affair would have passed without doing him any particular damage.

Having soothed himself a little by such reflections, Karl was just discreetly counting the tips he'd taken that night, because he had the feeling it had been a particularly good one when the Head Waiter put the inventory down on the table with the words 'Would you just wait a moment longer please, Feodor,' sprang lithely to his feet, and screamed at Karl so loudly that he could only stare in terror at his large, black, cavernous mouth.

'You left your post without permission. Do you know what that means? It means dismissal. I want no excuses, you can keep your lying excuses to yourself, for me the mere fact that you weren't there is quite enough.

If I condone that even just once, all forty lift-boys will be running off when on duty, and I'll be left to carry five thousand guests up the stairs by myself.'

Karl said nothing. The porter had come closer and tweaked at Karl's little jacket which was a bit creased, no doubt to draw the Head Waiter's attention to this minor flaw in Karl's appearance.

'Did you suddenly feel sick?' the Head Waiter asked cunningly. Karl looked at him searchingly and replied 'No.' 'So you didn't even feel sick?' screamed the Head Waiter even more loudly. 'Then you must have some truly wonderful excuse. All right, let's hear it. What's your story?' 'I didn't know you had to ask for permission by telephone,' said Karl. 'Now that is priceless,' said the Head Waiter, and grabbed Karl by the lapels and lifted him bodily up to a copy of the lift regulations which was pinned on the wall. The porter also followed them across to the wall. 'There! Read that!' said the Head Waiter, indicating one of the paragraphs. Karl thought he was meant to read it to himself. 'Out loud!' ordered the Head Waiter. But instead of reading it aloud, hoping it would calm the Head Waiter more effectively, Karl said: 'I know the paragraph, I was given a copy of the rules myself and read them carefully. But that sort of rule, which you never use, is most easily forgotten. I've been serving for two months, and never once left my post.' 'But you're about to leave it now,' said the Head Waiter, and walked over to the table, picked up the inventory as though to go on reading from it, but instead smacked it down on the table like a useless piece of bumf and, with scarlet cheek and brow, began criss-crossing the room. 'That a rascal like you should be the cause of such commotion on night duty!' he exclaimed from time to time. 'Do you know who was waiting to take the lift up at the time when this fellow walked off?' he asked the porter. And he gave a name that caused the porter (who must have a pretty shrewd idea of all the guests) to shudder violently, and cast a quick look at Karl, as if his mere presence was proof that the man who bore that name had had to wait in vain for the lift the boy had forsaken. 'But that's terrible!' said the porter, and slowly, in infinite disquiet, shook his head at Karl, who looked at him sorrowfully and thought he would now have to pay for the man's slow-wittedness on top of everything else. 'I know you too,' said the porter, jabbing out a big fat stiff index finger. 'You are the only boy not in the habit of greeting me. Who do you think you are! Everyone who goes past the porter's lodge has to greet me. You can do what you like with the other porters, but I insist on being greeted. I may sometimes behave as though I weren't paying attention, but rest assured, I know all too well who greets me and who doesn't, you rapscallion.' And he turned away from Karl and strode loftily over to the Head Waiter, who, instead of commenting on the porter's case, was finishing his breakfast and perusing a morning newspaper which a servant had just delivered into the room.

'Head Porter, sir,' said Karl, who wanted, at least while the Head Waiter's attention was elsewhere, to settle the dispute with the porter, because he realized that while the porter's complaint might not damage him, the man's enmity certainly could, 'of course I greet you. I haven't been in America long, and I come from Europe where people are known for greeting one another far more than is necessary. Of course I haven't been completely able to shake off the habit yet, and just two months ago in New York, where I happened to be moving in rather elevated circles, I was continually being admonished to give up my excessive politeness. And yet you say I failed to greet you. I greeted you several times a day. But of course not every time I saw you, because I must pass you hundreds of times a day.' 'You're supposed to greet me every time without exception, while you're speaking to me I want you to hold your cap in your hands, and you must always address me as "Sir" and not "you". And all of that every time, you hear, every time!' 'Every time?' Karl repeated quietly and questioningly, he remembered now how the whole time he had been here he had always been looked at sternly and reproachfully by the porter, from the very first morning, when, not yet used to his servile role, he had been a little too bold in asking the porter urgently and insistently whether two men hadn't come looking for him, or perhaps left a photograph for him. 'Now you see where such behaviour gets you,' said the porter, who had once more walked right up to Karl and pointed to the Head Waiter who was still reading, as though he was merely the person who was delegated to execute his revenge. 'In your next job you'll learn to greet the porter, even if it's just in a wretched doss-house.'

Karl realized that to all intents and purposes he had already lost his job, because the Head Waiter had said as much, the Head Porter had referred to it as a foregone conclusion, and in the case of a mere lift-boy the approval of the management would hardly be necessary. It had all happened rather faster than he had expected, because he had served for two months as well as he could, and certainly better than one or two other boys he could think of. But such things, when it came down to it, were obviously of no importance, neither in Europe nor in America, rather matters are decided by whatever impetuous judgement the initial rage of one's superiors might dictate. Perhaps it would have been best now if he had said goodbye and left right away, the Head Cook and Therese were perhaps both still asleep, he could take his leave of them in writing, to save them the upset and disappointment of a farewell in person, could quickly pack his things and slink away. Whereas if he stayed for one more day – and he could use a little sleep – all he had to look forward to would be the mushrooming of his affair into a full-blown scandal, reproaches from all sides, the insufferable sight of Therese in tears, and perhaps the Head Cook as well, and maybe on top of everything else some further punishment. On the other hand, it confused him to be confronting two enemies at once, either of whom might object to and misinterpret any words he might use on his own behalf. He therefore said nothing, and enjoyed the quiet in the room while he could, because the Head Waiter was still reading the newspaper and the Head Porter was putting the papers from his inventory, that had been scattered all over the table, back in numerical order, which with his evident short-sightedness was obviously proving rather difficult.

Finally with a yawn the Head Waiter laid the newspaper aside, looked to see that Karl was still present, and wound up the telephone on the table. He said 'Hallo' into it a few times, but no one answered. 'No one's answering,' he said to the Head Porter. He, who, it seemed to Karl, was following the telephoning with particular interest, said, 'It's already a quarter to six. She's bound to be awake. Ring louder.' At that moment, without further prompting, the reply signal came. 'Head Waiter Isbary speaking,' said the Head Waiter. 'Good morning, Head Cook. I haven't woken you up, have I. I'm so sorry. Yes, yes, it's a quarter to six already. Oh, I'm so sorry to give you a start. You ought to disconnect the telephone while you're asleep. No, no, absolutely, it's quite unpardonable, especially in view of the trifling matter I'm calling about. Yes, of course I have time, by all means, I'll hold the line if that's all right.' 'She must have run over to the telephone in her nightgown,' said the Head Waiter with a smile to the Head Porter, who was crouching over the telephone box with an anxious expression on his face. 'I really did wake her up, usually the little girl who does her typing wakes her, and she must have overslept today. It's a shame I woke her, she's nervous enough as it is.' 'Why isn't she back yet?' 'She's gone to see what's the matter with the girl,' replied the Head Waiter, with the earpiece pressed against his ear, as it was ringing again. 'She'll turn up,' he said into the mouthpiece. 'You mustn't be so put out by everything, you need a good holiday. Now, what I wanted to discuss with you. There's a lift-boy by the name of' – he turned inquiringly to Karl, who, having been following closely, said his name – 'by the name of Karl Rossmann, if I remember rightly, you took him under your wing a bit; I'm sorry to say he's given you a poor reward for your kindness, he's gone and left his post without permission, thereby causing me serious even incalculable consequences, and I have just fired him. I hope you won't take it amiss. What's that? Fired, yes, fired. But I told you, he left his post. No, I really can't give in to you over this, my dear Head Cook. It's a question of my authority, there's a lot at stake, one rotten apple will spoil the whole barrelful. You need eyes in the back of your head, especially with those lift-boys. No, no, I'm afraid I can't do you such a favour in this instance, anxious though I am always to be of service to you. And if I did let him stay in spite of everything, simply to keep my spleen functioning, it's for your sake, yes yours, that he can't stay. You look out for him in a way he certainly doesn't deserve, and knowing both him and yourself as I do, I know that could only lead to your being gravely disappointed, which is something I want to spare you at any price. I say so quite openly, though the fellow's buttoned his lip and is standing just a few feet away. He will be fired, no, no, Head Cook, dismissed, no no, he will be transferred to no other line of work, he is completely useless. Complaints are being voiced against him all the time. For example, the Head Porter, what's that, Feodor, is incensed at the boy's rudeness and impertinence. What, that's not enough? My dear Head Cook, you're denying your true nature on account of this boy. No please don't give me such a hard time over this.'

At that moment the porter leaned forward and whispered something into the Head Waiter's ear. At first the Head Waiter looked at him in amazement, and then spoke into the telephone at such a rate that to begin with Karl was unable to follow him quite, and advanced a couple of paces on tiptoe.

'My dear Head Cook,' he was saying, 'in all candour I would never have thought you such a poor judge of character. I have just now heard something about your paragon that will completely change your view of him, and I'm sorry to have to be the one who must break it to you. This excellent boy, then, whom you call a model of rectitude, spends every one of his free evenings running off into the city, and never returns till the following morning. Yes, yes, Head Cook, I have it on good authority, yes, quite unimpeachable authority. Now could you tell me perhaps from where he has the money for such pursuits? How he is supposed to remain alert while on duty? And would you perhaps like me to describe to you the kind of things he gets up to in the city? I really can't get rid of this boy too fast. And I should like you to be warned by his example to be more circumspect about boys who turn up on your doorstep.'

'But sir, Head Waiter,' cried Karl, quite relieved by the gross error that had evidently been perpetrated, and that might best lead to an unexpected improvement in his situation, 'there seems to be some confusion here. I believe the Head Porter told you that I go out every night. That's not the case at all, I spend every night in the dormitory, as all the boys will confirm. Whenever I'm not asleep, I'm studying business correspondence, but in any case I never set foot outside the dormitory at night. It's easily proved. The Head Porter is evidently confusing me with someone else, now I understand too why he thinks I don't greet him.'

'Will you shut up,' shouted the Head Porter and waved his fist – where others might have contented themselves with wagging a finger – 'So I'm confusing you with someone else. If that were so, then I couldn't go on being Head Porter, if I get people mixed up. Listen, Mr Isbary, I can't go on being Head Porter, can I, if I get people mixed up. In my thirty years of duty I have never once mixed anyone up, as hundreds of head waiters who've been here in that time will be happy to confirm, but now, with you, wretched boy, I've suddenly started getting confused. With you, and your strikingly smooth features. How could I possibly be confused, you could have slunk off into the city every night while my back was turned, but I'm telling you that your face is that of a no-good scoundrel.'

'That's enough, Feodor!' said the Head Waiter, whose telephone conversation with the Head Cook seemed to have come to an abrupt end. 'It's a very straightforward matter. It's not primarily a question of his nocturnal amusements. Perhaps before he leaves us he'd like to get some elaborate investigation started into his nocturnal habits. That would just suit him down to the ground. He would have all forty lift-boys summoned to give evidence, and of course all of them would have got him mixed up too, so by and by the entire hotel staff would be subpoenaed, the business of the hotel would grind to a halt for the duration, and at the end of it all when he was finally thrown out, he would have had a good laugh at our expense. So let's not fall for that. He's already made a monkey of that good woman, the Head Cook, so let that be enough. I won't hear any more, you are dismissed with immediate effect for dereliction of duty. I'll give you a slip for the cashier, so that your wages will be paid up to today. And between you and me, when I think of how you've behaved, that's pure generosity on my part, and I only do it out of regard for the Head Cook.'

The Head Waiter was about to put his name to the slip, when the telephone rang again. 'The lift-boys are playing up today!' he exclaimed after hearing a few words. 'That's outrageous!' he called, a while later. And he turned to the hotel porter and said: 'Feodor, will you keep hold of this fellow for a minute, we need to have further words with him.' And into the telephone he gave the order: 'Come up right away!'

Now at least the Head Porter could get something out of his system that his words hadn't succeeded in doing. He gripped Karl's upper arm, but not with a steady grip, which could have been borne, but periodically loosening it and then gradually making it tighter and tighter, which, with his great strength, seemed to have no limit, and made Karl see stars. Nor was he content to hold him, but, as though he had been ordered to stretch him at the same time, he lifted him up in the air from time to time and shook him, and half-inquired of the Head Waiter: 'I'm not mistaking him for someone else now, am I, I'm not mistaking him.'

Karl was relieved when the head lift-boy, one Bess, a forever panting fat boy, entered and distracted the attention of the Head Porter. Karl was so exhausted that he could barely manage a greeting, when, to his amazement, he saw a ghostly pale Therese slip into the room after the boy, untidily dressed and with loose, piled-up hair. In an instant she was at his side, whispering: 'Does the Head Cook know?' 'The Head Waiter told her on the telephone,' replied Karl. 'Then everything's all right, everything's all right,' she said quickly, with shining eyes. 'No,' said Karl, 'you don't know what it is they are accusing me of. I'll have to leave, the Head Cook is persuaded of that as well. Please don't stay here, go back upstairs, I'll come and say goodbye to you later.' 'Rossmann, honestly, what are you saying. You'll stay here with us as long as you like. The Head Waiter will do anything the Head Cook wants, he's in love with her, I discovered quite by chance recently. So set your mind at rest.' 'Please, Therese, leave me now. I can't speak so well in my defence when you're here with me. And I must defend myself carefully, because false accusations are being brought against me. But the more I keep my wits about me and defend myself, the more hope I have of being allowed to stay. So, Therese –' Unfortunately, in a sudden spasm of pain, he couldn't stop himself quietly adding: 'If only the Head Porter would let go of me! I didn't know he was my enemy. But he keeps squeezing me and lifting me up.' 'Why am I saying that!' he asked himself at the same time, 'no woman can stand to hear that,' and indeed Therese turned round and, undeterred by the waving of his free hand, said to the Head Porter: 'Head Porter, sir, will you please let go of Rossmann. You're hurting him. The Head Cook will be here any minute, and then we'll see that he's been unfairly treated. Let him go, how can you take pleasure in tormenting him.' And she even reached out for the Head Porter's hand. 'Orders, missy, orders,' said the Head Porter, and with his free hand he pulled Therese affectionately to himself, while with the other he squeezed Karl particularly hard, as though not only intending to cause him pain, but as though he had some design on the arm in his possession which was still far from being achieved.

It took Therese a while to twist away from the embrace of the Head Porter, and she was just about to intervene on Karl's behalf with the Head Waiter, who was listening to some rather elaborate account of Bess's, when the Head Cook strode into the room. 'Thank God,' cried Therese, and for a moment those were the only words that were heard in the room. Then the Head Waiter leapt up and thrust Bess aside: 'So you've come in person, Madam. Over this trifling business? Following our telephone conversation I guessed it, but I couldn't quite bring myself to believe it. And all the time the situation of your protégé is getting worse and worse. It looks as though I won't be dismissing him, but will have to have him locked up instead. Hear for yourself!' And he motioned Bess to come forward. 'I want to have a few words with Rossmann first,' said the Head Cook, taking a seat offered by the Head Waiter. 'Karl, please come closer,' she said. Karl did so, or rather was dragged there by the Head Porter. 'Let go of him,' the Head Cook said crossly, 'he's not a murderer.' The Head Porter released him, but not before giving him one final squeeze, so hard that tears came to his own eyes from the effort.

'Karl,' said the Head Cook, folding her hands calmly in her lap, and looking at him with her head slightly tilted – this wasn't like a cross-examination at all – 'first of all let me say that I still have complete trust in you. Also the Head Waiter is a just man, I can vouch for that. Both of us would dearly like to keep you here.' She glanced across at the Head Waiter, as though begging not to be contradicted. Nor was she – 'So forget whatever may have been said to you so far. In particular you mustn't take too hard what the Head Porter may have said to you. He is an excitable man, which is no wonder when you think about his job, but he has a wife and children, and he knows that it's not necessary to torment a boy who's all on his own, because the rest of the world will see to that anyway.'

It was very quiet in the room. The Head Porter looked to the Head Waiter for some explanation, but he went on looking at the Head Cook, and shook his head. The lift-boy Bess was grinning fatuously behind the Head Waiter's back. Therese was sobbing quietly with joy and worry, trying hard to keep the others from noticing.

Karl was looking – although this might be taken to be a bad sign – not at the Head Cook, who was certainly trying to catch his eye, but at the floor in front of him. His arm was throbbing wildly with pain, his sleeve was sticking to it, and he would have liked to take off his jacket and inspect the place. What the Head Cook was saying was of course very well intentioned, but unfortunately it seemed to him that her manner would make it even clearer that he didn't deserve any such kindness, that he had for the past two months enjoyed quite unmerited benevolence from the Head Cook, and actually the fittest thing for him was to be given into the Head Porter's hands.

123

'I say as much,' continued the Head Cook, 'so that you may be quite candid in your replies, which as I know you, you would probably have been anyway.'

'Can I go and get the doctor, the man might bleed to death in the meantime,' the lift-boy Bess piped up suddenly, very politely, but also very disruptively.

'Go on,' said the Head Waiter to Bess, who scurried off. And then, to the Head Cook: 'The thing is this. The Head Porter hasn't been detaining the boy for the fun of it. A stranger has been found down in the lift-boys' dormitory, heavily intoxicated, and carefully wrapped up in one of the beds. He was of course woken up and an attempt was made to remove him. But then the fellow started to make a great racket, and kept shouting that the dormitory belonged to Karl Rossmann, whose guest he was, who had brought him there and would punish anyone who dared to lay a finger on him. He had to wait for Karl Rossmann now because he had promised him money, and had just gone to get it. Mark this, Head Cook: Promised him money and had just gone to get it. You pay attention too, Rossmann,' said the Head Waiter in an aside to Karl, who had just turned to Therese, who was staring spellbound at the Head Waiter, and kept brushing some hair off her brow, or was at least making as if to do so. 'But perhaps I can remind you of some further commitments of yours. The man downstairs went on to say that, following your return, the two of you would be going on to pay a night visit to some singer or other, whose name unfortunately no one could make out, as the man would insist on singing it.'

At this point the Head Waiter broke off, because the Head Cook, now visibly pale, had risen from her chair, pushing it back a little. 'I'll spare you the rest,' said the Head Waiter. 'No, no, please,' said the Head Cook, taking his hand, 'go on, I want to hear everything, that's what I'm here for.' The Head Porter, who stepped forward, and, in indication of the fact that he had seen it all coming, beat his breast loudly, was simultaneously rebuked and pacified by the Head Waiter's words: 'Yes, Feodor, you were absolutely right!'

'There's not much more to report,' said the Head Waiter. 'The way the lads are, they first laughed at the man, then they got into an argument with him, and, as there are always some good boxers among them, they just punched him out, and I didn't dare ask how many places he's bleeding from, because the lads are tremendous boxers, and they would make short work of a drunk.'

'Well,' said the Head Cook, holding the back of the chair, and looking at the place where she had been sitting. 'Well, won't you say something please, Rossmann!' she said. Therese had left her original place and run across to the Head Cook, and, something Karl had never seen her do before, linked arms with her. The Head Waiter was standing just behind the Head Cook, and was slowly smoothing down a modest little lace collar of hers that had turned up slightly. The Head Porter, standing next to Karl said: 'Well get on with it,' but only to mask a jab in the back he gave him at the same time.

'It is true', said Karl, sounding more uncertain than he meant to as a result of the jab, 'that I brought the man into the dormitory.'

'That's all we want to know,' said the porter in the name of everyone there. The Head Cook turned silently to the Head Waiter and then to Therese.

'I had no other option,' Karl went on. 'The man used to be my companion, he came here after we hadn't seen each other for two months, to visit me, but he was so drunk he was unable to leave unaided.'

Standing beside the Head Cook, the Head Waiter said softly under his breath: 'He means to say he visited him, and then got so drunk he couldn't leave.' The Head Cook whispered something back over her shoulder to the Head Waiter, who, with a smile on his face that obviously had nothing to do with the present business, seemed to be making some demurral. Therese – Karl was looking now only to her – had seen enough, and pressed her face in complete helplessness against the Head Cook. The only person who was completely satisfied with Karl's explanation was the Head Porter, who repeated several times: 'Quite right, you have to help your drinking buddy,' and sought to impress this explanation on each of those present by looks and gestures.

'So it's my fault,' said Karl, and paused, as though waiting for a kind word from his judges, that might encourage him to further defence, but none came, 'but I'm only to blame for bringing the man, Robinson is his name, he's Irish, into the dormitory. Everything else he said because he was drunk, and it isn't true.'

'So you didn't promise him any money?' asked the Head Waiter.

'Yes, I did,' said Karl, and he was sorry he'd forgotten to mention that, and out of thoughtlessness or vagueness he had stated his innocence in too decisive terms. 'I did promise him money, because he asked me for some. But I wasn't going to get him any, I was only going to give him whatever tips I'd earned in the night.' And, as proof, he pulled the money out of his pocket and pointed to a few small coins in the palm of his hand.

'That's a tangled web you're weaving,' said the Head Waiter. 'In order to believe anything you say, one would have to forget whatever else you had said before. First of all you took the fellow – I don't believe he's called Robinson, no Irishman in that country's history has ever been called Robinson – first of all, you only took him to the dormitory, which is enough in itself to have you out on your ear – but without promising him money, then another question catches you out, and you say you did promise him money. But this isn't a question and answer session, we're here to let you justify yourself. Now first you didn't want to get the money, but give him your tips, but then it appears that you still have them on your person, so you obviously had need of other money, for which your long absence argues too. For me there'd be nothing out of the ordinary if you'd wanted to get him some money out of your box, but the vehemence with which you deny that is quite extraordinary. As is the way you kept seeking to deny that you made the man drunk here in the hotel, of which there isn't the slightest doubt, because you yourself conceded that he arrived on his own, but couldn't leave on his own, and he himself was shouting in the dormitory that he was your guest. So two things remain at issue, which, if you want to simplify matters, you can answer yourself, but which can also be determined without any assistance from you: first, how did you gain access to the storerooms, and second, how did you come by money to give away?'

'It's impossible to mount a defence of oneself without a certain amount of good will,' said Karl to himself, and didn't reply to the Head Waiter, however much Therese might suffer as a result. He knew that whatever he said would look quite different in retrospect from the way he had meant it to sound, and that whether it was good or bad depended solely on the way it was judged.

'He's not answering,' said the Head Cook.

'It's the most sensible thing he can do,' said the Head Waiter.

'He'll think of something,' said the Head Porter, and with his lately violent hand, gently stroked his beard.

'Stop it,' said the Head Cook to Therese, who had started sobbing beside her. 'You can see he's not answering, so how can I do anything for him. Remember I'm the one who's been proved wrong by the Head Waiter. Tell me, Therese, is there anything, do you think, that I haven't tried on his behalf?' How was Therese to know that, and what did it help, openly asking such a question of the little girl and thereby surely losing face in front of the two men?

'Madam,' said Karl, making one last effort, but for the sole purpose of saving Therese from having to make some reply, 'I don't think I have disgraced you in any way, and on closer inspection I don't think anyone would claim that I had.'

'Anyone,' said the Head Porter, and pointed at the Head Waiter, 'that's a dig at you, Mr Isbary.'

'Well now, Head Cook,' said the latter, 'it's half past six, time to move on. I think you'd better leave me the last word in this affair on which we have expended too much patience already.'

Little Giacomo had come in and wanted to go over to Karl, but was frightened off by the general silence, so he stood back and waited.

Since Karl's last words, the Head Cook had not taken her eyes off him, and there was nothing to suggest that she had heard the Head Waiter's words. She levelled her eyes at him, they were large and blue, if a little dimmed by age and so much work. To see her standing there, feebly rocking the chair in front of her, one might have expected her to go on to say: 'Well, Karl, the thing isn't quite clear to me yet, on reflection, and as you quite rightly said, it calls for closer investigation. So let's set that in motion now, whether we all agree to it or not, because that's what justice demands.'

Instead of which, after a short silence which no one dared to break – only the clock supplied confirmation of the Head Waiter's words by striking the half hour, and at the same time, as everyone knew, all the other clocks in the whole hotel also struck, an audible and an imagined chime, like the twofold twitching of a single great impatience, the Head Cook said: 'No, Karl, no, no! Don't let's get involved in all that. Just causes have a certain distinctive aspect, and yours, I must confess, doesn't. I say so and I am bound to say so as I came here most predisposed in your favour. You see, even Therese is silent.' (But she wasn't silent at all, she was crying.)

Taken by a sudden impulse, the Head Cook stopped and said: 'Karl, will you come here a minute,' and when he had gone to her – straight away the Head Waiter and Head Porter conferred animatedly behind his back – she put her left arm round him, and followed quite helplessly by Therese, went with him to the other end of the room, and walked to and fro for a while with both of them, and said: 'It is possible, Karl, and this is what you have put your trust in, otherwise I couldn't understand you at all, that an investigation may show you to be right in one or two details. And why not? Perhaps you did greet the Head Porter. I even believe you did, I have my own opinion of the Head Porter, you see, I'm even now being quite open with you. But these vindications are no use to you really. The Head Waiter, whose judgement I have learned to respect in the course of many years, and who is the most reliable man I know anywhere, has clearly found you culpable, and that seems to me irrefutably the case. Perhaps you merely acted rashly, but then again, perhaps I was deceived in you. And yet,' she said, virtually contradicting herself, and glancing across at the two men, 'I can't help thinking you're still a good boy at heart.'

'Head Cook! Head Cook! Come along now,' called the Head Waiter, who had caught her glance.

'We're just finishing,' said the Head Cook, and addressed Karl with greater urgency now: 'Listen, Karl, as I see it, I'm glad the Head Waiter isn't going to launch an investigation, because if he did, I'd have to try and stop him for your sake. No one must learn how and with what you entertained the man, who, incidentally, can't have been one of your former companions as you claim, because you had such a falling out with them when you broke up, so you would hardly have been looking after him now. So it can only be some acquaintance you foolishly made in some bar in the city. How could you keep all these things from me, Karl? If you found the dormitory so unbearable, and for that innocent reason you took to your nightlife, you had only to tell me, you know I wanted to get you a room of your own, and only desisted at your request. It now appears that you preferred the general dormitory because you could feel less constrained there. And you kept your money in my chest, and brought me your tips every week, where in God's name did you get the money to pay for your amusements, and where were you going to get the money for your friend from? All these are of course things I daren't even suggest to the Head Waiter, for the moment, because then an investigation might become unavoidable. So you must leave the hotel, and as quickly as possible. Go straight to the Pension Brenner – you've been there several times with Therese – they'll take you in for free on my recommendation' – and taking a golden crayon from her blouse, the Head Cook scribbled a few lines on a visiting card, but carried on speaking at the same time – 'I'll have your suitcase sent on after you, Therese, go to the lift-boys' cloakroom and pack his suitcase' (but Therese still refused to move, having endured so much misery, she now wanted to witness this sudden turn for the better in Karl's affairs, thanks to the kindness of the Head Cook).

Someone opened the door a crack, without showing himself, and then shut it again. It must have been for Giacomo, because he now stepped forward and said: 'Rossmann, I have something for you.' 'In a minute,' said the Head Cook, and pushed the visiting card into Karl's pocket as he stood and listened with bowed head, 'I'll keep your money for the moment, you know it's safe with me. Stay in today and think about everything, and tomorrow – I've no time today, I've spent far too long here already – I'll visit you at the Brenner, and we'll see what we can do for you then. I'm not abandoning you, I'm telling you right now. You're not to worry about the future, just about the recent past.' Thereupon she patted him on the back and went over to the Head Waiter, Karl raised his head and watched the large stately woman walking calmly and easily away from him.

'Aren't you even a bit pleased', said Therese, who had stayed behind with him, 'that everything has turned out so well?' 'Oh yes,' said Karl, and smiled at her, but he didn't know why he should be pleased to be called a thief and be sent packing. But joy gleamed in Therese's eyes, it was as though she was completely indifferent as to whether Karl had done wrong or not, whether he had been correctly judged or not, so long as he was allowed to get away somehow, with honour or in disgrace. And this was Therese, who was so scrupulous in her own affairs, turning over and inspecting some just slightly unclear sentence of the Head Cook's in her head for weeks. He asked her deliberately: 'Will you pack my suitcase and send it on promptly?' He had to shake his head in disbelief at the way Therese grasped the question and how her conviction that there were items in the suitcase that needed to be kept concealed from view meant that she didn't even look at Karl or shake hands, but merely whispered: 'Of course, Karl, right away, I'll pack it right now.' And she was gone.

Now there was no more stopping Giacomo, and excited after his long wait he called out: 'Rossmann, the man is rolling about in the corridor downstairs and refuses to be taken away. They wanted to have him taken to hospital but he wouldn't go and says you'd never let him be sent to a hospital. He wants to be driven home in a car, and says you'll pay for the car. Will you?'

'There's a trusting fellow,' said the Head Waiter. Karl shrugged his shoulders and handed his money over to Giacomo: 'It's all I've got,' he said.

'And I'm to ask you if you want to go in the car with him,' Giacomo asked, jingling the money.

'He won't be going in the car with him,' said the Head Cook.

'Now Rossmann,' said the Head Waiter quickly, without even waiting for Giacomo to leave the room, 'you're dismissed with immediate effect.'

The Head Porter nodded several times, as though these were his words, which the Head Waiter was merely repeating.

'I am not able to state the grounds for your dismissal, because if I did I would have to have you locked up.'

The Head Porter looked across at the Head Cook with notable severity, because it had not escaped him that she was the cause of this unduly mild treatment.

'Go to Bess now, get changed, give Bess your livery, and leave the premises at once, and I mean at once.'

The Head Cook closed her eyes, she did it to soothe Karl. As he bowed in farewell, he just caught a glimpse of the Head Waiter's hand discreetly taking the Head Cook's hand and playing with it. The Head Porter, with heavy tread, accompanied Karl to the door, which he wouldn't let him close, but kept open in order to be able to call after him: 'In a quarter of a minute I want to see you going past my office at the main gate, just remember that.'

Karl hurried as much as he could, to avoid a scene at the main entrance, but everything took much longer than he meant it to. To begin with, Bess couldn't be met with right away, and as it was now breakfast time there were people everywhere, and then it turned out that another boy had borrowed Karl's old trousers, and Karl was forced to look through most of the clothes stands next to the beds before he could find them, so that five minutes must have elapsed before Karl reached the main entrance. In front of him was a lady, accompanied by four gentlemen. They all went up to a large automobile which was waiting for them, and whose rear doors were being held open by a lackey who had his left arm extended stiffly behind him, which looked terribly impressive. But Karl's hope to slip out unobserved with this posh group was a vain one. The Head Porter had him by the hand and pulled him out between two of the gentlemen, begging their pardon as he did. 'That was never a quarter of a minute,' he said and looked askance at Karl, like a man inspecting a faulty watch. 'Come in here will you,' he said, and led him into the large porter's lodge, which Karl had been longing to see for ages, but which he now entered, propelled by the porter, full only of suspicion. He was already in the doorway when he turned round and tried to push the porter aside and get away. 'Oh no you don't, this is the way in,' said the Head Porter, spinning Karl round again. 'But I've already been dismissed,' said Karl, implying that no one in the hotel could order him about any longer. 'As long as I've got you in my grip, you're not dismissed,' said the porter, which was indeed the case.

Karl finally could think of no reason why he should defend himself against the porter. What worse thing could befall him? Besides, the walls of the porter's lodge were entirely made up of enormous glass panels, through which you could see the crowds of people flowing into one another in the lobby, just as clearly as if one were in their midst. Yes, there seemed to be no corner in the whole porter's lodge where one could be concealed from the eyes of those outside. And in however much of a hurry they all seemed to be as they made their way in or out, with outstretched arms, lowered heads and darting eyes, and luggage held aloft, yet hardly one of them failed to throw a glance into the porter's lodge, for behind its glass panels there were always announcements and messages hanging that were of importance to the guests as well as the hotel staff. In addition, there was direct commerce between the porter's lodge and the lobby, because of the two sliding windows which were manned by two under-porters, who were uninterruptedly engaged in giving out information on all kinds of subjects. These men were really overburdened, and Karl could have sworn that the Head Porter, as he knew him, must have got around doing this job in his past career. These two information dispensers had – you really couldn't get a sense of it from outside – at least ten inquiring faces at the windows in front of them. These ten questioners, who were continually changing, spoke in a babel of different languages, as though each one of them had been sent from a different country. There were always some asking their questions at the same time, while some others were talking amongst themselves. For the most part, they wanted to collect something from the porter's lodge or leave something there, and so you could always see hands waving impatiently out of the mass of people. Now someone wanted some newspaper, which was abruptly unfolded from above and briefly covered everyone's faces. And the two under-porters had to stand up to all this. Mere speaking would not have been enough, they had to babble, and one of them especially, a gloomy man with a beard that surrounded his whole face, gave information without the slightest break. He looked neither at the desk in front of him, where he had various things to do too, nor at the faces of any of his inquisitors, but just in front of him, obviously to save his strength. His beard must have impeded the clarity of his speech, and in the few moments Karl stood beside him, he could understand very little of what he said, although perhaps, for all that it still sounded like English, he might just have been replying in some foreign language. Besides, it was confusing, the way one piece of information followed on the heels of another, and merged with it, so that a questioner was often listening with a tense expression on his face in the belief that he was still hearing something intended for himself, only to realize a while later that he had been taken care of already. You also had to get used to the fact that the under-porter never asked for a question to be repeated, even if it was generally comprehensible and only asked in some slightly unclear way, a barely perceptible shake of the head would indicate that he didn't intend to reply to the question, and it was up to the questioner to realize his own shortcoming and reformulate his question in some better way. This kept some people at the counter for a very long time. To assist the under-porters, they each had an errand-boy, who had to run and get whatever the under-porter happened to need from a bookshelf and various files. These were the best-paid, if also the most exhausting, jobs for young people in the hotel, in a certain sense they were even worse off than the under-porters, who merely had to think and speak, whereas these young people had to think and run. If they happened to bring something inappropriate, the under-porter in his haste of course couldn't take the time to give them a long lecture, he would just sweep what they had laid in front of him on to the floor. Very interesting was the change-over of under-porters, which took place just after Karl's entry. Such change-overs must take place fairly frequently during the day at least, because the person probably didn't exist who could stand behind the counter for more than an hour. At the change-over time a bell sounded, and from two side doors the two under-porters whose turn it now was, emerged, each followed by his errand-boy. They stood for a while impassively by the counter to determine the current state of the answering process. When the right moment seemed to them to have come, they tapped on the shoulder of the under-porter they were relieving, who, though he had paid no attention to what had been going on behind his back, straightaway understood, and vacated his place. The whole thing happened so quickly that the people outside were often taken by surprise and almost shrank back from the new face that had so suddenly appeared in front of them. The men who had been relieved stretched, and from two basins that stood ready they poured water over their hot heads, the relieved errand-boys though were not yet permitted to stretch, they were still busy a while longer with picking up items that had been thrown on the floor during their hours of duty, and putting them back in their rightful places.

Karl had taken in all this in a few moments of the raptest attention, and he felt a slight headache as he quietly followed the Head Porter onward. Evidently the Head Porter had noticed how greatly impressed Karl was by this style of information-giving, and he suddenly tugged at Karl's hand, and said: 'You see, that's how people work here.' Karl himself hadn't actually been idle in the hotel, but he had had no notion of work such as this, and almost forgetting that the Head Porter was his sworn enemy, he looked up at him, and nodded in silent recognition. But that in turn struck the Head Porter as an overestimation of the under-porters and an implicit slight against his own person, because, as though he had been kidding Karl, he called out, without worrying about being overheard: 'Of course this is the most stupid work in the whole hotel; if you listen for an hour, you know pretty well all the questions that are asked, and the rest you don't need to answer. If you hadn't been so cheeky and impertinent, if you hadn't lied and tricked and boozed and stolen, I might have put you at one of these windows, because it's only numb-skulls I can use there.' Karl quite failed to hear the abuse directed at himself, such was his indignation at the way the honest and difficult work of the under-porters, far from being recognized, was mocked, and mocked at that by a man who if he had dared to sit at one of those counters would surely have been forced to quit within a matter of minutes, to the derision of all the questioners. 'Let me go,' said Karl, his curiosity about the porter's lodge now more than satisfied, 'I don't want anything more to do with you.' 'That's not going to get you out of here,' said the Head Porter, and pinned Karl's arms so that he couldn't even move them, and carried him bodily up to the other end of the porter's lodge. Could the people outside not see this violence by the Head Porter? And if they saw it, how on earth did they interpret it, because no one seemed at all exercised by it, no one so much as knocked on the window to let the Head Porter know he was under observation, and couldn't treat Karl as he pleased.

Soon, though, Karl had no more hope of getting help from the lobby, for the Head Porter pulled a string and instantly half the porter's lodge was screened right to the very top by black curtains. There were people in this part of the porter's lodge too, but they were all hard at work, and had no eyes or ears for anything that wasn't to do with their work. Besides, they were completely dependent upon the Head Porter, and, sooner than helping Karl, they would rather have helped to conceal whatever it was the Head Porter might have it in mind to do to him. For instance there were six under-porters manning six telephones. The principle, you could see at a glance, was that one would jot down conversations, while from his notes, the man next to him would pass on the orders by telephone. They were the very latest type of telephone that needed no telephone cubicles, for the ringing was no louder than a cheep, you could whisper into the mouthpiece, and, thanks to special electrical amplification, your words would boom out at the other end. And so one could barely hear the three speakers on their telephones, and might have supposed they were murmuringly observing some process in the telephone mouthpiece, while the other three drooped their heads over the paper it was their job to cover, as though stunned by the deafening volume in their ears that was inaudible to everyone else in the room. Once again there was a boy standing by each of the three speakers; these three boys did nothing but crane their necks to listen to their masters, and then hurriedly, as though stung, look up telephone numbers in enormous yellow books – the rustling of the volumes of paper easily drowning out all the noise of the telephones.

Karl simply couldn't resist observing it all closely, even though the Head Porter had sat down, holding him in front of him in a kind of embrace. 'It is my duty,' said the Head Porter, and shook Karl, as though to get him to face him, 'in the name of hotel management, at least to some extent, to catch up on what the Head Waiter, for whatever reason, has failed to do. We always stand in for each other here. Otherwise such a great enterprise would be impossible. You may say that I'm not your immediate superior, but that only makes it more creditable of me to interest myself in this otherwise neglected business. Besides, as Head Porter, I am in a certain sense put in charge of everything, because I am in charge of all the hotel entrances, this main entrance here, the three central and ten side entrances, not to mention the innumerable little doors and other exits. Of course all the service teams concerned have a duty of unconditional obedience to me. In return for these signal honours, I am charged by the management not to let anyone out who is in the slightest degree suspicious to me. You, I would say, are strongly suspicious.' And delighted with that he lifted his hands off Karl and let them fall again, which made a smacking noise and hurt. 'It is possible', he went on, enjoying himself hugely, 'that you might have managed to slip out unobserved at one of the other gates, because it's not worth my while issuing special instructions just for you. But seeing as you're here now, I'd like to make the most of you. In fact I never had any doubt in my mind that you would keep our appointment at the main entrance, because it is a rule that a cheeky and insubordinate party will only forsake his vices where it will do him the most damage. You will be able to observe this in yourself many times yet.'

'Don't imagine,' said Karl, and breathed in the strangely musty smell that emanated from the Head Porter, and only noticed for the first time now that he had been standing so close to him for so long, 'don't imagine', he said, 'that I am completely in your power, I can scream.' 'And I can gag you,' said the Head Porter, as calmly and quietly as he would gag him, if it ever came to that. 'And do you really think, if anyone should come in on your account, that he would back your version against the Head Porter's. You must concede your hopes are nonsensical. You know, when you were still in uniform, you had something vaguely impressive about you, but in this suit, which has Europe written all over it.' And he tugged at various bits of the suit, which indeed, although it had been almost new five months ago, was now worn, creased, and above all stained, which was largely to be attributed to the ruthlessness of the lift-boys, who every day, under instruction to keep the floor of the dormitory clean and free of dust, undertook no proper cleaning out of laziness, but merely squirted a kind of oil over the floor, which did terrible damage to all the clothes in the clothes stands. You could keep your clothes wherever you liked, there would always be someone who happened not to have his own to hand, but was easily able to find those that someone else had hidden, and borrow them for himself. And he might be one of the very ones who had to clean the room that day, and so the clothes wouldn't just get the odd squirt of oil on them, but a veritable dunking from top to bottom. Only Renell had managed to keep his exquisite wardrobe in some secret place where hardly anyone had managed to find them, especially as it appeared people didn't borrow out of malice or greed, but just helped themselves from haste and negligence. But even Renell's jacket had a perfectly round reddish oil stain in the middle of the back, by which an expert in the town might have identified even that elegant young man as a lift-boy.

Remembering all this, Karl told himself he had suffered enough as a lift-boy, and it had still all been in vain, because his lift-boy work hadn't, as he'd hoped, turned out to be a prelude to some higher position, rather he had been pushed out of it into something still lower, and was even very close to going to prison. On top of that he was in the grip of the Head Porter, who was probably thinking how he might further humiliate Karl. And completely forgetting that the Head Porter was certainly not a man who was open to persuasion, Karl shouted, hitting his brow with his momentarily relinquished hand as he did: 'And if I really did forget to greet you, how can a grown man get so vengeful over an omitted greeting!'

'I'm not vengeful,' said the Head Porter. 'I just want to look through your pockets. Of course I won't find anything in them, because I am sure you will have taken the precaution of letting your friend remove a little every day. But searched you must be.' And he reached into Karl's jacket pocket with such force that the stitching split at the side. 'Well, nothing there,' he said, as he picked over the contents of the pocket in his hand, a calendar advertising the hotel, a sheet of paper with an exercise in business correspondence on it, a few jacket and trouser buttons, the Head Cook's visiting card, a nail-file that a guest had tossed him while packing his suitcase, an old pocket mirror that Renell had given him in return for the dozen or so times he'd stood in for him, and a few more bits and pieces besides. 'Nothing there,' repeated the Head Porter, and threw everything under the seat, as though it were self-evident that any property of Karl's that hadn't been stolen belonged there. 'I've had enough,' said Karl to himself – his face must be scarlet – and when the Head Porter, incautious in his greed, started digging around in Karl's other pocket, Karl quickly slid out of his sleeves, leaped aside, knocking an under-porter quite hard against his telephone, ran rather more slowly through the humid air than he'd meant to, to the door, but was happily outside before the Head Porter had even been able to pick himself up in his heavy coat. The organization of the hotel security couldn't have been that exemplary after all, he heard bells ringing from several quarters, but God knows what they were ringing for, hotel employees were swarming around the entrance in such numbers that one could almost imagine they were unobtrusively making it impassable, because he really couldn't see much purpose in all their toing and froing – anyway, Karl quickly got outside, but was then forced to walk along the pavement in front of the hotel, he couldn't get to the public street, as an unbroken line of cars was driving haltingly past the entrance. These cars, trying to get as quickly as possible to their passengers waiting for them, had practically driven into one another, each one was being pushed along by the one behind. Pedestrians who were in a particular hurry to get to the street did occasionally walk through an individual car here and there, as though it were some public thoroughfare, and they were quite indifferent as to whether the car contained just chauffeur and servants or the most distinguished people. Such behaviour seemed overdone to Karl, and you probably had to be familiar with the conditions to try it, it would be very easy to try it with a car whose occupants might object, throw him out and cause a scandal, and there was nothing he had to fear more than that as a runaway, suspicious hotel employee in shirtsleeves. After all, this line of cars couldn't go on for ever, and for as long as he stuck close to the hotel it was actually the least obtrusive place for him. Finally Karl came to a place where the line of cars, though not actually broken, did loosen a little as it converged with the street. He was just about to slip into the traffic, which contained far more suspicious-looking persons than himself, running around without a care in the world, when he heard his name being called. He turned round and saw two lift-boys he knew well, at a low doorway that looked like the entrance to a tomb, with immense effort pulling out a litter, on which, as Karl could now determine, lay Robinson, indeed, head, face and arms all swathed in bandages. It was horrid to see him rubbing at his eyes bringing his arms up to his face in order to wipe away with the bandage the tears he was shedding out of pain or some other suffering, or even possibly joy at seeing Karl once more. 'Rossmann,' he called out reproachfully, 'why have you kept me waiting so long. I've spent the last hour trying to keep them from shipping me off before you arrived. These fellows' – and he nodded in the direction of one of the lift-boys, as though guaranteed immunity by his bandages from further blows – 'are devils incarnate. Oh Rossmann, how my visit to you has cost me.' 'What happened to you?' asked Karl, and stepped up to the litter which the lift boys laughingly put down for a rest. 'How can you ask,' sighed Robinson, 'just look at me. Consider! In all probability I've been crippled for life. I'm in excruciating pain from here to here' – and he indicated first his head then his toes – 'I only wish you could have seen my nose bleed. My waistcoat is completely ruined, I had to leave it behind, my trousers are ripped, I'm in my underpants' – and he raised the blanket a little so that Karl could take a look. 'What's going to become of me? I'll have to spend several months recuperating minimum, and I can tell you this right now, I have no one but you who can look after me, Delamarche is far too impatient. Rossmann, little Rossmann!' And Robinson stretched out his hand to Karl, who had stepped back a little, to win him over by stroking him. 'Why did I have to go and visit you!' he said repeatedly, lest Karl forget his part in his misfortune. Karl recognized at once that Robinson's lamentations stemmed not from his wounds, but from the incredible hangover he must be suffering, as one who had barely dropped off, heavily drunk, had been awoken straight afterwards, to his amazement beaten to a pulp, and was now completely disorientated in the waking world. The trivial nature of his injuries was already evident from his unsightly bandages of old rags which the lift-boys had completely swaddled him in, evidently for a lark. The two lift-boys at either end of the litter burst out giggling from time to time too. But this wasn't the place to bring Robinson round, pedestrians rushed past without paying any attention to the little group around the litter, people regularly hurdled athletically over Robinson's body, the driver paid with Karl's money was calling: 'Come on, come on,' the lift-boys, at the end of their strength, hoisted up the litter once more, Robinson took Karl's hand and said wheedlingly, 'Oh come on, come on,' and wasn't the darkness of an automobile the best place for Karl in his present predicament? And so he sat down next to Robinson, who rested his head against him, the lift-boys staying behind, heartily shook his hand through the window, as their former colleague, and the car turned sharply into the road, it seemed as though an accident were bound to happen, but then the all-encompassing traffic calmly accommodated the arrowy thrust of their car into itself.

The automobile came to a stop in what appeared to be a remote suburban street, because all around there was silence, children squatted on the edge of the pavement playing, a man with a lot of old clothes over his shoulders called up watchfully to the windows of the houses, Karl felt uncomfortably tired as he climbed out of the car on to the asphalt, on which the morning sun was shining warmly and brightly. 'Do you really live here?' he called into the car. Robinson, having slept peacefully for the whole drive, grunted unclearly in the affirmative, and seemed to be waiting for Karl to lift him out of the car. 'Well, I've done all I need to do here. Goodbye,' said Karl, and he set off down the street which sloped gently downhill. 'Karl, what are you doing?' cried Robinson, and in his alarm practically stood straight up in the car, although his knees were still a little trembly. 'I have to go,' said Karl, witnessing the sudden improvement in Robinson's condition. 'In your shirtsleeves?' he asked. 'I should think I'll earn enough for a jacket,' replied Karl, nodded confidently at Robinson, waved goodbye and would really have left him, if the driver hadn't called: 'One moment please, sir.' Unpleasantly, it turned out that the driver was claiming some further payment, because the wait in front of the hotel hadn't been included. 'That's right,' called Robinson from the car, in corroboration, 'you kept me waiting for such a long time. You'll have to give him a bit extra.' 'Quite so,' said the driver. 'If I had anything,' said Karl, reaching into his trouser pockets, even though he knew it was pointless. 'I'm going to have to stick by you,' said the driver and stood up, feet apart, 'I can't expect anything from the invalid in the back.' A young fellow with a chewed-up nose came over from the doorway and stopped to listen a few feet away. A policeman who was just doing his rounds in the street, took in the shirtsleeved man with lowered gaze, and stopped. Robinson, also spotting the policeman, was foolish enough to call to him out of the other window: 'It's nothing,

nothing at all,' as though it were possible to shoo away a policeman like a fly. The children, observing the policeman and seeing him stop, transferred their attention to Karl and the driver, and trotted over to have a look. In the gate opposite stood an old woman, watching stiffly.

Then a voice from above called out: 'Rossmann.' It was Delamarche, calling down from the top-floor balcony. He was hard to make out against the blueish-white sky, but was evidently wearing a dressing-gown, and surveying the street with opera glasses. Next to him was a red parasol under which a woman appeared to be seated. 'Hallo,' he cried at the top of his voice, in order to make himself heard, 'have you brought Robinson?' 'Yes,' replied Karl, powerfully seconded by another, far louder 'Yes,' from Robinson in the car. 'Hallo,' came the reply, 'I'm coming down.' Robinson leaned out of the car. 'What a man,' he said, and his praise for Delamarche was directed at Karl, at the driver, at the police-man, and at anyone else who cared to hear it. Up on the balcony, which everyone was still looking up at in distrait fashion, even though Delamarche had already left it, there was indeed a strongly built woman in a red dress under the parasol, who now got up, took the opera glasses off the parapet, and looked through them at the people below, who gradually turned their attention away. In expectation of Delamarche, Karl looked at the gateway and beyond it the yard, which was being crossed by an almost uninterrupted stream of commercial porters, each of whom was carrying on his shoulder a small, but evidently very heavy chest. The chauffeur had gone back to his car, and, making the most of the delay was polishing his lamps with a rag. Robinson palped his limbs, seemingly astonished at the small degree of discomfort he felt, in spite of paying very close attention, and gingerly bending down began to undo one of the thick bandages round his leg. The policeman held his black truncheon horizontally in front of him, and with the great patience required of policemen, whether on normal duty or undercover, waited quietly. The fellow with the chewed-up nose sat down on a bollard by the gate and stretched his legs. The children gradually tiptoed up to Karl, because even though he was paying them no attention, he seemed to them to be the most important of everyone on account of his blue shirtsleeves.

One gained a sense of the enormous height of the building from the length of time it took for Delamarche to appear. And when he did come, it was at a great pace, with his dressing-gown barely done up. 'So there you are!' he cried, at once pleased and severe. At each of his long strides, there was a flash of colourful underclothing. Karl didn't quite understand how Delamarche could walk around here in the city, in the enormous tenement block and on the public street, as comfortably clad as though he were in his private villa. Like Robinson, Delamarche too was greatly changed. His dark, clean-shaven, scrupulously clean face with its raw musculature looked proud and respectable. The harsh glint of his rather narrowed eyes was surprising. His violet dressing-gown was old and stained and rather too big for him, but out of that ugly garment sprouted a mighty dark cravat of heavy silk. 'Well?' he inquired, looking round. The policeman advanced a little, and leaned against the car bonnet. Karl gave a little explanation. 'Robinson is a little decrepit, but if he makes an effort he'll be able to walk up the stairs all right; the driver here wants a supplement to the fare which I've already paid him. And now I'm going. Good day.' 'You're not going anywhere,' said Delamarche. 'That's what I told him too,' piped up Robinson from the car. 'Oh yes I am going,' said Karl, and began to walk off. But Delamarche was after him already, and held him back forcibly. 'And I say you're staying,' he cried. 'Leave me alone,' said Karl, and got ready to fight his way out with his fists if need be, however little prospect of success that might have against a man of Delamarche's stamp. But there stood the policeman, there was the driver, here and there groups of workers passed through the otherwise peaceful street, would they permit him to be treated unfairly by Delamarche? He wouldn't like to have been shut up in a room with him, but what about here? Delamarche was now calmly paying off the driver, who, with many bows, pocketed the undeservedly large sum, and out of gratitude went over to Robinson, obviously to advise him on how best to get out of the car. Karl felt unobserved, perhaps Delamarche would be more disposed to accept a quiet departure, if a quarrel could be avoided that would of course be better, and so Karl simply walked out on to the road in order to get away as quickly as he could. The children flocked over to Delamarche to draw his attention to Karl's flight, but he didn't even have to intervene in person, because the policeman extended his truncheon and said: 'Stop!'

'What's your name,' he asked, tucking his truncheon under his arm, and slowly pulling out a notepad. Karl looked closely at him for the first time, he was a powerful man, but his hair was almost completely white. 'Karl Rossmann,' he said. 'Rossmann,' repeated the policeman, no doubt purely because he was a calm and conscientious officer, but Karl, for whom this was actually his first dealing with American officialdom, saw in that mere repetition the voicing of a certain suspicion. And his affair was probably looking bad, because even Robinson, who had so many worries of his own, leaned out of the car and gesticulated mutely and animatedly to Delamarche, to help Karl. But Delamarche refused with a hasty shake of the head and looked on impassively, his hands in his over-large pockets. The fellow on the bollard explained the whole affair from the beginning to a woman who had just come out of the gate. The children stood in a semicircle behind Karl and looked silently up at the policeman.

'Let me see your papers,' said the policeman. It was probably just a matter of form, because if you don't have a jacket, you won't have much in the way of papers either. Karl therefore made no reply, in order to answer the next question the more fully, and thereby perhaps gloss over the lack of documents. But the next question was: 'So you have no papers?' and Karl could only reply: 'Not on me.' 'That's not good,' said the policeman, and looked at everyone thoughtfully, and tapped the cover of his notebook with two fingers. 'Have you some kind of work?' he finally asked. 'I was a lift-boy,' said Karl. 'You were a lift-boy, but you aren't one any more, and so what do you live off now?' 'I'm going to look for a new job now.' 'So you were sacked from your job?' 'Yes, an hour ago.' 'Suddenly?' 'Yes,' said Karl, and raised his hand apologetically. He couldn't tell the whole story here, and even if it had been possible, it still seemed hopeless to try and avert a threatened injustice by telling of one already suffered. And if he hadn't received justice from the kindly Head Cook and the perspicacious Head Waiter, he certainly couldn't expect it from this group of people here on the street.

'And you were dismissed without your jacket?' asked the policeman. 'Well, yes,' said Karl, apparently even in America the authorities liked to ask about things they could perfectly well see with their own eyes. (How his father in obtaining his passport had been annoyed by the pointless questioning of the authorities.) Karl was sorely tempted to run away somewhere and not have to endure any more questions. But then the policeman asked the one question that Karl had most been afraid

143

of, and in fearful anticipation of which he had probably behaved more thoughtlessly than he would have done otherwise: 'In what hotel were you employed?' He lowered his head and didn't answer, he really didn't want to answer that question. He must at all costs avoid being taken back to the Hotel Occidental under police escort, facing further inquiries to which his friends and enemies would be summoned to appear, the Head Cook completely abandoning her already somewhat qualified good opinion of Karl, seeing him, whom she had supposed to be at the Pension Brenner, picked up by a policeman, in shirtsleeves, returned without her visiting card; the Head Waiter might perhaps merely nod sagely, the Head Porter though speak of the hand of god that had finally nabbed the scoundrel.

'He was working at the Hotel Occidental,' said Delamarche, repositioning himself next to the policeman. 'No,' cried Karl and stamped his foot, 'that's not true.' Delamarche looked at him with a sardonic twist of his lips, as though he could if he liked make other, far more damaging revelations about him. Karl's unexpected agitation caused a great commotion among the children, who all moved across to Delamarche, in order to have a better view of Karl. Robinson had stuck his head right out of the window by now, and, in his nervousness, was behaving very quietly; the occasional blink of an eye, nothing more. The fellow in the gateway clapped his hands with glee, the woman next to him jabbed him with her elbow to quieten him down. The porters were just having their breakfast-break, and they all trooped out with large mugs of black coffee, which they were stirring with breadsticks. A few sat down on the edge of the pavement, they all drank their coffee very noisily.

'You appear to know this boy,' the policeman asked Delamarche. 'Better than I should like to,' he replied. 'I once showed him a lot of kindness, but he paid me back very ill, which won't surprise you, even after the short interview you've had with him.' 'Yes,' said the policeman, 'he seems to be a surly fellow all right.' 'That he is,' said Delamarche, 'but that's not even the worst thing about him.' 'Oh?' said the policeman. 'Yes,' said Delamarche, who was now in full flight and with his hands in his pockets, swinging his dressing-gown this way and that, 'he's a nasty piece of work. Me and my friend over in the car took him in when he was in a very bad way, at the time he had no idea about things in America, he had just arrived here from Europe, where they had no use for him either, so we took him along with us, let him live with us, explained everything to him, tried to get him a job, for all the indications to the contrary thought we'd be able to turn him into a useful member of society, and then one night he simply disappeared, he just went, and that under circumstances I'd sooner not have to go into. Is that right or not?' Delamarche asked finally, tweaking at Karl's sleeve. 'Step back please, children,' called the policeman, because they had pressed forward so much that Delamarche almost tripped over one of them. And the porters too, who had previously underestimated the interest of the interview, had pricked up their ears, and assembled in a tight circle behind Karl, so that he couldn't take a backward step and moreover now had the babel of their voices in his ears, they were speaking or rather barking a quite incomprehensible English possibly mixed with words of Slavic.

'Thank you for that information,' said the policeman, saluting Delamarche. 'I'm certainly taking him in now, and I'll have him returned to the Hotel Occidental.' But Delamarche said: 'Might I ask you to leave the boy with me for the time being, I've got a couple of things to settle with him. I'll undertake to deliver him to the hotel myself afterwards.' 'I'm afraid I can't do that,' said the policeman. 'Here is my visiting card,' said Delamarche, giving him a little card. The policeman looked at it appreciatively, but said, with a pleasant smile: 'No, nothing doing.'

Though Karl had shown the utmost wariness of Delamarche hitherto, he now saw in him his only possible salvation. It was admittedly rather suspicious, the way he was pleading with the policeman to be given Karl, but it should finally prove easier to persuade Delamarche than the policeman not to take him back to the hotel. And even if Karl were delivered back to the hotel by Delamarche, that was still infinitely preferable to it happening under police escort. For now, Karl mustn't let on that he preferred to be with Delamarche, that would ruin everything. And he looked nervously at the hand of the policeman which might be raised at any moment to apprehend him.

'I should at least find out why he was so suddenly dismissed,' the policeman said at last, while Delamarche was looking dispiritedly off to the side, crushing his visiting card between his fingertips. 'But he wasn't dismissed at all,' Robinson called out suddenly and to the general astonishment, and leaning on the driver, he thrust himself as far out of the window as he could. 'On the contrary, he's got a good job there. He's in charge of the dormitory, and can bring in anyone he likes. Only he is incredibly busy, and if you want something from him, you have to wait for ages. He's forever closeted with the Head Waiter and the Head Cook and enjoys their confidence. He's certainly not been dismissed. I've no idea why he said he had been. How can he have been dismissed? I was seriously injured in the hotel, and he was instructed to get me home, and as he happened to be in his shirtsleeves he just came along in his shirtsleeves. I couldn't possibly have waited while he got his jacket.' 'Now then,' said Delamarche, with arms outspread, as though accusing the policeman of being a poor judge of character, and these two words of his seemed to bring the vague declaration of Robinson's into undeniable focus.

'But is that really the case?' asked the policeman, weakening already. 'And if it is, why is the boy claiming he was dismissed?' 'You say,' said Delamarche. Karl looked at the policeman, who was supposed to bring order among strangers who had only their own interests in mind, and a little of his general concerns affected Karl too. He didn't want to lie, and he kept his hands firmly clasped behind his back.

A supervisor appeared in the gateway and clapped his hands to indicate to the porters that it was time to get back to work. They tipped the coffee grounds out of their mugs, and with rolling strides and abating noise went back inside. 'We're not really getting anywhere like this,' said the policeman, and reached out to take Karl's arm. Karl instinctively drew back, sensed the space behind him that had been vacated by the porters, turned round, and with a few initial bounds, started running. The children all called out as one, and ran after him, for a few steps, stretching out their little hands. 'Stop that man!' the policeman shouted down the long, almost deserted road, and regularly repeating his cry, set off in pursuit of Karl, in a silent running style that indicated excellent condition and practice. It was as well for Karl that the chase took place in a working-class district. The workers don't side with the authorities. Karl ran down the middle of the road, where he had the fewest obstacles in his path, and from time to time he saw workers stopping on the edge of the pavement coolly watching him, while the policeman called out his 'Stop that man!' and stretched out his truncheon in Karl's direction as he ran, wisely choosing the smooth pavement for his terrain. Karl had little hope, and almost abandoned that when the policeman, as they were approaching some cross-streets, that almost certainly had some police patrols in them, began emitting a piercing whistle. Karl's only advantage was his light clothing, he flew or rather plunged down the middle of the street – the slope was getting steeper all the time – only, because of his sleepiness, he wasted his energy in very high, wasteful bounds that cost him time. But besides that, the policeman had his objective right in front of him, and didn't need to think about it, whereas for Karl, the running was actually a secondary concern, he had to think, to choose between various possibilities, to keep making decisions. His rather desperate plan was to avoid the cross-streets for now, as he couldn't know what they might contain, perhaps he might run straight into the purlieus of a police station; for as long as possible he wanted to stick to this street where he could see a long way down, until right at the bottom it debouched on to a bridge which had barely begun before disappearing into a haze of sun and water. In accordance with this decision, he was just gathering up his strength to pass the first cross-street at a sprint, when, not far ahead of him, he spied a policeman lurking, pressed flat against the dark wall of a house in shadow, all set to leap out at Karl at the right moment. Now there was nothing for it but the side-street, and when he heard his name being called out from there too, quite innocently – he thought at first it must be an illusion, because he had had a rushing in his ears for some time now, he didn't hesitate and, trying to catch the police out if possible, he leaped off one foot and jinked at a right angle into the little street.

No sooner had he taken a couple of bounds down this street – already he had forgotten that his name had been called, because now the second policeman was blowing his whistle as well, you could sense he was new to the chase, and far-off pedestrians in the street seemed to walk at a brisker pace – than a hand came out of a little doorway and with the words 'Keep shtum,' pulled Karl into a dark passageway. It was Delamarche, quite out of breath, with flushed cheeks, and hair plastered to his head. He was carrying his dressing-gown under his arm, and was dressed only in shirt and underpants. The door, which wasn't the front door of the house, but an unobtrusive side-entrance, he immediately shut and locked behind them. 'Just a second,' he said, leaned his head back against the wall, and panted. Karl, virtually in his arms, and half insensate, pressed his face against his chest. 'There they go,' said

Delamarche, and pointed to the door as he listened. And indeed the two policemen were running past, their footfall echoed in the empty street, ringing like steel on stone. 'You're all in, aren't you,' said Delamarche to Karl, who was still choking on his breath and unable to get a word out. Delamarche put him down carefully on the floor, knelt down beside him, stroked his brow a few times and watched. 'That's better,' said Karl at last, and struggled to his feet. 'Let's go then,' said Delamarche, putting his dressing-gown on again, and pushing Karl, still too weak to raise his head, in front of him. From time to time he gave him a little shake to freshen him up. 'How come you're so tired?' he said. 'You were able to gallop about like a horse in the open, while I had to crawl through the goddamned yards and passages. Luckily I'm a good runner too.' In his satisfaction he gave Karl a terrific thump on the back. 'The occasional race against the police is good practice.' 'I was already tired when I started running,' said Karl. 'There's no excuse for bad running,' said Delamarche. 'If it hadn't been for me, they'd have nabbed you long ago.' 'I think so too,' said Karl, 'I'm very indebted to you.' 'No doubt about it,' said Delamarche.

They were going down a long, narrow passage which was paved with smooth, dark stones. Occasionally, to right or left, there was a flight of stairs or you could see another, larger passage. There were hardly any grown-ups to be seen, only children playing on the empty stairs. On one balustrade there was a little girl crying so hard that her face was quite shiny with tears. No sooner had she spotted Delamarche than she ran up the stairs, gasping open-mouthed for breath, and only calmed herself when she had climbed several flights, looking round frequently to make sure no one was following her or was about to follow her. 'I ran her down just a moment ago,' said Delamarche laughing, and waved his fist at her, whereupon she screamed and ran up some more steps.

The yards they crossed were almost deserted as well. Only from time to time an errand-man came pushing a handcart, a woman filled a can with water at a pump, a postman crossed the yard with calm strides, an old man with a white moustache sat cross-legged in front of a glass door, smoking a pipe, boxes were being unloaded outside a removal firm, the idle horses turned their heads indifferently, a man in a work coat, with a piece of paper in his hand supervised all the work, there was an open window in an office and an employee sitting at a desk had turned away

148

from it and looked thoughtfully out at Karl and Delamarche as they passed.

'One really couldn't wish for a quieter neighbourhood than this,' said Delamarche. 'It's very noisy for a couple of hours in the evening but during the daytime it's exemplary.' Karl nodded, the quiet seemed a little excessive to him. 'I couldn't live anywhere else,' said Delamarche, 'because Brunelda is terribly sensitive to the slightest noise. Have you met Brunelda? Well, you will soon. I would urge you to be as quiet as possible when you're with her.'

When they reached the staircase that led up to Delamarche's apartment, the automobile had already driven off, and the fellow with the chewed-up nose – without remarking at Karl's reappearance – reported that he had carried Robinson up the stairs. Delamarche merely nodded to him, as though the man were his servant, who had performed a self-evident task, and pulled Karl, who was gazing out at the sunny street with some longing, up the stairs with him. 'We'll be up in a jiffy,' Delamarche said several times as they climbed, but his assurances refused to become true, at the end of each flight of stairs, another would begin in a slightly different direction. Once Karl even came to a stop, not really out of exhaustion, but sheer helplessness in the face of all these stairs. 'The apartment is very high up,' said Delamarche as they went on, 'but that has its advantages too. We very rarely go out, I go around in my dressing-gown all day, it's all very cosy. Of course we're too high to be troubled by visitors.' 'Where would they get visitors from,' Karl wondered.

Finally Robinson appeared on a landing in front of a closed front door, and they had arrived; the staircase wasn't even at an end, but led on into the penumbra, without any suggestion that it might soon be over. 'I knew it,' said Robinson quietly, as though still in pain, 'Delamarche is bringing him! Rossmann, where would you be without Delamarche!' Robinson stood there in his undergarments, trying to wrap himself up in the small blanket that he had been given at the Hotel Occidental, it was not clear why he hadn't gone into the apartment, instead of running the risk of making himself a laughing stock to possible passers-by on the stairs. 'Is she asleep?' asked Delamarche. 'I don't think so,' said Robinson, 'but I thought I'd better wait for you to come.' 'First we'll have to see whether she's sleeping or not,' said Delamarche, and bent down to the keyhole. After spending a long time looking, twisting his head this way and that, he got up and said: 'I can't quite make her out, the blinds are down. She's sitting on the sofa, maybe she's asleep.' 'Is she ill or something?' asked Karl, because Delamarche stood there, as though in need of advice. But he retorted sharply: 'Ill?' 'He doesn't know her,' said Robinson, in extenuation.

A few doors along, two women had stepped out on to the corridor, they wiped their hands on their aprons, looked at Delamarche and Robinson, and appeared to be discussing them. From another door, a very young girl with shiny blond hair jumped out, linked arms with the two women, and pressed herself against them.

'Those women are disgusting,' said Delamarche quietly, but evidently only out of respect for the sleeping Brunelda. 'I mean to report them to the police soon, and then we'll have some peace for a couple of years. Don't look,' he hissed at Karl, who saw nothing wrong with looking at the women, if they were forced to wait in the corridor for Brunelda to wake up. And he shook his head crossly, as though he didn't need to take any instructions from Delamarche, and, to make it even clearer, he moved in the direction of the women, but Robinson said: 'Rossmann, I wouldn't,' and held on to his sleeve, and Delamarche, already irritated by Karl, was so furious when the girl laughed aloud, that he rushed up to the women in a whirlwind of arms and legs, at which they disappeared behind their respective doors as though blown away. 'The corridor needs sweeping from time to time,' explained Delamarche; then he remembered Karl's opposition and said: 'I expect rather different behaviour from you, otherwise you'll have a hard time of it with me.'

Just then a tired voice in mild and gentle tones inquired from within: 'Delamarche?' 'Yes,' answered Delamarche, and smiled at the door, 'may we come in?' 'Oh yes,' came the reply, and after briefly glaring at the other two waiting behind him, Delamarche slowly opened the door.

Inside it was pitch black. The curtain over the balcony door – there were no windows – hung down to the floor and was barely translucent, but in addition the way the room was cluttered with furniture and had clothes hanging everywhere contributed much to its darkening. The air was musty and you could actually smell the dust that had collected in all the corners, where it was obviously safe from any human hand. The first things Karl noticed on entering were three chests set up one just behind the other.

On the sofa lay the woman who had been looking down from the balcony earlier. Her red dress had become a little rucked, and a great twist of it hung down to the floor, you could see her legs almost to the knee, she was wearing thick white woollen stockings and no shoes. 'It's so hot, Delamarche,' she said, turned her face from the wall, dangled her hand casually in the general direction of Delamarche, who took it and kissed it. Karl had eyes only for her double chin, which rolled along with the turn of her head. 'Should I have the curtain pulled up a little?' asked Delamarche. 'Anything but that,' she said with eyes shut, and as though in despair, 'that would only make it worse.' Karl had gone up to the foot of the sofa to have a closer look at the woman, he was astonished by her complaining, because the heat wasn't that excessive at all. 'Wait, I'll make you a bit more comfortable,' said Delamarche anxiously, undid a couple of buttons, and opened her dress out, so that her throat and some of her bosom were revealed, and the fine yellowish lace trim of her undergarment. 'Who's that,' the woman said suddenly, pointing a finger at Karl, 'why is he staring at me like that?' 'You'd better start making yourself useful soon,' said Delamarche, and shoved Karl out of the way, while reassuring the woman with the words: 'He's just the boy I brought along to attend on you.' 'But I don't want anyone,' she said, 'why are you bringing strangers into my apartment?' 'But you've been wishing you could have an attendant the whole time,' said Delamarche, falling to his knees; in spite of its great breadth, there was no room left on the sofa at all when Brunelda was on it. 'Oh Delamarche,' she said, 'you don't understand me, you don't understand me at all.' 'In that case I don't understand you,' said Delamarche, taking her face in his hands. 'But nothing's settled, if you like, I can throw him out on the spot.' 'Oh seeing as he's here, let him stay,' she said, and Karl, in his exhaustion, was so grateful for these words, even though they might not have been meant well, that, with the endless stairs that he might have had to go down again now always vaguely at the back of his mind, he stepped over the body of Robinson peacefully asleep in his blanket, and, ignoring Delamarche's irritated hand-flapping, said: 'I'd like to thank you for letting me stay here for a little. I haven't slept for twenty-four hours, but worked hard, and had a lot of other excitements too. I am dreadfully tired. I barely know where I am. But once I've had a couple of hours' sleep, you can send me packing just like that, and I'll be glad to go.' 'It's all right, you can stay,' said the woman, and she added, ironically: 'As you can see, we've more than enough room.' 'You'd better go then,' said Delamarche, 'we've no use for you here.' 'No, let him stay,' said the woman, this time seriously. And Delamarche said to Karl, as though enacting her wish: 'All right, go and lie down somewhere.' 'He can lie down on the curtains, but he has to take his boots off first, so he doesn't make any tears in them.' Delamarche showed Karl the place she meant. Between the door and the three chests many different sorts of curtains had been thrown on to one great heap. If you had folded them all up properly, put the heavy ones at the bottom and the lighter ones on top, and remembered to pull out all the various wooden planks and curtain-rings that were buried in the pile, then it might have made a passable bed, but as it was, it was just a swaying, sliding mass, on which Karl nevertheless straightaway lay down, because he was far too tired for any preliminaries, and, mindful of his hosts, he had to avoid making any sort of fuss.

He was already almost asleep when he heard a loud scream, got up and saw Brunelda sitting up on the sofa, her arms spread to embrace Delamarche who was kneeling in front of her. Embarrassed by the sight, Karl lay back and bedded down on the curtains to go back to sleep. It seemed obvious to him that he would not last so much as two days here, which made it all the more essential that he get some proper sleep, in order to be able to take future decisions quickly, rationally and correctly.

But Brunelda had seen Karl's staring eyes, which had alarmed her once already, and she cried: 'Delamarche, I can't stand this heat, I'm on fire, I must take my clothes off, I must bathe, send those two others away, anywhere you like, the corridor, the balcony, just out of my sight. We're in our own home, and yet we're continually being disturbed. If only I could be alone with you, Delamarche. Oh God, there they are still! How that brazen Robinson can stretch out in his underwear in the presence of a lady. And that stranger boy, who looked at me with wild eyes only a moment ago, and has lain down again in an attempt to trick me. Send them packing, Delamarche, they are a burden to me, they weigh on my mind. If I perish now, it will be on account of them.'

'I'll have them out right away, you go ahead and undress,' said Delamarche, and went over to Robinson, set his foot on his chest and shook it. At the same time he called over to Karl: 'Rossmann, get up! You're both to go out on the balcony! And woe betide either one of you that tries to come back in before you're sent for! Get a move on, Robinson' – and he shook him a bit harder – 'and you too, Rossmann, unless you want me to pay you a call as well' – and he clapped his hands loudly twice. 'It's taking so long!' cried Brunelda from the sofa, as she sat, she had her legs wide apart to give her excessive bulk a little more room, only with the utmost effort, with much panting and frequent rests could she bend down to reach the top of her stockings and roll them down a little, she was incapable of taking them off herself, that had to be done by Delamarche, for whom she was impatiently waiting.

Numb with exhaustion, Karl crawled off his pile, and slowly went over to the French window, a bit of curtain material had wrapped itself round his foot, and apathetically he dragged it along with him. In his absent-mindedness he even said: 'I bid you good night,' as he passed Brunelda, and then drifted past Delamarche, who was holding the curtain of the French window open a little, and then out on to the balcony. Immediately behind Karl came Robinson, in all probability just as tired, as he was muttering to himself: 'I'm fed up with the continual maltreatment here! I'm not going out on the balcony unless Brunelda's coming too.' But in spite of his protestation, he went out without any resistance at all, and, Karl having already collapsed on to the deck-chair, he curled up on the stone floor.

When Karl awoke it was already evening, the stars were out in the sky, and the radiance of the rising moon was visible behind the tall buildings opposite. Karl looked around at the unfamiliar sights, breathed in the cool refreshing air for some time before it came to him where he was. How careless he had been, disregarding all the advice of the Head Cook, the warnings of Therese, his own anxieties, now quietly sitting out on Delamarche's balcony, having slept through half the day here, as though the other side of the curtain there wasn't his arch-enemy, Delamarche. On the floor that lazy Robinson was just stretching and pulling at Karl's foot, that must have been what had woken him up, because he said: 'Rossmann, you sleep like a baby! That's carefree youth for you. How long are you proposing to sleep for? I could have let you sleep even longer, but in the first place it was getting a bit boring for me down on the floor, and in the second place I'm famished. Will you get up a moment, I've kept something to eat in the bottom of the chair, I'd just like to get it out. You can have a bit too.' And Karl, getting up, watched as Robinson, without getting up, crept over on his belly, and reaching out his hands, from under the chair pulled out a silver-gilt dish of the sort that, say, visiting cards are usually kept in. This dish, however, contained one half of a very black sausage, a few thin cigarettes, an already opened but still rather full sardine tin spilling oil, and a mess of mainly squashed and caked together sweets. Then he produced a large piece of bread and a sort of perfume bottle, which seemed to contain something other than perfume because Robinson pointed it out with particular gusto, and smacked his lips, to Karl. 'You see, Rossmann,' said Robinson, consuming one sardine after another, and from time to time wiping his hands on a woollen cloth that must have been left out on the balcony by Brunelda: 'You see, Rossmann, you need to put some food aside like me, if you're not to starve. You know, I'm an outcast. And if you're treated like a dog the whole time, you end up thinking that's what you are. I'm glad you're here, Rossmann, at least I've someone to talk to now. No one in the building talks to me. We're pariahs. And all because of Brunelda. Of course she's a splendid woman. You know' – and he beckoned Karl down, to whisper in his ear – 'I once saw her without any clothes on. Oh!' – and in recollection of his delight, he began to squeeze and pat Karl's legs, till Karl cried: 'Robinson, you're mad,' took his hands and pushed them away.

'You're still just a baby, Rossmann,' said Robinson, pulled out a dagger he wore on a string round his neck, uncapped it and cut up the hard sausage. 'You've got a lot to learn still. You've come to the right place for that, though. Sit down. Don't you want anything to eat? Well, maybe watching me will give you an appetite. Or to drink either? Well, what do you want? You're not exactly chatty either. But I don't mind who's out on the balcony with me, so long as I've got someone. I spend a lot of time out here. Brunelda gets a kick out of that. Any excuse is good enough, either she's cold or she's hot or she wants to sleep or comb her hair, or she wants to take off her corset or put it on, and each time I get put out on the balcony. Sometimes she does what she says, but usually she just stays lying on the sofa just as before, and doesn't move a muscle. I used to pull the curtain open a crack and take a peep inside, but ever since Delamarche caught me like that once – I know for a fact he didn't want to do it, he just did it because Brunelda asked him – and hit me in the face a few times with his whip – do you see the welt? – I haven't dared do it any more. And so I lie out here on the balcony, and my only pleasure is eating. The day before yesterday as I was lying out here alone of an evening – then I still had my elegant clothes, which I unfortunately lost in your hotel – those bastards! ripping the expensive gear off your back! – so, as I was lying there alone, looking down through the railing, I felt so sad I started to cry. Then, without my noticing it at first, Brunelda came out in her red dress – that's the one that suits her best if you ask me – watched me a while, and finally said: "Little Robinson, why are you crying?" Then she picked up her skirts and dried my eyes on the hem. Who knows what more she might have done if Delamarche hadn't shouted for her, and she didn't have to go back inside at once. Of course I thought it's my turn now, and I called through the curtain to ask if I could go back in the room. And what do you suppose she said? She said "No!" and "Who do you think you are?"'

'Why do you stay here then, if you're treated like that?' asked Karl.

'I'm sorry, Rossmann, that's not a very sensible question,' replied Robinson. 'You'll be staying here yourself, even if you get far worse treatment. Anyway, my treatment's not as bad as all that.'

'No,' said Karl, 'I'm definitely leaving, tonight if possible. I'm not staying with you.'

'Now how do you propose going about that, leaving tonight?' asked Robinson, who had chiselled out the soft part of the bread and was carefully dunking it in the oil in the sardine can. 'How are you going to leave, if you're not even allowed in the room.'

'Why aren't we allowed in the room?'

'As long as they haven't rung, we aren't allowed in,' said Robinson, keeping his mouth as wide open as he could while eating the oily bread, and catching the oil that dripped from the bread in his other hand, and using it as a reservoir, dunked the rest of the bread in it from time to time. 'Everything's been tightened up here. At first there was just a thin curtain, you couldn't quite see through it, but you could at least make out the shadows in the evening. That was disagreeable to Brunelda, and I had to alter one of her old theatre coats into a curtain and hang it up here in place of the old curtain. Now you can't see anything at all. Then

I used to be allowed to ask if I might go back inside yet and they replied "yes" or "no" according to the circumstances, but I expect I took advantage of that and asked once too often. Brunelda couldn't stand that, in spite of her fatness she has a frail constitution, she often suffers headaches and has gout in her legs the whole time – and so it was decided that I can't ask any more, but when I can go in, they'll ring the bell on the table. That has such a loud ring that it even wakes me out of my sleep – I used to keep a cat here for company, and the ringing gave her such a scare that she ran off and never came back. So it hasn't rung yet today – because if it rings it doesn't just mean I'm allowed to go in, I have to go in – and if it hasn't rung for a long time, then it could be a long time yet before it does.'

'Yes,' said Karl, 'but what applies to you doesn't have to apply to me as well. Besides these sort of things only hold good if you agree to be bound by them.'

'But', exclaimed Robinson, 'why shouldn't it apply to you too? Of course it applies to you as well. Stay here quietly with me, until it rings. Then you can see if you can get away.'

'Why don't you get out of here yourself? Just because Delamarche is your friend, or rather used to be? What kind of life is this? Wouldn't you be better off in Butterford, where you were headed for originally? Or in California, where you have some friends.'

'Yes,' said Robinson, 'who could have predicted it.' And before he resumed his tale, he said: 'Your health, my dear Rossmann,' and he took a long pull from the perfume bottle. 'Back then when you ditched us so meanly, we were in a bad way. In the first few days we couldn't find any work, that is Delamarche didn't want to work, he would have found something I'm sure, but he just sent me off to look, and I'm unlucky like that. He just hung around, but when it was almost dark he brought back a ladies' purse, it was very pretty, beads, he's given it to Brunelda now, but there wasn't much in it. Then he said we ought to go and beg in people's apartments, that way we might come across a few useful items, so we went begging, and to make a better impression, I sang on people's doorsteps. And, Delamarche is such a lucky devil, we were on our second doorstep, a wealthy ground-floor apartment, singing to a cook and a butler, and then who should come up the stairs but the lady the flat belongs to, Brunelda in fact. Maybe her corset was too tight, and she couldn't manage the few steps. But she was so beautiful, Rossmann! She had a white dress and a red parasol. I could have licked her all over. I could have gobbled her up. God, God she was beautiful. What a woman! No, tell me how can such a woman be allowed to exist? Of course the butler and the girl ran up to her and all but carried her up the stairs. We stood either side of the door and saluted, that's what they do here. She stopped awhile, she still hadn't got her breath, and I can't remember how it happened exactly, maybe I'd had so little to eat that it was starting to affect my judgement, and close up she was still more beautiful and enormous and wide and, because of a special corset she had on, I can show you in the chest, she was so firm all over – well, I just brushed against her behind, you know, ever so gently. Of course that's not permissible, a beggar touching a rich lady. It almost wasn't a touch at all, but I suppose in the end it sort of was. Who knows what consequences it might have had, if Delamarche hadn't slapped me right away, and slapped me so hard that both my hands flew up to my cheek.'

'Such goings on,' said Karl, quite captivated by the story, and sat down on the ground. 'So that was Brunelda?'

'That's right,' said Robinson, 'that was Brunelda.'

'Didn't you once say she was a singer?' asked Karl.

'Of course she's a singer, and a great singer too,' replied Robinson, revolving a huge mass of sweets on his tongue and now and then pushing a bit that was falling out of his mouth back in with his fingers. 'But of course we didn't know that then, we only saw that she was a rich and very distinguished lady. She acted as though nothing had happened, because I really only just tapped her with my fingertips. But she kept staring at Delamarche, who looked her – how does he manage it – straight in the eye. Then she said: "Come in for a bit," and with her parasol she ushered Delamarche into the apartment ahead of her. Then they both went inside and the servants shut the door after them. They just left me outside, and I thought it won't take all that long, and I sat down on the steps to wait for Delamarche. Then instead of Delamarche the butler came out and he brought me a whole bowl of soup, "compliments of Delamarche!" I thought to myself. The butler hung around for a while as I ate, and told me a few things about Brunelda, and then I saw what importance the visit to Brunelda could have for us. Because

Brunelda was a divorcee, she had a large fortune, and she was completely independent. Her ex-husband, a chocolate manufacturer, still loved her, but she didn't want anything more to do with him. He visited the apartment frequently, always dressed terribly smartly, as if for a wedding – that's literally true, I saw him myself – but in spite of all kinds of bribes, the butler didn't dare ask Brunelda whether she would receive him, because he had already asked a few times, and each time she had thrown in his face whatever she had to hand. Once it was even her large full hot-water bottle, and that knocked out one of his front teeth. Yes, Rossmann, you're amazed.'

'How do you know the man?' asked Karl.

'He still comes up here sometimes,' said Robinson.

'Up here?' in his astonishment, Karl patted the floor with his hand.

'You might well be amazed,' Robinson continued, 'I was amazed too, when the servant told me that at the time. Imagine, when Brunelda was out of the house, the man had himself admitted into her room by the butler, and he always took away some little nick-nack as a memento, and left something very fine and expensive in its place for Brunelda, with strict instructions to the butler not to say who it was from. But on one occasion – I have it from the butler, and I believe him – he left some absolutely priceless piece of porcelain, and Brunelda must have recognized it somehow, and she threw it on the floor and trod on it and spat on it, and did a few other things besides, so that the man was almost too disgusted to carry it outside.'

'What had her husband done to her?' asked Karl.

'I don't really know,' said Robinson. 'I don't think it was anything too terrible, he doesn't really know himself. I've spoken to him about it a few times. He waits for me down on the corner every day, if I come, I have to give him some bit of news, and if I can't, he waits for half an hour, and then goes away again. It was a good source of income for me, because he pays handsomely for any news, but since Delamarche got wind of it, I have to hand everything over to him, and so I don't go so often any more.'

'But what does the man want?' asked Karl, 'what does he want? He must know she won't have him back.'

'Yes,' sighed Robinson, lit a cigarette, and, waving his arms expansively, blew the smoke into the sky. Then something else seemed to occur to him, and he said: 'What do I care? All I know is he'd give a lot of money to lie here on the balcony, like us.'

Karl stood up, leaned against the railing and looked down on the street. The moon was now visible, but its light didn't yet reach into the depths of the street. The street, so empty by day, was now crammed full of people, especially the entrances to the buildings, everyone was in slow cumbersome movement, the shirtsleeves of the men and the light dresses of the women stood out a little from the darkness, all were bareheaded. The many balconies round about were all occupied now, there by the light of an electric lamp sat families, either round a small table or on a row of chairs, whatever suited the size of their particular balcony, or at the very least, they stuck their heads out of windows. The men sat there, legs apart, feet pushed through the railings, reading newspapers that reached down almost to the floor, or they played cards, apparently wordlessly, but smacking the cards down powerfully on the table, the women had their laps full of mending, and only occasionally allowed themselves a quick glance at their surroundings or at the street below, a frail blonde woman on the next door balcony kept yawning, rolling her eyes as she did, and covering her mouth with a garment she was just patching, even on the smallest balconies children seemed able to chase one another, which was tremendously irritating to the parents. Gramophones had been put on inside many of the rooms, and pumped out vocal or orchestral music, people weren't particularly bothered about the music, only from time to time the head of the family would gesture, and someone would run into the room to put on a new record. At some of the windows you could see completely motionless lovers, one such couple stood at a window facing Karl, the young man had his arm round the girl and was squeezing her breast with his hand.

'Do you know any of the neighbours,' Karl asked Robinson, who had got up now, and because he was cold had wrapped himself up in Brunelda's blanket in addition to his own.

'Almost no one. That's the drawback to my position,' said Robinson, and pulled Karl closer to whisper in his ear, 'otherwise I wouldn't have so much to complain about just now. Brunelda sold everything she had on account of Delamarche, and with all her wealth she moved into this apartment in the suburbs with him, so that she could devote herself entirely to him without anyone to bother her, which is what Delamarche wanted as well.'

'So she dismissed her servants?' Karl asked.

'That's right,' said Robinson. 'Where was there for them to stay here anyway? These servants are a very pampered lot. Once at Brunelda's, Delamarche drove one of them out of the room with a succession of slaps, left and right, until the fellow was out of the door. Then of course all the other servants got together with him and made a noise outside the door, and then Delamarche came out (in those days I wasn't a servant, I was a friend of the family's, though I mostly hung around with the servants), and asked: "What d'you want?" The oldest servant, a fellow by the name of Isidor, said: "You have nothing to say to us, madam is our mistress." As you probably noticed, they worshipped Brunelda. But Brunelda ran over to Delamarche without bothering about them, she wasn't so heavy then as she is now, and hugged and kissed him in front of them all, and called him "darling Delamarche". "And get rid of those jackanapes" she finally said. Jackanapes – she was referring to the servants, you should have seen their expression. Then Brunelda pulled Delamarche's hand down to the purse that she wore round her waist, and Delamarche reached into it and started paying off the servants, Brunelda played no part in it, other than standing there with an open purse at her waist. Delamarche had to reach into it a lot, because he handed out the money without counting it and without checking the claims they made. Finally he said: "Since you don't want to talk to me, I'd just like to tell you in Brunelda's name: Get out of here, and make it fast." And that was how they were dismissed, there was some wrangling after that, Delamarche even had to go to court once, but I don't really know what happened there. But immediately the servants were all gone, Delamarche said to Brunelda: "So now you've got no servants?" She said: "But what about Robinson." And Delamarche gave me a slap on the back and said: "All right, you can be our servant." And Brunelda gave me a pat on the cheek, if you ever get a chance, Rossmann, get her to pat you on the cheek, there's nothing like it.'

'So you became Delamarche's servant?' asked Karl, summing up.

Robinson heard the note of pity in the question, and replied: 'I'm the servant, but very few people realize that. Remember, you didn't notice it yourself, even though you've been with us a while. You saw the way

I was dressed that night in the hotel with you. Nothing but the best, and do servants go around like that? Only, the thing is this: I'm rarely allowed to go out, I always have to be around, there's always something needs doing in the house. One person just isn't enough for so much work. Perhaps you noticed, we've got lots of things standing around in the room, whatever we weren't able to sell when we moved out we had to take with us. Of course we could have given it away, but that's not how Brunelda operates. Just imagine the labour of carrying those things up the stairs.'

'Do you mean to say you carried all that up the stairs, Robinson?' Karl exclaimed.

'Who else?' said Robinson. 'There was a man to help me, a lazy beggar, I had to do most of it by myself. Brunelda stayed downstairs by the car, Delamarche gave the instructions upstairs, where to put things, and I kept going back and forth. It took two days, a long time, isn't it? but you've no idea how many things are up here in the room, all the boxes are full and behind the boxes everything's stacked up to the ceiling. If we'd taken on a couple of people to do the removal, it could all have been done very quickly, but Brunelda didn't want to entrust it to anyone else but me. That's very nice, but I ruined my health for the rest of my days doing it, and what else have I got but my health. If I exert myself even a tiny bit, I feel it here and here and here. Do you imagine those boys in the hotel, those bullfrogs – what else can you call them? – could ever have beaten me, if I'd been fit. But whatever's the matter with me, I'll never breathe a word to Delamarche and Brunelda, I'll go on working for as long as I can until I'm completely incapacitated, and then I'll lay myself down and die, and only then, too late, they'll see I was sick and in spite of that went on and on working, and finally worked myself to death in their service. Oh Rossmann,' he said finally, drying his eyes on Karl's sleeve. After a little while he said: 'Aren't you cold, standing there in your shirt.'

'Come on, Robinson,' said Karl, 'you're forever crying. I don't think you're that sick. You look pretty healthy to me, but because you always lie out on the balcony, you've been having thoughts. Maybe you do have an occasional pain in your chest, so do I, so does everyone. If everyone in the world would cry like that over every trifling thing, they'd all be crying on all the balconies.'

'No, I know better,' said Robinson, now wiping his eyes on the corner of his blanket. 'The student who lives with our landlady next door, who also used to cook for us, he said to me as I was taking back the plates recently: "I say, Robinson, you do look unwell." I'm not allowed to talk to those people, so I just put the plates down and turned to leave. Then he went up to me and said: "Listen, man, don't overdo it, you're sick." "Very well, then tell me what to do about it," I asked. "That's your affair," he said, and turned away. The others sitting at the table laughed, we have enemies all over, and so I preferred just to leave.'

'And so you believe people who are making a fool of you, and not those who mean well by you.'

'But I'm the one who knows how I feel,' Robinson exploded, but straightaway burst into tears again.

'That's just it, you don't know what the matter is with you, you should look for some proper job for yourself, instead of being Delamarche's servant here. As far as I can tell from what you've told me, and from what I've seen for myself, this isn't service, it's slavery. No one can stand that, I'm sure you're right there. But you think that because you're Delamarche's friend, you can't leave him. That's wrong, if he refuses to see what a miserable life you've got, then you've no obligation to him whatever.'

'So Rossmann, you really believe I'll get better if I stop serving here?'

'I'm convinced of it,' said Karl.

'Convinced?' Robinson repeated.

'Utterly,' said Karl, with a smile.

'Then I could start feeling better very soon,' said Robinson, looking at Karl.

'How's that?' he asked.

'Well, because you're due to take over from me here,' replied Robinson.

'Who told you that?' asked Karl.

'That's a well-established plan. We've been talking about that for several days now. It began with Brunelda ticking me off for not keeping the apartment clean enough. Of course I promised to fix it all right away. But that's far from easy. For example, in my condition, I can't crawl around everywhere to wipe up the dust, you can't even move freely in the middle of the room, so how could you amongst all the furniture and supplies. And if you want to clean anything really properly, that means moving the furniture and how can I do that by myself? And then it would all have to be done very quietly, because Brunelda hardly ever leaves the room, and she mustn't be disturbed. So I promised I would clean everything, but in fact I didn't. When Brunelda noticed, she told Delamarche that it couldn't go on like that, and they'd have to take on some more help. "Delamarche" she said, "I don't want you to reproach me for my running of the household. I'm not allowed to strain myself, you understand that, and Robinson isn't enough on his own, at first he was willing and looked around everywhere, but now he's tired the whole time, and just mopes in a corner. But a room with as many things in it as ours doesn't just look after itself." Then Delamarche went and had a think about what to do, because of course you can't just take anyone into a household like ours, not even for a trial period, because people are always gossiping about us. But because I'm a good friend of yours, and heard from Renell how they were making you sweat in the hotel, I thought of you. Delamarche agreed to it right away, even though you were so cheeky to him before, and of course I was very happy to be able to do you such a service. Because this job might have been made for you, you're young, strong and adroit, while I'm not up to anything any more. Only I just have to warn you that it's not quite a foregone conclusion yet, if Brunelda doesn't like you, we couldn't keep you. So try and make an effort to please her, and I'll see to the rest myself.'

'And what will you do once I'm the servant here?' Karl took the liberty of asking, once the initial shock of Robinson's news had worn off. So Delamarche had nothing worse in store for him than making him into his servant – if he'd had any worse intentions, that blabbermouthed Robinson would certainly have revealed them – but if this was how things stood, then Karl thought he might go through with his departure this very night. And while it had been Karl's concern previously, following his dismissal from the hotel, to find another job in short order so he didn't go hungry, a proper job, if possible, as respectable as his last, now, in comparison to this job proposed here, which was repulsive to him, any other job would be welcome, and even a period of hunger and unemployment would be preferable to this. He made no attempt to explain as much to Robinson, though, not least as Robinson's views would be coloured by his hopes of being relieved by Karl.

'So,' said Robinson, accompanying his speech with complacent hand movements – he had his elbows propped on the railing – 'so I'll explain everything to you and show you the supplies. You're educated, and I'm sure you write a clear hand, so you could draw up an inventory of all the things we have here. Brunelda has been wanting that for ages. If it's fine tomorrow morning, we'll ask Brunelda to sit out on the balcony, and then we'll be able to work quietly inside without disturbing her. Because one thing you have to bear in mind, Rossmann, above all. Don't disturb Brunelda. She hears everything, it's probably because she's a singer that she has such terribly sensitive ears. For instance if you roll out the brandy barrel behind the chests, that makes a noise just because it's so heavy, and then there are various things lying in its path, so you can't roll it away at one fell swoop. Say Brunelda is lying quietly on the sofa, catching flies, which are a terrific nuisance for her. You think she's not paying any attention, and carry on rolling the barrel. She's still lying peacefully. But in a moment, and when you're least expecting it, and when you're making the least amount of noise, she suddenly sits bolt upright, bangs the sofa with both hands, so that she disappears in a cloud of dust – I haven't been able to beat the sofa in all the time we've been here, after all how can I, she's always lying on it – and starts this terrible shouting like a man, and goes on for hours. The neighbours have stopped her from singing, but no one can stop her from shouting, she has to shout, it only happens quite rarely nowadays by the way, Delamarche and I are very careful. It did her a lot of harm as well. Once she became unconscious, so – Delamarche was away at the time – I had to fetch the student from next door, who sprayed her with some liquid from a big bottle, and it helped too, but the liquid had an insufferable smell, even now if you stick your nose in the sofa, you can still smell it. That student is definitely an enemy of ours, like everyone here, you should be wary of everyone and not get involved with any of them.'

'I say, Robinson,' said Karl, 'that all sounds like hard work. This is some job you've put me up for.'

'Don't worry,' said Robinson, and shook his head with serenely closed eyes, to dispel all possible worries of Karl's, 'the job also brings advantages with it like no other. You're in continual close proximity with a lady like Brunelda, sometimes you sleep in the same room as her, that, as you can imagine, has various amenities associated with it. You will be generously paid, money is there in copious amounts, as a friend of Delamarche's I wasn't actually given any, except when I went out Brunelda gave me some, but of course you will be paid just like a regular servant. Because that's all you'll be. The most important thing for you, though, is that I will be able to make it a great deal easier for you. To begin with, of course, I won't do anything so I can recuperate, but as soon as I feel a little better, you'll be able to count on me. The actual attendance on Brunelda I'm going to keep as my preserve, which is to say dressing her and doing her hair, inasmuch as that isn't done by Delamarche. You'll only have to deal with the tidying of the room, the shopping and the heavy housework.'

'No, Robinson,' said Karl, 'I'm really not tempted.'

'Don't be an idiot, Rossmann,' said Robinson, very close to Karl's face, 'don't pass up this fine opportunity. Where else will you get a job right away? Who knows you? Whom do you know?' We, two men who have knocked around a lot and have a lot of experience, went around for weeks without finding any work. It's not easy, in fact it's desperately hard.'

Karl nodded, surprised how sensible Robinson could be at times. Admittedly, these tips didn't apply to himself, he mustn't stay here, in the big city there would surely be some little thing he could do, all night, he knew, the inns were overflowing, they needed men to serve the customers, he already had some practice in that, he would slot quickly and unobtrusively into some business. In fact, on the ground floor of the building opposite, there was a little bar, from which rhythmic music came. The main entrance was covered by a large yellow curtain, which would sometimes be seized by a draught, and blow right out into the street. Apart from that, it had grown a lot quieter in the street. The majority of the balconies were now in darkness, only here and there in the distance was there still the odd light, but no sooner did you look at it than the people over there got up, and while they filed back into the apartment, a man reached up to the lamp and, as the last person out on the balcony, he had a final look down at the street, and turned off the lamp.

'It's getting to be night,' Karl told himself, 'if I stay here much longer, I'll be one of them.' He turned round to draw the curtain away from the apartment door. 'What are you doing?' said Robinson, and got between Karl and the curtain. 'I'm leaving,' said Karl, 'let me go, let me go!' 'You're going to disturb them,' cried Robinson, 'what do you think you're doing.' And he put his arms round Karl's neck and hung on to him with all his weight, twined his legs round Karl's legs and in an instant had him down on the ground. But Karl had learned how to look after himself from being among the lift-boys, and he brought his fist up against Robinson's chin, but only gently and with forbearance. His opponent, though, quickly and violently drove his knee hard into Karl's belly, and then, clutching his chin with both hands, started howling so loud that on the next door balcony a man clapped his hands frenziedly and called out 'Quiet'. Karl lay there a while, to get over the pain from Robinson's blow. He only turned his face to the curtain, which hung quiet and heavy in front of the evidently darkened room. There seemed to be no one in the room any more, maybe Delamarche and Brunelda had gone out, and Karl was already completely at liberty. Robinson, who really was behaving like a guard dog, had been completely shaken off.

Then from the far end of the street there came bursts of trumpets and drums. A few isolated shouts from people gradually amalgamated into a general hubbub. Karl turned his head and saw life returning to the balconies. He slowly rose, he couldn't quite stand upright yet, and had to lean hard against the railing. Down on the pavements were young fellows marching with great strides, arms out, caps in their raised hands, heads thrown far back. The actual road was still clear. Some individuals were swinging lanterns on long poles, which were swathed in yellowish smoke. Just then the drummers and trumpeters emerged into the light in broad ranks, and Karl was amazed at the numbers, then behind him he heard voices, and turned to see Delamarche raising the heavy curtain and Brunelda stepping out of the darkened room in her red dress, with a lace shawl over her shoulders, a dark bonnet over her probably unkempt hair that was merely piled up on her head, and tendrils of which peeped out here and there. In her hand she held a little open fan, but rather than using it, she kept it pressed against her face.

Karl moved along the railing a little to make room for the two of them. Surely no one would compel him to remain here, and if Delamarche tried to, then Brunelda would let him go, he had only to ask. After all she didn't like him, she was frightened of his eyes. But when he made a move in the direction of the door, she noticed and said: 'Where are you off to, little man?' Karl froze at Delamarche's stern expression, and Brunelda pulled him to herself. 'Don't you want to watch the procession down there?' she said, and pushed him against the railing in front of her. 'Do you know what it's about?' Karl heard her saying behind him, and he made an involuntary attempt to get away from her pressure, which failed. He looked sadly down at the street, as though it were his own bottomless sadness.

At first Delamarche stood behind Brunelda with arms crossed, then he ran into the room and fetched Brunelda the opera glasses. Down on the street, the main part of the procession had appeared behind the musicians. On the shoulders of one colossal man sat a gentleman, of whom nothing more could be seen from that height than his dully gleaming pate, over which he held his top hat aloft in perpetual greeting. Round about him some wooden placards were clearly being carried, they looked completely white from up on the balcony; their disposition was such that these placards seemed to lean against the gentleman on every side, and he soared up from their midst. As everything was continually on the move, the wall of placards was continually loosening and then re-forming itself. In a wider radius, the whole breadth of the street, though, so far as one could tell in the darkness, not much of its depth, was filled with supporters of the gentleman, all of them clapping their hands and calling out what was in all probability his name, which was short and unfortunately incomprehensible, in a long-drawn-out chanting. Individuals, cleverly distributed in the crowd, held car headlamps with extremely powerful light, which they ran slowly up and down the buildings on either side. At Karl's elevation, the light was no longer bothersome, but on the lower balconies you could see the people whom it brushed hurriedly shielding their eyes with their hands.

At Brunelda's plea, Delamarche asked the people on the neighbouring balcony what the procession was for. Karl was a little curious as to whether he would receive an answer, and what it would be. And indeed Delamarche had to ask three times, without getting a reply. Already he was leaning dangerously out over the edge. Brunelda was stamping her feet a little in irritation at the neighbours, Karl could feel her knees moving. Finally there was some reply, but at the same time everyone on that balcony, which was full of people, exploded with laughter.

Delamarche shouted something at them, so loud, that if at that moment there hadn't been a lot of noise on the whole street, everyone would have turned to look in astonishment. At least it had the effect that the laughter did die down rather prematurely.

'They are electing a new judge in our district tomorrow, and the man they're carrying down there is one of the candidates,' Delamarche reported, perfectly calmly returning to Brunelda. 'Honestly!' he said, tapping Brunelda's back affectionately. 'We're quite out of touch with what's going on in the world.'

'Delamarche,' said Brunelda, going back to the neighbours' behaviour, 'I should so like to move, if only it weren't such a strain. Unfortunately, I daren't risk it.' And sighing deeply, distracted and agitated, she fiddled about with Karl's shirt, who tried as unobtrusively as he could to push away those plump little hands of hers, which turned out to be easy, because Brunelda wasn't thinking about him, she was preoccupied with quite different thoughts.

Then Karl in turn quite forgot Brunelda, and suffered the weight of her arms on his shoulders, because he was quite absorbed by the goings-on down in the street. On the instruction of a small group of gesticulating men who were walking just in front of the candidate, and whose discussions seemed to have particular importance, because all around one could see listening faces bending towards them, a halt was suddenly called in front of the bar. One of these crucial figures raised his hand in a signal that was meant both for the crowd and the candidate. The multitude fell silent, and the candidate, trying repeatedly to get up on the shoulders of his bearer and repeatedly falling back, held a little address, in the course of which he waved his hat about at great speed, this way and that. That was very clearly visible, because while he spoke, all the car headlamps had been turned on to him, so that he found himself at the centre of a bright star.

Now too you could see the interest the whole street took in the occasion. On balconies that were occupied by partisans of the candidate, they began chanting his name and clapping their hands mechanically, leaning far over their railings. On the other balconies, which were actually the greater number, there was a strong counter-chant, which admittedly had no united effect, as these were supporters of several different candidates. On the other hand, all the opponents of the present candidate went on to unite in a general whistling, and even gramophones were turned on in many places. Between individual balconies political arguments were carried on with a vehemence that was accentuated by the late hour. The majority were already dressed for bed and had coats thrown over their shoulders, the women draped themselves in large dark cloths, the unattended children clambered alarmingly on the outside of the balconies, and emerged in ever-growing numbers from the darkened rooms, in which they had already been sleeping. Occasionally, odd unidentifiable items were thrown by particularly irate parties in the direction of their enemies, sometimes these hit, but for the most part they fell into the street below, often provoking cries of rage. If it got too noisy down below for the leading men, then the drummers and trumpeters were ordered to strike up, and their seemingly never-ending brassy fanfare, executed with all their strength, suppressed all human voices right up to the rooftops. And then, when all of a sudden – you could hardly believe it – they stopped, the obviously well-drilled crowd on the street roared out their party song into the momentary silence – in the light of the headlamps you could see the mouths of everyone wide open – until their opponents, recovering themselves, roared back ten times as loud as before from all the balconies and windows, and brought the party below, after their brief triumph, to complete silence, at least from what you could tell up there.

'Well, how do you like it, little fellow?' asked Brunelda, who was swivelling this way and that at Karl's back, to see all she could with her binoculars. Karl merely gave a nod back. He noticed out of the corner of his eyes how Robinson was eagerly giving Delamarche various reports evidently to do with Karl's behaviour, but Delamarche obviously seemed to think them completely unimportant, because with his left hand – he was embracing Brunelda with the right – he kept trying to push him away. 'Wouldn't you like to try looking through the glasses?' asked Brunelda, and tapped Karl on the chest, to show that she meant him.

'I can see well enough,' said Karl.

'Try it,' she said, 'you'll have a better view.'

'My eyesight is very good,' replied Karl, 'I can see it all.' He didn't find it a kindness, more a nuisance when she put the glasses up to his eyes and said just the one word 'You!' melodiously, but also with menace. And then Karl had the glasses in front of him, and could see nothing at all.

'I can't see a thing,' he said, and tried to remove the glasses, but she held them in place, while his head, was so cushioned on her breast he could move it neither sideways nor back.

'But now you can see,' she said, and turned the screw on the glasses.

'No, I still can't see anything,' said Karl, and thought that, even without wanting to, he had indeed relieved Robinson, because Brunelda's insufferable moods were now being taken out on him.

'When are you going to be able to see?' she said, and went on – Karl now had his whole face in her heavy breathing – turning at the screw. 'Now?' she asked.

'No, no, no!' cried Karl, even though in fact, he could, still dimly, begin to make out the scene. But just then Brunelda had some business with Delamarche, she held the glasses more loosely in front of Karl's face, and Karl could, without her particularly minding it, look out from under the glasses down on to the street. After that she no longer insisted on having her way, and used the glasses for herself.

Down below a waiter had stepped out of the bar and rushing from side to side on the doorstep, was taking the orders of the leaders. You could see him straining to look back in the direction of the bar, and call over as much assistance as he could muster. In the course of what were obviously preparations for a great round of free drinks the candidate never stopped speaking for a moment. His bearer, the colossal man who seemed to be subordinate exclusively to him, kept making little turns after every few sentences, to distribute the speech equally to all parts of the crowd. The candidate's position was generally hunched over and he tried with jerky movements of his free hand, and with his top hat in the other, to lend emphasis to what he was saying. Sometimes, almost at regular intervals, he went into a kind of convulsion, he rose up with outspread arms, he no longer addressed a group but the generality, he spoke to the dwellers of the houses right up to the topmost storeys, and yet it was perfectly obvious that even in the lowest floors no one could hear him, yes, and that even had the possibility existed, no one wanted to hear him, because every window and every balcony was tenanted by at least one shouting speaker of its own. By now a few waiters had emerged from the bar with a board the size of a billiard table, weighed down with filled and shining glasses. The leaders organized their distribution, which took place in the form of a march past the door of the bar. But even though the glasses on the board kept being refilled, they weren't enough for the crowd, and two lines of barmen had to slip out to either side of the board to serve the crowd. The candidate had of course stopped speaking by now, and was using the pause to get his strength back. His bearer was carrying him slowly back and forth away from the crowd and the bright lights, and only a few of his closest associates accompanied him and spoke up to him.

'Look at the little chap,' said Brunelda. 'He's forgotten where he is for looking.' And she took Karl by surprise, and with both hands turned his face towards her, so that she was looking straight into his eyes. It lasted only for a second, though, because Karl quickly shook off her hands, and annoyed not to be left in peace even for a little while, and at the same time longing to go down to the street and see everything up close, he tried with all his might to free himself from Brunelda's pressure, and said:

'Please let me go.'

'You're saying with us,' said Delamarche, without taking his eye off the street, merely extending a hand to prevent Karl from going.

'It's all right,' said Brunelda, and pushed Delamarche's hand away, 'he wants to stay.' And she pressed Karl even harder against the railing, he would have had to fight her to get free of her. And even if he'd succeeded in that, what would he have accomplished. To his left was Delamarche, Robinson was to his right, he was well and truly imprisoned.

'You should be thankful we're not throwing you out,' said Robinson, and tapped at Karl with the hand he had pushed through under Brunelda's arm.

'Throwing you out?' said Delamarche. 'A runaway thief isn't thrown out. He's handed over to the police. And that can happen as early as tomorrow morning, unless he keeps absolutely quiet.'

From that moment on, Karl could take no more pleasure in the spectacle down below. He leaned over the railing a bit but only because he was forced to, unable to stand upright because of Brunelda. Full of his own worries, with a distracted gaze, he watched the people down there as they went up to the bar door in groups of twenty or so, took their glasses, turned and raised them in the direction of the now preoccupied candidate, called out a party greeting, emptied their glasses and set them down on the board, surely with a crash, but inaudibly at this height, and then made way for a new, rowdy and impatient, group. At the instruction of the leaders, the band, who had been playing inside the bar, now stepped out on to the street, their large brass instruments glittered in the midst of the dark crowd, but their playing was all but drowned by the general hubbub. The street, at least the opposite side of it where the bar was, was filled with people almost as far as you could see. They were streaming down from the heights, where Karl had driven along in the car that morning, and they were coming up the hill from the bridge, and even the people in the buildings had been unable to resist the temptation to take a hand in the proceedings themselves, the balconies and windows were now occupied almost exclusively by women and children, while the men were swarming out through the entrances. But now the music and the hospitality had achieved their objective, the crowd was big enough, a leader flanked by two car headlights motioned to the music to stop, emitted a piercing whistle, and you could now see the somewhat errant bearer with the candidate hurrying down through a space cleared for him by his supporters.

The moment he reached the door of the bar, the candidate, in the beam of a tight circle of headlamps, embarked on his next speech. But now everything was much harder than before, the bearer no longer had the slightest freedom of movement, the crush was too great. The closest supporters, who previously had tried everything to contribute to the effectiveness of the candidate's speech, were now struggling to remain in his proximity, some twenty of them were desperately clinging on to the bearer. But strong as he was, he couldn't take a single step as he pleased, there was no possibility of influencing the crowd by revolving or advancing or retreating at given moments. The crowd was in chaotic flux, each man was leaning against his neighbour, none was standing upright any more, the opponents seemed to have gained strength greatly from the new arrivals, the bearer had stood long in the vicinity of the bar door, but now, apparently unresistingly, he allowed himself to drift up and down the street, the candidate was speaking all the time, but it wasn't quite clear any more whether he was laying out his programme or asking for help, and there was every indication that a rival candidate had appeared, or even several, because from time to time in a sudden blaze of light you could see a man raised aloft in the crowd, speaking with pale face and clenched fists to loud cheers of approval.

'What's going on now?' asked Karl, turning in breathless confusion to his guards.

'The little one's all excited,' said Brunelda to Delamarche, and took Karl by the chin to pull his head over to her. But Karl wasn't willing, and, with a ruthlessness inspired by the goings-on below, he shook himself so hard that Brunelda not only let go of him, but shrank back and set him free. 'You've seen enough now,' she said, obviously angered by Karl's behaviour, 'go inside, make the beds and get everything ready for the night.' She pointed to the room. That was the direction Karl had wanted to go in for several hours now, and he did not demur. Then was heard from the street the crunch of breaking glass. Unable to resist, Karl leapt back to the railing for a last quick look down. The opponents had mounted an attack, perhaps even a decisive attack, and the car headlamps of the supporters, whose powerful beams had ensured that at least the principal actions took place in full view of the public, and thus kept everything within bounds, had all been smashed at once, the candidate and his bearer were now caught in the same general, uncertain illumination, whose sudden expansion had the same effect as utter darkness. You couldn't have said, even approximately, where the candidate was, and the deceptiveness of the dark was actually heightened by a swelling, universal chant that was moving up from the area of the bridge.

'Didn't I tell you what you had to do,' said Brunelda, 'hurry up. I'm tired,' she added, and stretched her arms up in the air, so that her breasts arced even more pronouncedly than they did otherwise. Delamarche, who was still holding her in his embrace, pulled her across to a corner of the balcony. Robinson went after them, to remove the last traces of his meal, which he had left there.

Karl had to make the most of this favourable opportunity, this was not the time to go on looking down, he would see enough of the goings-on in the street when he got there himself, far more than from up here. In a couple of bounds he hurried through the reddish illuminated room, but the door was locked and the key had been removed. That had to be found now, but how could anyone find a key in all this mess, still less in whatever precious little time Karl had at his disposal. He should have been on the stairs by now, running for all he was worth. But instead he was looking for the key! He looked in all the drawers he could find, rummaged around on the table where various items of cutlery, napkins and a half-completed piece of embroidery were all lying around, was attracted by an easy chair on which was a balled-up pile of old clothes, where the key might perhaps be lurking, but could never be found, finally throwing himself on the sofa – which did indeed have an awful smell – to grope in all its corners and crannies for the key. Then he stopped his search and stood still in the middle of the room. Brunelda must have the key attached to her belt, he told himself, she had so many things hanging there, all his searching was in vain.

And blindly Karl grabbed a couple of knives and pushed them in between the two wings of the door, one at the top, one at the bottom, so that he might have two separate points of attack. No sooner had he begun to lever on the knives, than of course their blades snapped off. He could have wished for nothing better, their stumps, which he would be able to drive in deeper, would hold more securely. And then with all his strength he pulled, arms and legs wide apart, groaning and watching the door like a hawk. It wouldn't be able to withstand him forever, he realized that with delight from the audible loosening of the lock, but the more slowly it happened, the better for him, the lock mustn't burst open, because then they would hear it from the balcony, rather he had to loosen the lock very slowly, and Karl was working towards that end with immense care, his eyes closer and closer to the lock.

'Will you look at that,' he heard the voice of Delamarche saying. All three of them were in the room, the curtains had been drawn behind them already, Karl must have failed to hear them come in, and at the sight his hands let go of the knives. He had no time to offer a word of explanation or apology, because in a fit of rage that went far beyond the immediate situation, Delamarche – his loose dressing-gown cord describing a great arc in the air – flew at Karl. Karl was able to get out of the way of the attack at the last moment, he might have pulled the knives out of the door, but he didn't, instead crouching and leaping up in the air, he snatched the broad collar of Delamarche's dressing-gown, pulled it up and then pulled it higher – the dressing-gown was far too big for Delamarche after all – and now happily he had Delamarche's head in his grip, who, completely taken by surprise, first groped about blindly with his hands, and after a little while but still not very effectively began to batter Karl's back with his fists, who, to protect his face, had thrown himself at Delamarche's chest. Karl could stand the buffeting, though he was squirming with pain, and the blows were getting stronger all the time, but then how could he not have done, he had victory in his sights. With his hands on Delamarche's head, his thumbs probably directly over his eyes, he pulled him along in front of him into the worst of the furniture chaos, at the same time trying with his feet to loop the dressing cord round Delamarche's ankles, and so bring him to a fall.

Thus entirely preoccupied with Delamarche, especially as he could feel his resistance growing stronger by the minute, felt his sinewy enemy body pressing against his more powerfully all the time, he quite forgot he wasn't alone with Delamarche. But all too soon he was reminded of the fact, because all at once he felt his feet going from under him, Robinson, throwing himself to the ground behind him, was pushing them apart and shouting. With a sigh, Karl let go of Delamarche, who took a further step back, Brunelda was standing there, feet apart, knees bent, in all her breadth in the middle of the room, observing the goings-on with shining eyes. As though participating in the fight herself, she was panting, moving her fists and glowering. Delamarche folded his collar down, now he could see again, and now the fight as such was over, and what followed was merely punishment. He grabbed Karl by his shirt front, almost lifted him off his feet, and hurled him, not even deigning to look at him as he did, with such force against a cupboard just a couple of paces away, that at first Karl thought that the piercing pains in his head and back from his impact against the closet were caused directly by Delamarche's hand. 'You rotter!' he heard Delamarche call out as it grew dark in front of his eyes. And collapsing in exhaustion in front of the closet he heard the words 'just you wait' like a distant echo in his ears.

When he regained consciousness, everything was in darkness, it was probably deep in the night, from the balcony a pale glimmer of moonlight crept into the room under the curtain. You could hear the calm breathing of the three sleepers, the loudest of whom by far was Brunelda, she snorted in her sleep, as she did occasionally while speaking; but it wasn't easy to tell where each of the three was, as the whole room was filled with the sounds of their breathing. Only after examining his surroundings a little did Karl think of himself, and then he got a great shock, because though he felt quite crooked and stiff with pain, it hadn't occurred to him that he might have sustained a serious and bloody injury. But now he had the feeling of a weight on his head, and his whole face, his throat, his chest under his shirt felt moist with blood. He had to get to the light, to find out the extent of his injuries, perhaps he had been crippled for life, then Delamarche would probably let him go, but what would he do, there were really no prospects for him then. The fellow in the gateway with the chewed-up nose came to mind, and for a moment he buried his face in his hands.

Automatically he first turned towards the door, and groped his way there on all fours. Before long, he came upon a boot with his fingertips, and then a leg. That had to be Robinson, who else would sleep in his boots? He had been ordered to lie across the doorway to prevent Karl from escaping. But did they not know what condition he was in? What he wanted now wasn't to escape, but to get at the light. If he couldn't get out by the door, he would have to go out on the balcony.

The dining-table was obviously somewhere completely different from where it had been in the evening, the sofa, which Karl of course approached with extreme caution was surprisingly enough unoccupied, but instead, in the middle of the room he encountered a high pile of albeit crushed clothes, blankets, curtains, pillows and rugs. To begin with he thought it was just a little pile like the one he had found on the sofa in the evening, and that had maybe rolled down on to the floor, but to his amazement, as he crept on, he realized it was a whole cartload of such stuff that had probably been taken out of the boxes for the night, where it was kept in the daytime. He crawled round the pile and soon recognized that the whole thing was a kind of bed, high on top of which, as his most cautious probing told him, Delamarche and Brunelda were resting.

So now he knew where everyone was sleeping, and he made haste to get out on the balcony. It was a completely different world in which, once past the curtain, he quickly got to his feet. In the cool night air, by the full light of the moon, he paced up and down the balcony a few times. He looked down at the street, it was completely quiet, music still sounded from the bar, but only quietly, outside the door a man was sweeping the pavement, in the street where in the evening amidst the confused general babble the shouting of an election candidate couldn't be told from a thousand other voices, you could now hear the scratching of a broom on the paving stones.

The sound of a table being moved on the neighbouring balcony alerted Karl to the fact that there was someone sitting there, studying. It was a young man with a goatee beard which he kept twirling as he read, with rapid lip movements. He sat, facing Karl, at a small table covered with books, he had taken the lamp off the wall, and jammed it between two large books, and was bathed in its harsh light.

'Good evening,' said Karl, thinking he had seen the young man looking across at him.

But he must have been mistaken, because the young man seemed not to have noticed him at all, shielded his eyes with his hand to avoid the glare of the light and see who had suddenly greeted him, and then, still not seeing anything, picked the lamp up to shed a little of its light on the balcony next door.

At length he replied 'Good evening,' glowered for an instant, and added: 'Will that be all?'

'Am I disturbing you?' asked Karl.

'Absolutely, absolutely,' said the man, returning the lamp to its former spot.

With those words any attempt at contact had been rejected, but still Karl didn't leave the corner of the balcony nearest to the man. He looked silently across as the man read his book, turned the pages, occasionally looked something up in another book which he always took down with lightning speed, and several times jotted something down in a notebook, bending surprisingly low over it as he did.

Could this man be a student? He gave every appearance of studying. In much the same way – a long time ago now – Karl had sat at the table in his parents' home, doing his homework, while his father read the paper or did the bookkeeping and correspondence for a club, and his mother busied herself with some sewing, pulling the thread high up into the air. In order not to impede his father, Karl kept only his notebook and his pens on the table, and his other books on chairs to either side of him. How quiet it had been there! How rarely strangers had set foot in that room! Even as a little boy, Karl had always liked it in the evening when his mother locked the front door with her key. What would she say if she knew that her Karl was now reduced to trying to prise open strange doors with knives.

And what had been the point of all his studying! He had forgotten everything; if he'd had to take up his studies again here, he would have found it very hard. He remembered how once he had been ill at home for a month – and how hard it had been then to make up for the lost time. And now, apart from his English business correspondence textbook, it was such a long time since he'd read a book.

'You, young man,' Karl suddenly heard himself being addressed, 'couldn't you go somewhere else? You're bothering me no end, the way you're standing and staring at me. It's two in the morning: surely it's not too much to ask, to be allowed to study in peace on my own balcony. Is there something you want from me?'

'You're studying?' asked Karl.

'Yes, yes,' said the man, and used these few moments that were lost for studying to rearrange his books.

'Then I won't trouble you,' said Karl. 'I was going to go back inside anyway. Good night.'

The man didn't even reply, with a sudden resolve after the removal of the distraction, he had returned to his studies, and propped his forehead on his right hand.

Then, just by the curtain, Karl remembered why he had come outside in the first place, he didn't even know yet about his state of health. What was it pressing down on his head? He put up his hand, and was surprised, there was no bloody wound as he had feared in the dark room, it was nothing more than a still damp turban-like bandage. To judge from the odd scraps of lace still dangling from it, it must have been torn from some old undergarment of Brunelda's, that Robinson had quickly wound round Karl's head. Only he'd forgotten to wring it dry, and so, while Karl had lain unconscious, all the water had run down his face and under his shirt, and so given Karl such a fright.

'You're not still there?' asked the man, blinking at him.

'I'm just on my way,' said Karl, 'I just wanted to look at something, it's pitch dark in the room.'

'Who are you anyway?' said the man, and laid his pen down on his open book, and walked up to the railing. 'What's your name? How did you come to be with those people? Have you been here long? What did you want to look at? Turn your lamp on, so that I can have a look at you.'

Karl did so, but before he replied, he pulled the curtain across a little more, so that they wouldn't notice anything indoors. 'Excuse me,' he said in a whisper, 'for talking so quietly. If they hear me in there, I'll be in trouble again.'

'Again?' asked the man.

'Yes,' said Karl, 'earlier this evening I had a great fight with them. I must have a terrible bump there.' And he felt the back of his head.

'What kind of argument?' asked the man, and, as Karl didn't answer immediately he added, 'It's all right, you can tell me everything you have against those people. I hate all three of them, and especially your Señora. I would be surprised if they hadn't already tried to poison you against me. My name's Josef Mendel, and I'm a student.'

'Yes,' said Karl, 'they did talk about you, but nothing bad. It was you who treated Miss Brunelda once, isn't that so?'

'That's right,' said the student, with a laugh, 'does the sofa still smell of it?'

'Oh yes,' said Karl.

'I'm glad to hear it,' said the student, and ran his hand through his hair. 'And why are they taking lumps out of you?'

'There was an argument,' said Karl, thinking about how he could explain it to the student. But then he interrupted himself, and said: 'Are you sure I'm not bothering you?'

'In the first place,' said the student, 'you've already bothered me, and unfortunately I'm so nervous that it takes me a long time to get back into it. I haven't done a stroke of work since you've started strolling about on your balcony. Secondly, I always have a break at about three o'clock. So go on, tell me about it. I'm interested.'

'It's very straightforward,' said Karl, 'Delamarche wants me to be his servant. But I don't want to. I wanted to leave right away last night. But he didn't want to let me go, and locked the door, I tried to break it open, and then we had our fight. I'm sorry I'm still here.'

'Have you another job to go to?' asked the student.

'No,' said Karl, 'but I don't care about that, so long as I can get away from here.'

'Well now,' said the student, 'you don't care about that?' And they were both silent for a while.

'Why don't you want to stay with those people?' the student finally asked.

'Delamarche is a bad lot,' said Karl, 'I've had dealings with him before. Once I walked with him for a day, and I was glad when we parted company. And now I'm to be his servant?'

'If all servants were as pernickety as you are when it comes to choosing a master!' said the student, seemingly amused. 'You see, in the daytime, I'm a salesman, the lowest grade of salesman, more of an errand-boy really, in Montly's department store. That Montly is most certainly a crook, but I'm not bothered about that, I'm just furious I'm paid so badly. So take an example from me.'

'What?' said Karl, 'you're a salesman in the daytime, and you study at night?'

'Yes,' said the student, 'it's the only way. I've tried everything, but this way is still the best. Years ago I was only a student, day and night you know, and I almost starved doing it, I slept in a pigsty, and I didn't dare enter the lecture halls in the suit I was wearing. But that's over.'

'So when do you sleep?' asked Karl, and looked at the student in astonishment.

'Aye, aye, sleep!' said the student, 'I'll sleep when I've finished my studies. For now I drink black coffee.' And he turned round, pulled out a large flask from under his studying table, poured some black coffee from it into a little cup, and knocked it back, as you swallow medicine as quickly as possible, to get the least taste of it.

'Wonderful stuff, black coffee,' said the student, 'I'm sorry you're so far away that I can't give you some to try.'

'I don't like black coffee,' said Karl.

'Nor do I,' said the student and laughed. 'But where would I be without it. Without black coffee, I wouldn't last five minutes with Montly. I keep saying Montly, even though he wouldn't know me from Adam. I can't positively say how I would fare at work if I didn't keep a flask of coffee just as big as this one ready prepared at my desk, because I've never yet dared to stop drinking coffee, but believe me, I'd soon be curled up on my desk, asleep. Unfortunately they half suspect that anyway, they call me "Black coffee", which is a stupid joke, and has I'm sure already damaged my career prospects there.'

'And when will you be finished with studying?' asked Karl.

'It's going very slowly,' said the student with lowered head. He left the railing and sat down at the table again; with his elbows resting on his open book, running his hands through his hair he said: 'It could take another year or two.'

'I wanted to study too,' said Karl, as though that fact entitled him to more confidence than the now more taciturn student had already shown him.

'I see,' said the student, and it wasn't quite clear whether he'd started reading his book again, or was merely staring at it absent-mindedly, 'you should be glad you've given it up. For some years now I've only been studying out of bloody-mindedness. It brings me little satisfaction, and even less in the way of future prospects. What prospects am I supposed to have! America is full of quack doctors.'

'I wanted to be an engineer,' said Karl quickly to the student who now seemed wholly indifferent.

'And now you're going to be a servant for those people,' said the student looking up quickly, 'that must hurt.'

This conclusion on the part of the student was a misunderstanding, but Karl thought it might help him with the student. And so he asked: 'Is there any chance I might get a job at the department store?'

The question tore the student away from his book; it didn't even occur to him that he might help Karl to apply for a job. 'Try it,' he said, 'or rather don't. Getting my job at Montly's has been the greatest success of my life to date. If I had to choose between my studies and my job, I would choose my job every time. Although of course I'm doing my best to see that I never have to make the choice.'

'So that's how hard it is to get a job there,' said Karl, musingly.

'You have no idea,' said the student, 'it's easier to become the district judge here than the doorman at Montly's.'

Karl didn't say anything. That student, who was so much more experienced than himself, and who hated Delamarche for reasons Karl had yet to learn, and who certainly wished no ill upon Karl, didn't offer so much as a word of encouragement to Karl to walk out on Delamarche. And he didn't even know about the threat that was posed by the police, and from which Delamarche offered the only possible source of protection.

'You watched the demonstration down there earlier in the evening, didn't you? If you didn't know the circumstances, you might think that candidate, Lobter's his name, might have some prospects, or at least was a possibility, no?'

'I don't know anything about politics,' said Karl.

'You're making a mistake,' said the student. 'But be that as it may, you've still got eyes and ears in your head. The man certainly had his friends and his enemies, that can't have escaped your attention. Well, in my opinion the man hasn't the faintest chance of being returned. I happen to know all about him, someone who lives here with us knows him. He's not an untalented man, and his political opinions and his political career to date would seem to qualify him as a suitable judge for this district. But no one gives him the slightest chance, he'll fail just as comprehensively as it's possible to fail, he'll have blown his few dollars on his election campaign, and that's all.'

Karl and the student looked at one another in silence for a while. The student nodded with a smile, and rubbed his tired eyes with one hand.

'Well, aren't you going to bed yet?' he asked, 'I have to get back to my studies. You see how much I still have to do.' And he riffled through half a volume, to give Karl some idea of how much work was still waiting for him.

'Well, good night then,' said Karl, and bowed.

'Come over and see us some time,' said the student, seated at his table again by now, 'of course only if you'd like to. There are always a lot of people here. Between nine and ten in the evening I'd have some time for you myself.'

'So you advise me to stay with Delamarche?' asked Karl.

'Definitely,' said the student, and already his head was bent over his books. It was as though he hadn't said the word at all; it echoed in Karl's ears, as though it had come from a far deeper voice than the student's. Slowly he made his way to the curtain, took a final look at the student, now sitting immobile in his pool of light, surrounded by all the darkness, and slipped into the room. The combined breathing of the three sleepers met him. He felt along the wall for the sofa, and when he had found it, he stretched out on it quietly, as though it was his regular bed. As the student, who knew Delamarche and circumstances here well, and was moreover a cultivated man, had counselled him to stay, he had no qualms for the moment. He didn't have such lofty aims as the student, who could say if he would have managed to complete his studies if he'd stayed at home, and what barely seemed possible at home no one could demand that he did in a foreign land. But the hope of finding a job where he could do something and find recognition for it was certainly greater if he took the servant's job with Delamarche, and from the security that offered, waited for a favourable opening. This street seemed to contain many small and medium-sized offices that might not be all that choosy when it came to filling a vacancy. He was happy to be a porter, if need be, but really it wasn't out of the question that he might be chosen for actual office work and might one day sit as an office worker at his desk and look out of his open window with no worries for a while, just like that official he had seen in the morning while walking through the courtyards. It comforted him, even as he shut his eyes that he was still young, and that Delamarche would at some stage let him go: this household really didn't give the impression of being made to last. But once Karl had got a job in an office, then he would occupy himself with nothing but his office work, and not fritter away his strength the way the student did. If need be, he would do night work at the office too, which would be asked of him anyway, in view of his limited business experience. He would think exclusively of the interest of the business where he was employed, and accept all manner of work, even what other employees saw as demeaning to them. Good resolutions crowded into his mind, as though his future boss were standing by his sofa, and could read them in his face.

Thinking such thoughts, Karl fell asleep and as he was drifting off, he was disturbed once more by a vast sigh from Brunelda who, evidently plagued by troubling dreams, tossed and turned on her bed.

'Up! Up!' cried Robinson, the moment Karl opened his eyes in the morning. The curtain in the doorway had not yet been drawn, but you could see from the even way the sun poured through the cracks that the morning was already well advanced. Robinson was bustling about here and there, with a worried expression on his face, now he was carrying a towel, now a bucket of water, now sundry items of clothing and underwear, and every time he passed Karl, he would nod in his direction to induce him to get up, and show him, by holding up whatever he happened to be carrying, how he was exerting himself on Karl's behalf, today and for the last time, seeing as he couldn't of course grasp the intricacies of serving on his very first morning.

After a time Karl saw whom Robinson was in the process of waiting on. In an alcove which Karl had failed to notice before, separated from the rest of the room by a couple of chests of drawers, great ablutions were in progress. You could see Brunelda's head, her bare throat – the hair had just been pushed into her face – and the nape of her neck, over the chests of drawers, and Delamarche's raised hand waving in and out of view, holding a liberally dripping bath sponge, with which Brunelda was being scrubbed and washed. You could hear the short commands Delamarche gave Robinson, who didn't pass things through the now blocked-off entrance to the alcove, but was restricted to a little gap between one of the chests of drawers and a screen, and was made to hold out each new item with extended arms and averted face. 'The towel! The towel,' shouted Delamarche. And just as Robinson, who had been looking for something else under the table, started at this call and withdrew his head from under the table, there was already a different command: 'Water, I want the water goddammit,' and the enraged face of Delamarche loomed over the chest of drawers. All those things that Karl thought were needed only once in the course of washing and dressing were here called for and brought repeatedly, and in every possible order. A large pan full of water was always kept to heat up on a little electric stove, and time and again, with legs wide apart, Robinson lugged it into the washroom. In view of the amount of work it was understandable that he didn't always follow his orders to the letter, and once, when another towel was called for, he simply pulled a shirt off the great sleeping platform in the middle of the room, and tossed it in a tangled mass over the chest of drawers.

But Delamarche had his hands full as well, and perhaps was only so irritated with Robinson – and far too irritated even to notice Karl – because he was unable to satisfy Brunelda himself. 'Oh!' she cried, and even the otherwise uninvolved Karl shrank at that. 'You're hurting me! Go away! I'd sooner wash myself than go on suffering like this! I won't be able to lift my arm again because of you. You're squeezing me so hard, it's making me ill. I just know my back is covered with bruises. Of course, you'll never tell me if it is. Just you wait, I'll get Robinson to look at me, or the little new chap. All right, I won't but just be a bit more careful. Just show a little sensitivity, Delamarche, but that's what I say every morning, and it makes no difference. Robinson,' she cried suddenly, waving some frilly knickers in the air, 'come to my rescue, see how I'm suffering, he calls this torment washing, that Delamarche. Robinson, Robinson, what's keeping you, have you no pity either?' Karl silently motioned to Robinson with one finger to go to her, but Robinson lowered his eyes and shook his head in a superior fashion, he knew better than that. 'Are you crazy?' he whispered into Karl's ear. 'She doesn't mean it literally. One time I did go in, and never again. Both of them grabbed hold of me and held me down in the bath, I almost drowned. And for days afterwards Brunelda taunted me for being dirty-minded, she kept saying: "You haven't been to see me in my bath for a while now," or "When will you come and inspect me in my bath?" I had to get down on my knees and beg before she agreed to stop. I'll never forget that.' And all the time Robinson was talking, Brunelda kept calling: 'Robinson! Robinson! What's keeping that Robinson!'

In spite of the fact that no one came to her assistance, and there wasn't even a reply – Robinson had sat down next to Karl, and the two of them looked silently across at the chests of drawers, above which the heads of Brunelda and Delamarche were visible from time to time – in spite of that, Brunelda didn't stop her loud complaining about Delamarche. 'Come on, Delamarche,' she cried, 'you're not washing me at all. What have you done with the sponge? Get a grip! If only I could bend down, if only I could move! I'd soon show you what washing is. Where are the days of my girlhood when I used to swim in the Colorado every morning on my parents' estate, the supplest of all my girlfriends. And now! When will you learn to wash me, Delamarche, you're just waving the sponge around, you're trying as hard as you can, but still I can't feel anything at all. When I told you not to scrub me raw, I didn't mean to say that I just wanted to stand around and catch cold. I feel like hopping out of the bath and running off, just as I am.'

But then she didn't carry out her threat – which she wasn't actually in a position to do anyway – because Delamarche, worried that she might catch cold, seemed to have seized her and pushed her down into the tub, because there was an almighty splash.

'That's typical of you, Delamarche,' said Brunelda, a little more quietly, 'you make a bad job of something, and then try and get out of it by flattering me unmercifully.' Then there was silence for a while. 'They're kissing now,' said Robinson, and raised his eyebrows.

'What work is there to do now?' asked Karl. Now that he had decided to stay here, he wanted to get to work. He left Robinson, who didn't reply, behind on the sofa, and started to pull apart the great bed, still compacted by the weight of the sleepers who had lain on it all night, in order to fold each single item of it neatly, as probably hadn't been done for weeks.

'Do go and see what's happening, Delamarche,' said Brunelda, 'I think they're attacking our bed. You need to be on your guard the whole time, there's never a moment's peace. You'll have to be stricter with those two, or they'll just do as they please.' 'It's bound to be the little fellow with his bloody industriousness,' said Delamarche, and it sounded as though he was about to erupt out of the washroom, Karl hurriedly dropped everything, but fortunately Brunelda said: 'Don't leave me, Delamarche, don't leave me. Oh, the water's so hot, it's making me so tired. Stay here with me, Delamarche.' Only then did Karl really notice how there were swathes of steam rising incessantly behind the dressers.

Robinson's hand flew to his cheek, as though Karl had done something terrible. 'I want everything left just exactly as it was before,' came Delamarche's voice, 'don't you know Brunelda likes to lie down for an hour after her bath? What a wretched household! You wait, you'll catch it from me. Robinson, are you daydreaming again. I'm making you responsible for everything that happens. It's up to you to keep that boy in check, we're not going to change the way we do things here to suit him. Whenever we want anything done, you're useless, and if nothing needs doing, you're as busy as bees. Go and skulk in a corner somewhere and wait until you're needed.'

But all that was straightaway forgotten, because Brunelda whispered very feebly, as though overcome by the hot water: 'My perfume! I want my perfume!' 'Her perfume!' shouted Delamarche. 'Get to it.' Yes, but where was the perfume? Karl looked at Robinson, Robinson looked at Karl. Karl saw that he would have to take the responsibility on his own shoulders, Robinson evidently had no idea where the perfume was, he just lay down on the floor and kept waving both his arms about under the sofa, bringing to light nothing more than tangles of dust and woman's hair. Karl first hurried to the washstand that was right by the door, but its drawers contained nothing but old English novels, journals and sheet music, and all of them so crammed full that it was impossible to shut them again, once they'd been opened. 'The perfume!' groaned Brunelda in the meantime. 'How long it's taking! I wonder if I'll get my perfume today!' In view of her impatience, Karl of course couldn't possibly look thoroughly anywhere, he had to rely on cursory impressions. The bottle wasn't in the washstand, and on top of it were only old jars of medicine and ointments, everything else must have already been taken into the washroom. Maybe the bottle was in the drawer of the dining-table. But, on the way to the table – Karl had only the perfume in his thoughts, nothing else – he collided violently with Robinson, who had finally given up looking under the sofa, and following some dim notion where the perfume might be, had walked blindly into Karl. The clash of heads was clearly audible. Karl remained mute, Robinson carried on on his way, but to relieve his pain, let out a long and exaggeratedly loud howl.

'Instead of trying to find my perfume, they're ragging,' said Brunelda. 'This household is making me ill, Delamarche, I can just tell I'm going to die in your arms. I must have the perfume,' she then cried, pulling herself together, 'I simply must have it. I'm not leaving the bath until they bring it, even if I have to stay here all day.' And she petulantly brought her fist down into the water, so that it splashed.

But the perfume wasn't in the dining-table drawer either, though that was full of Brunelda's toiletries, such things as old powder puffs, jars of cream, hairbrushes, curls and lots of tangled and stuck-together things, but not the perfume. And Robinson, still wailing, in a corner where there were about a hundred stacked-up boxes and cartons, opening and rummaging through them all one after another, each time causing half the contents, sewing things and letters for the most part, to fall to the floor where they remained, could find nothing either as he occasionally signified to Karl by shaking his head and shrugging his shoulders.

Then Delamarche in his underwear leapt out of the washroom, while Brunelda could be heard crying hysterically. Karl and Robinson stopped their search and looked at Delamarche, who, soaked to the skin, and with water pouring off his face and hair as well, exclaimed: 'Now will you kindly start looking.' 'Here!' he commanded Karl, and 'You there!' Robinson. Karl really did look, and even checked places that had already been assigned to Robinson, but he was no more able to find the perfume than Robinson, who devoted most of his energy to keeping an eye out for Delamarche, who was stamping up and down the room as far as it went, undoubtedly longing to give both Karl and Robinson a good thrashing.

'Delamarche!' cried Brunelda, 'come and dry me at least. Those two won't manage to find the perfume, and will only make a mess. Tell them to stop looking. Right away! And put everything down! And not touch anything! They'll turn our apartment into a pigsty. Grab hold of them, Delamarche, if they don't stop! But they're still at it, I heard a box falling. They're not to pick it up, leave everything where it is, and just get out of the room! Bolt the door behind them, and come back to me. I've been lying in the water far too long already, my legs are getting quite cold.'

'All right, Brunelda, all right,' cried Delamarche, and hurried to the door with Karl and Robinson. Before he let them go, though, he instructed them to get some breakfast and if possible to borrow a good perfume for Brunelda.

'It's so dirty and messy in your flat,' said Karl once they were in the corridor, 'as soon as we're back with the breakfast, we'll have to start tidying up.'

'If only I wasn't in such pain,' said Robinson. 'The way I'm treated!' Robinson was certainly offended that Brunelda didn't draw the slightest distinction between himself, who had been serving her for months, and Karl, who had only been recruited yesterday. But that was really all he deserved, and Karl said: 'You must pull yourself together.' But in order not to consign him to complete despair, he said: 'It's a job that just needs doing once, and then it'll be done. I'll make a bed for you behind the chests, and once everything's a bit neater, you'll be able to lie there all day and not have to bother about anything, and then you'll have your health back soon enough.'

'So you've seen for yourself what my condition is like,' said Robinson, and turned away from Karl, to be alone with his suffering self. 'But will they ever let me lie in peace?'

'If you like, I'll mention it to Delamarche and Brunelda myself.'

'When has Brunelda ever shown any compassion?' cried Robinson, and with his fist – for which Karl was quite unprepared – he banged open the door they were just passing.

They found themselves in a kitchen, from whose stove, which seemed in need of repair, little black clouds were rising. Kneeling by the oven door was one of the women Karl had seen in the corridor yesterday, putting large lumps of coal into the fire with her bare hands, while inspecting it from all angles. All the while she was groaning with the discomfort of having to kneel at her age.

'It had to be, didn't it, this pestilence,' she said, on seeing Robinson, got to her feet with some difficulty, resting her hand on the coal box, and shut the oven door, around whose handle she wrapped her apron. 'It's four in the afternoon' – Karl looked in astonishment at the kitchen clock – 'and you want your breakfast? What a bunch!'

'Sit down,' she said, 'and wait till I can see to you.'

Robinson made Karl sit down next to him on a little bench by the door, and whispered to him: 'We have to do whatever she says. We depend on her, you see. We rent our room from her, so she can evict us any time she likes. Whereas we can't possibly change apartments, we could never manage to move all our things out, and above all Brunelda isn't transportable.'

'And isn't there any other room to be had on the passage?' Karl asked.

'No one would have us,' replied Robinson, 'no one will have us in the whole building.'

So they sat quietly and waited on their little bench. The woman kept running between a pair of tables, a washtub and the stove. From her exclamations it could be gleaned that her daughter was poorly, and that as a result she had to do all the work by herself, which meant the serving and catering for thirty tenants. As if that weren't enough on its own, the oven had something wrong with it, the food refused to cook, a thick soup was being prepared in two enormous saucepans, and however many times the woman inspected it with her ladles and poured it out from a height, the soup wasn't ready, it was certainly the fault of the poor fire, and so she almost squatted down on the floor by the door of the oven, and with a poker prodded around in the glowing coals. The smoke that filled the kitchen made her cough so much that sometimes she had to reach for a chair and for minutes on end, do nothing but cough. She quite regularly remarked that she would not supply any more breakfasts today, because she had neither the time nor the inclination. As Karl and Robinson had been detailed on the one hand to get the breakfast, and on the other had no possibility of compelling her, they simply ignored such remarks of hers, and just sat quietly as before.

All around on chairs and footstools and on and underneath the tables, yes, even stacked in a corner of the floor, were the dirty breakfast dishes of the tenants. There were jugs which probably still contained a little coffee or milk, some of the little plates had scraps of butter on them, there was a large tin can that had fallen over, and some biscuits had rolled a long way across the floor. It was quite feasible to make all that into a breakfast that even Brunelda, as long as she was kept ignorant of its origins, wouldn't have been able to turn her nose up at. When that occurred to Karl, and a glance at the clock told him that they had been waiting for half an hour already, and Brunelda might be raging and turning Delamarche against the servants, the woman was just calling out, in the midst of a fit of coughing – in the course of which she stared at Karl – 'You can sit here as long as you like, you're not getting any breakfast. But if you want, you can have supper in a couple of hours.'

'Come on, Robinson,' said Karl, 'we'll put our own breakfast together.'

'What?' cried the woman tilting her head. 'Be reasonable,' said Karl, 'why won't you give us our breakfast? We've been waiting for half an hour, that's long enough. It's all included in what we pay, and I'm sure we pay more than some of your other tenants. The fact that we breakfast so late may be burdensome for you, but we are your tenants, we're in the habit of breakfasting late, so you should cater for us a little bit as well. Of course it's particularly difficult for you today, what with your daughter's sickness, but then again we're prepared to make our own breakfast from the leftovers, if that's all there is and you won't make us any fresh.'

But the woman wouldn't let herself in for a friendly discussion with anyone, for these particular tenants even the general leftovers were too good; but on the other hand she was quite fed up with the intrusiveness of these two servants, so she grabbed a cup, thrust it at Robinson's midriff, who, after sitting for some time with an injured expression, realized that he was supposed to hold on to it, to collect whatever food the woman could get together. She then loaded the cup in a great hurry with an assortment of things, but the overall appearance was that of a lot of dirty crockery, not like a presentable breakfast. Even as the woman pushed them outside, and they hurried towards the door, shoulders hunched as though expecting blows or abuse, Karl took the cup out of Robinson's hands, because it didn't seem to him that Robinson would look after it well enough.

Once they were in the corridor, sufficiently far away from the land-lady's door, Karl sat down on the floor with the cup, first of all to give it a good clean, then to gather together what belonged together, to pour all the milk into one container, to scrape the various pats of butter on to one plate, and then to remove every appearance of use, thus cleaning the knives and spoons, trimming the half-eaten bread rolls, and so put a better complexion on the whole thing. To Robinson this work seemed superfluous, and he insisted that breakfast had often looked much worse, but Karl wouldn't be talked out of it, and was even glad that Robinson with his dirty fingers wasn't interested in helping. To keep him quiet, Karl had right away, but, as he told him, in final settlement, given him a few biscuits and the thick sediment of a jug once containing cocoa.

When they reached their apartment, and Robinson casually grasped the door handle, Karl held him back, since he wasn't yet sure whether it was all right to go in. 'Oh yes,' said Robinson, 'he's just doing her hair.' And indeed, in the still unaired and darkened room there sat Brunelda in the armchair with her legs apart, while Delamarche stood behind her, bending low over her, combing her short and probably very tangled hair. Brunelda was wearing another of her very loose dresses, this time a pale pink one, if anything it was a little shorter than yesterday's, at any rate you could see the coarse woven white stockings up to the knee. Impatient with the time it was taking to comb her hair, Brunelda pushed her thick red tongue between her lips this way and that, sometimes, with the exclamation 'Oh Delamarche!', she even completely broke away from Delamarche, who waited with raised comb for her to lay her head back again.

'That took a long time,' said Brunelda in a general way, and to Karl in particular she said: 'You'll have to speed up a bit if you want to give satisfaction. That lazy guzzling Robinson is not a good example for you. I expect you've already breakfasted on the way somewhere, well, I tell you, I won't stand for that on another occasion.'

This was most unfair, and Robinson too shook his head and his lips moved although they didn't make any sound, but Karl for his part could see that the only way of impressing his masters was by showing clear evidence of work. He therefore pulled a low Japanese table out of a corner, laid a cloth over it, and put out the things he had brought. Anyone who had seen the origins of this breakfast could not fail to be impressed with it, but for those others who hadn't, as Karl had to admit, there were some grounds for criticism.

Luckily, Brunelda was hungry. She nodded graciously at Karl, as he set everything out, and often got in his way by filching little morsels for herself before he was ready, with her soft, fat, potentially all-flattening hand. 'He's done well,' she said, smacking her lips, and pulled Delamarche, who left the comb in her hair for a later resumption, down next to her on a chair. Delamarche too was mollified by the sight of the meal, both of them were very hungry, their hands hurried this way and that across the little table. Karl saw that to give satisfaction he should be sure to bring as much as possible, and, remembering he had left various eatables on the floor of the kitchen, he said: 'For this first time, I wasn't sure how to go about it, next time I'll do better.' But even as he spoke, he remembered whom he was addressing, he had concentrated too much on the thing itself. Brunelda nodded contentedly at Delamarche, and fed Karl a handful of crumbs by way of reward.

FRAGMENTS

(I) BRUNELDA'S DEPARTURE

One morning Karl pushed the Bath chair in which Brunelda sat out of the gate. It was rather later than he had planned. They had agreed to arrange the exodus for night-time, to attract none of the attention in the street which would have been inevitable by day, however demurely Brunelda offered to cover herself with a large grey cloth. But getting her down the steps had taken too long, in spite of the eager cooperation of the student, who, as it now transpired, was nothing like as strong as Karl. Brunelda comported herself very bravely, hardly groaning at all, and trying in every way to make it easier for her two bearers. But there was no other way of doing it than setting her down on every fifth step, to give themselves, and her too, time for a minimal rest. It was a chilly morning, a cold subterranean sort of breeze was blowing in the corridors, but Karl and the student were covered in sweat, and each time they stopped kept having to wipe their faces with a corner of Brunelda's cloth, which she kindly let them have. And so it was fully two hours till they reached the bottom, where the little handcart had been waiting since the previous evening. The lifting of Brunelda into it was again a laborious process, but then one could see the whole enterprise as crowned with success, because the pushing of the wagon couldn't be that difficult, with its high wheels, although there was always the chance that the wagon might fall apart under Brunelda's weight. That was a risk that had to be taken, though, one could hardly travel with a spare conveyance, although the student had half jokingly volunteered to get hold of one and push it. Next they had to take leave of the student, which was actually very cordial. All the past disagreements between Brunelda and the student appeared forgotten, he even apologized for the old insult to Brunelda he had perpetrated during her illness, but Brunelda said that had been long forgotten and more than made up for. She ended up asking the student to be so good as to accept a dollar from her as a keepsake, which she had some trouble finding among her skirts. In the light of Brunelda's famous avarice, this gift was really very significant, and the student was quite delighted with it, and in his delight tossed the coin high up in the air. Then, though, he had to look for it on the ground, and Karl had to help him, and it was Karl in the end who found it under Brunelda's cart. The farewell between the student and Karl was of course much more straightforward, they simply shook hands, and said they were sure they would meet again, by which time at least one of them – the student insisted it would be Karl, Karl that it would be the student – would have achieved fame, as unfortunately hadn't happened yet. Then Karl, in good heart, picked up the wagon handle, and pushed it out of the gate. The student watched them as long as they were in sight, and waved his handkerchief. Karl frequently turned round and nodded goodbye, even Brunelda would have liked to turn round, but such a movement was too strenuous for her. At the end of the street, in order to make a last farewell possible for her, Karl described a circle with the wagon, so that Brunelda could see the student too, who used the opportunity to wave especially vigorously with his handkerchief.

But then Karl said they mustn't have any more stops, they had a long way ahead of them, and had set out much later than they'd meant to. And indeed, one could already see the occasional vehicle, and even the odd pedestrian too, on his way to work. Karl had meant nothing more by his remark than what he had said, but Brunelda with her sensitivity had a different interpretation and completely covered herself with her grey cloth. Karl made no objection; a handcart with a grey cloth draped over it was still a very arresting sight but incomparably less than a clearly visible Brunelda would have been. He navigated very carefully; before turning a corner, he would look down the street; if it seemed necessary, he even left the wagon and went on alone a few paces, if he could see some potentially disagreeable encounter looming, then he waited until it might be avoided, or even followed a different route down a new street. But even then, as he'd previously studied all possible routes in detail, he never risked making a long detour. Even so, there were obstacles that might have been anticipated, but couldn't be foreseen individually. Suddenly, for instance, in a street that climbed gently, enjoyed good visibility, and was happily completely deserted, something that Karl sought to make the most of by especial haste, a policeman emerged from the dark corner of an entry way, and asked Karl what he was pushing in his carefully covered cart. Though he had looked quite stern to begin with, he had to smile when he lifted the cloth and saw the hot and apprehensive form of Brunelda. 'Hello!' he said. 'There I was thinking you had about ten sacks of potatoes, and it's just one female? Where are you headed for? Who are you?' Brunelda didn't even dare look at the policeman, but kept her eyes on Karl, evidently doubting that even he would be able to save her. But Karl had had enough dealings with policemen, the whole affair didn't seem so terribly threatening to him. 'Miss, why don't you show him', he said, 'the piece of paper you were given?' 'Oh yes,' said Brunelda, and started looking, but in such a hopeless fashion that she really would arouse suspicion. 'Miss', said the policeman with manifest irony, 'seems unable to find her paper.' 'Not at all,' said Karl calmly, 'she's got it all right, she's just mislaid it.' He began looking for it himself, and soon pulled it out from behind Brunelda's back. The policeman gave it a perfunctory glance. 'So that's you, is it,' said the policeman with a smile, 'Miss? And what about you, little fellow, in charge of transport and arrangements? Can't you find any better occupation?' Karl merely shrugged his shoulders, that was just typical police nosiness. 'Well, have a good trip then,' said the policeman, when he didn't get an answer. There was probably contempt in the policeman's tone, and so Karl went away without saying goodbye, the contempt of the police was still preferable to their interest.

Shortly afterwards he had a possibly even more disagreeable encounter. A man approached him, pushing a handcart full of milk churns, and obviously burning to know what was under the grey cloth on Karl's cart. It was hardly possible that he had exactly the same route as Karl, but he stuck to his side, whatever surprising turns Karl made. At first he contented himself with exclamations, such as: 'That looks like a heavy load' or 'Your load looks badly balanced, something's about to fall off the top.' Then, later, he put direct questions: 'What have you got under that cloth?' Karl replied: 'What's it to you?' But as that only made the man still more curious, Karl finally said: 'Apples.' 'What a lot of apples,' said the man in amazement, and he repeated it a few times yet. 'That's a whole apple harvest,' he said. 'That's right,' said Karl. But, either because he didn't believe Karl, or because he wanted to annoy him, he went further, he started – all the while they were moving – reaching out playfully for the cloth, and finally went so far as to tug at it. How Brunelda must be suffering! Out of consideration for her, Karl wanted to avoid an argument with the man, and he turned abruptly into the next open gate, as though that were his destination. 'Here we are,' he said, 'thanks for your company.' The man stopped in amazement in front of the gate, and watched Karl calmly going in, prepared if need be, to cross the whole of the first courtyard. Surely the man could be in no more doubt, but to satisfy his wickedness one more time, he left his wagon standing, tiptoed after Karl and tugged so hard on the cloth that he almost bared Brunelda's face. 'Your apples need to breathe,' he said, and off he ran. Even that Karl put up with, since it finally rid him of the man. He pulled the cart into a corner of the courtyard, where there were some large empty crates, in the lee of which he wanted to say some comforting words to Brunelda under her cloth. But he had to talk to her a long time, because she was in tears, and quite seriously beseeched him to let her stay behind the crates all day, and only go on at night. He might not have been able to convince her how mistaken that would have been on his own, but when someone at the other end of the pile of crates hurled an empty crate on to the ground, so that it made a dreadful noise that echoed round the empty courtyard, she was so terrified that, without another word, she pulled the cloth back over her again, and was probably delighted when Karl quickly got moving again.

The streets were now getting more and more populous, but the wagon aroused rather less attention than Karl had feared. Perhaps it might even have been wiser to choose a different time for the move. If another journey like this should become necessary, Karl decided to try it at noon. Without any further serious incident, he finally turned into the dark narrow alleyway where Enterprise No. 25 was. In front of the door stood the squinting administrator with his watch in his hand. 'Are you always this late?' he asked. 'We had various obstacles,' explained Karl. 'You always get those,' said the administrator. 'In this firm, they're not an excuse. Kindly remember that!' Karl barely listened to talk like that any more, everyone used their own power and belaboured the next man. Once you'd gotten used to it, it wasn't really much more than the regular striking of a clock. But what did alarm him as he pulled the wagon into the corridor was the dirt there, although he'd been expecting it too. It wasn't, when he looked at it more closely, any tangible sort of dirt. The stone flags in the passage had been swept almost clean, the whitewash on the walls wasn't old, the artificial palms only slightly dusty, and yet everything was greasy and repulsive, it was as though everything had been somehow misused, and no cleaning on earth could ever make it better. Whenever Karl came to a new place, he liked to think what improvements could be made to it, and how pleasant it must be to roll up his sleeves and get down to it, regardless of the almost infinite labour it would take. But here he didn't know where to start. Slowly he took the cloth off Brunelda. 'Welcome, Miss,' said the administrator affectedly, there was no question that Brunelda had made a good impression on him. No sooner had Brunelda sensed that than, as Karl observed with satisfaction, she began to exploit it. The fear of the last few hours vanished. She [*text ends here*]

(2)

On a street corner, Karl saw a poster with the following announcement: 'At the racecourse in Clayton, today from 6 a.m. till midnight, personnel is being hired for the Theatre in Oklahoma! The great Theatre of Oklahoma is calling you! It's calling you today only! If you miss this opportunity, there will never be another! Anyone thinking of his future, your place is with us! All welcome! Anyone who wants to be an artist, step forward! We are the theatre that has a place for everyone, everyone in his place! If you decide to join us, we congratulate you here and now! But hurry, be sure not to miss the midnight deadline! We shut down at midnight, never to reopen! Accursed be anyone who doesn't believe us! Clayton here we come!'

There were a lot of people standing in front of the poster, but it didn't seem to excite much enthusiasm. There were so many posters, no one believed posters any more. And this poster was still more incredible than posters usually are. Above all, it had one great drawback, there wasn't a single word in it about payment. If it had been at all worth mentioning, then surely the poster would have mentioned it; it wouldn't have left out the most alluring thing of all. No one wanted to be an artist, but everyone wanted to be paid for his work.

But for Karl there was a great lure in the poster. 'All welcome' it said. All, even Karl. Everything he had done up until now would be forgotten, no one would hold it against him. He could turn up for work that was not a disgrace, something for which people were openly invited to apply! And just as open was the promise that he would be taken on as well. He could ask for nothing better, he wanted to begin a proper career at last, and perhaps this was the way. Maybe all the grandiloquence of the poster was just a trick, maybe the great Theatre of Oklahoma was just a little touring circus, but it was taking people on, and that was enough.

Karl didn't read the poster through again, he just looked out the sentence 'All welcome' once more.

At first he thought of going to Clayton on foot, but that would have meant a three-hour slog, and he might arrive just in time to hear that all the places had been filled. Admittedly, according to the poster, there was an unlimited number of vacancies to be filled, but vacant position ads always put it like that. Karl realized that he would either have to decide against it on the spot, or take public transport. He counted up his money, without the trip it was enough for eight days, he pushed the little coins around on the palm of his hand. A gentleman who had been watching him patted him on the back and said: 'All the best for the ride to Clayton.' Karl nodded silently, and went on calculating. But he decided soon enough, took out the money for the ride, and went to the subway.

When he got out in Clayton, the sound of many trumpets greeted his ears. It was a confused noise, the trumpets weren't playing in tune, there was just wild playing. But that didn't bother Karl, rather it confirmed to him what a great enterprise the Theatre of Oklahoma was. But when he left the station and saw the whole racecourse ahead of him, he saw that everything was much bigger than he could possibly have imagined, and he couldn't understand how an organization could go to such lengths merely for the recruitment of personnel. Outside the entrance to the racecourse was a long low stage, on which a hundred women dressed as angels in white cloths, with great wings on their backs were blowing into golden trumpets. They weren't standing directly on the stage though, each of them stood on an individual pedestal that couldn't be seen, because the long billowing robes of the angel costumes completely covered them. As the pedestals were very high, as much as six feet, the figures of the women looked gigantic, only their little heads looked somewhat out of scale, and their hair, which they wore loose, looked too short and almost laughable, hanging between the big wings and down the side of them. To avoid uniformity, pedestals of all different sizes had been used, there were some quite low women, not much above life size, but others next to them seemed to scale such heights that they were surely in danger from every breath of wind. And now all these women were blowing trumpets.

There weren't many listeners. Small by comparison to their great forms, about a dozen or so youths walked up and down in front of the stage, looking up at the women. They pointed at this one or that one, but didn't seem to have any intention of joining up or going inside. Only one slightly older man was to be seen, he stood a little to one side. He had brought along his wife and a baby in a pram. The woman held the pram with one hand, with the other she supported herself on the man's shoulder. They admired the performance, but you could see they were disappointed too. They were probably expecting to find a work opportunity, and were confused by the trumpeting.

It was the same with Karl. He went over to the man, listened to the trumpets a while and said: 'Is this not the reception point for the Theatre of Oklahoma?' 'I thought so too,' said the man, 'but we've been waiting here for an hour, and have heard nothing but trumpets. There's not a poster anywhere, no announcers, no one to get any information from.' Karl said: 'Perhaps they're waiting for more people to come. There really aren't very many here yet.' 'Could be,' said the man, and they were both silent again. It was difficult to conduct a conversation with all the noise of the trumpets. But then the woman whispered something to her husband, he nodded, and she promptly called out to Karl: 'Couldn't you go across to the racecourse and ask where the reception takes place?' 'Yes,' said Karl, 'but that would mean walking right across the stage, through the angels.' 'Is that so difficult?' asked the woman. She thought it was a simple matter for Karl, but was reluctant to let her husband go. 'Well, all right,' said Karl, 'I'll go.' 'That's very good of you,' said the woman, and she and her husband shook Karl's hand. The youths clustered together to watch Karl climbing on to the stage. It felt as though the women blew louder, to welcome the first job applicant. And yet the ones whose pedestals Karl passed on his way actually took their trumpets from their lips, and leaned over to watch him. At the far end of the stage, Karl saw a man walking restlessly back and forth, obviously just waiting for people, to give them all the information they could possibly wish for. Karl was on the point of going over to him, when above him, he heard the sound of his name: 'Karl,' called one of the angels. Karl looked up, and was so pleasantly surprised he started to laugh: it was Fanny. 'Fanny,' he cried, and waved up at her. 'Come here!' called Fanny. 'Don't just walk past me.' And she parted her robes, revealing her pedestal and a narrow flight of steps leading up it. 'Am I allowed to go up?' asked Karl. 'Who's going to tell me we can't shake hands with each other,' cried Fanny, and looked around wrathfully, as if in fact someone with just such a message was coming. Karl ran up the stairs. 'Not so fast!' cried Fanny. 'The pedestal and the pair of us will fall over.' But they didn't, Karl successfully reached the last step. 'Look,' said Fanny, after they'd greeted one another, 'see what a good job I've got.' 'It's very nice,' said Karl, looking round. All the women nearby had noticed Karl, and were giggling. 'You're almost the tallest of them,' said Karl, and put out a hand to measure the height of the others. 'I saw you right away,' said Fanny, 'as soon as you came out of the station, but unfortunately I'm in the back row, so you couldn't see me, and I wasn't able to call you either. I did try and blow especially loud, but you didn't spot me.' 'You do all play very badly,' said Karl. 'Let me have a go.' 'Sure,' said Fanny, and gave him the trumpet, 'but don't spoil the chorus, or I'll lose my job.' Karl began to play, he had imagined it would be a crude version of a trumpet, really just for making a noise, but it turned out to be an instrument that was capable of almost infinite expression. If all the instruments were like that one, then they were being seriously misused. Undisturbed by the noise of the others all around, Karl played a tune he had heard once in a bar somewhere at the top of his lungs. He was glad to have run into an old friend, to be privileged to play the trumpet in front of everyone, and to be on the verge, possibly, of getting a good job. A lot of the women stopped playing and listened: when he suddenly stopped, barely half the trumpets were in use, and it took a while for the previous volume to return. 'You're an artist,' said Fanny, as Karl handed the trumpet back to her. 'You should get a job as a trumpeter.' 'Do they take men too?' asked Karl. 'Yes,' said Fanny, 'we play for two hours. Then we are relieved by the men, who are dressed as devils. Half of them are trumpeters, the other half drummers. It's very nice, just as the whole design is very beautiful. Don't you like our costumes? What about the wings?' She looked down her body. 'Do you think,' asked Karl, 'I'll manage to get a job here too?' 'Definitely,' said Fanny, 'it's the greatest theatre in the world. How lucky that we're going to be together again. Although that depends on what sort of job you get too. Because it's quite possible that even if we both have jobs here, we might never see each other.' 'Is the whole thing really that big?' Karl asked. 'It's the greatest theatre in the world,' Fanny said again, 'I have to admit I haven't seen it myself yet, but some of my colleagues who have been to Oklahoma, say it's almost boundless.' 'There aren't many people applying,' said Karl, pointing down at the youths and the little family. 'That's true,' said Fanny. 'But bear in mind that we recruit in every major city, that our publicity team is continually on the move, and that we are only one of many such teams.' 'Has the theatre not opened yet?' asked Karl. 'Oh yes,' said Fanny, 'it's an old theatre, but it's being extended all the time.' 'It surprises me,' Karl said, 'that there aren't more people coming in.' 'Yes,' said Fanny, 'it is strange.' 'Could it be,' said Karl, 'that the lavish displays with angels and devils put off more people than they attract?' 'Hard to say,' said Fanny. 'But it's a possibility. You should tell our leader about it, perhaps you can help him by doing that.' 'Where is he?' asked Karl. 'In the racecourse,' said Fanny, 'in the stewards' box.' 'That's another thing,' said Karl, 'why is the recruiting taking place at a racecourse?' 'Well,' said Fanny, 'wherever we go, we make the biggest preparations for the biggest demand. There's so much space in a racecourse. We put our processing offices in the little booths where they usually take bets. There are said to be more than two hundred of them.' 'But,' Karl exclaimed, 'does the Theatre of Oklahoma have sufficient income to pay for such publicity teams?' 'What's it to us,' said Fanny. 'But now, Karl, you'd better go, in case you miss out, and I need to start playing again. Try in any case to get a job on our team, and come back and tell me. Remember I'll be on tenterhooks.' She pressed his hand, told him to be careful going down the steps, put the trumpet to her lips again, but didn't start blowing until she saw that Karl was safely back on the ground. Karl arranged her robes round the steps as they had been before, Fanny thanked him with a nod of her head, and Karl went, pondering all that he had heard in various ways, up to the man who had already seen Karl up with Fanny, and had approached the pedestal to meet him.

'Do you want to join us?' asked the man. 'I'm the team's head of personnel, and would like to welcome you.' He stood leaning forward slightly, perhaps out of politeness, swaying on the spot, and playing with his watch chain. 'Thank you,' said Karl. 'I read your company's poster, and have reported here as asked.' 'Quite right,' said the man, approvingly, 'unfortunately not everyone behaves as correctly as you do.' Karl wondered if this might be the moment to let the man know that the inducements of the publicity team, by their very magnificence, might be counter-productive. But he didn't say anything, because this man wasn't the head of the team, and besides it wouldn't have made a good impression if, before he had even been taken on, he started suggesting what improvements might be made. And so he merely said: 'There's someone else waiting outside, who wants to report as well and sent me on ahead. Can I go back and get him?' 'Of course,' said the man, 'the more people the better.' 'He has his wife with him, and a baby in a pram. Should they come too?' 'Of course,' said the man, who seemed to be amused by Karl's doubts. 'We can use everyone.' 'I'll be back right away,' said Karl, and ran to the edge of the stage. He waved to the couple and called out that they could all come. He helped lift the pram on to the stage, and they went on together as a group. The youths, seeing that, held a discussion, then, hesitating until the very last moment, they slowly climbed the steps, hands in pockets, and finally followed Karl and the family. Just then more passengers emerged from the underground station, and seeing the stage with the angels, threw up their arms in amazement. It did appear as though the rate of job applications might pick up somewhat. Karl was very glad to have come so early, perhaps the first of all, the couple were anxious and asked various questions about what would be expected of them. Karl said he knew nothing definite as yet, but he had really received the impression that everyone without exception would be taken. He thought one could have confidence.

The head of personnel came to meet them, he was very pleased so many people were coming, he rubbed his hands, greeted everyone individually with a little bow, and put them all in a line. Karl was first, then the couple, and only then everyone else. When they had all lined up, the youths at first barged and shoved each other, and it took a while for them to settle down, then the head of personnel said, as the trumpeters ceased: 'On behalf of the Theatre of Oklahoma, I'd like to welcome you. You've come early' – actually, it was almost noon – 'the crush isn't yet great, and so the formalities of your recruitment will soon be concluded. I trust you all have your legitimation papers on you.' The youths straightaway pulled some old papers out of their pockets and waved them at the head of personnel, the husband nudged his wife, who pulled a whole bundle of papers from underneath the baby's coverlet in the pram, only Karl had none. Would that get in the way of his recruitment? It was quite possible. But Karl knew from past experience that, with a little determination, such regulations could be circumvented. The head of personnel looked down the line, to check that everyone had their papers, and as Karl had raised his hand as well, even though it was an empty hand, he took it that he too was provided for. 'That's fine,' said the head of personnel, and waved the youths away, as they pressed to have their papers inspected immediately, 'the papers will be examined in the reception suites. As you've already seen from our posters, we can use everyone. But of course we need to know what an applicant's previous occupation was, so that we can put him somewhere where his experience will be of use to us.' But it's a theatre, Karl thought dubiously, and listened very closely. 'Therefore,' continued the head of personnel, 'we have set up reception suites in the bookmakers' booths, one office for each type of profession. So I want you all to tell me your previous occupations, families generally go to the office of the man, then I will lead you to your respective offices, where first your papers and then your qualifications will be tested by experts in the field – just a very short test, nothing to be afraid of. Then you'll be taken on, and will receive further instructions from there. All right, let's begin. The first office, as the sign will tell you, is for engineers. Do there happen to be any engineers among you?' Karl stepped forward. It seemed to him, precisely because he had no papers, that he should aim to get through all the formalities as quickly as possible, and he did have a certain justification for stepping forward too, as he had wanted to become an engineer. But when the youths saw him step forward, they became envious, and stepped forward too, every one of them. The head of personnel drew himself up to his full height and said to the youths: 'You're all engineers?' Then they all slowly put their hands down again, while Karl stood his ground. The head of personnel looked at him with some incredulity, because Karl seemed to him both too badly dressed and too young to be an engineer, but he made no comment, perhaps out of gratitude, because Karl, or so it must have seemed to him anyway, had brought along all these applicants. He merely pointed courteously to the office in question, and Karl went there while the head of personnel turned to the others.

In the office for engineers were two men seated at two sides of a right-angled desk, comparing two large inventories they had lying in front of them. One of them read from a list of names, the other ticked them off in his inventory. When Karl stepped in front of them and said hello, they immediately put aside their inventories, and both took out large ledgers, which they clapped open. One of them, obviously just a secretary, said: 'May I see your legitimation papers.' 'I'm afraid I don't have them with me,' said Karl. 'Doesn't have them,' said the secretary to the other man, and made a note of it in his ledger. 'Are you an engineer?' inquired the other, who seemed to be the head of the office. 'Not as such,' said Karl quickly, 'but –' 'All right,' said the gentleman, even more quickly, 'then you've come to the wrong place. I'd ask you to pay attention to the sign.' Karl gritted his teeth, the gentleman must have noticed it, because he said: 'No cause for disquiet. We can use everyone.' And he beckoned to one of the servants who were going around unoccupied between the barriers: 'Would you lead this gentleman to the office for people with technical qualifications.' The servant took the command literally, and took Karl by the hand. They went between many booths, in one of which Karl saw one of the lads, already taken on, thanking the gentleman there with a handshake. In the office where Karl was brought, as he had anticipated, the same thing happened. Only from here, having heard that he'd been to a secondary school, he was taken to the office for former secondary schoolboys. But then, when Karl said he'd been to a secondary school in Europe, they declared this wasn't the right place either, and had him brought to the office for people who had attended secondary school in Europe. This was a booth on the very periphery, not merely smaller than all the others, but lower too. The servant who brought him there was livid about his long errand, and the many referrals, for which in his opinion Karl bore sole responsibility. He wouldn't wait for any questions here, but dashed off at once. This office seemed to be the end of the line anyway. When Karl saw the head of the office, he was alarmed by his close resemblance to one of his former teachers, who was probably still teaching at the secondary school back home. The resemblance, however, on closer inspection, turned out to be a matter of details only, but the spectacles perched on the broad nose, the beautifully trimmed blond beard, the gentle curve of the back, and the surprisingly loud voice all kept Karl in amazement for a while yet. Luckily, he didn't have to pay much attention, because the procedure here was much simpler than in the other offices. Here too, however, they noted that his legitimation papers were missing, and the head of the office referred to it as extraordinarily negligent of him, but the secretary, who had the whip hand here, glossed over it, and after a few short questions from the head, and while he was just gathering himself for a major question, he declared that Karl had been taken on. The head of the office turned to the secretary open-mouthed, but he merely made a dismissive gesture, said: 'Hired,' and immediately entered the decision in his ledger. Evidently the secretary was of the opinion that coming from a secondary school in Europe was something so lowly that anyone claiming to fall in that category could be taken at his word. Karl for his part was nothing loath, and went up to him to thank him. But there was one further delay, when he was asked for his name. He didn't reply right away, he was reluctant to give his real name and have that entered. If he got the smallest job, and was able to perform that satisfactorily, then he would happily divulge his name, but not now, he had kept it secret for too long to betray it now. Therefore, as nothing else came to mind just then, he gave what had been his nickname on his last jobs: 'Negro.' 'Negro?' asked the boss, turning his head and pulling a face, as though Karl had now reached the height of preposterousness. The secretary too looked at Karl a while, but then he repeated 'Negro' and wrote it down. 'You didn't write down Negro, did you,' the boss shouted at him. 'Yes, Negro,' said the secretary placidly, and gestured to the boss to conclude the formalities. The boss restrained himself, stood up and said: 'I hereby proclaim that the Theatre of Oklahoma –' But he got no further, he couldn't violate his conscience, sat down, and said: 'His name is not Negro.' The secretary raised his eyebrows, got up in turn, and said: 'I inform you that you have been hired by the Theatre of Oklahoma, and that you will now be presented to our leader.' A servant was sent for, and Karl was escorted to the stewards' stand.

Karl saw the pram at the foot of the stairs, and just then the couple came down, the woman carrying the baby in her arms. 'Have you been taken on?' asked the man, he was much livelier now than before, and the woman behind him was smiling too. When Karl replied that he had just been taken on, and was just going to be presented, the man said: 'Then I congratulate you. We too have just been taken, it seems to be a good company, admittedly it's hard to know your way around, but then it's like that everywhere.' They said 'Goodbye,' and Karl climbed up to the stand. He took it slowly, because the little room at the top seemed to be bursting with people, and he didn't want to barge in. He even stopped and looked over the large racecourse that stretched away in every direction to the distant forests. He felt like seeing a horse race again, he hadn't had a chance to do that yet in America. In Europe he had been taken along to one as a small child once, but all he could remember of that was how his mother had pulled him through a crowd of people who didn't want to let him through. In effect, he had never really seen a proper race. He heard some machinery clanking behind him, turned round and watched the mechanism that shows the names of the winners at races now raising the following line into the air: 'Businessman Kalle with wife and child.' So that was where the names of the recruits were communicated to the offices.

Just then several gentlemen, engaged in a lively discussion, holding pencils and notebooks, came running down the stairs, Karl pressed himself against the bannister to let them pass, and as there was now room at the top he went on up. In a corner of the wooden-railed platform – it looked like the flat roof of a narrow tower – sat, with his arms spread out along the wooden rails, a gentleman wearing a broad white silk sash that said: Leader of the 10th Promotional Team of the Theatre of Oklahoma. On a little table next to him was a telephone, that was probably also used in the races, by which the leader could obviously learn all necessary information about each individual applicant before they were presented to him, because he asked Karl no questions to begin with, but merely observed to another gentleman who was leaning next to him, with feet crossed, and his chin cupped in his hand: 'Negro, a secondary schoolboy from Europe.' And as though that were all that was required of the deeply bowing Karl, he looked past him down the stairs, to see if there wasn't anyone else coming along after him. But, as there wasn't anyone, he occasionally listened in to the conversation the other gentleman was having with Karl, but mainly just looked out over the racetrack and drummed on the railing with his fingers. These delicate and yet sinewy fingers, long and in rapid motion, occasionally distracted Karl, in spite of the fact that the other gentleman was really sufficiently taxing on his own.

'You've been out of work?' that gentleman began by asking. This question, like almost every other question he put, was very simple, quite straightforward, and Karl's replies to them were not tested by any follow-up questions, but in spite of that the gentleman, by the way he stared as he asked them, observing their effect with torso leaning forward, taking the answers with head sunk on his chest, and occasionally repeating them aloud, seemed to give them a special significance, which one couldn't understand, but some sense of which made one awkward and self-conscious. It happened on several occasions that Karl felt like recalling an answer he'd just given and offering another instead which might find more favour, but he always managed to restrain himself, knowing what a bad impression such vacillation must make, and how, anyway, the effect of his replies was generally impossible to gauge. Besides, though, he took considerable comfort from the fact that his acceptance seemed already to have been concluded.

The question whether he had been out of work, he answered with a straightforward 'Yes.' 'Where were you last employed?' the gentleman then asked. Karl was about to reply, when he lifted his finger and said: 'I stress: last!' Karl had understood the original question anyway, and now involuntarily shook his head at this confusing remark, and replied: 'In an office.' This was indeed the case, but if the gentleman happened to want to know a little more about the type of office, he would be forced to lie to him. But the gentleman did not do that, and instead asked a question which was very easy to answer truthfully: 'Were you happy there?' 'No,' cried Karl, almost before he had finished. Looking out of the corner of his eye, Karl noticed that the leader was smiling a little, Karl regretted the impulsiveness of his last reply, but it had been too tempting to shout out that 'No,' because during the whole of his last employment, he had been simply longing for some new employer to come along and ask him precisely that question. But his answer could have another drawback too, because the gentleman could now go on to ask him why he hadn't been happy. Instead, though, he asked: 'What sort of job do you think would suit you?' That might be a trick question, because why was it being asked, if Karl had already been taken on as an actor: although he saw that, he still couldn't bring himself to claim that he felt particularly suited for the profession of acting. And so he avoided the question, and, at the risk of seeming obstinate, he said: 'I read the poster in the city, and as it said that all were welcome, I came along.' 'We know that,' said the gentleman, and his ensuing silence indicated that he insisted on an answer to his question. 'I was taken on as an actor,' Karl said hesitantly, to make it clear to the gentleman how difficult he found this last question. 'That's right,' said the gentleman, and was once more silent. 'Well,' said Karl, and all his hopes of having found a job began to shake, 'I don't know if I'm right for acting. But I will do my best, and try to do everything I'm asked.' The gentleman turned to the leader, and they both nodded, Karl seemed to have given a good answer, he plucked up courage again, and awaited the next question, a little more hopefully. That was: 'What were you originally going to study?' To narrow the question down – the gentleman seemed at pains to do that – he added: 'I mean, in Europe.' At the same time, he took his hand away from his chin, and waved it feebly, as though to indicate at one and the same time the remoteness of Europe and the insignificance of whatever plans might have been made there. Karl said: 'I wanted to be an engineer.' The answer went against the grain, it was absurd in the context of his career so far in America to bring out that old chestnut – and would he ever have succeeded, even in Europe? – but it was the only answer he had and for that reason he gave it. The gentleman, though, took it seriously, as he took everything seriously. 'Well,' he said, 'we probably can't make an engineer out of you right away, but maybe it would suit you for the time being to work on some fairly simple technical tasks.' 'Certainly,' said Karl, he was very happy, of course if he accepted the offer it would mean being plucked out of the acting profession, and put with the technical workers, but he really believed he would make a much better fist of that. Anyway, he kept saying to himself, what mattered wasn't so much the type of work as one's ability to stick it out, whatever it might be. 'Are you strong enough for such demanding work?' asked the gentleman. 'Oh yes,' said Karl. Thereupon the gentleman had Karl come up to him, and felt his arm. 'He's a strong lad,' he said, pulling Karl by the arm over to the leader. The leader nodded and smiled, then without getting off the railing, he gave Karl his hand and said: 'Well, that's it then. In Oklahoma, we'll check everything over again. Be sure to be a credit to our publicity team!' Karl gave a final bow, and he wanted to take leave of the other gentleman too, but he was already walking up and down the platform, looking up, as though completely finished with his task. As Karl climbed down the stairs, next to him the scoreboard was pulled up, and on it the words: 'Negro, Technical Worker'. As everything had gone so well,

Karl wouldn't have minded too much if it had been his real name up on the board. Everything was very well organized, because at the foot of the stairs, Karl was met by a servant who put an armband round his arm. When Karl lifted his arm to see what was on the band, it was, quite rightly, 'technical worker'.

Wherever Karl was supposed to be taken next, first he wanted to go and tell Fanny how well everything had gone. But, to his regret, he learned that both the angels and the devils had already left for the next point on the publicity team's itinerary, to announce the arrival of the whole team the next day. 'Shame,' said Karl, and it was the first disappointment he had experienced in this enterprise, 'there was someone I knew among the angels.' 'You'll see her again in Oklahoma,' said the servant, 'now come along please, you're the last.' He led Karl along the back of the stage, where the angels had been standing earlier, now there were just their empty pedestals. Karl's assumption that more applicants might come, now that there was no more music from the angels turned out to be wrong, because there were no grown-ups at all in front of the stage, just a few children fighting over a long white feather that must have come from an angel's wing. One boy held it up in the air, while the other children tried with one hand to push his head down and reached for the feather with the other.

Karl pointed to the children, but the servant said without looking: 'Hurry up, it took a very long time before you were taken. I expect they had their doubts?' 'I really don't know,' said Karl, astonished, but he didn't think so. Always, even in circumstances that were clear as crystal, someone could be found who liked to alarm his fellow-humans. But at the wonderful sight of the large public enclosure to which they had now come, Karl quickly forgot the servant's remark. On the stand was a long bench covered with a white cloth, and all those who had been accepted sat on the bench below it, with their backs to the racetrack, and were being catered for. All were excited and in high spirits, just as Karl sat down unnoticed, the last to arrive, on the bench, a number of them stood up with glasses aloft, and someone proposed a toast to the leader of the 10th publicity team, to whom he referred as 'The father of all the unemployed everywhere'. Someone pointed out that he could be seen from there, and indeed there was the stewards' tribune, with the two gentlemen, not too far away at all. Then everyone raised their glasses

214

in that direction, and Karl too picked up the glass in front of him, but however loudly they called and however hard they tried to get their attention, nothing on the stewards' stand indicated that they had noticed, or more precisely wanted to notice the ovation. The leader was leaning in the corner as before, and the other gentleman stood beside him, cupping his chin in his hand.

A little disappointed, they all sat down again, now and then someone would turn to look at the stewards' stand, but soon they were quite preoccupied by the plentiful meal, some poultry bigger than any Karl had ever seen, with many forks stuck in their crisply roasted flesh, were carried around, and wine glasses kept being replenished by the servants – one almost didn't notice it, bending over one's plate, and a thin stream of red wine fell into one's glass – and anyone who didn't care to participate in the general conversation could look at pictures of the Theatre in Oklahoma, which had been piled up at one end of the table, from where they were supposed to be passed from hand to hand. But no very great attention was paid to the pictures, and so it happened that Karl, at the end of the row, got to see only one of them. To go by this one picture, though, they must all have been very well worth seeing. This picture showed the box of the President of the United States. At first sight, one might think it wasn't a box at all, but the stage, so far did the curved balustrades jut out into empty space. The balustrades were entirely made of gold. In between little pillars that might have been cut out by the minutest scissors, there was a row of portraits of former presidents, one had a strikingly straight nose, thickish lips and stubbornly lowered eyes under bulging lids. The box was brightly lit from all sides and from above; white and yet somehow mild light laid bare the front of the box, whereas its recesses, deepening pleats of red velvet falling full length and swagged by cords, were a darkly glimmering void. It was hardly possible to imagine people in this box, so sumptuously self-sufficient did it look. Karl didn't forget to eat, but he often looked at the picture too, having put it next to his plate.

He would have liked very much to see at least one of the other pictures, but didn't want to fetch it himself because a servant had his hand on the stack of them, and some sequence had to be kept to, so instead he just turned to look down the table and see if there might not be a picture on its way to him. Then to his astonishment – at first he couldn't believe it – among those faces bent furthest over their plates he saw one that was very familiar to him – Giacomo. He ran over to him at once. 'Giacomo,' he called. He, shy as he always was when taken by surprise, got up from his plate, turned round in the little space between the benches, wiped his mouth with his hands, and was finally very glad to see Karl, asked him to sit with him, or offered to go over to Karl's place, they wanted to tell each other everything, and stay together for always. Karl didn't want to bother the others, so each of them agreed to stay in his place for now, the meal would soon be over, and then they would never be parted. But Karl stayed close to Giacomo, just to watch him. What memories of past times! Where was the Head Cook? What was Therese doing? Giacomo's appearance had hardly changed at all, the Head Cook's prediction that within six months he would turn into a raw-boned American hadn't come to pass, he was just as delicate as ever, hollow-cheeked as ever, although at the moment his cheeks were bulging, because he had a huge piece of meat in his mouth, from which he was slowly pulling out the superfluous bones and throwing them on to his plate. As Karl saw from his armband, Giacomo had not been taken on as an actor, but as a lift-boy, the Theatre of Oklahoma really did, it seemed, have use for everyone.

Lost looking at Giacomo, Karl had stayed away from his place far too long, he was just about to go back to it, when the head of personnel came along, stood on one of the higher benches, clapped his hands, and gave a little speech, for which the majority stood, and those who remained seated, unable to tear themselves away from their food, were finally compelled to stand too by nudges from the others. 'I hope', he said, Karl had tiptoed back to his place, 'you were happy with your welcome dinner. In general, the food for our publicity team is held in high regard. Unfortunately I have to bring the meal to a speedy conclusion, because the train that will take you to Oklahoma is leaving in five minutes. It's a long journey, but as you'll see, you will be well looked after. Let me present to you the gentleman who will be responsible for transporting you, and whom you must obey.' A skinny little gentleman clambered up on to the same bench as the head of personnel, barely found time for a perfunctory bow, but began right away by indicating with gestures of his nervous hands how he wanted everyone to assemble, get in line and start moving. But for a time no one did any of this, because the same individual who had proposed a toast earlier now banged on the table with his hand and embarked on a lengthy vote of thanks, even though – Karl was getting quite agitated – it had just been announced that their train would be leaving shortly. But the speaker, not even seeming to care that the head of personnel wasn't listening, he was giving the transport organizer some instructions, was now well into his speech, he listed all the dishes that had been served, gave his verdicts on each of them, and concluded with the cry: 'And that, gentleman, is the way to our hearts.' Everyone laughed, except those he had addressed, but there was more truth than humour in his remarks.

The comeuppance for the speech was that they now needed to run to the station. That wasn't very difficult, though, for – Karl only noticed it now – no one had any luggage – really the only luggage was the pram, which, pushed along by the father at the head of the column, bounced wildly up and down. Suspicious, unpropertied people had assembled here, and had been so well received and looked after! And the head of transport in particular was so involved. At one moment he was helping to push the pram with one hand, while raising the other to exhort the recruits, at the next he was behind the last of the stragglers, driving them on, the next he was running down the flanks, fixing some of the slower ones in the middle with his eye, and by waving his arm, demonstrating to them how they should be running.

When they reached the station, the train was already standing there. The people in the station pointed to the group, called out such things as: 'They all belong to the Theatre of Oklahoma,' the theatre seemed to be far better known than Karl had supposed, although of course he'd never been at all interested in theatrical matters previously. A whole carriage had been reserved for the group, the head of transport was more assiduous than the conductor in urging them in. First he looked into each compartment, arranging a thing or two here and there, and only then did he climb in himself. Karl had managed to get a window seat, and pulled Giacomo in next to him. So they sat pressed together, and both were really looking forward to the trip, they had yet to travel in such a carefree manner in America. When the train began to move, they put their hands out of the window to wave, at which the youths opposite dug each other in the ribs and found it stupid.

They rode for two days and two nights. Only now did Karl begin to grasp the size of America. He looked out of the window tirelessly, and Giacomo craned towards it with him, until the youths opposite, more interested in playing cards, had had enough, and gave him the window seat opposite. Karl thanked them – Giacomo's English wasn't comprehensible to everyone – and as time passed, as happens with people sharing a compartment, they became much friendlier, though their friendliness often took trying forms, for instance each time they dropped a card and looked for it on the floor, they pinched Karl or Giacomo in the leg as hard as they could. Giacomo would cry out, and pull his legs up, Karl sometimes tried to reply with a kick, but otherwise bore it in silence. Everything that happened in the little smoke-filled compartment – even though the windows were open – paled into insignificance compared to what was outside.

On the first day they travelled over a high mountain range. Blue-black formations of rock approached the train in sharp wedges, they leaned out of the window and tried in vain to see their peaks, narrow dark cloven valleys opened, with a finger they traced the direction in which they disappeared, broad mountain streams came rushing like great waves on their hilly courses, and, pushing thousands of little foaming wavelets ahead of them, they plunged under the bridges over which the train passed, so close that the chill breath of them made their faces shudder.

READ MORE IN PENGUIN

In every corner of the world, on every subject under the sun, Penguin represents quality and variety – the very best in publishing today.

For complete information about books available from Penguin – including Puffins, Penguin Classics and Arkana – and how to order them, write to us at the appropriate address below. Please note that for copyright reasons the selection of books varies from country to country.

In the United Kingdom: Please write to *Dept. EP, Penguin Books Ltd, Bath Road, Harmondsworth, West Drayton, Middlesex UB7 ODA*

In the United States: Please write to *Consumer Sales, Penguin USA, P.O. Box 999, Dept. 17109, Bergenfield, New Jersey 07621-0120.* VISA and MasterCard holders call 1-800-253-6476 to order Penguin titles

In Canada: Please write to *Penguin Books Canada Ltd, 10 Alcorn Avenue, Suite 300, Toronto, Ontario M4V 3B2*

In Australia: Please write to *Penguin Books Australia Ltd, P.O. Box 257, Ringwood, Victoria 3134*

In New Zealand: Please write to *Penguin Books (NZ) Ltd, Private Bag 102902, North Shore Mail Centre, Auckland 10*

In India: Please write to *Penguin Books India Pvt Ltd, 706 Eros Apartments, 56 Nehru Place, New Delhi 110 019*

In the Netherlands: Please write to *Penguin Books Netherlands bv, Postbus 3507, NL-1001 AH Amsterdam*

In Germany: Please write to *Penguin Books Deutschland GmbH, Metzlerstrasse 26, 60594 Frankfurt am Main*

In Spain: Please write to *Penguin Books S. A., Bravo Murillo 19, 1° B, 28015 Madrid*

In Italy: Please write to *Penguin Italia s.r.l., Via Felice Casati 20, I–20124 Milano*

In France: Please write to *Penguin France S. A., 17 rue Lejeune, F–31000 Toulouse*

In Japan: Please write to *Penguin Books Japan, Ishikiribashi Building, 2–5–4, Suido, Bunkyo-ku, Tokyo 112*

In South Africa: Please write to *Longman Penguin Southern Africa (Pty) Ltd, Private Bag X08, Bertsham 2013*

READ MORE IN PENGUIN

Penguin Twentieth-Century Classics offer a selection of the finest works of literature published this century. Spanning the globe from Argentina to America, from France to India, the masters of prose and poetry are represented by the Penguin.

If you would like a catalogue of the Twentieth-Century Classics library, please write to:

Penguin Marketing, 27 Wrights Lane, London W8 5TZ

(Available while stocks last)

BY THE SAME AUTHOR

The Transformation ('Metamorphosis') and Other Stories

This volume contains Kafka's most famous story, 'The Transformation', more popularly known as 'Metamorphosis'. Other works include, 'Meditation', a collection of his earlier studies; 'The Judgement', written in a single night of frenzied creativity; 'The Stoker', the first chapter of a novel set in America; and 'A Fasting Artist', a collection of stories written towards the end of Kafka's life. There is also a fascinating occasional piece, 'The Aeroplanes at Brescia', Kafka's eye-witness account of an air display in 1909. Taken together, these stories reveal the breadth of Kafka's literary vision and the extraordinary imaginative depth of his thought.

The Great Wall of China and Other Short Works

This edition has been prepared directly from the author's manuscripts and contains the major short works left by Kafka, including *Blumfeld, an Elderly Bachelor*, *The Great Wall of China* and *Investigations of a Dog*, together with *The Collected Aphorisms* and *He: Aphorisms from the 1920 Diary*.

The Trial

'Only our concept of time makes us call the Last Judgement by that name; it is a court in standing session' – Franz Kafka

'Somebody must have laid false information against Josef K., for he was arrested one morning without having done anything wrong.' From this first sentence onwards, Josef K. is on trial for his very existence in a novel which is infinitely perceptive about the nature of terror.

Metamorphosis *and* The Trial, *both read by Steven Berkoff, are also available as Penguin Audiobooks*